The Sorrows of Young Werther

Die Leiden des jungen Werther

The Sorrows of Young Werther

Die Leiden des jungen Werther

JOHANN WOLFGANG VON GOETHE

A Dual-Language Book

Edited and Translated by
STANLEY APPELBAUM

DOVER PUBLICATIONS, INC.
Mineola, New York

Bibliographical Note

This Dover edition, first published in 2004, contains the complete German text of the revised edition of *Die Leiden des jungen Werther*, which was originally published by Georg Joachim Göschen, Leipzig, in 1787. (See the Introduction for further bibliographical details.) The German text is accompanied by a new English translation by Stanley Appelbaum, who also provided the Introduction and footnotes.

Library of Congress Cataloging-in-Publication Data

Goethe, Johann Wolfgang von, 1749–1832.
    [Werther. English & German]
    The sorrows of young Werther = Die Leiden des jungen Werther : a dual-language book / Johann Wolfgang von Goethe ; edited and translated by Stanley Appelbaum.
        p. cm.
    Contains the complete German text of the revised edition of Die Leiden des jungen Werther, originally published in Leipzig in 1787.
       ISBN-13: 978-0-486-43363-9 (pbk.)
       ISBN-10: 0-486-43363-3 (pbk.)
      I. Title: Leiden des jungen Werther. II. Appelbaum, Stanley. III. Title.

PT2027.W3A664 2004
833'.6—dc22

                                     2003070110

Manufactured in the United States by LSC Communications
43363308   2021
www.doverpublications.com

Contents

Introduction   v

Die Leiden des jungen Werther / The Sorrows of Young Werther
    Erstes Buch / Book One   2/3
    Zweites Buch / Book Two   92/93

Appendix One: Poem Written by Goethe for a 1775 Printing   204

Appendix Two: Original English Text of the Principal
    Ossian Passage   204

INTRODUCTION

Johann Wolfgang Goethe (1749–1832) was born in Frankfurt am Main. His well-to-do patrician father had purchased a "Councilor" title, but was chiefly a gentleman of leisure who tried to forget that his inherited wealth had come from plebeian trade. The boy, extremely bright (his earliest extant poem was written at age eight), received a remarkable education, largely from private tutors, acquiring: Latin, Greek, French, English, and Hebrew; drawing and calligraphy; clavier playing, fencing, and riding. His talent for art was stimulated during the Seven Years' War, when Frankfurt was occupied by the French and a French commandant, quartered in the boy's home, gave commissions to numerous local painters.

In 1765 Goethe went to Leipzig to study law at the university. He also pursued literature, art, and women, writing conventional erotic poems for and about the first of his lengthy line of flesh-and-blood muses (some biographers designate the periods of his career by the names of his mistresses-in-chief, who, from 1774 on, were principally married women). A casual acquaintance in Leipzig was Karl Wilhelm Jerusalem (1747–1772), son of an eminent theologian; his father was a friend of the great dramatist Gotthold Ephraim Lessing (1729–1781), who was a patron of young Karl. The young man found Goethe a vapid fop, while Goethe considered him an unsociable brooder. Goethe contracted a serious illness in 1768 and returned home.

By March 1770 he was in Strasbourg, where he remained for eighteen months and finally received a law degree of sorts. While there he fell in love with Friederike Brion, the daughter of a rural pastor, and began writing love poems of a force and originality new to German poetry. He also met one of the major influences on his mental progress, Johann Gottfried Herder (1744–1803), who inspired him with a serious interest in folk poetry, nature, medieval art, Homer, Shakespeare, and Ossian (on Ossian, see footnote 8, page 53); Goethe translated some passages from Ossian and sent them to Friederike after returning home in 1771.

Back in Frankfurt, he practiced law lackadaisically, but continued to

write very actively. Now he became associated with a group of young writers (mockingly called "geniuses") in the movement that came to be known as *Sturm und Drang* (Storm and Stress) after the name of a play by one of its leaders, Friedrich Maximilian Klinger (1752–1831). This movement (1771–1778) advocated a return to Nature, political freedom, and boldness, if not savagery, in writing; other than Herder, its idols were Rousseau and such pre-Romantic English authors as Edward Young. From 1771 to 1773 Goethe worked on the long, wild, anti-classical play *Götz von Berlichingen,* which made a reputation for him when it was produced in Berlin in 1774.

Meanwhile, in the spring of 1772 Goethe had gone to the Hessian town of Wetzlar, which was the seat of the supreme court and court of appeals of the Holy Roman Empire from 1693 until Napoleon dissolved the Empire in 1806; his father wanted him to observe the operations of that court and to make useful connections. In Wetzlar, Goethe once again came across Jerusalem, who was posted there in the diplomatic service of his native Duchy of Brunswick (Braunschweig).

On June 9, 1772, Goethe met Charlotte (Lotte) Buff (1753–1828), the daughter of the local representative of the Teutonic Order (a medieval order of knighthood that had once conquered parts of northeastern Europe and had invaded Russia, and still had many commercial interests to protect). Since 1768 Lotte had been engaged to Johann Georg Christian Kestner (1741–1800), who was then an attaché at Wetzlar in the service of his native Electorate of Hanover (Hannover; later he participated in his land's administration). Lotte became the great love of Goethe's Wetzlar months and the inspiration for *Werther,* but it is questionable how serious he really was about her, and whether, as claimed by him and many after him, he was really valiantly rescuing his life and career by his precipitous departure from Wetzlar on September 11, 1772. One major biographer suspects that the extremely intelligent and broadminded Kestner was gallantly prepared to relinquish Lotte to Goethe, and it was that entanglement from which the poet was escaping!

Only a month and a half later, on the night of October 29/30, Jerusalem killed himself out of both career and romantic disappointments. A week later Goethe visited Wetzlar for three days, and learned many details from Kestner, with whom he continued on good terms and maintained a correspondence.

Back in Frankfurt, Goethe became one of the inner circle of the *Sturm und Drang* movement, and wrote some of his boldest and finest anti-establishment poems. He was also making life miserable

for even more husbands; apparently he was not crushed by his "loss" of Lotte. When the Kestners married in 1773, he sent them their wedding rings, and they sent him the bridal bouquet, which he once wore. A novel based on the Wetzlar days was also germinating in his mind. In a letter to Kestner of September 15, 1773, he reports that he is working on a novel, which is going slowly. But it appears that *Die Leiden des jungen Werthers*,[1] which has been regarded by some as the epitome of *Sturm und Drang*, and by others as Goethe's farewell to that phase of his career, was principally composed very rapidly between February and April of 1774.

The publisher Christian Friedrich Weygand, who had moved his operation to Leipzig in 1773, wrote to Goethe (now known for *Götz*) for new material. Goethe sent him the play *Clavigo*, which he completed in May 1774; Weygand published it in July (it was the first of Goethe's publications with his name on it). Goethe sent *Werther* to Weygand in May. On September 19 he received three pre-publication copies, one of which he sent to the Kestners; the actual publication was at Michaelmas (September 29), the date of the annual Leipzig book fair. In three parts, the novel contained vignettes by the eminent Leipzig artist and art-school director Adam Friedrich Oeser (1717–1799), from whom Goethe had taken lessons while a law student. Though *Werther* was published anonymously, the identity of the author soon became known, and for the rest of his life (often to his chagrin, because he felt he had advanced much further) Goethe was known as "the author of *Werther*."

The book was an immediate sensation; in fact, it has been called the greatest literary success of all time, and the book that established the notion of the author-as-genius. It rapidly went into additional printings by Weygand in 1774 and 1775. For one of the 1775 printings, issued as a "second, genuine edition," Goethe wrote the inconsequential little poem that is reprinted and translated as Appendix One of this Dover volume. (He also wrote a few humorous verses about the book, including one extremely scatological retort to adverse criticism.) There were some twenty pirated editions by 1787; there were parodies, there were (apparently) copycat suicides (the novel was banned here and there for glorifying self-destruction), and there were countless commercial spinoffs. Six French translations appeared from 1775

---

1. The title is usually translated, not incorrectly, as "The Sorrows of Young Werther," but some scholars insist that "Sufferings" is a truer rendition of *Leiden*. The genitive ending -*s* was not dropped from the hero's name in the title until the 1824 edition (to be mentioned later).

to 1778, an English one in 1779, an Italian one in 1781, and a Russian one in 1788. (Jules Massenet's 1891 opera *Werther* is the most famous work based on the novel, but far from the only one.)

Kestner's reaction was not violent, but he did complain that Albert, the character in the novel that everyone in the know easily identified with him, was so dull, a complete stick, merely a foil for Werther. In a fervent letter to him, dated November 21, 1774, Goethe assured him that he wasn't Albert, but refused to cease publication: "Werther must, must continue to exist! You don't feel *him*, you feel only *yourself* and *me*." Goethe called the book an "innocent mixture of truth and fabrication"; in a letter to Lotte of August 26, announcing the imminent publication, he had spoken of it as "a prayer book, a little treasure chest, or whatever you wish to call it."

Goethe had identified himself with Werther in a number of ways, and had used many true incidents: Werther is an amateur artist, born on the same day of the year as Goethe, and he leaves Wetzlar on almost the same day of the year that Goethe did. The novel contains a luscious Friederike, also the daughter of a country parson. The Kestners had actually given Goethe a copy of the Wetstein printing of Homer, as well as Lotte's pink bow and a silhouette of her. Goethe's own translations from Ossian are incorporated into the text. Jerusalem had really borrowed Kestner's pistols for his suicide, and the note requesting them had had the same wording as Werther's note to Albert; Jerusalem *had* been reading Lessing's play *Emilia Galotti* before he killed himself.

The epistolary form of the novel was common at the time, having been made especially popular by the novels of Samuel Richardson and by Rousseau's *Nouvelle Héloïse*, but in Werther there is only one correspondent. Goethe's book has been called lyrical and dramatic rather than novelistic.

Goethe continued writing. In 1775 he got engaged and broke it off; went on a tour of Switzerland; and was invited to Weimar by the Duke of Saxe-Weimar. The duke took a great liking to him, and he became a major figure in the administration of the duchy from 1776 until 1786, when he took an unauthorized leave of two years in Italy; he was made a nobleman in 1782, the *von* being added to his name at that time. In his first ten years in Weimar, he wrote less than previously, but the quality of his work was high, and he became increasingly a classicist and conservative in literature and in life. Many of his social rough edges were planed away by a congenial (married) lady-in-waiting.

In 1782 his thoughts reverted to *Werther,* and he began planning a revision, which he worked on into 1783, and then with renewed vigor

in 1786, receiving valuable advice from Herder and from the eminent poet and novelist Christoph Martin Wieland (1733–1813). In a letter to Kestner of May 2, 1783, he assures him that in the new version Albert will be a much more sympathetic figure, a hero to everyone except poor jealousy-ridden Werther. The new version was published by Georg Joachim Göschen (1752–1828), who founded his Leipzig house in 1785 and communicated with Goethe by way of Wieland and Friedrich Schiller (1759–1805), the great poet and playwright who was soon to initiate a literary (not very warm personally) friendship with "the author of *Werther*." Negotiations between Göschen and Goethe for an eight-volume collected-works edition (Goethe's first) began in June 1786, and the contract was signed in September. The edition, *Goethe's Schriften*, which unfortunately sold very poorly, appeared between 1787 and 1790; the revised *Werther* was in the first volume, published 1787, and was also published separately. It is this version of *Werther* that is now almost universally reprinted in German, and translated, and it is the basis for this Dover edition, as well.

For the 1787 edition Goethe not only rehabilitated the character of Albert; he also added a number of entire letters and other passages, including Lotte's canary and the entire subplot of the enamored farmhand (a reflection of Werther's own plight), and he totally overhauled and expanded the final section of the book, the "editor's narrative." Oddly enough, he couldn't locate a copy of the original Weygand edition, and he used a pirated edition as the basis for his revision, so that the wording differed even more than it might have otherwise. In a few places his alterations contradict earlier material that was left in.

It is unnecessary here to go into great detail about the remainder of Goethe's long life. After his return to Weimar from Italy in 1788, he was forgiven for the escapade, and was still *persona grata*, but had less to do with governing the duchy. He served as director of the Weimar theater from 1791 to 1817, and wrote a vast amount more, including the plays *Egmont* (1788) and *Torquato Tasso* (1790); the novels *Wilhelm Meisters Lehrjahre* (W. M.'s Years of Apprenticeship; 1795–96) and *Wilhelm Meisters Wanderjahre* (W. M.'s Years of Wandering; 1821); the two parts of *Faust* (part 1 published 1808; part 2 completed 1832 [published posthumously 1833]); the autobiography *Dichtung und Wahrheit* (Poetry and Truth; 1811–32); and innumerable lyric poems, which may constitute his most abiding legacy. In his old age he was a grand old man, a sage of European reputation, whom travelers to Weimar visited as the town's main attraction. A few more things can be said about *Werther* in particular:

In 1808, in the course of his central European campaigns,
Napoleon had conversations with Goethe in Erfurt and Weimar. The
empereur told the great author that he had read *Werther* several times
as a young man, and criticized Goethe for having burdened his hero
with disappointments in both love *and* his diplomatic career; one
would have been enough. Goethe, a diplomat himself, replied that
Napoleon was the very first to have put his finger on that "error."

In 1816, Charlotte Buff Kestner, a widow since 1800, visited
Goethe in Weimar with some personal request, and was disappointed
to find that he was no longer ablaze with love for her. This incident
was the basis for Thomas Mann's clever 1939 novel *Lotte in Weimar*
(in English, aka *The Beloved Returns*).

In later years Goethe often claimed to be frightened at his youthful
ardor, and the "dangers" he had escaped, whenever he dipped into
Werther again. Although he *had* said in the past that the novel had a
seminal place in the course of human history (some people even
blamed it for the French Revolution!), in a conversation with his
sounding board Johann Peter Eckermann (1792–1854) on January 2,
1824, he stated: "When considered more closely, the much-discussed
Werther period does not actually belong to the course of world culture, but to the life development of every individual who, with an in-
born free sense of Nature, finds himself in the cramping molds of an
obsolete world and must learn to live in it. Thwarted happiness, confined activity, and unsatisfied wishes are not faults of a given period,
but the problems of every single person, and it would be a bad thing
if, once in his life, everyone did not have a period in which he felt that
Werther had been written exclusively for him."

The year 1824 also marked the fiftieth anniversary of Weygand's
first publication of *Werther,* and the then owners of that firm asked
Goethe to supply a new introduction for a new printing. He re-
sponded with the profound and brilliant poem "An Werther."[2]

The English translation in the present Dover dual-language edition
(based on the 1787 text) is as complete as possible.[3]

---

2. Original text and translation (by the present translator) in: Goethe, *103 Great
Poems / 103 Meistergedichte,* Dover, 1999 (ISBN 0-486-40667-9). 3. By contrast, the
currently available translation in the Modern Library, New York, though admirably accurate and elegant, lacks the preamble to Book One and all the original footnotes, and
occasionally omits phrases and clauses, and in one case an entire paragraph. (Not to
mention that its Introduction and Foreword are nearly devoid of factual information
pertaining directly to the novel, and there is no identification at all of historical figures
or other cultural references.)

The Sorrows of Young Werther

Die Leiden des jungen Werther

Was ich von der Geschichte des armen Werther nur habe auffinden
können, habe ich mit Fleiß gesammelt, und lege es euch hier vor, und
weiß, daß ihr mirs danken werdet. Ihr könnt seinem Geiste und
seinem Charakter eure Bewunderung und Liebe, seinem Schicksale
eure Tränen nicht versagen.

Und du, gute Seele, die du eben den Drang fühlst wie er, schöpfe
Trost aus seinem Leiden, und laß das Büchlein deinen Freund sein,
wenn du aus Geschick oder eigener Schuld keinen nähern finden
kannst.

Erstes Buch

Am 4. Mai 1771.

Wie froh bin ich, daß ich weg bin! Bester Freund, was ist das Herz des
Menschen! Dich zu verlassen, den ich so liebe, von dem ich unzer-
trennlich war, und froh zu sein! Ich weiß, du verzeihst mirs. Waren
nicht meine übrigen Verbindungen recht ausgesucht vom Schicksal,
um ein Herz wie das meine zu ängstigen? Die arme Leonore! Und
doch war ich unschuldig. Konnt ich dafür, daß, während die eigensin-
nigen Reize ihrer Schwester mir eine angenehme Unterhaltung ver-
schafften, daß eine Leidenschaft in dem armen Herzen sich bildete!
Und doch – bin ich ganz unschuldig? Hab ich nicht ihre
Empfindungen genährt? hab ich mich nicht an den ganz wahren
Ausdrücken der Natur, die uns so oft zu lachen machten, so wenig
lächerlich sie waren, selbst ergötzt, hab ich nicht – O was ist der
Mensch, daß er über sich klagen darf! Ich will, lieber Freund, ich verspreche dirs, ich will mich bessern, will nicht mehr ein bißchen Übel,
das uns das Schicksal vorlegt, wiederkäuen, wie ichs immer getan
habe; ich will das Gegenwärtige genießen, und das Vergangene soll mir
vergangen sein. Gewiß, du hast recht, Bester, der Schmerzen wären
minder unter den Menschen, wenn sie nicht – Gott weiß, warum sie so

I have diligently collected everything I could locate concerning the history of poor Werther, and I herewith present it to you in the knowledge that you will thank me for it. You cannot fail to admire and love his mind and nature, or to weep over his fate.

And you, good soul, you that feel the same pressures he did, derive consolation from his suffering, and let this little book be your friend, if you cannot find any closer one, thanks to fate or your own fault!

Book One

May 4, 1771

How glad I am to have come away! Best of friends, what the human heart is like! To leave you behind, you whom I love so much, from whom I was inseparable, and to be glad! I know you'll forgive me. Weren't all my other connections as if precisely chosen by fate to oppress a heart such as mine? Poor Leonore! And yet I was blameless. Was it my fault if a passion developed in my poor heart while her sister's willful charms created a pleasing diversion for me? And yet—am I completely blameless? Didn't I encourage her feelings? Didn't I myself take delight in the quite genuine utterances of nature, which made us laugh so often, though they were so far from laughable? Didn't I— Oh, what is man, that he should complain about himself? Dear friend, I promise you, I will, I will improve; no longer will I endlessly ruminate over some trifling woe that fate presents to us, as I've always done; I shall enjoy the present moment, and let bygones be bygones. You're certainly right, good friend, people would have fewer sorrows if they didn't (God knows why they're made that way!), if they didn't occupy themselves, with such

3

gemacht sind – mit so viel Emsigkeit der Einbildungskraft sich beschäftigten, die Erinnerungen des vergangenen Übels zurückzurufen, eher als eine gleichgültige Gegenwart zu ertragen.

Du bist so gut, meiner Mutter zu sagen, daß ich ihr Geschäft bestens betreiben und ihr ehstens Nachricht davon geben werde. Ich habe meine Tante gesprochen und bei weitem das böse Weib nicht gefunden, das man bei uns aus ihr macht. Sie ist eine muntere, heftige Frau von dem besten Herzen. Ich erklärte ihr meiner Mutter Beschwerden über den zurückgehaltenen Erbschaftsanteil; sie sagte mir ihre Gründe, Ursachen und die Bedingungen, unter welchen sie bereit wäre, alles herauszugeben, und mehr als wir verlangten – Kurz, ich mag jetzt nichts davon schreiben; sage meiner Mutter, es werde alles gut gehen. Und ich habe, mein Lieber, wieder bei diesem kleinen Geschäft gefunden, daß Mißverständnisse und Trägheit vielleicht mehr Irrungen in der Welt machen als List und Bosheit. Wenigstens sind die beiden letzteren gewiß seltener.

Übrigens befinde ich mich hier gar wohl, die Einsamkeit ist meinem Herzen köstlicher Balsam in dieser paradiesischen Gegend, und diese Jahrszeit der Jugend wärmt mit aller Fülle mein oft schauderndes Herz. Jeder Baum, jede Hecke ist ein Strauß von Blüten, und man möchte zum Maikäfer werden, um in dem Meer von Wohlgerüchen herumschweben und alle seine Nahrung darin finden zu können.

Die Stadt selbst ist unangenehm, dagegen ringsumher eine unaussprechliche Schönheit der Natur. Das bewog den verstorbenen Grafen von M . . . , seinen Garten auf einem der Hügel anzulegen, die mit der schönsten Mannigfaltigkeit sich kreuzen und die lieblichsten Täler bilden. Der Garten ist einfach, und man fühlt gleich bei dem Eintritte, daß nicht ein wissenschaftlicher Gärtner, sondern ein fühlendes Herz den Plan gezeichnet, das seiner selbst hier genießen wollte. Schon manche Träne hab ich dem Abgeschiedenen in dem verfallenen Kabinettchen geweint, das sein Lieblingsplätzchen war und auch meines ist. Bald werde ich Herr vom Garten sein; der Gärtner ist mir zugetan, nur seit den paar Tagen, und er wird sich nicht übel dabei befinden.

Am 10. Mai.

Eine wunderbare Heiterkeit hat meine ganze Seele eingenommen, gleich den süßen Frühlingsmorgen, die ich mit ganzem Herzen genieße. Ich bin allein und freue mich meines Lebens in dieser Gegend, die für solche Seelen geschaffen ist wie die meine. Ich bin so glück-

great diligence of their imagination, in recalling the woes of the past instead of putting up with their neutral present.

Be so kind as to tell my mother that I shall carry out her errand to the best of my ability, and report to her about it very soon. I've spoken with my aunt, who is far from being the evil woman she's considered to be in my household. She's a lively, high-spirited lady with the kindest heart. I put before her my mother's complaints about the share of the inheritance which she has held back; she told me her reasons, the causes, and the conditions on which she'd be ready to hand everything over, even more than we were asking for—. In short, I don't feel like writing about it now; tell my mother it will all work out. And, dear friend, in this transaction I have found once again that misunderstandings and inertia may cause more confusion in the world than cunning and malice do. At least, the latter two are certainly rarer.

For the rest, I feel quite comfortable here; solitude is a precious balm to my heart in this heavenly region, and this season of youth thoroughly warms my often shuddering heart. Every tree, every hedge is a bouquet of blossom, and I'd like to become a junebug so I could float around in this sea of fragrances and find all my nourishment in it.

The town itself is unpleasant, but on the other hand, the natural features all around it are indescribably beautiful. That induced the late Count von M—— to lay out his garden on one of the hills that intersect one another with the loveliest variety, forming the most charming valleys. The garden is simple, and as soon as you enter it you feel that its plan was traced not by some scientific garden designer, but by a sensitive heart which wanted to enjoy its own self here. I have already shed many a tear in honor of the departed count in the dilapidated little pavilion which was his favorite spot, and is now mine as well. Soon I shall be master of the garden; the gardener is fond of me, though I've been here only a couple of days, and he won't find himself the worse off for it.

May 10

A peculiar serenity has taken over my whole soul, like the sweet spring mornings that I enjoy with all my heart. I'm alone and I take joy in my life in this region, which was just made for souls like mine. I'm so happy, dear friend, so deeply immersed in the feel-

lich, mein Bester, so ganz in dem Gefühle von ruhigem Dasein versunken, daß meine Kunst darunter leidet. Ich könnte jetzt nicht
zeichnen, nicht einen Strich, und bin nie ein größerer Maler gewesen
als in diesen Augenblicken. Wenn das liebe Tal um mich dampft und
die hohe Sonne an der Oberfläche der undurchdringlichen Finsternis
meines Waldes ruht und nur einzelne Strahlen sich in das innere
Heiligtum stehlen, ich dann im hohen Grase am fallenden Bache
liege und näher an der Erde tausend mannigfaltige Gräschen mir
merkwürdig werden; wenn ich das Wimmeln der kleinen Welt zwischen Halmen, die unzähligen, unergründlichen Gestalten der
Würmchen, der Mückchen näher an meinem Herzen fühle, und fühle
die Gegenwart des Allmächtigen, der uns nach seinem Bilde schuf,
das Wehen des All-liebenden, der uns in ewiger Wonne schwebend
trägt und erhält; mein Freund! wenns dann um meine Augen däm-
mert und die Welt um mich her und der Himmel ganz in meiner
Seele ruhn wie die Gestalt einer Geliebten – dann sehne ich mich oft
und denke: ach könntest du das wieder ausdrücken, könntest du dem
Papiere das einhauchen, was so voll, so warm in dir lebt; daß es würde
der Spiegel deiner Seele, wie deine Seele ist der Spiegel des unendlichen Gottes! – Mein Freund – Aber ich gehe darüber zugrunde,
ich erliege unter der Gewalt der Herrlichkeit dieser Erscheinungen.

Am 12. Mai.

Ich weiß nicht, ob täuschende Geister um diese Gegend schweben,
oder ob die warme himmlische Phantasie in meinem Herzen ist, die
mir alles ringsumher so paradiesisch macht. Da ist gleich vor dem
Orte ein Brunnen, ein Brunnen, an den ich gebannt bin wie Melusine
mit ihren Schwestern. – Du gehst einen kleinen Hügel hinunter und
findest dich vor einem Gewölbe, da wohl zwanzig Stufen hinabgehen,
wo unten das klarste Wasser aus Marmorfelsen quillt. Die kleine
Mauer, die oben umher die Einfassung macht, die hohen Bäume, die
den Platz ringsumher bedecken, die Kühle des Ortes: das hat alles so
was Anzügliches, was Schauerliches. Es vergeht kein Tag, daß ich
nicht eine Stunde da sitze. Da kommen dann die Mädchen aus der
Stadt und holen Wasser, das harmloseste Geschäft und das nötigste,
das ehemals die Töchter der Könige selbst verrichteten. Wenn ich da
sitze, so lebt die patriarchalische Idee so lebhaft um mich, wie sie alle,
die Altväter, am Brunnen Bekanntschaft machen und freien, und wie
um die Brunnen und Quellen wohltätige Geister schweben. O der
muß nie nach einer schweren Sommertagswanderung sich an des
Brunnens Kühle gelabt haben, der das nicht mitempfinden kann.

ing of a tranquil existence, that my art is suffering from it. Right now I couldn't do any drawing, not even a stroke, but I've never been a greater painter than in these moments. When the dear valley's vapors rise around me, and the sun, high in the sky, reposes on the surface of my forest's impenetrable darkness, while only a few beams steal into the innermost sanctum, and when I then lie in the tall grass by the plunging brook and, closer to the ground, a thousand different grasses attract my attention; when I feel, closer to my heart, the swarming microcosm between their blades, the innumerable, unfathomable forms of the grubs and gnats; and when I feel the presence of the Almighty, who created us in his image, the motion of the All-Loving One, who bears us aloft in eternal rapture and sustains us; my friend, when dusk then falls before my eyes, and the world around me, and the sky, repose totally in my soul like the form of a beloved woman—then I often feel a yearning, and I think: oh, if you could only reproduce this, if you could breathe onto the paper that which lives within you with such fullness and warmth, so that it might become the mirror of your soul, just as your soul is the mirror of eternal God!— My friend— But these thoughts are killing me, I'm succumbing to the power of the splendor of these phenomena.

May 12

I don't know whether deceptive spirits hover over this region, or whether it's the warm, heavenly imagination in my heart that makes everything around me so much like Paradise. Among other things, right outside my place there's a fountain, a fountain to which I'm spellbound like Melusine and her sister water nymphs.—You walk down a low hill and you find yourself in front of a stone vault, where about twenty steps lead down to a place where the clearest water emerges from blocks of marble. The low wall that encloses the fountain at the top, the tall trees that shade the spot all around, the coolness of the place: all of that is somehow alluring and deliciously thrilling. Not a day goes by when I don't sit there for an hour. Then the girls come from town to fetch water, the most innocent occupation and the most necessary, one that kings' daughters performed personally in olden days. When I sit there, the notion of the time of the Patriarchs revives in me with such force: how all of those men of yore used to make one another's acquaintance and woo at a well, and how beneficent spirits hovered around wells and springs. Oh, a man who can't share those feelings must never have refreshed himself at a cool well after a hard journey on a summer's day!

Am 13. Mai.

Du fragst, ob du mir meine Bücher schicken sollst? – Lieber, ich bitte dich um Gottes willen, laß mir sie vom Halse! Ich will nicht mehr geleitet, ermuntert, angefeuert sein, braust dieses Herz doch genug aus sich selbst; ich brauche Wiegengesang, und den habe ich in seiner Fülle gefunden in meinem Homer. Wie oft lull ich mein empörtes Blut zur Ruhe, denn so ungleich, so unstet hast du nichts gesehen als dieses Herz. Lieber! brauch ich dir das zu sagen, der du so oft die Last getragen hast, mich vom Kummer zur Ausschweifung, und von süßer Melancholie zur verderblichen Leidenschaft übergehen zu sehen? Auch halte ich mein Herzchen wie ein krankes Kind; jeder Wille wird ihm gestattet. Sage das nicht weiter; es gibt Leute, die mir es verübeln würden.

Am 15. Mai.

Die geringen Leute des Ortes kennen mich schon und lieben mich, besonders die Kinder. Wie ich im Anfange mich zu ihnen gesellte, sie freundschaftlich fragte über dies und das, glaubten einige, ich wollte ihrer spotten, und fertigten mich wohl gar grob ab. Ich ließ mich das nicht verdrießen; nur fühlte ich, was ich schon oft bemerkt habe, auf das lebhafteste: Leute von einigem Stande werden sich immer in kalter Entfernung vom gemeinen Volke halten, als glaubten sie durch Annäherung zu verlieren; und dann gibts Flüchtlinge und üble Spaßvögel, die sich herabzulassen scheinen, um ihren Übermut dem armen Volke desto empfindlicher zu machen.

Ich weiß wohl, daß wir nicht gleich sind, noch sein können; aber ich halte dafür, daß der, der nötig zu haben glaubt, vom sogenannten Pöbel sich zu entfernen, um den Respekt zu erhalten, ebenso tadelhaft ist als ein Feiger, der sich vor seinem Feinde verbirgt, weil er zu unterliegen fürchtet.

Letzthin kam ich zum Brunnen, und fand ein junges Dienstmädchen, das ihr Gefäß auf die unterste Treppe gesetzt hatte und sich umsah, ob keine Kamerädin kommen wollte, ihr es auf den Kopf zu helfen. Ich stieg hinunter und sah sie an. – Soll ich Ihr helfen, Jungfer? sagte ich. – Sie ward rot über und über. – O nein, Herr! sagte sie. – Ohne Umstände! – Sie legte ihren Kringen zurecht, und ich half ihr. Sie dankte und stieg hinauf.

Den 17. Mai.

Ich habe allerlei Bekanntschaft gemacht, Gesellschaft habe ich noch keine gefunden. Ich weiß nicht, was ich Anzügliches für die

May 13

You ask whether you should send me my books.—Dear friend, I beg you for God's sake not to saddle me with them! I don't want to be guided, encouraged, or inspired any more; my heart is sufficiently active on its own; I need lullabies, and I've found them in abundance in my Homer. How often I croon my overexcited blood to rest (for you've never seen anything as changeable and unsteady as my heart)! Dear friend, do I need to tell you this, when you've so often borne the burden of watching me shift from grief to reckless dreams, from sweet melancholy to disastrous passion? Besides, I treat my heart like a sick child; I let it have anything it wants. Don't let that get around; there are people who'd hold it against me.

May 15

The local people of humble degree already know and love me, especially the children. When I first approached them, asking friendly questions about this and that, a few of them thought I wanted to make fun of them, and gave me some quite rude answers. I didn't let that bother me; I merely felt, and quite keenly, what I've often noticed before: people of some station in life will always maintain a cool distance from the common people, as if they thought they'd lose something by the contact; and then there are superficial types and sorry jokers who pretend to condescend, in order to make the poor commoners more acutely aware of their arrogance.

I know quite well that we aren't equal, and can't be; but, on the other hand, I consider that a man who feels it necessary to shun the so-called riffraff, in order to retain their respect, is just as blameworthy as a coward who hides from his enemy out of fear of being defeated.

Recently I visited the fountain and found a young servant girl who had set down her pitcher on the lowest step and was looking around to see whether some companion might arrive and help her hoist it onto her head. I walked down and looked at her. "May I help you, miss?" I asked. She blushed all over her face. "Oh, no, sir!" she said. "Don't make a fuss!" She arranged the carrying pad on her head, and I aided her. She thanked me and climbed up.

May 17

I've made all sorts of acquaintances, but I haven't found anyone yet to keep company with. I don't know what I have that attracts

Menschen haben muß; es mögen mich ihrer so viele und hängen sich an mich, und da tut mirs weh, wenn unser Weg nur eine kleine Strecke miteinander geht. Wenn du fragst, wie die Leute hier sind, muß ich dir sagen: wie überall! Es ist ein einförmiges Ding um das Menschengeschlecht. Die meisten verarbeiten den größten Teil der Zeit, um zu leben, und das bißchen, das ihnen von Freiheit übrig bleibt, ängstigt sie so, daß sie alle Mittel aufsuchen, um es loszuwerden. O Bestimmung des Menschen!

Aber eine recht gute Art Volks! Wenn ich mich manchmal vergesse, manchmal mit ihnen die Freuden genieße, die den Menschen noch gewährt sind, an einem artig besetzten Tisch mit aller Offen- und Treuherzigkeit sich herumzuspaßen, eine Spazierfahrt, einen Tanz zur rechten Zeit anzuordnen, und dergleichen, das tut eine ganz gute Wirkung auf mich; nur muß mir nicht einfallen, daß noch so viele andere Kräfte in mir ruhen, die alle ungenutzt vermodern und die ich sorgfältig verbergen muß. Ach, das engt das ganze Herz so ein – Und doch! mißverstanden zu werden, ist das Schicksal von unser einem.

Ach, daß die Freundin meiner Jugend dahin ist! ach, daß ich sie je gekannt habe! – Ich würde sagen: du bist ein Tor! du suchst, was hienieden nicht zu finden ist. Aber ich habe sie gehabt, ich habe das Herz gefühlt, die große Seele, in deren Gegenwart ich mir schien mehr zu sein, als ich war, weil ich alles war, was ich sein konnte. Guter Gott! blieb da eine einzige Kraft meiner Seele ungenutzt? Konnt ich nicht vor ihr das ganze wunderbare Gefühl entwickeln, mit dem mein Herz die Natur umfaßt? War unser Umgang nicht ein ewiges Weben von der feinsten Empfindung, dem schärfsten Witze, dessen Modifikationen, bis zur Unart, alle mit dem Stempel des Genies bezeichnet waren? Und nun! – Ach, ihre Jahre, die sie voraus hatte, führten sie früher ans Grab als mich. Nie werde ich sie vergessen, nie ihren festen Sinn und ihre göttliche Duldung.

Vor wenig Tagen traf ich einen jungen V . . . an, einen offnen Jungen, mit einer gar glücklichen Gesichtsbildung. Er kommt erst von Akademieen, dünkt sich eben nicht weise, aber glaubt doch, er wisse mehr als andere. Auch war er fleißig, wie ich an allerlei spüre; kurz, er hat hübsche Kenntnisse. Da er hörte, daß ich viel zeichnete und Griechisch könnte (zwei Meteore hierzulande), wandte er sich an mich und kramte viel Wissens aus, von Batteux bis zu Wood, von de

people; so many like me and become attached to me, and then I feel bad when our ways part after only a short distance. If you ask what the people here are like, I must say: like everywhere else! The human race is pretty uniform. Most people spend the bulk of their time working for a living, and the little bit of leisure they have left bothers them so, that they seek every means of getting rid of it. The human condition!

But the people hereabout are a fine lot! When I sometimes let myself go and share with them those joys that are still permitted to people—to joke around a well-set table with complete candor and artlessness, to arrange an outing or a dance at an appropriate time, and the like—the effect on me is quite beneficial, as long as I don't stop to think that there are so many other powers within me that are all moldering away unused, powers which I must carefully conceal. Oh, that oppresses my heart so badly— and yet, to be misunderstood is the lot of people like us.

Too bad that the friend of my younger days is gone! Too bad that I ever came to know her![1]—I'd say: "You're a fool! You're seeking something not to be found on earth." But I *did* have her as a friend, I did feel that heart, that great soul in whose presence I seemed to be more than I actually was, because I was all that I was capable of being. Good God! Was even a single power of my soul left unused at that time? Wasn't I able, in her presence, to unfold all of that strange emotion by means of which my heart comprehends nature? Wasn't our relationship an endless interweaving of the subtlest sensations and the keenest intelligence, all the gradations of which, even bad behavior, bore the stamp of genius? And now!—Alas, her age, which was more advanced, led her to the grave before me. I shall never forget her, her steadfast mind, and her divine tolerance.

A few days ago I met a young man called V——, a candid fellow with a truly felicitous set of features. He's just out of the university, doesn't imagine he's overwise, but still thinks he knows more than other people. He was industrious, too, as I can tell from many indications; in short, he's got plenty of knowledge. When he heard that I draw a lot and that I know Greek (two marvels in these parts), he turned his attention to me and un-

---

1. Some scholars take this as a reference to the pietistic Susanna Katharina von Klettenberg (1723–1774), the "beautiful soul" who befriended Goethe during his illness in 1768, but the description that follows contains features that couldn't be ascribed to her.

Piles zu Winckelmann, und versicherte mich, er habe Sulzers
Theorie, den ersten Teil, ganz durchgelesen, und besitze ein
Manuskript von Heynen über das Studium der Antike. Ich ließ das
gut sein.
Noch gar einen braven Mann habe ich kennen lernen, den
fürstlichen Amtmann, einen offenen, treuherzigen Menschen. Man
sagt, es soll eine Seelenfreude sein, ihn unter seinen Kindern zu
sehen, deren er neun hat; besonders macht man viel Wesens von
seiner ältesten Tochter. Er hat mich zu sich gebeten, und ich will ihn
ehster Tage besuchen. Er wohnt auf einem fürstlichen Jagdhofe, anderthalb Stunden von hier, wohin er nach dem Tode seiner Frau zu
ziehen die Erlaubnis erhielt, da ihm der Aufenthalt hier in der Stadt
und im Amthause zu weh tat.
Sonst sind mir einige verzerrte Originale in den Weg gelaufen, an
denen alles unausstehlich ist, am unerträglichsten ihre Freundschafts-
bezeigungen.
Leb wohl! der Brief wird dir recht sein, er ist ganz historisch.

Am 22. Mai.

Daß das Leben des Menschen nur ein Traum sei, ist manchem schon
so vorgekommen, und auch mit mir zieht dieses Gefühl immer
herum. Wenn ich die Einschränkung ansehe, in welcher die tätigen
und forschenden Kräfte des Menschen eingesperrt sind; wenn ich
sehe, wie alle Wirksamkeit dahinaus läuft, sich die Befriedigung von
Bedürfnissen zu verschaffen, die wieder keinen Zweck haben, als unsere arme Existenz zu verlängern, und dann, daß alle Beruhigung
über gewisse Punkte des Nachforschens nur eine träumende
Resignation ist, da man sich die Wände, zwischen denen man gefangen sitzt, mit bunten Gestalten und lichten Aussichten bemalt – das
alles, Wilhelm, macht mich stumm. Ich kehre in mich selbst zurück,
und finde eine Welt! Wieder mehr in Ahnung und dunkler Begier als
in Darstellung und lebendiger Kraft. Und da schwimmt alles vor
meinen Sinnen, und ich lächle dann so träumend weiter in die Welt.
Daß die Kinder nicht wissen, warum sie wollen, darin sind alle
hochgelahrte Schul- und Hofmeister einig; daß aber auch
Erwachsene gleich Kindern auf diesem Erdboden herumtaumeln,
und wie jene nicht wissen, woher sie kommen und wohin sie gehen,

loaded a lot of knowledge, from Batteux to Wood, from de Piles to Winckelmann, and he assured me that he had thoroughly perused the first part of Sulzer's theory and that he owned a manuscript by Heyne on Greco-Roman studies.[2] I left it at that.

I've met another, quite fine man, the prince's bailiff, a candid, ingenuous person. They say it's a joy to the soul to see him in the midst of his children, of whom he has nine; people make a great to-do about his eldest daughter especially. He has invited me to visit him, and I will do so very soon. He lives in a hunting lodge belonging to his employer which is located an hour and a half away from here; after his wife died, he got permission to move there because it hurt him too much to live here in town in his official residence.

Otherwise, a few odd eccentrics have crossed my path; everything about them is intolerable, the most unbearable thing being their displays of friendship.

Farewell! You'll like this letter, it's completely expository.

May 22

Many a one before me has felt as if human existence were merely a dream, and that feeling is always with me as well. When I observe the limitations within which man's powers of activity and inquiry are enclosed; when I see how all our activity is aimed at satisfying our needs, which in turn have no other purpose than to prolong our wretched existence; and then, when I observe that all our contentment over certain points into which we have inquired is merely dreamy resignation, a painting of the walls between which we are confined with colorful figures and bright landscapes—all of that, Wilhelm, makes me silent. I withdraw into myself, and I discover a world! More as a premonition and an obscure desire than as a clear vision and a living force. Then everything becomes blurred to my senses, and I merely go on facing the world with the smile of a dreamer.

All learned schoolmasters and tutors agree that children don't know what they want; but that adults, too, stagger around this world just like children, and, like them, don't know where they've come from or where they're going—that they have

---

2. All the men named were theoreticians and researchers in the fine arts: Charles Batteux (1713–1780), Robert Wood (1717–1771), Roger de Piles (1635–1709), Johann Joachim Winckelmann (1717–1768), Johann Georg Sulzer (1720–1779), Christian Gottlob Heyne (1729–1812).

ebensowenig nach wahren Zwecken handeln, ebenso durch Biskuit
und Kuchen und Birkenreiser regiert werden: das will niemand gern
glauben, und mich dünkt, man kann es mit Händen greifen.

Ich gestehe dir gern, denn ich weiß, was du mir hierauf sagen
möchtest, daß diejenigen die Glücklichsten sind, die gleich den
Kindern in den Tag hineinleben, ihre Puppen herumschleppen, aus-
und anziehen und mit großem Respekt um die Schublade umher-
schleichen, wo Mama das Zuckerbrot hineingeschlossen hat, und
wenn sie das gewünschte endlich erhaschen, es mit vollen Backen
verzehren und rufen: Mehr! – Das sind glückliche Geschöpfe. Auch
denen ists wohl, die ihren Lumpenbeschäftigungen oder wohl gar
ihren Leidenschaften prächtige Titel geben, und sie dem
Menschengeschlechte als Riesenoperationen zu dessen Heil und
Wohlfahrt anschreiben. – Wohl dem, der so sein kann! Wer aber in
seiner Demut erkennt, wo das alles hinausläuft, wer da sieht, wie artig
jeder Bürger, dem es wohl ist, sein Gärtchen zum Paradiese zuzu-
stutzen weiß, und wie unverdrossen auch der Unglückliche unter der
Bürde seinen Weg fortkeucht und alle gleich interessiert sind, das
Licht dieser Sonne noch eine Minute länger zu sehen – ja, der ist still
und bildet auch seine Welt aus sich selbst, und ist auch glücklich, weil
er ein Mensch ist. Und dann, so eingeschränkt er ist, hält er doch
immer im Herzen das süße Gefühl der Freiheit, und daß er diesen
Kerker verlassen kann, wann er will.

Am 26. Mai.

Du kennst von altersher meine Art, mich anzubauen, mir irgend an
einem vertraulichen Ort ein Hüttchen aufzuschlagen und da mit aller
Einschränkung zu herbergen. Auch hier hab ich wieder ein Plätzchen
angetroffen, das mich angezogen hat.

Ungefähr eine Stunde von der Stadt liegt ein Ort, den sie Wahlheim°
nennen. Die Lage an einem Hügel ist sehr interessant, und wenn man
oben auf dem Fußpfade zum Dorf herausgeht, übersieht man auf
Einmal das ganze Tal. Eine gute Wirtin, die gefällig und munter in
ihrem Alter ist, schenkt Wein, Bier, Kaffee; und was über alles geht,
sind zwei Linden, die mit ihren ausgebreiteten Ästen den kleinen Platz
vor der Kirche bedecken, der ringsum mit Bauerhäusern, Scheuern

---

°Der Leser wird sich keine Mühe geben, die hier genannten Orte zu suchen; man
hat sich genötigt gesehen, die im Originale befindlichen wahren Namen zu verändern.

equally unreal goals and are equally governed by biscuits, cake, and birch rods—no one is willing to believe, though it seems so obvious to me.

I gladly admit to you (because I know how you'd like to respond) that the luckiest people are those who live one day at a time, like children, dragging around their dolls, dressing and undressing them, and skulking with great respect around the drawer where Mother has locked away the pastry; when they finally seize what they've longed for, they stuff their mouths with it and shout: "More!" Those are fortunate creatures. Those people, too, get along who bestow glowing titles on their paltry activities, or even their passions, and announce them to the human race as being monumental undertakings for its salvation and welfare.—Fine for those who can be that way! But the man who humbly realizes what it all amounts to, who observes how neatly every well-off townsman can trim his garden until it's the Garden of Eden, and how tirelessly even the unfortunate continue on their way, though panting beneath their load, and how all people are equally concerned to behold the light of the sun one minute longer—yes, that man is quiet and creates his world out of himself, and is also happy because he's a human being. And then, with all his limitations, he nevertheless always has in his heart the sweet feeling that he's free, and can leave this prison any time he wants.

                                                              May 26
You've long known my way of settling in, of erecting some little cottage in a congenial place and taking shelter in it, with all its limitations. Here, too, I've come across a spot that has attracted me.

About an hour's journey from town there's a village called Wahlheim.° Its position on a hill is very intriguing, and when you walk out of the village on the footpath up there, you suddenly catch sight of the entire valley. A kind innkeeper, a woman obliging and alert for her age, serves wine, beer, and coffee; and, best of all, two lime trees shade the little square in front of the church with their spreading branches; this square is completely

---

°The reader shouldn't take the trouble to locate the places named here; I've felt compelled to change the real names that are found in the original letters. [Footnote in the German original. The real name of the village was Garbenheim. "Wahlheim" connotes a "chosen place," a place to which one has an elective affinity.]

und Höfen eingeschlossen ist. So vertraulich, so heimlich hab ich nicht leicht ein Plätzchen gefunden, und dahin laß ich mein Tischchen aus dem Wirtshause bringen und meinen Stuhl, trinke meinen Kaffee da und lese meinen Homer. Das erste Mal, als ich durch einen Zufall an einem schönen Nachmittage unter die Linden kam, fand ich das Plätzchen so einsam. Es war alles im Felde, nur ein Knabe von ungefähr vier Jahren saß an der Erde, und hielt ein anderes, etwa halbjähriges, vor ihm zwischen seinen Füßen sitzendes Kind mit beiden Armen wider seine Brust, so daß er ihm zu einer Art von Sessel diente und, ungeachtet der Munterkeit, womit er aus seinen schwarzen Augen herumschaute, ganz ruhig saß. Mich vergnügte der Anblick: ich setzte mich auf einen Pflug, der gegenüberstand, und zeichnete die brüderliche Stellung mit vielem Ergötzen. Ich fügte den nächsten Zaun, ein Scheunentor und einige gebrochene Wagenräder bei, alles wie es hintereinander stand, und fand nach Verlauf einer Stunde, daß ich eine wohlgeordnete, sehr interessante Zeichnung verfertiget hatte, ohne das mindeste von dem Meinen hinzuzutun. Das bestärkte mich in meinem Vorsatze, mich künftig allein an die Natur zu halten. Sie allein ist unendlich reich, und sie allein bildet den großen Künstler. Man kann zum Vorteile der Regeln viel sagen, ungefähr was man zum Lobe der bürgerlichen Gesellschaft sagen kann. Ein Mensch, der sich nach ihnen bildet, wird nie etwas Abgeschmacktes und Schlechtes hervorbringen, wie einer, der sich durch Gesetze und Wohlstand modeln läßt, nie ein unerträglicher Nachbar, nie ein merkwürdiger Bösewicht werden kann; dagegen wird aber auch alle Regel, man rede was man wolle, das wahre Gefühl von Natur und den wahren Ausdruck derselben zerstören! Sag du, das ist zu hart! sie schränkt nur ein, beschneidet die geilen Reben etc. – Guter Freund, soll ich dir ein Gleichnis geben? Es ist damit wie mit der Liebe. Ein junges Herz hängt ganz an einem Mädchen, bringt alle Stunden seines Tages bei ihr zu, verschwendet alle seine Kräfte, all sein Vermögen, um ihr jeden Augenblick auszudrücken, daß er sich ganz ihr hingibt. Und da käme ein Philister, ein Mann, der in einem öffentlichen Amte steht, und sagte zu ihm: Feiner junger Herr! lieben ist menschlich, nur müßt Ihr menschlich lieben! Teilet Eure Stunden ein, die einen zur Arbeit, und die Erholungsstunden widmet Eurem Mädchen. Berechnet Euer Vermögen, und was Euch von Eurer Notdurft übrig bleibt, davon verwehr ich Euch nicht, ihr ein Geschenk, nur nicht zu oft, zu machen, etwa zu ihrem Geburts- und Namenstage etc. – Folgt der Mensch, so gibts einen brauchbaren jungen Menschen, und ich will selbst jedem Fürsten raten, ihn in ein Kollegium zu setzen; nur mit seiner Liebe ists am Ende, und wenn er ein Künstler ist, mit

surrounded by farmhouses, barns, and yards. I have rarely found a spot so congenial and homelike; I have my little table and my chair brought out there from the inn, I drink my coffee and read my Homer there. The first time I arrived beneath the lime trees, accidentally one fine afternoon, I found the spot rather deserted. Everyone was in the fields, only a boy of about four was sitting on the ground, while clasping to his chest with both arms another child, about six months old, who was sitting in front of him between his legs, so that the older child served the younger one as a sort of seat; despite the lively look in his dark eyes as he gazed around, the older child remained quite calm. I enjoyed the sight: I sat down on a plow that was standing opposite, and I drew the brothers in that pose with great delight. I added the nearest fence, a barn door, and a few broken cartwheels, everything in its relative position; and after an hour had gone by, I found that I had produced a well-composed, very interesting drawing, without adding a thing from my own imagination. That confirmed my resolve to stick to nature in the future. Nature alone is infinitely rich, nature alone forms a great artist. Much can be said on behalf of rules, more or less the same that can be said in praise of society. A person who forms his style on them will never produce anything tasteless or bad, just as a man who lets himself be fashioned by laws and propriety can never become an unbearable neighbor or a remarkable criminal; but, on the other hand, say what you will, every rule will destroy the true feeling for nature and the true expression of it! Go on, say that's too extreme! "The rule merely curbs our excesses, prunes away luxuriant vines, etc." My good friend, may I give you a comparison? It's the same way as with love. A young man's heart is completely attached to some girl, he spends every hour of the day with her, he spends all his strength and fortune to let her know every moment that he's entirely devoted to her. Then some philistine may perhaps come along, a man in public office, and say to him: "My good young man! To love is human, but you must love in a human way! Divide up your time, so many hours for work, etc., and devote your leisure hours to your girl. Calculate your fortune and, from what you have left over after seeing to your needs, I gladly allow you to give her a gift, but not too often, let's say for her birthday, name day, and the like." If the young man obeys, he will be a useful fellow, and I'd even advise any ruler to give him some administrative post; but his love

seiner Kunst. O meine Freunde! warum der Strom des Genies so selten ausbricht, so selten in hohen Fluten hereinbraust und eure
staunende Seele erschüttert? – Liebe Freunde, da wohnen die gelasse-
nen Herren auf beiden Seiten des Ufers, denen ihre Gartenhäuschen,
Tulpenbeete und Krautfelder zugrunde gehen würden, die daher
inzeiten mit Dämmen und Ableiten der künftig drohenden Gefahr
abzuwehren wissen.

Am 27. Mai.

Ich bin, wie ich sehe, in Verzückung, Gleichnisse und Deklamation
verfallen und habe darüber vergessen, dir auszuerzählen, was mit den
Kindern weiter geworden ist. Ich saß, ganz in malerische Empfindung
vertieft, die dir mein gestriges Blatt sehr zerstückt darlegt, auf
meinem Pfluge wohl zwei Stunden. Da kommt gegen Abend eine
junge Frau auf die Kinder los, die sich indes nicht gerührt hatten, mit
einem Körbchen am Arm, und ruft von weitem: Philipps, du bist
recht brav. – Sie grüßte mich, ich dankte ihr, stand auf, trat näher hin
und fragte sie, ob sie Mutter von den Kindern wäre. Sie bejahte es,
und indem sie dem ältesten einen halben Weck gab, nahm sie das
kleine auf und küßte es mit aller mütterlichen Liebe. – Ich habe,
sagte sie, meinem Philipps das Kleine zu halten gegeben, und bin mit
meinem Ältesten in die Stadt gegangen, um Weißbrot zu holen und
Zucker und ein irden Breipfännchen. – Ich sah das alles in dem
Korbe, dessen Deckel abgefallen war. – Ich will meinem Hans (das
war der Name des Jüngsten) ein Süppchen kochen zum Abende; der
lose Vogel, der Große, hat mir gestern das Pfännchen zerbrochen, als
er sich mit Philippsen um die Scharre des Breis zankte. – Ich fragte
nach dem Ältesten, und sie hatte mir kaum gesagt, daß er auf der
Wiese sich mit ein paar Gänsen herumjage, als er gesprungen kam
und dem Zweiten eine Haselgerte mitbrachte. Ich unterhielt mich
weiter mit dem Weibe und erfuhr, daß sie des Schulmeisters Tochter
sei, und daß ihr Mann eine Reise in die Schweiz gemacht habe, um
die Erbschaft eines Vetters zu holen. – Sie haben ihn drum betrügen
wollen, sagte sie, und ihm auf seine Briefe nicht geantwortet; da ist er
selbst hineingegangen. Wenn ihm nur kein Unglück widerfahren ist!
ich höre nichts von ihm. – Es ward mir schwer, mich von dem Weibe
loszumachen, gab jedem der Kinder einen Kreuzer, und auch fürs
jüngste gab ich ihr einen, ihm einen Weck zur Suppe mitzubringen,
wenn sie in die Stadt ginge, und so schieden wir von einander.
Ich sage dir, mein Schatz, wenn meine Sinnen gar nicht mehr halten wollen, so lindert all den Tumult der Anblick eines solchen

is a thing of the past, and so is his art, if he's an artist. O my friends, why does genius so seldom gush forth, so seldom swell and flow torrentially, stirring your astonished soul?—Dear friends, the calm-and-collected gentlemen dwell on both banks, and their summerhouses, tulip beds, and cabbage patches would be ruined; and so in timely fashion they know how to ward off the future threat with dams and sluices.

May 27

As I see, I've lapsed into ecstatic utterances, similes, and declamation, which have made me forget to tell you the rest of the incident with the children. Completely immersed in the painterly sensations which my letter of yesterday depicted to you very disjointedly, I sat on my plow for about two hours. Then, toward evening, a young woman went up to the children, who hadn't budged in the meantime, with a little basket on her arm, calling from a distance: "Philipps, you're a very good boy!" She greeted me, I thanked her; I stood up, came closer, and asked her whether she was the mother of the children. She said she was, and, while handing the older boy half a bread roll, she picked up the younger one and kissed him with strong maternal affection. She said: "I told my Philipps to hold onto the little one, and I went to town with my oldest boy to buy white bread, sugar, and a clay porridge pot." I saw all of that in the basket, the lid of which had opened. "I want to cook soup for supper for my Hans" (that was the name of the youngest); "yesterday the big boy, that wild rascal, broke the old pot while fighting with Philipps over the porridge scrapings." I asked about the eldest boy, and scarcely had she told me that he was traipsing around the meadow with a few geese, when he came running up, bringing along a hazel switch for the four-year-old. I spoke a little more with the woman and learned that she's the schoolmaster's daughter and that her husband is away in Switzerland to receive a cousin's inheritance. "They wanted to cheat him out of it," she said, "and they wouldn't answer his letters, so he went himself. I hope he hasn't met with any misfortune! I haven't heard a word from him." I found it hard to break away from the woman; I gave each child a small coin, and I also gave her one for her youngest, to buy him a roll to eat with his soup whenever she went to town; and so we said good-bye.

I tell you, my friend, whenever my mind is at its lowest ebb, all my confusion is relieved at the sight of such a person, tracing

Geschöpfs, das in glücklicher Gelassenheit den engen Kreis seines
Daseins hingeht, von einem Tage zum andern sich durchhilft, die
Blätter abfallen sieht und nichts dabei denkt, als daß der Winter
kommt.

Seit der Zeit bin ich oft draußen. Die Kinder sind ganz an mich
gewöhnt, sie kriegen Zucker, wenn ich Kaffee trinke, und teilen das
Butterbrot und die saure Milch mit mir des Abends. Sonntags fehlt
ihnen der Kreuzer nie, und wenn ich nicht nach der Betstunde da bin,
so hat die Wirtin Ordre, ihn auszuzahlen.

Sie sind vertraut, erzählen mir allerhand, und besonders ergötze
ich mich an ihren Leidenschaften und simpeln Ausbrüchen des
Begehrens, wenn mehr Kinder aus dem Dorfe sich versammeln.

Viel Mühe hat michs gekostet, der Mutter ihre Besorgnis zu
nehmen, sie möchten den Herrn inkommodieren.

Am 30. Mai.

Was ich dir neulich von der Malerei sagte, gilt gewiß auch von der
Dichtkunst; es ist nur, daß man das Vortreffliche erkenne und es
auszusprechen wage, und das ist freilich mit wenigem viel gesagt. Ich
habe heut eine Szene gehabt, die, rein abgeschrieben, die schönste
Idylle von der Welt gäbe; doch was soll Dichtung, Szene und Idylle?
muß es denn immer gebosselt sein, wenn wir teil an einer
Naturerscheinung nehmen sollen?

Wenn du auf diesen Eingang viel Hohes und Vornehmes erwartest,
so bist du wieder übel betrogen; es ist nichts als ein Bauerbursch, der
mich zu dieser lebhaften Teilnehmung hingerissen hat. – Ich werde,
wie gewöhnlich, schlecht erzählen, und du wirst mich, wie gewöhnlich, denk ich, übertrieben finden; es ist wieder Wahlheim, und
immer Wahlheim, das diese Seltenheiten hervorbringt.

Es war eine Gesellschaft draußen unter den Linden, Kaffee zu
trinken. Weil sie mir nicht ganz anstand, so blieb ich unter einem
Vorwande zurück.

Ein Bauerbursch kam aus einem benachbarten Hause und beschäftigte sich, an dem Pfluge, den ich neulich gezeichnet hatte, etwas
zurechtzumachen. Da mir sein Wesen gefiel, redete ich ihn an, fragte
nach seinen Umständen, wir waren bald bekannt und, wie mirs
gewöhnlich mit dieser Art Leuten geht, bald vertraut. Er erzählte mir,
daß er bei einer Witwe in Diensten sei und von ihr gar wohl gehalten
werde. Er sprach so vieles von ihr und lobte sie dergestalt, daß ich

the narrow circle of her existence in happy tranquillity, taking each day as it comes, seeing the leaves fall with no other thought than that winter is coming. Ever since then, I've been outdoors frequently. The children are quite used to me; they get sugar when I drink coffee, and share my bread and butter and sour milk in the evening. On Sundays they always receive their little coin, and when I'm not there after services, the innkeeper has orders to distribute the money.

They take me into their confidence and tell me all sorts of things; I'm particularly delighted by their passions and naïve outbreaks of covetousness when several village children assemble.

It's given me a lot of trouble to make their mother stop worrying that they might be "annoying the gentleman."

May 30[3]

What I said to you recently about painting certainly holds for literature as well; one must merely recognize what is excellent and be bold enough to utter it, but, of course, that's saying a lot in just a few words. Today I lived a scene which, if neatly written down, would furnish the most beautiful idyll in the world; but where do literature, scene, and idyll come in? When we take part in a natural event, must it always be tidily rearranged?

If this preamble leads you to expect something lofty and aristocratic, you'll be badly cheated once again; it's a mere farmhand that has inspired this acute sympathy in me.—As usual, I'll narrate this badly and, as usual, you'll find that I've exaggerated, I think; once again it's Wahlheim, always Wahlheim, that produces these rarities.

There was a party of people outside under the lime trees drinking coffee. Because I didn't completely approve of them, I stayed behind on some pretext.

A farmhand came out of a nearby house and occupied himself with some repairs on the plow I had recently drawn. Since I liked the look of him, I spoke to him and asked about his circumstances; soon we had gotten to know each other and, as usually happens to me with people of this sort, we were soon on a confidential basis. He told me that he worked for a widow who treated him very well. He said so much about her and praised her so highly that I could

---

3. This entire letter was a new addition to the 1787 version of the novel.

bald merken konnte, er sei ihr mit Leib und Seele zugetan. Sie sei nicht mehr jung, sagte er, sie sei von ihrem ersten Mann übel gehalten worden, wolle nicht mehr heiraten, und aus seiner Erzählung leuchtete so merklich hervor, wie schön, wie reizend sie für ihn sei, wie sehr er wünsche, daß sie ihn wählen möchte, um das Andenken der Fehler ihres ersten Mannes auszulöschen, daß ich Wort für Wort wiederholen müßte, um dir die reine Neigung, die Liebe und Treue dieses Menschen anschaulich zu machen. Ja, ich müßte die Gabe des größten Dichters besitzen, um dir zugleich den Ausdruck seiner Gebärden, die Harmonie seiner Stimme, das heimliche Feuer seiner Blicke lebendig darstellen zu können. Nein, es sprechen keine Worte die Zartheit aus, die in seinem ganzen Wesen und Ausdruck war; es ist alles nur plump, was ich wieder vorbringen könnte. Besonders rührte mich, wie er fürchtete, ich möchte über sein Verhältnis zu ihr ungleich denken und an ihrer guten Aufführung zweifeln. Wie reizend es war, wenn er von ihrer Gestalt, von ihrem Körper sprach, der ihn ohne jugendliche Reize gewaltsam an sich zog und fesselte, kann ich mir nur in meiner innersten Seele wiederholen. Ich hab in meinem Leben die dringende Begierde und das heiße, sehnliche Verlangen nicht in dieser Reinheit gesehen, ja wohl kann ich sagen: in dieser Reinheit nicht gedacht und geträumt. Schelte mich nicht, wenn ich dir sage, daß bei der Erinnerung dieser Unschuld und Wahrheit mir die innerste Seele glüht, und daß mich das Bild dieser Treue und Zärtlichkeit überall verfolgt, und daß ich, wie selbst davon entzündet, lechze und schmachte.

Ich will nun suchen, auch sie ehstens zu sehn, oder vielmehr, wenn ichs recht bedenke, ich wills vermeiden. Es ist besser, ich sehe sie durch die Augen ihres Liebhabers; vielleicht erscheint sie mir vor meinen eignen Augen nicht so, wie sie jetzt vor mir steht, und warum soll ich mir das schöne Bild verderben?

Am 16. Junius.

Warum ich dir nicht schreibe? – Fragst du das und bist doch auch der Gelehrten einer. Du solltest raten, daß ich mich wohl befinde, und zwar – Kurz und gut, ich habe eine Bekanntschaft gemacht, die mein Herz näher angeht. Ich habe – ich weiß nicht.

Dir in der Ordnung zu erzählen, wie's zugegangen ist, daß ich eines der liebenswürdigsten Geschöpfe habe kennen lernen, wird schwer halten. Ich bin vergnügt und glücklich, und also kein guter Historienschreiber.

Einen Engel! – Pfui! das sagt jeder von der Seinigen, nicht wahr? Und doch bin ich nicht imstande, dir zu sagen, wie sie vollkommen

He &'s passion
and imagination
over reality

to her body and soul. She wasn't
had been treated badly by her hus-
rry; it was so crystal clear from his
ning he found her, how much he
der to erase the memory of her first
to repeat each of his words exactly
to give you an idea of this man's pure affection, love, and loyalty.
Yes, I'd have to possess the talent of the greatest writer to be able
to depict for you in lively fashion at the same time the expressiveness of his gestures, the harmony of his voice, the secret fire in his
glances. No, no words can describe the tenderness that lay in his
entire being and expression; whatever I could say to portray it
would be too coarse. I was particularly moved by his fear lest I
form an unjust opinion about his relationship with her, and conceive doubts as to her good conduct. How charming it was when
he spoke about her form, her body, which, even without the
charms of youth, attracted him to her powerfully and held him
captive—this I can only repeat to myself deep down in my heart.
In my whole life I've never come across urgent desire and hot, ardent longing in such an unadulterated form; I can even say I've
never even imagined or dreamed of it in such purity. Don't scold
me if I tell you that, when I recall such innocence and truth, my
soul glows within me, and that the image of such fidelity and tenderness pursues me everywhere, and that, as if I were inflamed
with them myself, I languish and yearn.

Now I'll try to see her, too, as soon as possible; no, now that I
think it over, I'll avoid doing so. It's better if I see her through
her lover's eyes; perhaps in my own eyes she won't look the same
as she stands before me right now, and why should I spoil that
beautiful image for myself?

June 16

Why I haven't written to you?—You ask that question, even
though you're a scholar! You ought to guess that I'm feeling well,
and in fact— To be brief, I've met somebody who is close to my
heart. I've—I don't know.

To tell you in proper sequence how I came to meet one of the
most adorable beings will be difficult. I'm contented and happy,
and so I can't be a good historian.

"An angel!" Bah! That's what every man calls his sweetheart,
isn't it? And yet I'm incapable of telling you how perfect she is,

ist, warum sie vollkommen ist; genug, sie hat allen meinen Sinn gefangen genommen.

So viel Einfalt bei so viel Verstand, so viele Güte bei so viel Festigkeit, und die Ruhe der Seele bei dem wahren Leben und der Tätigkeit. – Das ist alles garstiges Gewäsch, was ich da von ihr sage, leidige Abstraktionen, die nicht einen Zug ihres Selbst ausdrücken. Ein andermal – Nein, nicht ein andermal, jetzt gleich will ich dirs erzählen. Tu ichs jetzt nicht, so geschäh es niemals. Denn, unter uns, seit ich angefangen habe zu schreiben, war ich schon dreimal im Begriffe, die Feder niederzulegen, mein Pferd satteln zu lassen und hinauszureiten. Und doch schwur ich mir heute früh, nicht hinauszureiten, und gehe doch alle Augenblick ans Fenster, zu sehen, wie hoch die Sonne noch steht. – – –

Ich habs nicht überwinden können, ich mußte zu ihr hinaus. Da bin ich wieder, Wilhelm, will mein Butterbrot zu Nacht essen und dir schreiben. Welch eine Wonne das für meine Seele ist, sie in dem Kreise der lieben muntern Kinder, ihrer acht Geschwister zu sehen! –

Wenn ich so fortfahre, wirst du am Ende so klug sein wie am Anfange. Höre denn, ich will mich zwingen, ins Detail zu gehen.

Ich schrieb dir neulich, wie ich den Amtmann S . . . habe kennen lernen und wie er mich gebeten habe, ihn bald in seiner Einsiedelei, oder vielmehr seinem kleinen Königreiche zu besuchen. Ich vernachlässigte das und wäre vielleicht nie hingekommen, hätte mir der Zufall nicht den Schatz entdeckt, der in der stillen Gegend verborgen liegt.

Unsere jungen Leute hatten einen Ball auf dem Lande angestellt, zu dem ich mich denn auch willig finden ließ. Ich bot einem hiesigen guten, schönen, übrigens unbedeutenden Mädchen die Hand, und es wurde ausgemacht, daß ich eine Kutsche nehmen, mit meiner Tänzerin und ihrer Base nach dem Orte der Lustbarkeit hinausfahren und auf dem Wege Charlotten S . . . mitnehmen sollte. – Sie werden ein schönes Frauenzimmer kennen lernen, sagte meine Gesellschafterin, da wir durch den weiten ausgehauenen Wald nach dem Jagdhause fuhren. – Nehmen Sie sich in acht, versetzte die Base, daß Sie sich nicht verlieben! – Wie so? sagte ich. – Sie ist schon vergeben, antwortete jene, an einen sehr braven Mann, der weggereist ist, seine Sachen in Ordnung zu bringen, weil sein Vater gestorben ist, und sich um eine ansehnliche Versorgung zu bewerben. – Die Nachricht war mir ziemlich gleichgültig.

Die Sonne war noch eine Viertelstunde vom Gebirge, als wir vor dem Hoftore anfuhren. Es war sehr schwül, und die Frauenzimmer äußerten ihre Besorgnis wegen eines Gewitters, das sich in weiß-

Beginning of his love

a   to say that she has taken my
v
n   th so much intelligence, so
m   h firmness of character, and
m   and activeness!—

...... twaddle, that I'm saying about her, nasty abstractions which don't express even one feature of her personality. Another time— No, not another time, I'll tell you about it right now! If I don't do it now, it may never happen. Because, between you and me, three times since starting to write this, I was on the point of laying down my pen, having my horse saddled, and riding out to see her. And yet I swore to myself this morning that I wouldn't ride out there; but every minute I go to the window to see how high the sun still is in the sky. — — —

I was unable to resist, I had to go see her. Now I'm back, Wilhelm; I'll have my nighttime bread and butter and I'll write to you. What rapture it is for my soul to see her in the circle of those dear, lively children, her eight brothers and sisters!

If I go on like this, you'll be as poorly informed at the end as at the beginning. So listen, I'll force myself to go into the details.

I wrote to you recently about meeting the bailiff S—— and his inviting me to visit him soon in his hermitage, or rather his little kingdom. I neglected to do so, and I might never have gone there, if chance hadn't disclosed to me the treasure hidden in that quiet neighborhood.

Our young people had arranged a country ball, which I consented to attend. I offered myself as partner to a local girl who's kind and pretty but otherwise insignificant, and it was agreed that I would hire a coach, ride out to the place where the dance was to be held along with my partner and her female cousin, and pick up Charlotte S—— on the way. "You'll get to meet a beautiful woman," my partner said as we were riding through the wide cleared woods toward the hunting lodge. "Watch out," her cousin interjected, "so you don't fall in love!" "Why is that?" I asked. "She's already engaged," she replied, "to a very fine man who's away on a trip to straighten out his affairs, because his father died, and to apply for a post with a lucrative income." The news left me rather cold.

The sun was still at a quarter-hour's distance from the hills when we arrived in front of the outer gate. It was very sultry, and the ladies expressed their concern over a rainstorm which seemed to

grauen dumpfichten Wölkchen rings am Horizonte zusammen-
zuziehen schien. Ich täuschte ihre Furcht mit anmaßlicher Wetter-
kunde, ob mir gleich selbst zu ahnen anfing, unsere Lustbarkeit
werde einen Stoß leiden.

Ich war ausgestiegen, und eine Magd, die ans Tor kam, bat uns,
einen Augenblick zu verziehen, Mamsell Lottchen würde gleich kommen. Ich ging durch den Hof nach dem wohlgebauten Hause, und da
ich die vorliegenden Treppen hinaufgestiegen war und in die Tür trat,
fiel mir das reizendste Schauspiel in die Augen, das ich je gesehen
habe. In dem Vorsaale wimmelten sechs Kinder, von eilf zu zwei
Jahren, um ein Mädchen von schöner Gestalt, mittlerer Größe, die
ein simples weißes Kleid, mit blaßroten Schleifen an Arm und Brust,
anhatte. Sie hielt ein schwarzes Brot und schnitt ihren Kleinen ringsherum jedem sein Stück nach Proportion ihres Alters und Appetits
ab, gabs jedem mit solcher Freundlichkeit, und jedes rufte so unge-
künstelt sein: Danke! indem es mit den kleinen Händchen lange in
die Höhe gereicht hatte, ehe es noch abgeschnitten war, und nun mit
seinem Abendbrote vergnügt entweder wegsprang, oder nach seinem
stillern Charakter gelassen davonging nach dem Hoftore zu, um die
Fremden und die Kutsche zu sehen, darinnen ihre Lotte wegfahren
sollte. – Ich bitte um Vergebung, sagte sie, daß ich Sie hereinbemühe
und die Frauenzimmer warten lasse. Über dem Anziehen und allerlei
Bestellungen fürs Haus in meiner Abwesenheit habe ich vergessen,
meinen Kindern ihr Vesperbrot zu geben, und sie wollen von nie-
manden Brot geschnitten haben als von mir. – Ich machte ihr ein
unbedeutendes Kompliment, meine ganze Seele ruhte auf der
Gestalt, dem Tone, dem Betragen, und ich hatte eben Zeit, mich von
der Überraschung zu erholen, als sie in die Stube lief, ihre Hand-
schuhe und den Fächer zu holen. Die Kleinen sahen mich in einiger
Entfernung so von der Seite an, und ich ging auf das jüngste los, das
ein Kind von der glücklichsten Gesichtsbildung war. Es zog sich
zurück, als eben Lotte zur Türe herauskam und sagte: Louis, gib dem
Herrn Vetter eine Hand. – Das tat der Knabe sehr freimütig, und ich
konnte mich nicht enthalten, ihn ungeachtet seines kleinen Rotz-
näschens herzlich zu küssen. – Vetter? sagte ich, indem ich ihr die
Hand reichte, glauben Sie, daß ich des Glücks wert sei, mit Ihnen ver-
wandt zu sein? – O, sagte sie mit einem leichtfertigen Lächeln, unsere
Vetterschaft ist sehr weitläufig, und es wäre mir leid, wenn Sie der
schlimmste drunter sein sollten. – Im Gehen gab sie Sophien, der ältesten Schwester nach ihr, einem Mädchen von ungefähr eilf Jahren,
den Auftrag, wohl auf die Kinder achtzuhaben und den Papa zu

be closing in all around the horizon in the form of grayish-white, steamy little clouds. I dispelled their fears with weather-wisdom I didn't really possess, even though I myself started to have a foreboding that our pleasure party was going to suffer a jolt.

I had left the coach when a maid came to the gate and asked us to be patient for a moment; Miss Lotte would soon be there. I walked through the yard toward the well-built house, and when I had ascended the front steps and entered the doorway, I caught sight of the most charming scene I have ever beheld. In the vestibule six children, ages two to eleven, were swarming around a shapely girl of middle height who was wearing a simple white gown with pink bows on her arms and bosom. She was holding a loaf of black bread and was cutting slices for the children around her, each slice proportioned to their age and appetite; she handed each one his slice with great warmth, and each one called out an artless "Thank you!" Each one had stretched out his little hands way up, even before the slice had been cut, and now, contented with their supper, they either dashed off or, if their nature was placid, they walked off calmly, all heading for the outer gate to observe the strangers and the coach in which their Lotte was to ride away. "Please pardon me," she said, "for putting you to the trouble of coming in, and for making the ladies wait. Because I had to dress up and leave all sorts of instructions for the household during my absence, I forgot to give my children their snack, and they won't let anyone else slice their bread but me." I said something routinely courteous, while my whole soul hung on her form, her voice, and her demeanor, and I had just enough time to recover from my surprise when she ran into the parlor to fetch her gloves and fan. The little ones were studying me from the sidelines at a little distance, and I went up to the youngest one, a child with extremely fine features. He recoiled, but just then Lotte came in the door and said: "Louis, give Cousin your hand." The boy did so quite unreservedly, and I couldn't resist giving him a hearty kiss in spite of his little snotty nose. "Cousin?" I said, holding out my hand to her; "do you think I deserve the good fortune of being related to you?" "Oh," she said with a playful smile, "we have a very extended family of cousins, and I'd be sorry if you were the worst of the lot." As we left, she gave Sophie, the next-eldest sister, a girl of about eleven, orders to tend to the children carefully and to greet their father when he came home

grüßen, wenn er vom Spazierritte nach Hause käme. Den Kleinen
sagte sie, sie sollten ihrer Schwester Sophie folgen, als wenn sie's selber wäre, das denn auch einige ausdrücklich versprachen. Eine kleine
naseweise Blondine aber, von ungefähr sechs Jahren, sagte: Du bists
doch nicht, Lottchen, wir haben dich doch lieber. – Die zwei ältesten
Knaben waren auf die Kutsche geklettert, und auf mein Vorbitten er-
laubte sie ihnen, bis vor den Wald mitzufahren, wenn sie versprächen,
sich nicht zu necken und sich recht festzuhalten.

Wir hatten uns kaum zurechtgesetzt, die Frauenzimmer sich be-
willkommet, wechselsweise über den Anzug, vorzüglich über die
Hüte, ihre Anmerkungen gemacht und die Gesellschaft, die man erwartete, gehörig durchgezogen, als Lotte den Kutscher halten und
ihre Brüder herabsteigen ließ, die noch einmal ihre Hand zu küssen
begehrten, das denn der älteste mit aller Zärtlichkeit, die dem Alter
von funfzehn Jahren eigen sein kann, der andere mit viel Heftigkeit
und Leichtsinn tat. Sie ließ die Kleinen noch einmal grüßen, und wir
fuhren weiter.

Die Base fragte, ob sie mit dem Buche fertig wäre, das sie ihr
neulich geschickt hätte. – Nein, sagte Lotte, es gefällt mir nicht; Sie
könnens wiederhaben. Das vorige war auch nicht besser. – Ich er-
staunte, als ich fragte, was es für Bücher wären, und sie mir
antwortete°: – Ich fand so viel Charakter in allem, was sie sagte, ich
sah mit jedem Wort neue Reize, neue Strahlen des Geistes aus ihren
Gesichtszügen hervorbrechen, die sich nach und nach vergnügt zu
entfalten schienen, weil sie an mir fühlte, daß ich sie verstand.

Wie ich jünger war, sagte sie, liebte ich nichts so sehr als Romane.
Weiß Gott, wie wohl mirs war, wenn ich mich Sonntags so in ein
Eckchen setzen und mit ganzem Herzen an dem Glück und Unstern
einer Miß Jenny teilnehmen konnte. Ich leugne auch nicht, daß die
Art noch einige Reize für mich hat. Doch da ich so selten an ein Buch
komme, so muß es auch recht nach meinem Geschmack sein. Und
der Autor ist mir der liebste, in dem ich meine Welt wiederfinde, bei
dem es zugeht wie um mich, und dessen Geschichte mir doch so
interessant und herzlich wird als mein eigen häuslich Leben, das

---

°Man sieht sich genötiget, diese Stelle des Briefes zu unterdrücken, um niemand
Gelegenheit zu einiger Beschwerde zu geben. Obgleich im Grunde jedem Autor
wenig an dem Urteile eines einzelnen Mädchens und eines jungen unsteten
Menschen gelegen sein kann.

from his ride. She told the little ones to obey their sister Sophie as if she were Lotte herself, and a few of them made an express promise to do so. But an impudent little blond girl of about six said: "But it won't be you, Lotte, and we love you more." The two oldest boys had clambered onto the coach, and at my request she allowed them to come along up to the edge of the woods if they promised not to indulge in horseplay, but to hold on tight.

Scarcely had we settled in; scarcely had the ladies greeted one another, made mutual comments on their attire, especially their hats, and thoroughly disparaged the other guests who were expected, when Lotte bade the coachman stop to let off her brothers; they insisted on kissing her hand once more, the older one doing so with all the tenderness that a boy of fifteen can muster up, and the other very roughly and playfully. She made the boys say good night again, and we rode on.

My partner's cousin asked whether she had finished the book she had recently sent her. "No," Lotte replied, "I don't like it, you can have it back. The one before that wasn't much better." I was astonished when I asked what books they were and she answered:—° I found so much character in everything she said; with every word I saw new charms, new rays of intelligence beaming from her features, which seemed gradually to settle into a pleased expression because she could tell that I understood her.

"When I was younger," she said, "I liked nothing better than novels. God knows what a pleasure it was when I could sit down in some corner on Sundays and participate wholeheartedly in the good fortunes and disasters of Miss Jenny.[4] And I don't deny that that genre still possesses some charms for me. But because I so seldom get to read a book, it really has to suit my taste. And I like best those authors in whom I rediscover my own world, in whose books things happen as they do in my environment, and whose stories are nevertheless as interesting and congenial to

---

°I feel compelled to suppress this passage of the letter, to avoid giving anyone cause for any complaints—although, fundamentally, no author can be too much concerned over the opinions of an individual girl and a flighty young man. [Footnote in the original.]   4. Either the heroine of a French novel by Marie-Jeanne Riccoboni (1714–1792); or else the heroine of the novel *Geschichte der Miß Fanny Wilkins* (1766) by Johann Timotheus Hermes (1738–1821).

freilich kein Paradies, aber doch im ganzen eine Quelle unsäglicher
Glückseligkeit ist.

Ich bemühte mich, meine Bewegungen über diese Worte zu verbergen. Das ging freilich nicht weit: denn da ich sie mit solcher
Wahrheit im Vorbeigehen vom Landpriester von Wakefield, vom –°
reden hörte, kam ich ganz außer mich, sagte ihr alles, was ich mußte,
und bemerkte erst nach einiger Zeit, da Lotte das Gespräch an die
anderen wendete, daß diese die Zeit über mit offenen Augen, als
säßen sie nicht da, dagesessen hatten. Die Base sah mich mehr als einmal mit einem spöttischen Näschen an, daran mir aber nichts gelegen
war.

Das Gespräch fiel aufs Vergnügen am Tanze. – Wenn diese
Leidenschaft ein Fehler ist, sagte Lotte, so gestehe ich Ihnen gern,
ich weiß mir nichts übers Tanzen. Und wenn ich was im Kopfe habe
und mir auf meinem verstimmten Klavier einen Contretanz
vortrommle, so ist alles wieder gut.

Wie ich mich unter dem Gespräche in den schwarzen Augen
weidete! wie die lebendigen Lippen und die frischen muntern
Wangen meine ganze Seele anzogen! wie ich, in den herrlichen
Sinn ihrer Rede ganz versunken, oft gar die Worte nicht hörte, mit
denen sie sich ausdrückte! – davon hast du eine Vorstellung, weil
du mich kennst. Kurz, ich stieg aus dem Wagen wie ein
Träumender, als wir vor dem Lusthause stillehielten, und war so in
Träumen rings in der dämmernden Welt verloren, daß ich auf die
Musik kaum achtete, die uns von dem erleuchteten Saal herunter
entgegenschallte.

Die zwei Herrn Audran und ein gewisser N. N. – wer behält alle
die Namen! – die der Base und Lottens Tänzer waren, empfingen uns
am Schlage, bemächtigten sich ihrer Frauenzimmer, und ich führte
das meinige hinauf.

Wir schlangen uns in Menuetts um einander herum; ich forderte
ein Frauenzimmer nach dem andern auf, und just die unleidlichsten
konnten nicht dazu kommen, einem die Hand zu reichen und ein
Ende zu machen. Lotte und ihr Tänzer fingen einen Englischen an,
und wie wohl mirs war, als sie auch in der Reihe die Figur mit uns anfing, magst du fühlen. Tanzen muß man sie sehen! Siehst du, sie ist so
mit ganzem Herzen und mit ganzer Seele dabei, ihr ganzer Körper

---

°Man hat auch hier die Namen einiger vaterländischen Autoren ausgelassen. Wer
teil an Lottens Beifall hat, wird es gewiß an seinem Herzen fühlen, wenn er diese
Stelle lesen sollte, und sonst braucht es ja niemand zu wissen.

me as my own domestic life, which is no paradise, to be sure, but is still on the whole a source of indescribable bliss."

I strove to conceal the emotions that these words aroused in me. To be sure, I couldn't keep it up for long, because when I heard her speak, in passing, with such truth about *The Vicar of Wakefield*,[5] and about ——,* I lost all my self-control and told her everything I felt compelled to; only some time later, when Lotte started speaking to the others, did I notice that during our conversation they had sat there with staring eyes, as if they had been elsewhere. My partner's cousin looked at me more than once, making a mocking face, for which I felt no concern, however.

The conversation turned to the pleasures of dancing. "If that passion is a fault," Lotte said, "I gladly confess, nothing delights me as much as dancing. And when something is bothering me, and I drum out a contredanse on my out-of-tune clavier, everything's all right again."

How I fed my gaze on her dark eyes during the conversation! How those lively lips and fresh, alert cheeks allured my whole soul! How often, totally immersed in the splendid meaning of her speech, I didn't even hear the words with which she expressed herself! You have some notion of all that because you know me. In short, I descended from the coach like a man in a dream when we came to a stop in front of the house where the dance was being held; and I was so lost in dreams in the twilight world around me that I scarcely paid attention to the music that reached our ears from the illuminated ballroom upstairs.

The two gentlemen, Audran and a certain Anonymous (who can remember all the names?), who were the partners of my partner's cousin and of Lotte, met us at the coach door and took their partners into tow, while I led mine upstairs.

We wound about one another in minuets; I invited one lady after another to dance, and it was precisely the most disagreeable ones who could never make up their mind to give me their hand and make an end of it. Lotte and her partner began an English contredanse, and you can surely tell how good I felt when, in the same rank, she began the dance figure along with us. You have to see her dance! You see, she gets into it with so

---

5. The 1766 novel by Oliver Goldsmith (1728–1774). *Here again the names of a few German authors have been omitted. Those who won Lotte's approval will certainly feel this in their hearts if they should happen to read this passage; otherwise, no one needs to know. [Footnote in the original.]

Eine Harmonie, so sorglos, so unbefangen, als wenn das eigentlich alles wäre, als wenn sie sonst nichts dächte, nichts empfände; und in dem Augenblicke gewiß schwindet alles andere vor ihr.

Ich bat sie um den zweiten Contretanz; sie sagte mir den dritten zu, und mit der liebenswürdigsten Freimütigkeit von der Welt versicherte sie mir, daß sie herzlich gern Deutsch tanze. – Es ist hier so Mode, fuhr sie fort, daß jedes Paar, das zusammengehört, beim Deutschen zusammenbleibt, und mein Chapeau walzt schlecht und dankt mirs, wenn ich ihm die Arbeit erlasse. Ihr Frauenzimmer kanns auch nicht und mag nicht, und ich habe im Englischen gesehen, daß Sie gut walzen; wenn Sie nun mein sein wollen fürs Deutsche, so gehen Sie und bitten sichs von meinem Herrn aus, und ich will zu Ihrer Dame gehen. – Ich gab ihr die Hand darauf, und wir machten aus, daß ihr Tänzer inzwischen meine Tänzerin unterhalten sollte.

Nun gings an! und wir ergötzten uns eine Weile an mannigfaltigen Schlingungen der Arme. Mit welchem Reize, mit welcher Flüchtigkeit bewegte sie sich! und da wir nun gar ans Walzen kamen und wie die Sphären um einander herumrollten, gings freilich anfangs, weils die wenigsten können, ein bißchen bunt durcheinander. Wir waren klug und ließen sie austoben, und als die Ungeschicktesten den Plan geräumt hatten, fielen wir ein und hielten mit noch einem Paare, mit Audran und seiner Tänzerin, wacker aus. Nie ist mirs so leicht vom Flecke gegangen. Ich war kein Mensch mehr. Das liebenswürdigste Geschöpf in den Armen zu haben und mit ihr herumzufliegen wie Wetter, daß alles ringsumher verging, und – Wilhelm, um ehrlich zu sein, tat ich aber doch den Schwur, daß ein Mädchen, das ich liebte, auf das ich Ansprüche hätte, mir nie mit einem andern walzen sollte als mit mir, und wenn ich drüber zugrunde gehen müßte. Du verstehst mich!

Wir machten einige Touren gehend im Saale, um zu verschnaufen. Dann setzte sie sich, und die Orangen, die ich beiseite gebracht hatte, die nun die einzigen noch übrigen waren, taten vortreffliche Wirkung, nur daß mir mit jedem Schnittchen, das sie einer unbescheidenen Nachbarin ehrenhalben zuteilte, ein Stich durchs Herz ging.

Beim dritten Englischen Tanz waren wir das zweite Paar. Wie wir die Reihe durchtanzten und ich, weiß Gott mit wieviel Wonne, an ihrem Arm und Auge hing, das voll vom wahresten Ausdruck des offensten, reinsten Vergnügens war, kommen wir an eine Frau, die mir wegen ihrer liebenswürdigen Miene auf einem nicht mehr ganz jungen Gesichte merkwürdig gewesen war. Sie sieht Lotten lächelnd an,

much heart and soul—her whole body one harmony, so carefree and unconstrained, as if it were really everything to her, as if she had no other thoughts or emotions; and at such moments everything else surely vanishes from her sight.

I asked her for the second contredanse; she promised me the third, and with the most charming candor in the world she assured me that she just loved to do German waltzes. "The fashion here," she continued, "is for every couple who belong together to stay together for the waltz, and my partner waltzes badly and is grateful to me for sparing him that effort. Your partner can't do it and doesn't like it, either, and during the contredanse I saw that you waltz well; so, if you want to be my partner in the waltz, go and ask my gentleman's permission, and I'll ask your lady's." I gave her my hand on it, and we came to an agreement that meanwhile her partner would chat with mine.

Now it began, and for a while we took pleasure in various twinings of the arms. With what charm, with what facility she moved! And when we got to the actual spinning about and circled each other like the spheres, it's true things got a little confused at the outset, because very few of the dancers were good at it. We were smart and we let them get exhausted, and after the clumsiest ones had cleared the floor, we moved in and with one more couple, Audran and his partner, we held our own manfully. I've never been so successful at it. I was no longer a mere human. To hold that most adorable being in my arms and to fly around with her like a stormwind, so that everything around me disappeared, and—Wilhelm, to be honest, I swore to myself that no girl I loved or had any claim to would ever waltz with any man but me, even if it cost my life. You know what I mean!

We walked around the ballroom a few times to catch our breath. Then she sat down, and the oranges I had set aside and were now the only ones left, had an excellent effect, except that, with each slice she offered for the sake of politeness to a presumptuous lady next to her, I felt a pang in my heart.

In the third contredanse we were the second couple. As we danced through the lines and (God knows with what great rapture) I was clinging to her arms and staring into her eyes, which were filled with the most genuine expression of the frankest, purest pleasure, we came across a woman who had attracted my attention by the charming expression on her no longer young face. She looked at Lotte with a smile, lifted a menacing finger,

hebt einen drohenden Finger auf und nennt den Namen Albert zweimal im Vorbeifliegen mit viel Bedeutung.

Wer ist Albert? sagte ich zu Lotten, wenns nicht Vermessenheit ist zu fragen. – Sie war im Begriff zu antworten, als wir uns scheiden mußten, um die große Achte zu machen, und mich dünkte einiges Nachdenken auf ihrer Stirn zu sehen, als wir so vor einander vorbeikreuzten. – Was soll ichs Ihnen leugnen, sagte sie, indem sie mir die Hand zur Promenade bot, Albert ist ein braver Mensch, dem ich so gut als verlobt bin. – Nun war mir das nichts Neues (denn die Mädchen hatten mirs auf dem Wege gesagt) und war mir doch so ganz neu, weil ich es noch nicht im Verhältnis auf sie, die mir in so wenig Augenblicken so wert geworden war, gedacht hatte. Genug, ich verwirrte mich, vergaß mich, und kam zwischen das unrechte Paar hinein, daß alles drunter und drüber ging, und Lottens ganze Gegenwart und Zerren und Ziehen nötig war, um es schnell wieder in Ordnung zu bringen.

Der Tanz war noch nicht zu Ende, als die Blitze, die wir schon lange am Horizonte leuchten gesehen, und die ich immer für Wetterkühlen ausgegeben hatte, viel stärker zu werden anfingen und der Donner die Musik überstimmte. Drei Frauenzimmer liefen aus der Reihe, denen ihre Herrn folgten; die Unordnung wurde allgemein, und die Musik hörte auf. Es ist natürlich, wenn uns ein Unglück oder etwas Schreckliches im Vergnügen überrascht, daß es stärkere Eindrücke auf uns macht als sonst, teils wegen des Gegensatzes, der sich so lebhaft empfinden läßt, teils und noch mehr, weil unsere Sinnen einmal der Fühlbarkeit geöffnet sind und also desto schneller einen Eindruck annehmen. Diesen Ursachen muß ich die wunderbaren Grimassen zuschreiben, in die ich mehrere Frauenzimmer ausbrechen sah. Die klügste setzte sich in eine Ecke, mit dem Rücken gegen das Fenster, und hielt die Ohren zu. Eine andere kniete vor ihr nieder und verbarg den Kopf in der ersten Schoß. Eine dritte schob sich zwischen beide hinein und umfaßte ihre Schwesterchen mit tausend Tränen. Einige wollten nach Hause; andere, die noch weniger wußten, was sie taten, hatten nicht so viel Besinnungskraft, den Keckheiten unserer jungen Schlucker zu steuern, die sehr beschäftigt zu sein schienen, alle die ängstlichen Gebete, die dem Himmel bestimmt waren, von den Lippen der schönen Bedrängten wegzufangen. Einige unserer Herren hatten sich hinabbegeben, um ein Pfeifchen in Ruhe zu rauchen; und die übrige Gesellschaft schlug es nicht aus, als die Wirtin auf den klugen Einfall kam, uns ein Zimmer anzuweisen, das Läden und Vorhänge hätte. Kaum waren wir

and spoke the name "Albert" twice, very significantly, as we whizzed apart.

"Who is Albert?" I asked Lotte," if it isn't presumptuous of me to ask." She was about to reply when we had to separate to form the big figure eight, and I thought I could detect some pensiveness on her brow as we crisscrossed in front of each other. "Why should I keep it from you?" she said, while giving me her hand for the promenade. "Albert is a fine man to whom I'm as good as engaged." Now, that was no news to me (because the girls had told me so on the way), and yet it was quite new to me, because I had not yet imagined it in relationship to a woman who had become so dear to me in such a short time. Enough! I got confused, forgot what I was doing, and danced into the wrong couple, so that everything became topsy-turvy, and it took all of Lotte's active tugging and pulling to put things in order again quickly.

The dance was not yet over when the lightning flashes we had been seeing on the horizon for some time, and which I had constantly identified as lightning that cools the atmosphere without portending rain, began to grow much stronger, and thunder drowned out the music. Three ladies broke ranks, followed by their partners; the chaos became general, and the music stopped. It's natural, when a disaster or something frightening takes us by surprise in the midst of pleasure, that it makes a stronger impression on us than at other times, partly because of the contrast that is so keenly experienced, partly, and even more, because our senses have already been opened to receptivity and thus accept impressions all the faster. It is to these causes that I must ascribe the odd grimaces I suddenly saw on the faces of several ladies. The cleverest one sat down in a corner with her back to the window and held her hands over her ears. Another woman knelt down in front of her and hid her head in the first woman's lap. A third thrust herself between those two and clasped her sisters-in-suffering while shedding a thousand tears. A few wanted to go home; others, who knew even less what they were doing, didn't have enough awareness to ward off the bold advances of our young epicureans, who seemed greatly occupied in catching on the lips of the nervous beauties every fearful prayer that was destined for heaven. A few of our gentlemen had gone downstairs to smoke a pipe in peace and quiet; and the other guests didn't refuse when our hostess hit upon the clever idea of leading us into

da angelangt, als Lotte beschäftiget war, einen Kreis von Stühlen zu
stellen, und, als sich die Gesellschaft auf ihre Bitte gesetzt hatte, den
Vortrag zu einem Spiele zu tun. Ich sah manchen, der in Hoffnung auf ein saftiges Pfand sein
Mäulchen spitzte und seine Glieder reckte. – Wir spielen Zählens,
sagte sie. Nun gebt acht! Ich geh im Kreise herum von der Rechten
zur Linken, und so zählt ihr auch ringsherum, jeder die Zahl, die an
ihn kommt, und das muß gehen wie ein Lauffeuer, und wer stockt
oder sich irrt, kriegt eine Ohrfeige, und so bis tausend. – Nun war das
lustig anzusehen. Sie ging mit ausgestrecktem Arm im Kreise herum.
Eins, fing der erste an, der Nachbar zwei, drei der folgende, und so
fort. Dann fing sie an, geschwinder zu gehen, immer geschwinder; da
versahs einer, patsch! eine Ohrfeige, und über das Gelächter der folgende auch patsch! Und immer geschwinder. Ich selbst kriegte zwei
Maulschellen und glaubte mit innigem Vergnügen zu bemerken, daß
sie stärker seien, als sie sie den übrigen zuzumessen pflegte. Ein allgemeines Gelächter und Geschwärm endigte das Spiel, ehe noch das
Tausend ausgezählt war. Die Vertrautesten zogen einander beiseite,
das Gewitter war vorüber, und ich folgte Lotten in den Saal.
Unterwegs sagte sie: Über die Ohrfeigen haben sie Wetter und alles
vergessen! – Ich konnte ihr nichts antworten. – Ich war, fuhr sie fort,
eine der Furchtsamsten, und indem ich mich herzhaft stellte, um den
andern Mut zu geben, bin ich mutig geworden. – Wir traten ans
Fenster. Es donnerte abseitwärts, und der herrliche Regen säuselte
auf das Land, und der erquickendste Wohlgeruch stieg in aller Fülle
einer warmen Luft zu uns auf. Sie stand auf ihren Ellenbogen
gestützt, ihr Blick durchdrang die Gegend, sie sah gen Himmel und
auf mich, ich sah ihr Auge tränenvoll, sie legte ihre Hand auf die
meinige und sagte: – Klopstock! – Ich erinnerte mich sogleich der
herrlichen Ode, die ihr in Gedanken lag, und versank in dem Strome
von Empfindungen, den sie in dieser Losung über mich ausgoß. Ich
ertrugs nicht, neigte mich auf ihre Hand und küßte sie unter den
wonnevollsten Tränen. Und sah nach ihrem Auge wieder – Edler!
hättest du deine Vergötterung in diesem Blicke gesehen, und möchte
ich nun deinen so oft entweihten Namen nie wieder nennen hören.

a room that had shutters and curtains. Scarcely had we arrived there when Lotte busied herself placing chairs in a circle; after the guests had sat down at her request, she suggested playing a game.

I saw many a man pursing his lips and stretching his limbs at the prospect of a juicy "forfeit." "We'll play counting," she said. "Now pay attention! I'll walk around in a circle from right to left, and all of you must count in turn, each one calling out the number matching his place, and it's got to go like a brush fire. Whoever hesitates or makes a mistake gets a slap on the face, and so on until we reach a thousand." Now, that was an amusing sight. She walked around in a circle with her arm extended. "One!" the first man began, his neighbor said "Two," the next man said "Three," and so on. Then she started to go faster, and ever faster; then someone got it wrong: whack, a slap! And because of his laughter, the next man, too: whack! And faster all the time. I myself received two slaps, and with an inner satisfaction, it seemed to me that they were harder than the ones she was normally dealing out to the others. The game ended amid universal laughter and noisy bustling, even before the count had reached a thousand. The most intimate couples drew each other aside, the storm was over, and I followed Lotte into the ballroom. On the way she said: "The slaps made them forget the storm and everything else!" I was unable to respond. She continued: "I was one of the most frightened, but by pretending to be brave in order to give the others courage, I became courageous myself." We stepped over to the window. There was thunder off to the side, and the splendid rain pattered onto the ground, and the most refreshing fragrance ascended to us in all the fullness of a warm breeze. She stood there, leaning on her elbows, her gaze penetrating the surroundings; she looked up at the sky and at me; I saw tears in her eyes; she placed her hand on mine and said: "Klopstock!"[6] I at once recalled the splendid ode she had in mind, and I became immersed in the torrent of emotions with which she had inundated me by speaking that watchword. I couldn't bear it; I stooped over her hand and kissed it with the most rapturous tears. And I looked at her eyes again.—Noble poet, if you could have seen how her gaze deified you! May I never again hear others speak your name, which has so often been profaned!

---

6. A reference to the ode "Die Frühlingsfeier" (The Spring Rite) by Friedrich Gottlob Klopstock (1724–1803). His odes, which he had begun writing in 1747, were published in 1771.

Wo ich neulich mit meiner Erzählung geblieben bin, weiß ich nicht
mehr; das weiß ich, daß es zwei Uhr des Nachts war, als ich zu Bette
kam, und daß, wenn ich dir hätte vorschwatzen können, statt zu
schreiben, ich dich vielleicht bis an den Morgen aufgehalten hätte.

Was auf unserer Hereinfahrt vom Balle geschehen ist, habe ich
noch nicht erzählt, habe auch heute keinen Tag dazu.

Es war der herrlichste Sonnenaufgang. Der tröpfelnde Wald, und
das erfrischte Feld umher! Unsere Gesellschafterinnen nickten ein.
Sie fragte mich, ob ich nicht auch von der Partie sein wollte? ihrent-
wegen sollt ich unbekümmert sein. – Solange ich diese Augen offen
sehe, sagte ich und sah sie fest an, so lange hats keine Gefahr. – Und
wir haben beide ausgehalten bis an ihr Tor, da ihr die Magd leise auf-
machte und auf ihr Fragen versicherte, daß Vater und Kleine wohl
seien und alle noch schliefen. Da verließ ich sie mit der Bitte, sie sel-
bigen Tages noch sehen zu dürfen; sie gestand mirs zu, und ich bin
gekommen; und seit der Zeit können Sonne, Mond und Sterne
geruhig ihre Wirtschaft treiben, ich weiß weder, daß Tag noch daß
Nacht ist, und die ganze Welt verliert sich um mich her.

Ich lebe so glückliche Tage, wie sie Gott seinen Heiligen ausspart;
und mit mir mag werden, was will, so darf ich nicht sagen, daß ich die
Freuden, die reinsten Freuden des Lebens nicht genossen habe. – Du
kennst mein Wahlheim; dort bin ich völlig etabliert, von da habe ich
nur eine halbe Stunde zu Lotten, dort fühl ich mich selbst und alles
Glück, das dem Menschen gegeben ist.

Hätt ich gedacht, als ich mir Wahlheim zum Zwecke meiner
Spaziergänge wählte, daß es so nahe am Himmel läge! Wie oft habe
ich das Jagdhaus, das nun alle meine Wünsche einschließt, auf
meinen weiten Wanderungen, bald vom Berge, bald von der Ebne
über den Fluß gesehen!

Lieber Wilhelm, ich habe allerlei nachgedacht, über die Begier im
Menschen, sich auszubreiten, neue Entdeckungen zu machen, her-
umzuschweifen; und dann wieder über den inneren Trieb, sich der
Einschränkung willig zu ergeben, in dem Gleise der Gewohnheit so
hinzufahren und sich weder um Rechts noch um Links zu beküm-
mern.

Es ist wunderbar: wie ich hierher kam und vom Hügel in das
schöne Tal schaute, wie es mich ringsumher anzog. – Dort das Wäld-
chen! – Ach könntest du dich in seine Schatten mischen! – Dort die

more love

June 19

I no long[er recall where I stopped in my] recent narrative; I do
know th[at it was two A.M. when I got to b]ed, and that, if I had
been ab[le to chat with you instead of writ]ing, I might have kept
you up [until the break of the morning.]

I have not yet told you [what happen]ed when we rode back
from the ball, and I don't have time for it today.

It was the most splendid sunrise. The dripping woods and the
refreshed fields all around us! Our companions dozed off. She
asked me whether I didn't want to join them; I shouldn't hesi-
tate on her account. "As long as I see your eyes open," I said,
gazing at her steadily, "there's no danger of it." And we both held
out until we reached her gate, when her maid quietly opened it
for her and, replying to her questions, assured her that her father and the children were well and that all of them were still
asleep. Then I took leave of her with the request that I might see
her again that very day; she consented, and I visited her; and
ever since then, the sun, moon, and stars can go about their job
with peace of mind; I don't know if it's day or night, and the
whole world around me is lost to my sight.

June 21

I am living days as happy as those which God reserves for his
saints; and no matter what happens to me, I can never honestly
say that I haven't tasted the joys, the purest joys of life.—You
know my Wahlheim; I'm a complete fixture there; from there I
have only a half-hour's ride to Lotte; there I can feel myself, and
all the happiness allotted to man.

If I had only imagined, when I made Wahlheim the goal of my
outings, that it was located so close to heaven! How often I es-
pied the hunting lodge, which now contains all my wishes, on my
extensive roamings, now from the mountain, now from the plain
across the river!

Dear Wilhelm, I've thought about all sorts of things, about
man's desire to spread out, make new discoveries, wander
around; and then about his inner urge to yield willingly to his
limitations, to continue on in the beaten track of his habits, looking neither to the right nor to the left.

It's a strange thing: how I came here and looked down from
the hill at the beautiful valley, how I was attracted by everything
around.—The little patch of woods over there!—Oh, if you only

Spitze des Berges! – Ach könntest du von da die weite Gegend über-
schauen! – Die ineinandergeketteten Hügel und vertraulichen Täler!
– O könnte ich mich in ihnen verlieren! – – Ich eilte hin und kehrte
zurück und hatte nicht gefunden, was ich hoffte. O es ist mit der
Ferne wie mit der Zukunft! Ein großes dämmerndes Ganze ruht vor
unserer Seele, unsere Empfindung verschwimmt darin wie unser
Auge, und wir sehnen uns, ach! unser ganzes Wesen hinzugeben, uns
mit aller Wonne eines einzigen, großen, herrlichen Gefühls ausfüllen
zu lassen – Und ach! wenn wir hinzueilen, wenn das Dort nun Hier
wird, ist alles vor wie nach, und wir stehen in unserer Armut, in unserer Eingeschränktheit, und unsere Seele lechzt nach entschlüpftem
Labsale.

So sehnt sich der unruhigste Vagabund zuletzt wieder nach seinem
Vaterlande und findet in seiner Hütte, an der Brust seiner Gattin, in
dem Kreise seiner Kinder, in den Geschäften zu ihrer Erhaltung die
Wonne, die er in der weiten Welt vergebens suchte.

Wenn ich des Morgens mit Sonnenaufgange hinausgehe nach
meinem Wahlheim und dort im Wirtsgarten mir meine Zuckererbsen
selbst pflücke, mich hinsetze, sie abfädne und dazwischen in meinem
Homer lese; wenn ich in der kleinen Küche mir einen Topf wähle, mir
Butter aussteche, Schoten ans Feuer stelle, zudecke und mich dazu
setze, sie manchmal umzuschütteln: da fühl ich so lebhaft, wie die
übermütigen Freier der Penelope Ochsen und Schweine schlachten,
zerlegen und braten. Es ist nichts, das mich so mit einer stillen,
wahren Empfindung ausfüllte als die Züge patriarchalischen Lebens,
die ich, Gott sei Dank, ohne Affektation in meine Lebensart ver-
weben kann.

Wie wohl ist mirs, daß mein Herz die simple harmlose Wonne des
Menschen fühlen kann, der ein Krauthaupt auf seinen Tisch bringt,
das er selbst gezogen, und nun nicht den Kohl allein, sondern all die
guten Tage, den schönen Morgen, da er ihn pflanzte, die lieblichen
Abende, da er ihn begoß und da er an dem fortschreitenden Wachs-
tum seine Freude hatte, alle in Einem Augenblicke wieder mitge-
nießt.

Am 29. Junius.

Vorgestern kam der Medikus hier aus der Stadt hinaus zum Amtmann
und fand mich auf der Erde unter Lottens Kindern, wie einige auf mir
herumkrabbelten, andere mich neckten, und wie ich sie kitzelte und
ein großes Geschrei mit ihnen erregte. Der Doktor, der eine sehr dog-
matische Drahtpuppe ist, unterm Reden seine Manschetten in Falten

could mingle with its shade!—The mountain peak over there!—
Oh, if you could survey the extensive region from that vantage
point!—The crisscrossing hills and the cozy valleys!—Oh, if I
could lose myself in them!——I hastened over and returned, and
I hadn't found what I'd been hoping for. Oh, distance is like the
future! A great entity looms in dusk before our soul; our emotions become blurred in it, as our sight does; and, alas, we long
to devote our whole being to it, to allow ourselves to be filled
with all the rapture of a single great, splendid feeling— And,
alas, when we hasten over to it, when the "there" becomes
"here," everything is the same as before, and we stand there in
our poverty, in our limitations, and our soul yearns for the comfort that has eluded it.

That's the way the most restless wanderer finally longs for his
homeland again, and finds in his cottage, on his wife's bosom, in
the circle of his children, in his work to support them, the bliss
that he had sought in vain out in the wide world.

When, in the morning, I go out to Wahlheim at sunrise, and
when in the inn garden there I pick my sugar peas myself, sit
down, and string them, reading my Homer at intervals; when, in
the little kitchen, I choose a pot, take a little butter, put peapods
on the fire, cover the pot, sit down next to it, and stir the peas
every so often: I feel so keenly how Penelope's boisterous suitors slaughter, cut up, and roast oxen and pigs. Nothing could fill
me with such a quiet, true sensation as the traits of patriarchal
life, which, thank God, I can weave into my mode of life without
affectation.

How good I feel that my heart can experience the simple, innocent bliss of a man who sets on his table a head of cabbage he
has grown himself, and who now enjoys not the cabbage alone,
but at one and the same time, enjoys once again all those good
days, the morning on which he planted it, the lovely evenings
when he watered it and when he took joy in its developing
growth.

June 29

The day before yesterday the doctor came from town to see the
bailiff here, and found me on the floor among Lotte's children,
some of them climbing over me, others teasing me, while I tickled them and made a lot of noise with them. The doctor, a very
dogmatic marionette who pleats his cuffs while he speaks and

legt und einen Kräusel ohne Ende herauszupft, fand dieses unter der
Würde eines gescheiten Menschen; das merkte ich an seiner Nase.
Ich ließ mich aber in nichts stören, ließ ihn sehr vernünftige Sachen
abhandeln und baute den Kindern ihre Kartenhäuser wieder, die sie
zerschlagen hatten. Auch ging er darauf in der Stadt herum und
beklagte: des Amtmanns Kinder wären so schon ungezogen genug,
der Werther verderbe sie nun völlig.
Ja, lieber Wilhelm, meinem Herzen sind die Kinder am nächsten
auf der Erde. Wenn ich ihnen zusehe und in dem kleinen Dinge die
Keime aller Tugenden, aller Kräfte sehe, die sie einmal so nötig
brauchen werden; wenn ich in dem Eigensinne künftige Standhaftig-
keit und Festigkeit des Charakters, in dem Mutwillen guten Humor
und Leichtigkeit, über die Gefahren der Welt hinzuschlüpfen,
erblicke, alles so unverdorben, so ganz! – immer, immer wiederhole
ich dann die goldenen Worte des Lehrers der Menschen: Wenn ihr
nicht werdet wie eines von diesen! Und nun, mein Bester, sie, die un-
seresgleichen sind, die wir als unsere Muster ansehen sollten, behan-
deln wir als Untertanen. Sie sollen keinen Willen haben! – Haben wir
denn keinen? Und wo liegt das Vorrecht? – Weil wir älter sind und
gescheiter! – Guter Gott von deinem Himmel, alte Kinder siehst du
und junge Kinder und nichts weiter; und an welchen du mehr Freude
hast, das hat dein Sohn schon lange verkündigt. Aber sie glauben an
ihn und hören ihn nicht, – das ist auch was Altes! – und bilden ihre
Kinder nach sich und – Adieu, Wilhelm! Ich mag darüber nicht weiter
radotieren.

Am 1. Julius.

Was Lotte einem Kranken sein muß, fühl ich an meinem eigenen
armen Herzen, das übler dran ist als manches, das auf dem Siechbette
verschmachtet. Sie wird einige Tage in der Stadt bei einer recht-
schaffnen Frau zubringen, die sich nach der Aussage der Ärzte ihrem
Ende naht und in diesen letzten Augenblicken Lotten um sich haben
will. Ich war vorige Woche mit ihr, den Pfarrer von St . . . zu besuchen;
ein Örtchen, das eine Stunde seitwärts im Gebirge liegt. Wir kamen
gegen vier dahin. Lotte hatte ihre zweite Schwester mitgenommen. Als
wir in den mit zwei hohen Nußbäumen überschatteten Pfarrhof traten,
saß der gute alte Mann auf einer Bank vor der Haustür, und da er
Lotten sah, ward er wie neu belebt, vergaß seinen Knotenstock und
wagte sich auf, ihr entgegen. Sie lief hin zu ihm, nötigte ihn, sich
niederzulassen, indem sie sich zu ihm setzte, brachte viele Grüße von
ihrem Vater, herzte seinen garstigen, schmutzigen jüngsten Buben, das

pulls an endless shirt frill out of his waistcoat, found this beneath the dignity of an intelligent person; I could tell by the way he wrinkled his nose. But I didn't let anything disturb me, I let him reel off very sensible arguments while I rebuilt the children's houses of cards, which they had demolished. Then he went around town complaining: the bailiff's children were already badly behaved, now Werther is spoiling them altogether.

Yes, dear Wilhelm, children are the things I love best on earth. When I watch them and I see in the little beings the germs of all the virtues, all the powers that they will need so urgently some day; when I see in their obstinacy future steadfastness and firmness of character, when I detect in their petulance good humor and ease in getting past the world's dangers, everything so unspoiled, so unalloyed—then I always, always repeat the golden words of the Teacher of humanity: "Unless ye become as one of these!" And now, dear friend, we treat them, our equals, whom we should look upon as models for us, as our subjects. They must have no will of their own!—Don't *we* have a will? And wherein does our privilege lie?—In that we're older and cleverer!—Good God, looking down from your heaven, you see old children and young children, and nothing more; and your Son proclaimed to us long ago which ones give you more joy. But people believe in him, and yet don't hear what he says—that's an old story, too!—and raise their children to be like themselves, and— Farewell, Wilhelm! I don't want to go on babbling about this.

July 1

What Lotte must mean to a sick person, I can feel from my own poor heart, which is worse off than many a one languishing on a sickbed. She's going to spend a few days in town with an honest woman who, according to her doctors, is nearing her end and wants to have Lotte beside her in her final moments. I went with her last week to visit the parson of St——, a hamlet located in the mountains an hour's distance away. We got there about four. Lotte had taken along her next-oldest sister. When we entered the parsonage yard, which is shaded by two tall walnut trees, the good old man was seated on a bench in front of his house door, and, upon seeing Lotte, he seemed to be reinvigorated; he forgot his knobby stick and tried to get up and meet her halfway. She ran over to him and made him sit back down; she sat down beside him, delivered kind regards from her father, and hugged his disgusting, filthy

Quakelchen seines Alters. Du hättest sie sehen sollen, wie sie den Alten beschäftigte, wie sie ihre Stimme erhob, um seinen halb tauben Ohren vernehmlich zu werden, wie sie ihm von jungen robusten Leuten erzählte, die unvermutet gestorben wären, von der Vortrefflichkeit des Karlsbades, und wie sie seinen Entschluß lobte, künftigen Sommer hinzugehen, wie sie fand, daß er viel besser aussähe, viel munterer sei als das letztemal, da sie ihn gesehn. Ich hatte indes der Frau Pfarrerin meine Höflichkeiten gemacht. Der Alte wurde ganz munter, und da ich nicht umhin konnte, die schönen Nußbäume zu loben, die uns so lieblich beschatteten, fing er an, uns, wiewohl mit einiger Beschwerlichkeit, die Geschichte davon zu geben. – Den alten, sagte er, wissen wir nicht, wer den gepflanzt hat: einige sagen dieser, andere jener Pfarrer. Der jüngere aber dort hinten ist so alt als meine Frau, im Oktober funfzig Jahr. Ihr Vater pflanzte ihn des Morgens, als sie gegen Abend geboren wurde. Er war mein Vorfahr im Amt, und wie lieb ihm der Baum war, ist nicht zu sagen; mir ist ers gewiß nicht weniger. Meine Frau saß darunter auf einem Balken und strickte, da ich vor siebenundzwanzig Jahren als ein armer Student zum ersten Male hier in den Hof kam. – Lotte fragte nach seiner Tochter: es hieß, sie sei mit Herrn Schmidt auf die Wiese hinaus zu den Arbeitern, und der Alte fuhr in seiner Erzählung fort: wie sein Vorfahr ihn liebgewonnen und die Tochter dazu, und wie er erst sein Vikar und dann sein Nachfolger geworden. Die Geschichte war nicht lange zu Ende, als die Jungfer Pfarrerin mit dem sogenannten Herrn Schmidt durch den Garten herkam; sie bewillkommte Lotten mit herzlicher Wärme, und ich muß sagen, sie gefiel mir nicht übel: eine rasche, wohlgewachsene Brünette, die einen die kurze Zeit über auf dem Lande wohl unterhalten hätte. Ihr Liebhaber (denn als solchen stellte sich Herr Schmidt gleich dar), ein feiner, doch stiller Mensch, der sich nicht in unsere Gespräche mischen wollte, ob ihn gleich Lotte immer hereinzog. Was mich am meisten betrübte, war, daß ich an seinen Gesichtszügen zu bemerken schien, es sei mehr Eigensinn und übler Humor als Eingeschränktheit des Verstandes, der ihn sich mitzuteilen hinderte. In der Folge ward dies leider nur zu deutlich; denn als Friederike beim Spazierengehen mit Lotten und gelegentlich auch mit mir ging, wurde des Herrn Angesicht, das ohnedies einer bräunlichen Farbe war, so sichtlich verdunkelt, daß es Zeit war, daß Lotte mich beim Ärmel zupfte und mir zu verstehn gab, daß ich mit Friederiken zu artig getan. Nun verdrießt mich nichts mehr, als wenn die Menschen einander plagen, am meisten, wenn junge Leute in der Blüte des Lebens, da sie am offensten für alle Freuden sein könnten, einander die paar guten Tage mit

youngest boy, the screeching pet of his old age. You should have seen her, keeping the old man busy, raising her voice so his half-deaf ears could hear her, telling him about sturdy young people who had died unexpectedly, about the excellence of the spa at Karlsbad, and how she approved of his decision to go there next summer, how she thought he was looking much better and was much livelier than the last time she had seen him. Meanwhile I had paid my comp   old man grew quite lively, and w   autiful walnut trees, which wer   e, he began, though with som   ry. "We don't know," he said, "v   t was one pastor, others say it v   ehind it there is exactly as old a   father planted it on the morning   rn. He was my predecessor in o   he loved that tree; I certainly love it no less. My wife was sitting under it on a tree trunk, knitting, when I first stepped into this yard, a poor student, twenty-seven years ago." Lotte inquired after his daughter; it seems she had gone out to the meadow with Mr. Schmidt to see the laborers, and the old man continued his story: how his predecessor had grown fond of him, as his daughter had also, and how he had become, first his curate and then his successor. The story wasn't long over when the parson's daughter came up through the garden along with the aforesaid Mr. Schmidt; she welcomed Lotte with cordial warmth, and I must say I liked her quite a lot: a quick-moving, well-shaped brunette who could well entertain a man during a brief rustic sojourn. Her suitor (for Mr. Schmidt immediately introduced himself as such) was a well-bred but quiet person who wouldn't take part in our conversations, even though Lotte kept trying to draw him in. What made me saddest was that I thought I could detect in his face that it was obstinacy and ill humor, rather than a circumscribed intelligence, that prevented him from participating. Later on, this became all too clear, unfortunately: when the four of us went for a stroll and Friederike walked with Lotte and occasionally with me, the gentleman's face, which was swarthy to begin with, darkened so visibly that it was time for Lotte to pluck my sleeve and give me to understand that I had been too attentive to Friederike. Now, nothing vexes me more than when people plague one another, especially when young people in the prime of life, when they could be most open to any pleasure, spoil one an-

Fratzen verderben und nur erst zu spät das Unersetzliche ihrer Verschwendung einsehen. Mich wurmte das, und ich konnte nicht umhin, da wir gegen Abend in den Pfarrhof zurückkehrten und an einem Tische Milch aßen, und das Gespräch auf Freude und Leid der Welt sich wendete, den Faden zu ergreifen und recht herzlich gegen die üble Laune zu reden. – Wir Menschen beklagen uns oft, fing ich an, daß der guten Tage so wenig sind und der schlimmen so viel, und wie mich dünkt, meist mit Unrecht. Wenn wir immer ein offenes Herz hätten, das Gute zu genießen, das uns Gott für jeden Tag bereitet, wir würden alsdann auch Kraft genug haben, das Übel zu tragen, wenn es kommt. – Wir haben aber unser Gemüt nicht in unserer Gewalt, versetzte die Pfarrerin; wie viel hängt vom Körper ab! wenn einem nicht wohl ist, ists einem überall nicht recht. – Ich gestand ihr das ein. – Wir wollen es also, fuhr ich fort, als eine Krankheit ansehen und fragen, ob dafür kein Mittel ist? – Das läßt sich hören, sagte Lotte: ich glaube wenigstens, daß viel von uns abhängt. Ich weiß es an mir. Wenn mich etwas neckt und mich verdrießlich machen will, spring ich auf und sing ein paar Contretänze den Garten auf und ab, gleich ists weg. – Das wars, was ich sagen wollte, versetzte ich: es ist mit der üblen Laune völlig wie mit der Trägheit, denn es ist eine Art von Trägheit. Unsere Natur hängt sehr dahin, und doch, wenn wir nur einmal die Kraft haben, uns zu ermannen, geht uns die Arbeit frisch von der Hand, und wir finden in der Tätigkeit ein wahres Vergnügen. – Friederike war sehr aufmerksam, und der junge Mensch wandte mir ein, daß man nicht Herr über sich selbst sei und am wenigsten über seine Empfindungen gebieten könne. – Es ist hier die Frage von einer unangenehmen Empfindung, versetzte ich, die doch jedermann gerne los ist; und niemand weiß, wie weit seine Kräfte gehen, bis er sie versucht hat. Gewiß, wer krank ist, wird bei allen Ärzten herumfragen, und die größten Resignationen, die bittersten Arzeneien wird er nicht abweisen, um seine gewünschte Gesundheit zu erhalten. – Ich bemerkte, daß der ehrliche Alte sein Gehör anstrengte, um an unserm Diskurse teilzunehmen, ich erhob die Stimme, indem ich die Rede gegen ihn wandte. Man predigt gegen so viele Laster, sagte ich; ich habe noch nie gehört, daß man gegen die üble Laune vom Predigtstuhle gearbeitet hätte.* – Das müssen die Stadtpfarrer tun, sagte er, die Bauern haben keinen bösen Humor; doch könnte es auch zuweilen nicht schaden, es wäre eine Lektion für seine Frau wenigstens und für den Herrn Amtmann. – Die Gesellschaft

---

*Wir haben nun von Lavatern eine treffliche Predigt hierüber, unter denen über das Buch Jonas.

other's good days (which are so few) with eccentric behavior, and only realize they have squandered something irreplaceable when it's too late. That irritated me, and when we returned to the parsonage toward evening and were drinking milk at a table, the conversation turning to the joys and sorrows of life, I couldn't refrain from picking up the thread and inveighing quite forcefully against spoilsports. "We humans often complain," I began, "that there are so few happy days and so many bad ones, and I think we're generally wrong. If we always had a heart receptive to the enjoyment of the good things God prepares for us every day, then we'd also have the strength to endure bad things when they arrive." "But our moods aren't in our power," the parson's wife retorted; "so much depends on our physical state! When someone doesn't feel well, nothing goes right for him." I admitted she was correct. "And so," I continued, "let's consider it to be an illness, and let's ask whether there's a remedy for it." "That sounds right to me," said Lotte; "at least, I believe that a lot depends on us. I know that from myself. When something bothers me and is apt to make me ill-tempered, I jump up and I hum a few contredanses while pacing to and fro in the garden, and it's gone right away." "That's what I meant to say," I chimed in; "a bad mood is just like sluggishness, because it *is* one type of sluggishness. Our nature is strongly inclined toward it, and yet if we once summon up the strength to get a grip on ourselves, our work proceeds briskly, and we find real pleasure in being active." Friederike was very attentive, and the young man raised the objection that a person can't control himself and certainly can't dominate his feelings. "What we're talking about here is an unpleasant feeling," I retorted, "one that everybody would surely be glad to get rid of; and no one knows how far his powers extend until he has tested them. Certainly a sick man will ask advice of every doctor, and he won't balk at the severest deprivations or the bitterest medicine to regain the health he desires." I noticed that the honorable old man was straining his ears to participate in our discussion; I raised my voice and addressed my remarks to him. "People preach against so many vices," I said, "but I have not yet heard about anyone combating surly temper from the pulpit."° "Town preachers need to do that," he said; "peasants don't have bad tempers. But it couldn't hurt occasionally; it would be a lesson

---

°Now we have an excellent sermon on the subject by Lavater, one of those based on the book of Jonah. [Footnote in the original. The Swiss preacher Johann Caspar Lavater (1741–1801) became most famous for his work on physiognomy. Goethe befriended him from 1774 to 1786, and ridiculed him later on.]

lachte, und er herzlich mit, bis er in einen Husten verfiel, der unsern Diskurs eine Zeitlang unterbrach; darauf denn der junge Mensch wieder das Wort nahm: Sie nannten den bösen Humor ein Laster; mich deucht, das ist übertrieben. – Mitnichten, gab ich zur Antwort, wenn das, womit man sich selbst und seinem Nächsten schadet, diesen Namen verdient. Ist es nicht genug, daß wir einander nicht glücklich machen können, müssen wir auch noch einander das Vergnügen rauben, das jedes Herz sich noch manchmal selbst gewähren kann? Und nennen Sie mir den Menschen, der übler Laune ist und so brav dabei, sie zu verbergen, sie allein zu tragen, ohne die Freude um sich her zu zerstören! Oder ist sie nicht vielmehr ein innerer Unmut über unsere eigene Unwürdigkeit, ein Mißfallen an uns selbst, das immer mit einem Neide verknüpft ist, der durch eine törichte Eitelkeit aufgehetzt wird? Wir sehen glückliche Menschen, die *wir* nicht glücklich machen, und das ist unerträglich. – Lotte lächelte mich an, da sie die Bewegung sah, mit der ich redete, und eine Träne in Friederikens Auge spornte mich fortzufahren. – Wehe denen, sagte ich, die sich der Gewalt bedienen, die sie über ein Herz haben, um ihm die einfachen Freuden zu rauben, die aus ihm selbst hervorkeimen. Alle Geschenke, alle Gefälligkeiten der Welt ersetzen nicht einen Augenblick Vergnügen an sich selbst, den uns eine neidische Unbehaglichkeit unsers Tyrannen vergällt hat.

Mein ganzes Herz war voll in diesem Augenblicke; die Erinnerung so manches Vergangenen drängte sich an meine Seele, und die Tränen kamen mir in die Augen.

Wer sich das nur täglich sagte, rief ich aus: du vermagst nichts auf deine Freunde, als ihnen ihre Freuden zu lassen und ihr Glück zu vermehren, indem du es mit ihnen genießest. Vermagst du, wenn ihre innere Seele von einer ängstigenden Leidenschaft gequält, vom Kummer zerrüttet ist, ihnen einen Tropfen Linderung zu geben?

Und wenn die letzte, bangste Krankheit dann über das Geschöpf herfällt, das du in blühenden Tagen untergraben hast, und sie nun daliegt in dem erbärmlichen Ermatten, das Auge gefühllos gen Himmel sieht, der Todesschweiß auf der blassen Stirne abwechselt, und du vor dem Bette stehst wie ein Verdammter, in dem innigsten Gefühl, daß du nichts vermagst mit deinem ganzen Vermögen, und die Angst dich inwendig krampft, daß du alles hingeben möchtest, dem untergehenden Geschöpfe einen Tropfen Stärkung, einen Funken Mut einflößen zu können.

Die Erinnerung einer solchen Szene, wobei ich gegenwärtig war, fiel mit ganzer Gewalt bei diesen Worten über mich. Ich nahm das Schnupftuch vor die Augen und verließ die Gesellschaft, und nur

for my wife, at least, and for the bailiff." Everyone laughed, and he joined in heartily until he was seized by a fit of coughing which interrupted our discussion for a time. Thereupon the young man took the floor again: "You called bad temper a vice; I find that an exaggeration." "Not at all," I replied, "not if something that injures oneself and one's neighbors deserves that name. Isn't it enough that we can't make one another happy without also depriving one another of the pleasure in which every heart can still sometimes indulge? And name me that man who is ill-tempered and at the same time so noble as to conceal it, to suffer it in silence without disrupting the joy all around him! Or, isn't ill temper rather an inward indignation over our own unworthiness, a self-dislike which is always combined with an envy that's stirred up by foolish vanity? We see happy people, who haven't been made happy by *us*, and that's unbearable." Lotte smiled at me upon observing my agitated delivery, and a tear in Friederike's eyes spurred me on to proceed. "Woe to those," I said, "who use the power they have over another's heart to rob it of the simple pleasures that germinate from it spontaneously. No amount of gifts or kind favors can replace one moment of self-satisfaction that an envious malaise of our tyrant has soured for us."

My whole heart was full at that moment; the recollection of so much in the past oppressed my soul, and tears welled up in my eyes.

I exclaimed: "If people would only tell themselves every day: you have no power over your friends except to let them have their pleasures and to increase their happiness by enjoying it along with them. When the depths of their soul are tortured by an alarming passion or torn apart by grief, do you have the power to offer them a drop of relief?

"And when the final, most frightening illness befalls the being whom you undermined when she was in the prime of life, and she now lies there in pitiful exhaustion, her eyes fixed unseeingly on heaven, the sweat of death coming and going on her pallid brow, and you stand in front of her bed like a damned soul, knowing full well that nothing in your power can help her, and anxiety attacks your vitals, so that you'd sacrifice anything to be able to give the perishing woman one drop of strength, one spark of courage—"

The recollection of just such a scene, at which I had been present, came over me with full force at these words. I pressed my handkerchief to my eyes and left the room; only Lotte's voice, call-

Lottens Stimme, die mir rief, wir wollten fort, brachte mich zu mir selbst. Und wie sie mich auf dem Wege schalt, über den zu warmen Anteil an allem, und daß ich drüber zugrunde gehen würde! daß ich mich schonen sollte! – O der Engel! Um deinetwillen muß ich leben!

Am 6. Julius.

Sie ist immer um ihre sterbende Freundin und ist immer dieselbe, immer das gegenwärtige, holde Geschöpf, das, wo sie hinsieht, Schmerzen lindert und Glückliche macht. Sie ging gestern abend mit Mariannen und dem kleinen Malchen spazieren; ich wußte es und traf sie an, und wir gingen zusammen. Nach einem Wege von anderthalb Stunden kamen wir gegen die Stadt zurück, an den Brunnen, der mir so wert und nun tausendmal werter ist. Lotte setzte sich aufs Mäuerchen, wir standen vor ihr. Ich sah umher, ach! und die Zeit, da mein Herz so allein war, lebte wieder vor mir auf. – Lieber Brunnen, sagte ich, seither hab ich nicht mehr an deiner Kühle geruht, hab in eilendem Vorübergehn dich manchmal nicht angesehn. – Ich blickte hinab und sah, daß Malchen mit einem Glase Wasser sehr beschäftigt heraufstieg. – Ich sah Lotten an und fühlte alles, was ich an ihr habe. Indem kommt Malchen mit einem Glase. Marianne wollt es ihr abnehmen – Nein! rief das Kind mit dem süßesten Ausdrucke, nein, Lottchen, *du* sollst zuerst trinken! – Ich ward über die Wahrheit, über die Güte, womit sie das ausrief, so entzückt, daß ich meine Empfindung mit nichts ausdrücken konnte, als ich nahm das Kind von der Erde und küßte es lebhaft, das sogleich zu schreien und zu weinen anfing. – Sie haben übel getan, sagte Lotte. – Ich war betroffen. – Komm, Malchen, fuhr sie fort, indem sie es bei der Hand nahm und die Stufen hinabführte, da wasche dich aus der frischen Quelle, geschwind, geschwind, da tuts nichts. – Wie ich so dastand und zusah, mit welcher Emsigkeit das Kleine mit seinen nassen Händchen die Backen rieb, mit welchem Glauben, daß durch die Wunderquelle alle Verunreinigung abgespült und die Schmach abgetan würde, einen häßlichen Bart zu kriegen; wie Lotte sagte: es ist genug, und das Kind doch immer eifrig fortwusch, als wenn viel mehr täte als wenig – ich sage dir, Wilhelm, ich habe mit mehr Respekt nie einer Taufhandlung beigewohnt, und als Lotte heraufkam, hätte ich mich gern vor ihr niedergeworfen wie vor einem Propheten, der die Schulden einer Nation weggeweiht hat.

Des Abends konnte ich nicht umhin, in der Freude meines Herzens

[handwritten annotation:] likes kissing kids

[handwritten annotation:] Shows what he likes about Lotte

y senses. And
empathy for
take care of
sake!

July 6
same, always
makes people
out walking
ut it and met
an hour and
ntain which
er. Lotte sat
down on the low wall, and we stood in front of her. I looked around and, alas, the days in which my heart was so alone were revived in my mind. "Dear fountain," I said, "since then I haven't rested by your coolness; in my hasty passing I sometimes haven't looked at you." I glanced down and saw that Malchen was climbing up very busily with a glass of water.—I looked at Lotte and felt all that she means to me. Meanwhile Malchen arrived with her[8] glass. Marianne wanted to take it from her. "No!" the child exclaimed in the sweetest tones; "no, Lotte, *you* must drink first!" The sincerity and lovingness in her exclamation delighted me so, that the only way I could express my emotion was to pick up the child and kiss her warmly; immediately she began to yell and cry. "You did wrong," said Lotte. I was hurt. "Come, Malchen," she continued, taking her by the hand and leading her down the steps; "go wash in the fresh spring, quickly, quickly, and nothing will happen." How I stood there watching the child rubbing her cheeks so diligently with her wet little hands, in the firm conviction that the miraculous spring would rinse away all contamination and remove the disgrace of getting an ugly beard; how Lotte said it was enough, but the child kept on washing eagerly, as if more were better than less—I tell you, Wilhelm, I've never attended a baptism with greater reverence. When Lotte came back up, I would have gladly prostrated myself before her as if she were a prophet whose sacrament had expunged the sins of a nation.

In the evening my heart was so joyous that I couldn't help nar-

---

7. No doubt a pet name for Amalie (a younger sister). Marianne is unidentified (a sister? a maid?).   8. Reading *seinem* for *einem*, as at least one German editor suggests.

den Vorfall einem Manne zu erzählen, dem ich Menschensinn zu-
traute, weil er Verstand hat; aber wie kam ich an! Er sagte, das sei sehr
übel von Lotten gewesen; man solle den Kindern nichts weismachen;
dergleichen gebe zu unzähligen Irrtümern und Aberglauben Anlaß,
wovor man die Kinder frühzeitig bewahren müsse. – Nun fiel mir ein,
daß der Mann vor acht Tagen hatte taufen lassen, drum ließ ichs vorbeigehen und blieb in meinem Herzen der Wahrheit getreu: wir sollen
es mit den Kindern machen, wie Gott mit uns, der uns am glücklichsten macht, wenn er uns in freundlichem Wahne so hintaumeln läßt.

Am 8. Julius.

Was man ein Kind ist! Was man nach so einem Blicke geizt! Was man
ein Kind ist! – Wir waren nach Wahlheim gegangen. Die Frauenzimmer fuhren hinaus, und während unserer Spaziergänge glaubte
ich in Lottens schwarzen Augen – ich bin ein Tor, verzeih mirs! du
solltest sie sehen, diese Augen! – Daß ich kurz bin (denn die Augen
fallen mir zu vor Schlaf), siehe, die Frauenzimmer stiegen ein, da
standen um die Kutsche der junge W . . . , Selstadt und Audran und
ich. Da ward aus dem Schlage geplaudert mit den Kerlchen, die
freilich leicht und lüftig genug waren. – Ich suchte Lottens Augen;
ach sie gingen von einem zum andern! Aber auf mich! mich! mich!
der ganz allein auf sie resigniert dastand, fielen sie nicht! – Mein Herz
sagte ihr tausend Adieu! Und sie sah mich nicht! Die Kutsche fuhr
vorbei, und eine Träne stand mir im Auge. Ich sah ihr nach und sah
Lottens Kopfputz sich zum Schlage herauslehnen, und sie wandte
sich um zu sehen, ach! nach mir? – Lieber! In dieser Ungewißheit
schwebe ich; das ist mein Trost: vielleicht hat sie sich nach mir umge-
sehen! Vielleicht! – Gute Nacht! O was ich ein Kind bin!

Am 10. Julius.

Die alberne Figur, die ich mache, wenn in Gesellschaft von ihr
gesprochen wird, solltest du sehen! Wenn man mich nun gar fragt,
wie sie mir gefällt – Gefällt! das Wort hasse ich auf den Tod. Was muß
das für ein Mensch sein, dem Lotte gefällt, dem sie nicht alle Sinnen,
alle Empfindungen ausfüllt! Gefällt! Neulich fragte mich einer, wie
mir Ossian gefiele!

rating the incident to a man whom I credited with human feelings because he's intelligent; but how wrong I was! He said that Lotte had acted very badly; children shouldn't be told any tall stories, because that gives rise to countless errors and superstitions from which children must be guarded at an early age.—It then occurred to me that the same man had celebrated a baptism a week earlier; so I let the matter drop, but remained faithful in my heart to the truth: we should treat children the way God treats us: he makes us happiest when he lets us reel along in a beneficent delusion.

July 8

How childish we are! How we long for such a glance! How childish we are!—We had gone to Wahlheim. The ladies drove out, and during our strolls I thought I could detect in Lotte's dark eyes—I'm a fool, forgive me! You ought to see those eyes!—To be brief (because I'm so sleepy, my eyes are closing), behold: the ladies got into the coach, while young W——, Selstadt, Audran, and I were standing around it. Then the ladies chatted through the coach door with the lads, who were certainly cheerful and breezy enough.—I sought Lotte's eyes; alas, they were turning from one man to another! But they didn't alight on me, me, me, the only one there devoted to her!—My heart made her a thousand farewells! And she didn't look at me! The coach drove past, and there were tears in my eyes. I watched her go, and I saw Lotte's headgear leaning out the coach door, and she turned her head to look back—ah, at me?—Dear friend! I'm adrift in this uncertainty; that is my consolation; perhaps she looked back at me! Perhaps!—Good night! Oh, how childish I am!

July 10

The foolish figure I cut when I'm in company and people talk about her—you should see it! Whenever they go so far as to ask me how I like her— "Like!" I hate that word mortally. What kind of person would merely "like" Lotte, and not have his whole mind and heart filled with her? "Like!" Recently someone asked me how I "liked" Ossian![8]

---

8. Ossian, son of Fingal, was a legendary Irish bard of the third century A.D. From 1760 to 1765 the Scotsman James Macpherson (1736–1796) published a number of pre-Romantic prose poems purporting to be translations from recently rediscovered manuscripts of Ossian's works; most readers believed him; Goethe was an Ossian enthusiast at this time.

Am 11. Julius.

Frau M . . . ist sehr schlecht; ich bete für ihr Leben, weil ich mit
Lotten dulde. Ich sehe sie selten bei meiner Freundin, und heute hat
sie mir einen wunderbaren Vorfall erzählt. – Der alte M . . . ist ein
geiziger, rangiger Filz, der seine Frau im Leben was rechts geplagt
und eingeschränkt hat; doch hat sich die Frau immer durchzuhelfen
gewußt. Vor wenigen Tagen, als der Arzt ihr das Leben abgesprochen
hatte, ließ sie ihren Mann kommen – Lotte war im Zimmer – und redete ihn also an: Ich muß dir eine Sache gestehen, die nach meinem
Tode Verwirrung und Verdruß machen könnte. Ich habe bisher die
Haushaltung geführt, so ordentlich und sparsam als möglich: allein du
wirst mir verzeihen, daß ich dich diese dreißig Jahre her hintergangen
habe. Du bestimmtest im Anfange unserer Heirat ein geringes für die
Bestreitung der Küche und anderer häuslichen Ausgaben. Als unsere
Haushaltung stärker wurde, unser Gewerbe größer, warst du nicht zu
bewegen, mein Wochengeld nach dem Verhältnisse zu vermehren;
kurz, du weißt, daß du in den Zeiten, da sie am größten war, ver-
langtest, ich solle mit sieben Gulden die Woche auskommen. Die
habe ich denn ohne Widerrede genommen und mir den Überschuß
wöchentlich aus der Losung geholt, da niemand vermutete, daß die
Frau die Kasse bestehlen würde. Ich habe nichts verschwendet und
wäre auch, ohne es zu bekennen, getrost der Ewigkeit entgegenge-
gangen, wenn nicht diejenige, die nach mir das Hauswesen zu führen
hat, sich nicht zu helfen wissen würde und du doch immer darauf
bestehen könntest, deine erste Frau sei damit ausgekommen.

Ich redete mit Lotten über die unglaubliche Verblendung des
Menschensinns, daß einer nicht argwohnen soll, dahinter müsse was
anders stecken, wenn eins mit sieben Gulden hinreicht, wo man den
Aufwand vielleicht um zweimal so viel sieht. Aber ich habe selbst
Leute gekannt, die des Propheten ewiges Ölkrüglein ohne Verwunde-
rung in ihrem Hause angenommen hätten.

Am 13. Julius.

Nein, ich betrüge mich nicht! Ich lese in ihren schwarzen Augen
wahre Teilnehmung an mir und meinem Schicksal! Ja ich fühle, und
darin darf ich meinem Herzen trauen, daß sie – o darf ich, kann ich
den Himmel in diesen Worten aussprechen? – daß sie mich liebt!

Mich liebt! – Und wie wert ich mir selbst werde, wie ich – dir darf

July 11

Mrs. M—— is very ill; I pray for her life because I am suffering along with Lotte. I see her rarely at my lady friend's house, and today she told me about an odd incident.—Old M—— is a greedy, avaricious miser, who has really tormented and confined his wife during her lifetime, but she always managed to get by. A few days ago, when the doctor gave her no chance of survival, she sent for her husband—Lotte was in the room—and addressed him as follows: "I must confess something to you which might create confusion and vexation after my death. Until now I've managed the household expenses as properly and thriftily as possible; but you'll forgive me for having deceived you for thirty years now. When we were just married, you allowed me a small sum for the kitchen and other domestic outlays. When our household expanded and our business grew, you couldn't be persuaded to increase my weekly allowance in proportion; in short, you know that, when the housekeeping demanded most, I had to make do with seven gulden a week. I took them from you without arguing, and I got whatever else I needed each week out of the till, because no one would imagine that the lady of the house would rob the cashbox. I didn't squander a cent and I would cheerfully have met my Maker without confessing it, if it weren't that the woman who'll manage the household after me would be unable to make ends meet, and you would still be able to affirm that your first wife got along with that amount."

I spoke with Lotte about the unbelievable blindness of human feelings which could prevent a man from suspecting that there must be a reason for his wife to get by with seven gulden while the outlay is obviously about twice that amount. But I myself have known people who would have received the prophet's self-replenishing oil jug[9] in their home without amazement.

July 13

No, I'm not mistaken! In her dark eyes I read true sympathy for me and my fate! Yes, I feel (and in this I can trust my heart) that she—oh, may I, can I express heaven in these words?—that she loves me!

[10]Loves me!—And how good I feel about myself, how I—I

---

9. Elisha caused the oil jug of the widow at Zarephath to be perpetually full (I Kings 17: 12–16).   10. This entire paragraph was a new addition in the 1787 version.

ichs wohl sagen, du hast Sinn für so etwas – wie ich mich selbst anbete, seitdem sie mich liebt!

Ob das Vermessenheit ist oder Gefühl des wahren Verhältnisses? – Ich kenne den Menschen nicht, von dem ich etwas in Lottens Herzen fürchtete. Und doch – wenn sie von ihrem Bräutigam spricht, mit solcher Wärme, solcher Liebe von ihm spricht – da ist mirs wie einem, der aller seiner Ehren und Würden entsetzt und dem der Degen genommen wird.

Am 16. Julius.

Ach wie mir das durch alle Adern läuft, wenn mein Finger unversehens den ihrigen berührt, wenn unsere Füße sich unter dem Tische begegnen! Ich ziehe zurück wie vom Feuer, und eine geheime Kraft zieht mich wieder vorwärts – mir wirds so schwindlig vor allen Sinnen. – O! und ihre Unschuld, ihre unbefangne Seele fühlt nicht, wie sehr mich die kleinen Vertraulichkeiten peinigen. Wenn sie gar im Gespräch ihre Hand auf die meinige legt und im Interesse der Unterredung näher zu mir rückt, daß der himmlische Atem ihres Mundes meine Lippen erreichen kann – ich glaube zu versinken, wie vom Wetter gerührt. – Und, Wilhelm! wenn ich mich jemals unterstehe, diesen Himmel, dieses Vertrauen –! Du verstehst mich. Nein, mein Herz ist so verderbt nicht! Schwach! schwach genug! – Und ist das nicht Verderben? –

Sie ist mir heilig. Alle Begier schweigt in ihrer Gegenwart. Ich weiß nie, wie mir ist, wenn ich bei ihr bin; es ist, als wenn die Seele sich mir in allen Nerven umkehrte. – Sie hat eine Melodie, die sie auf dem Klaviere spielet mit der Kraft eines Engels, so simpel und so geistvoll! Es ist ihr Leiblied, und mich stellt es von aller Pein, Verwirrung und Grillen her, wenn sie nur die erste Note davon greift.

Kein Wort von der alten Zauberkraft der Musik ist mir unwahrscheinlich. Wie mich der einfache Gesang angreift! Und wie sie ihn anzubringen weiß, oft zur Zeit, wo ich mir eine Kugel vor den Kopf schießen möchte! Die Irrung und Finsternis meiner Seele zerstreut sich, und ich atme wieder freier.

Am 18. Julius.

Wilhelm, was ist unserem Herzen die Welt ohne Liebe! Was eine Zauberlaterne ist ohne Licht! Kaum bringst du das Lämpchen hinein, so scheinen dir die buntesten Bilder an deine weiße Wand! Und wenns nichts wäre als das, als vorübergehende Phantome, so machts

can surely say this to you, you appreciate such things—how I worship myself now that she loves me!

Is this presumptuousness or the awareness of the real situation?—I don't know any man I'd fear as a rival in Lotte's affections. And yet—when she talks about her fiancé, talks about him with such warmth, so much love—then I feel like a man who has been shorn of all his honor and dignity and must surrender his sword.

July 16

Oh, what a thrill runs through my veins when my finger unexpectedly touches hers, when our feet make contact under the table! I pull back as if from a flame, and a secret force draws me forward again—all my senses are dazed.—Oh, and her innocent, naïve soul doesn't perceive how much those little intimacies torment me. When we're talking and she actually places her hand on mine and, carried away by the topic, she moves closer to me, so that the heavenly breath of her mouth can reach my lips—I feel as if I'm sinking, as if I'm struck by lightning.—And, Wilhelm, if I ever venture to take that heaven and that confidence, and—! You understand me. No, my heart isn't that corrupt! Weak, yes! Weak enough!—And isn't that corruption?—

She is sacred to me. All lust falls silent in her presence. I never know how I feel when I'm with her; it's as if my soul were overturned and I felt it in every nerve.—She has a melody which she plays on the clavier with the force of an angel, so simple and so spiritual! It's her favorite song, and it heals me of all pain, confusion, and daydreams as soon as she plays even the first note of it.

No legend about the ancient magic power of music is improbable to me. How that simple song grips me! And how opportunely she starts to play it, often when I feel like blowing my brains out! The confusion and darkness in my soul are dispelled, and I breathe more easily again.

July 18

Wilhelm, what is the world to our heart without love? The same as a magic lantern without light! As soon as you put the little lamp in it, the most variegated images show up on your white wall! And if it were no more than that, merely transitory phan-

doch immer unser Glück, wenn wir wie frische Jungen davorstehen
und uns über die Wundererscheinungen entzücken.

Heute konnte ich nicht zu Lotten, eine unvermeidliche Gesellschaft
hielt mich ab. Was war zu tun? Ich schickte meinen Diener hinaus, nur
um einen Menschen um mich zu haben, der ihr heute nahe gekommen wäre. Mit welcher Ungeduld ich ihn erwartete, mit welcher
Freude ich ihn wiedersah! Ich hätte ihn gern beim Kopfe genommen
und geküßt, wenn ich mich nicht geschämt hätte.

Man erzählt von dem Bononischen Steine, daß er, wenn man ihn in
die Sonne legt, ihre Strahlen anzieht und eine Weile bei Nacht leuchtet.
So war mirs mit dem Burschen. Das Gefühl, daß ihre Augen auf seinem
Gesichte, seinen Backen, seinen Rockknöpfen und dem Kragen am
Surtout geruht hatten, machte mir das alles so heilig, so wert! Ich hätte
in dem Augenblick den Jungen nicht um tausend Taler gegeben. Es war
mir so wohl in seiner Gegenwart. – Bewahre dich Gott, daß du darüber
lachest. Wilhelm, sind das Phantome, wenn es uns wohl ist?

Den 19. Julius.

Ich werde sie sehen! ruf ich morgens aus, wenn ich mich ermuntere
und mit aller Heiterkeit der schönen Sonne entgegenblicke; ich
werde sie sehen! Und da habe ich für den ganzen Tag keinen Wunsch
weiter. Alles, alles verschlingt sich in dieser Aussicht.

Den 20. Julius.

Eure Idee will noch nicht die meinige werden, daß ich mit dem
Gesandten nach *** gehen soll. Ich liebe die Subordination nicht
sehr, und wir wissen alle, daß der Mann noch dazu ein widriger
Mensch ist. Meine Mutter möchte mich gern in Aktivität haben, sagst
du; das hat mich zu lachen gemacht. Bin ich jetzt nicht auch aktiv?
und ists im Grunde nicht einerlei: ob ich Erbsen zähle oder Linsen?
Alles in der Welt läuft doch auf eine Lumperei hinaus, und ein
Mensch, der um anderer willen, ohne daß es seine eigene Leidenschaft, sein eigenes Bedürfnis ist, sich um Geld oder Ehre oder sonst
was abarbeitet, ist immer ein Tor.

Am 24. Julius.

Da dir so sehr daran gelegen ist, daß ich mein Zeichnen nicht ver-
nachlässige, möchte ich lieber die ganze Sache übergehen als dir
sagen, daß zeither wenig getan wird.

Noch nie war ich glücklicher, noch nie war meine Empfindung an
der Natur, bis aufs Steinchen, aufs Gräschen herunter, voller und in-

toms, still it always makes us happy when we stand there like young boys and delight in the miraculous phenomena.

Today I couldn't visit Lotte, an unavoidable get-together prevented me. What was I to do? I sent out my valet, merely to have a person around me who had come near her today. How impatiently I awaited him, how joyously I saw him again! I would gladly have held his head and kissed him, if I hadn't been ashamed to.

People say about Bolognese calcite that, when it's placed in sunlight, it attracts the sun's rays and glows for a time at night. That's how it was with me and that lad. The feeling that her eyes had rested on his face, his cheeks, his jacket buttons, and his topcoat collar made them all so sacred, so meaningful to me! At that moment I wouldn't have taken a thousand *taler* for the boy. I felt so good in his presence.—May God keep you from laughing at this! Wilhelm, are they phantoms when we feel so good?

July 19
"I'm going to see her!" I shout in the morning when I awaken and look into the lovely sunlight in total serenity; "I'm going to see her!" After that, I have no further desires for the whole day. Everything, everything else is swallowed up by that prospect.

July 20
I still can't concur with your notion that I should go to —— along with the ambassador. I'm not very fond of being a subordinate, and we all know that the man is a repellent person, besides. My mother would like to see me employed, you say; that made me laugh. Am I not active now? And, at bottom, isn't it all the same whether I count peas or lentils? After all, everything in the world is basically paltry and shabby, and a man who wears himself away working for money, honor, or anything else for the sake of others, without a personal passion or need to do so, is always a fool.

July 24
Since you are so concerned that I don't neglect my drawing, I'd rather skip the whole subject than tell you that I haven't done much lately.

Never before have I been happier, never before has my awareness of nature, down to every pebble, every blade of grass,

niger, und doch – Ich weiß nicht, wie ich mich ausdrücken soll, meine
vorstellende Kraft ist so schwach, alles schwimmt und schwankt so vor
meiner Seele, daß ich keinen Umriß packen kann; aber ich bilde mir
ein, wenn ich Ton hätte oder Wachs, so wollte ichs wohl herausbilden.
Ich werde auch Ton nehmen, wenns länger währt, und kneten, und
solltens Kuchen werden!

Lottens Porträt habe ich dreimal angefangen und habe mich
dreimal prostituiert; das mich um so mehr verdrießt, weil ich vor
einiger Zeit sehr glücklich im Treffen war. Darauf habe ich denn ihren
Schattenriß gemacht, und damit soll mir gnügen.

Am 26. Julius.

Ja, liebe Lotte, ich will alles besorgen und bestellen; geben Sie mir
nur mehr Aufträge, nur recht oft. Um eins bitte ich Sie: keinen Sand
mehr auf die Zettelchen, die Sie mir schreiben. Heute führte ich es
schnell nach der Lippe, und die Zähne knisterten mir.

Am 26. Julius.

Ich habe mir schon manchmal vorgenommen, sie nicht so oft zu
sehen. Ja wer das halten könnte! Alle Tage unterlieg ich der
Versuchung und verspreche mir heilig: morgen willst du einmal wegbleiben, und wenn der Morgen kommt, finde ich doch wieder eine
unwiderstehliche Ursache, und ehe ich michs versehe, bin ich bei ihr.
Entweder sie hat des Abends gesagt: Sie kommen doch morgen? –
Wer könnte da wegbleiben? Oder sie gibt mir einen Auftrag, und ich
finde schicklich, ihr selbst die Antwort zu bringen; oder der Tag ist gar
zu schön, ich gehe nach Wahlheim, und wenn ich nun da bin, ists nur
noch eine halbe Stunde zu ihr! – Ich bin zu nah in der Atmosphäre –
Zuck! so bin ich dort. Meine Großmutter hatte ein Märchen vom
Magnetenberg: die Schiffe, die zu nahe kamen, wurden auf einmal
alles Eisenwerks beraubt, die Nägel flogen dem Berge zu, und die
armen Elenden scheiterten zwischen den übereinanderstürzenden
Brettern.

Am 30. Julius.

Albert ist angekommen, und ich werde gehen; und wenn er der beste,
der edelste Mensch wäre, unter den ich mich in jeder Betrachtung zu
stellen bereit wäre, so wärs unerträglich, ihn vor meinem Angesicht
im Besitz so vieler Vollkommenheiten zu sehen. – Besitz! – Genug,

been fuller and keener, and yet— I don't know how to express it, my power to depict things is so weak, everything is so blurred and shaky in my soul that I can't manage a firm contour; but I tell myself that, if I had clay or wax, I'd be able to model something from it. And I will get some clay, if this keeps up, and mold it, even if only cookies result!

Three times I started a portrait of Lotte, and three times I made a fool of myself; this annoys me all the more because not long ago I was very good at seizing a likeness. I made a silhouette of her instead, and that will be enough for me.

July 26[11]

Yes, dear Lotte, I will take care of and arrange everything; just give me more errands, and often, too. One thing I ask of you: don't strew sand any more on the notes you write to me. Today I lifted your note to my lips quickly, and my teeth crackled.

July 26

I've already resolved more than once not to see her so often. But who can keep such promises? Every day I'm subject to temptation and swear a sacred oath: tomorrow for a change you'll stay away; and when tomorrow comes, I find another irresistible reason all the same, and before I realize it I'm with her. Either she said the evening before: "You're coming tomorrow, aren't you?" (Then who could stay away?) Or else she gives me some errand, and I find it proper to bring her the answer in person; or else the day is too fine, I go to Wahlheim and, once I'm there, it's just another half-hour to her place!—I'm too close, and in her atmosphere.—Zip! I'm there. My grandmother used to tell a tale about the magnetic mountain: ships that came too near were suddenly shorn of all their iron parts, the nails flew to the mountain, and the poor wretches were wrecked among the planks that collapsed in confusion.

July 30

Albert has arrived, and I shall depart; even if he were the best and noblest man in the world, one to whom I would willingly submit in every regard, it would still be unbearable to see him in possession of so many perfections right before my eyes.—

---

11. Entire letter a new 1787 addition.

Wilhelm, der Bräutigam ist da! Ein braver, lieber Mann, dem man gut
sein muß. Glücklicherweise war ich nicht beim Empfange! Das hätte
mir das Herz zerrissen. Auch ist er so ehrlich und hat Lotten in
meiner Gegenwart noch nicht ein einzig Mal geküßt. Das lohn ihm
Gott! Um des Respekts willen, den er vor dem Mädchen hat, muß ich
ihn lieben. Er will mir wohl, und ich vermute, das ist Lottens Werk
mehr, als seiner eigenen Empfindung: denn darin sind die Weiber
fein und haben recht: wenn sie zwei Verehrer in gutem Vernehmen
mit einander erhalten können, ist der Vorteil immer ihr, so selten es
auch angeht.

Indes kann ich Alberten meine Achtung nicht versagen. Seine
gelassene Außenseite sticht gegen die Unruhe meines Charakters
sehr lebhaft ab, die sich nicht verbergen läßt. Er hat viel Gefühl und
weiß, was er an Lotten hat. Er scheint wenig üble Laune zu haben,
und du weißt, das ist die Sünde, die ich ärger hasse am Menschen als
alle andere.

Er hält mich für einen Menschen von Sinn; und meine
Anhänglichkeit an Lotten, meine warme Freude, die ich an allen
ihren Handlungen habe, vermehrt seinen Triumph, und er liebt sie
nur desto mehr. Ob er sie nicht manchmal mit kleiner Eifersüchtelei
peinigt, das lasse ich dahingestellt sein, wenigstens würd ich an seinem Platze nicht ganz sicher vor diesem Teufel bleiben.

Dem sei nun wie ihm wolle! Meine Freude, bei Lotten zu sein, ist
hin. Soll ich das Torheit nennen oder Verblendung? – Was brauchts
Namen! erzählt die Sache an sich! – Ich wußte alles, was ich jetzt
weiß, ehe Albert kam; ich wußte, daß ich keine Prätension auf sie zu
machen hatte, machte auch keine – das heißt, insofern es möglich ist,
bei so viel Liebenswürdigkeit nicht zu begehren. – Und jetzt macht
der Fratze große Augen, da der andere nun wirklich kommt und ihm
das Mädchen wegnimmt.

Ich beiße die Zähne aufeinander und spotte über mein Elend und
spottete derer doppelt und dreifach, die sagen könnten, ich sollte
mich resignieren, und weil es nun einmal nicht anders sein könnte –
Schafft mir diese Strohmänner vom Halse! – Ich laufe in den Wäldern
herum, und wenn ich zu Lotten komme und Albert bei ihr sitzt im
Gärtchen unter der Laube und ich nicht weiter kann, so bin ich ausgelassen närrisch und fange viel Possen, viel verwirrtes Zeug an. –
Um Gottes willen, sagte mir Lotte heut, ich bitte Sie, keine Szene wie
die von gestern abend! Sie sind fürchterlich, wenn Sie so lustig sind.
– Unter uns, ich passe die Zeit ab, wenn er zu tun hat; wutsch! bin ich
drauß, und da ist mirs immer wohl, wenn ich sie allein finde.

Possession!—Suffice it to say, Wilhelm, her fiancé is here. A
fine, likable man, whom anyone must be fond of. Fortunately I
wasn't present when she welcomed him! That would have torn
my heart apart. Besides, he has such a sense of honor; he has not
yet kissed Lotte once while I was there. God reward him for
that! I must love him for the respect he shows the girl. He
wishes me well, and I assume that it's Lotte's doing rather than
the result of his own feelings: because women are clever that
way, and they're right: when they can maintain good relations
between two suitors, the advantage is always theirs, though it
can be managed only rarely.

Meanwhile, I can't deny Albert my esteem. His calm exterior
is in vivid contrast to the restlessness of my nature, which can't
be concealed. He has a lot of sensitivity, and he knows what a
prize he has in Lotte. He seems to have very little bad temper,
and, as you know, that's the sin I hate in people worse than anything else.

He considers me to be a sensible person; and my attachment
to Lotte, my sincere joy in all her doings, increases his triumph,
and he loves her all the more for it. I leave it an open question
whether he doesn't sometimes torment her with petty jealousy; at
least, in his place, I wouldn't be entirely immune from that devil.

Be that as it may! My joy in being with Lotte is over. Shall I
call that folly or blindness?—What's the need of names? The
matter proclaims itself!—I knew everything I now know before
Albert arrived; I knew I had no claim on her, and I made none—
that is, insofar as it's possible to feel no desire for someone so
adorable.—And now the big baby is amazed when the other
man actually arrives and takes away his girl.

I grit my teeth and laugh at my misery, and I'd laugh twice or
three times as hard at anyone who'd say I ought to resign myself, and because it has to be this way— Get those straw pup-
pets off my back!—I run around in the woods, and when I get
to Lotte's place and Albert is sitting in her little garden under
the arbor and I can't go any further, I become foolishly frolic-
some and come out with a lot of nonsense and gibberish. "For
God's sake," Lotte said to me today, "please don't make a scene
like the one yesterday evening! You're scary when you're that
jolly." Between you and me, I wait for a time when he's occupied; I'm out there in a whiz and then I always feel good when
I find her alone.

Am 8. August.

Ich bitte dich, lieber Wilhelm, es war gewiß nicht auf dich geredt, wenn ich die Menschen unerträglich schalt, die von uns Ergebung in unvermeidliche Schicksale fordern. Ich dachte wahrlich nicht daran, daß du von ähnlicher Meinung sein könntest. Und im Grunde hast du recht. Nur eins, mein Bester: in der Welt ist es sehr selten mit dem *Entweder-Oder* getan, die Empfindungen und Handlungsweisen schattieren sich so mannigfaltig, als Abfälle zwischen einer Habichts- und Stumpfnase sind.

Du wirst mir also nicht übelnehmen, wenn ich dir dein ganzes Argument einräume und mich doch zwischen dem *Entweder-Oder* durchzustehlen suche.

Entweder, sagst du, hast du Hoffnung auf Lotten, oder du hast keine. Gut, im ersten Fall suche sie durchzutreiben, suche die Erfüllung deiner Wünsche zu umfassen: im anderen Falle ermanne dich und suche einer elenden Empfindung loszuwerden, die alle deine Kräfte verzehren muß. – Bester! das ist wohl gesagt und – bald gesagt.

Und kannst du von dem Unglücklichen, dessen Leben unter einer schleichenden Krankheit unaufhaltsam allmählich abstirbt, kannst du von ihm verlangen, er solle durch einen Dolchstoß der Qual auf einmal ein Ende machen? Und raubt das Übel, das ihm die Kräfte verzehrt, ihm nicht auch zugleich den Mut, sich davon zu befreien?

Zwar könntest du mir mit einem verwandten Gleichnisse antworten: Wer ließe sich nicht lieber den Arm abnehmen, als daß er durch Zaudern und Zagen sein Leben aufs Spiel setzte? – Ich weiß nicht! – und wir wollen uns nicht in Gleichnissen herumbeißen. Genug – Ja, Wilhelm, ich habe manchmal so einen Augenblick aufspringenden, abschüttelnden Mutes, und da – wenn ich nur wüßte wohin? ich ginge wohl.

Abends.

Mein Tagebuch, das ich seit einiger Zeit vernachlässiget, fiel mir heut wieder in die Hände, und ich bin erstaunt, wie ich so wissentlich in das alles, Schritt vor Schritt, hineingegangen bin! Wie ich über meinen Zustand immer so klar gesehen und doch gehandelt habe wie ein Kind, jetzt noch so klar sehe, und es noch keinen Anschein zur Besserung hat.

Am 10. August.

Ich könnte das beste, glücklichste Leben führen, wenn ich nicht ein Tor wäre. So schöne Umstände vereinigen sich nicht leicht, eines

August 8

Please, dear Wilhelm, I certainly didn't have you in mind when I called people unbearable who demand we resign ourselves to an unavoidable fate. Really and truly, I didn't think you could be of that opinion. Basically you're right. Just one thing, best of friends: in this world things are very seldom "either or"; emotions and behavior have as many shadings as there are gradations from a hawklike nose to a snub nose.

So you won't hold it against me if I admit your entire argument but nevertheless attempt to slip through between the "either" and the "or."

You say: either you have hopes of winning Lotte or you don't. Good, in the former case try to achieve those hopes, try to attain the fulfillment of your wishes; in the latter case, get hold of yourself and try to shake off an unhappy feeling that has to consume all your strength.—Dear friend, that's well said—and easily said.

Can you ask an unfortunate man whose life is gradually but inexorably ebbing away because of an insidious illness, can you ask him to put an end to his torment all at once with a dagger blow? Doesn't the disease that's consuming his strength also deprive him at the same time of the requisite courage to liberate himself from it?

Of course, you could answer me with a related metaphor: What man wouldn't rather have an arm amputated than risking his life by hesitating and wavering?—I don't know!—And let's not tussle around with metaphors. Enough!—Yes, Wilhelm, at times I have such moments of courage that flares up and shakes things off, and then—if I only knew where I was heading, I'd go.

That evening.[12]

My diary, which I've neglected for some time, came into my hands again today, and I'm amazed at how consciously I've walked into all this, step by step! How I've always seen my condition so clearly and yet acted like a child, how I still see it clearly and yet detect no hint of an improvement.

August 10

I could be leading the best, the happiest life if I weren't a fool. It isn't often that such lovely circumstances combine to delight

---

12. This heading and paragraph new in 1787.

Menschen Seele zu ergötzen, als die sind, in denen ich mich jetzt befinde. Ach so gewiß ists, daß unser Herz allein sein Glück macht. – Ein Glied der liebenswürdigen Familie zu sein, von dem Alten geliebt zu werden wie ein Sohn, von den Kleinen wie ein Vater, und von Lotten! – dann der ehrliche Albert, der durch keine launische Unart mein Glück stört; der mich mit herzlicher Freundschaft umfaßt; dem ich nach Lotten das Liebste auf der Welt bin – Wilhelm, es ist eine Freude, uns zu hören, wenn wir spazierengehen und uns einander von Lotten unterhalten: es ist in der Welt nichts Lächerlichers erfunden worden als dieses Verhältnis, und doch kommen mir oft darüber die Tränen in die Augen.

Wenn er mir von ihrer rechtschaffenen Mutter erzählt: wie sie auf ihrem Todbette Lotten ihr Haus und ihre Kinder übergeben und ihm Lotten anbefohlen habe, wie seit der Zeit ein ganz anderer Geist Lotten belebt habe, wie sie, in der Sorge für ihre Wirtschaft und in dem Ernste, einen wahre Mutter geworden, wie kein Augenblick ihrer Zeit ohne tätige Liebe, ohne Arbeit verstrichen, und dennoch ihre Munterkeit, ihr leichter Sinn sie nie dabei verlassen habe. – Ich gehe so neben ihm hin und pflücke Blumen am Wege, füge sie sehr sorgfältig in einen Strauß und – werfe sie in den vorüberfließenden Strom und sehe ihnen nach, wie sie leise hinunterwallen. – Ich weiß nicht, ob ich dir geschrieben habe, daß Albert hierbleiben und ein Amt mit einem artigen Auskommen vom Hofe erhalten wird, wo er sehr beliebt ist. In Ordnung und Emsigkeit in Geschäften habe ich wenig seinesgleichen gesehen.

Am 12. August.

Gewiß, Albert ist der beste Mensch unter dem Himmel. Ich habe gestern eine wunderbare Szene mit ihm gehabt. Ich kam zu ihm, um Abschied von ihm zu nehmen; denn mich wandelte die Lust an, ins Gebirge zu reiten, von woher ich dir auch jetzt schreibe, und wie ich in der Stube auf und ab gehe, fallen mir seine Pistolen in die Augen. – Borge mir die Pistolen, sagte ich, zu meiner Reise. – Meinetwegen, sagte er, wenn du dir die Mühe nehmen willst, sie zu laden; bei mir hängen sie nur pro forma. – Ich nahm eine herunter, und er fuhr fort: Seit mir meine Vorsicht einen so unartigen Streich gespielt hat, mag ich mit dem Zeuge nichts mehr zu tun haben. – Ich war neugierig, die Geschichte zu wissen. – Ich hielt mich, erzählte er, wohl ein Vierteljahr auf dem Lande bei einem Freunde auf, hatte ein paar Terzerolen ungeladen und schlief ruhig. Einmal an einem regnichten Nachmittage, da ich müßig sitze, weiß ich nicht, wie mir einfällt: wir könnten überfallen werden, wir könnten die Terzerolen nötig haben und

a man's soul as those in which I now find myself. Ah, that's how undeniable it is that our heart alone creates its own happiness.— To be a member of that charming family, to be loved by the old man like a son, by the children like a father, and by Lotte! Then there's honest Albert, who doesn't disturb my happiness with any moody discourtesy, who receives me with cordial friendship, who likes me best in the world after Lotte—Wilhelm, it's a pleasure to hear us when we're strolling and discussing Lotte: there's never been anything in the world as comical as this relationship, and yet I often weep over it.

When he tells me about her respectable mother: how on her death bed she handed over her house and her children to Lotte, and entrusted Lotte to him; how since then a totally different spirit has invigorated Lotte; how, in her concern for her housekeeping and in her gravity, she has become a real mother; how not a moment of her time has gone by without active love and labor, while her liveliness and cheerfulness have never deserted her, nevertheless— I walk alongside him and pick flowers along the way, I assemble them very carefully into a bouquet and— throw them into the stream flowing past us and watch them gently float away.—I don't know whether I've written you that Albert will remain here and will be given a court position with a handsome income (he's greatly liked at court). As for orderliness and diligence in business, I've rarely seen his like.

August 12

Yes, Albert is the best of men on earth. Yesterday I had a strange scene with him. I went to see him to take leave of him, because I had the urge to ride into the mountains (I'm now writing to you from there); while I was pacing up and down his parlor, his pistols caught my eye. "Lend me the pistols for my trip," I said. "Fine with me," he said, "if you want to take the trouble to load them; in my place they're merely hanging on the wall for show." I took one down, and he continued: "Ever since my caution played such a nasty trick on me, I don't want to have anything more to do with those gadgets." I was curious to hear the story. He recounted: "I stayed at a friend's house in the country about three months; I had a brace of small pistols, unloaded, and I slept soundly. One rainy afternoon, while I was sitting idly, I don't know what got into my head: we might be attacked, we might need the pistols, we might—you know how that is. I gave

könnten – du weißt ja, wie das ist. – Ich gab sie dem Bedienten, sie zu putzen und zu laden; und der dahlt mit den Mädchen, will sie erschrecken, und Gott weiß wie, das Gewehr geht los, da der Ladstock noch drinsteckt, und schießt den Ladstock einem Mädchen zur Maus herein an der rechten Hand und zerschlägt ihr den Daumen. Da hatte ich das Lamentieren und die Kur zu bezahlen obendrein, und seit der Zeit laß ich alles Gewehr ungeladen. Lieber Schatz, was ist Vorsicht? Die Gefahr läßt sich nicht auslernen! Zwar – Nun weißt du, daß ich den Menschen sehr liebhabe bis auf seine *Zwar;* denn versteht sichs nicht von selbst, daß jeder allgemeine Satz Ausnahmen leidet? Aber so rechtfertig ist der Mensch! wenn er glaubt, etwas Übereiltes, Allgemeines, Halbwahres gesagt zu haben, so hört er dir nicht auf, zu limitieren, zu modifizieren und ab- und zuzutun, bis zuletzt gar nichts mehr an der Sache ist. Und bei diesem Anlaß kam er sehr tief in Text: ich hörte endlich gar nicht weiter auf ihn, verfiel in Grillen, und mit einer auffahrenden Gebärde drückte ich mir die Mündung der Pistole übers rechte Aug an die Stirn. – Pfui! sagte Albert, indem er mir die Pistole herabzog, was soll das? – Sie ist nicht geladen, sagte ich. – Und auch so, was solls? versetzte er ungeduldig. Ich kann mir nicht vorstellen, wie ein Mensch so töricht sein kann, sich zu erschießen; der bloße Gedanke erregt mir Widerwillen.

Daß ihr Menschen, rief ich aus, um von einer Sache zu reden, gleich sprechen müßt: das ist töricht, das ist klug, das ist gut, das ist bös! Und was will das alles heißen? Habt ihr deswegen die inneren Verhältnisse einer Handlung erforscht? wißt ihr mit Bestimmtheit die Ursachen zu entwickeln, warum sie geschah, warum sie geschehen mußte? Hättet ihr das, ihr würdet nicht so eilfertig mit euren Urteilen sein.

Du wirst mir zugeben, sagte Albert, daß gewisse Handlungen lasterhaft bleiben, sie mögen geschehen, aus welchem Beweggrunde sie wollen.

Ich zuckte die Achseln und gabs ihm zu. – Doch, mein Lieber, fuhr ich fort, finden sich auch hier einige Ausnahmen. Es ist wahr, der Diebstahl ist ein Laster; aber der Mensch, der, um sich und die Seinigen vom gegenwärtigen Hungertode zu erretten, auf Raub ausgeht, verdient der Mitleiden oder Strafe? Wer hebt den ersten Stein auf gegen den Ehemann, der im gerechten Zorne sein untreues Weib und ihren nichtswürdigen Verführer aufopfert? gegen das Mädchen, das in einer wonnevollen Stunde sich in den unaufhaltsamen Freuden der Liebe verliert? Unsere Gesetze selbst, diese kaltblütigen Pedanten, lassen sich rühren und halten ihre Strafe zurück.

them to my valet to clean and load; he fooled around with the maids, trying to scare them, and somehow or other the pistol went off with the ramrod still in it, and shot the ramrod into one girl's right hand, the ball of her thumb, and crushed her thumb. Then I had to put up with her howls, and I had to pay the doctor on top of it; ever since then I've left all pistols unloaded. My dear friend, what is caution? Danger can't be learned by heart! To be sure—" Now, you know I like the fellow very much except for his "to be sure"; because isn't it obvious that every generality admits of exceptions? But the man is so conscientious! Whenever he thinks he's said something over-hasty, too general, or only half-true, he doesn't cease adding limitations and modifications, taking away a little bit, putting back a little bit, until the subject is thoroughly flogged. And on this occasion he rambled on and on; finally I wasn't even listening to him any more, I lapsed into my capricious thoughts, and with an impetuous gesture I pressed the muzzle of the pistol against my forehead over my right eye. "Bah!" Albert said, lowering the pistol; "what are you doing?" "It's not loaded," I said. "Even so, what were you thinking of?" he replied impatiently. "I can't imagine how a man can be so foolish as to shoot himself; the very thought is repellent to me."

I exclaimed: "Why do you people, when speaking of anything, immediately have to say: that's foolish, that's wise, that's good, that's bad? What does it all mean? Have you studied the deeply-lying reasons for the person's action? Are you able to expound the accurate causes of the occurrence, the necessity for the occurrence? If you had done so, you wouldn't be so hasty with your judgments."

"You'll grant me," said Albert, "that certain actions remain blameworthy no matter from what motives they are performed."

I shrugged my shoulders and admitted it. "But, my friend," I continued, "here too there are a few exceptions. It's true that theft is a vice; but when a man goes out stealing in order to save himself and his family from imminent starvation, does he deserve sympathy or punishment? Who will cast the first stone at the husband who sacrifices his unfaithful wife and her ignoble seducer in his righteous wrath? Or at the girl who goes astray in the inexorable joys of love during an hour of rapture? Even our laws, those coldblooded pedants, allow themselves to be moved to pity, and restrain their penalties."

Das ist ganz was anders, versetzte Albert, weil ein Mensch, den seine Leidenschaften hinreißen, alle Besinnungskraft verliert und als ein Trunkener, als ein Wahnsinniger angesehen wird.

Ach ihr vernünftigen Leute! rief ich lächelnd aus. Leidenschaft! Trunkenheit! Wahnsinn! Ihr steht so gelassen, so ohne Teilnehmung da, ihr sittlichen Menschen! scheltet den Trinker, verabscheut den Unsinnigen, geht vorbei wie der Priester und dankt Gott wie der Pharisäer, daß er euch nicht gemacht hat wie einen von diesen. Ich bin mehr als einmal trunken gewesen, meine Leidenschaften waren nie weit vom Wahnsinn, und beides reut mich nicht: denn ich habe in meinem Maße begreifen lernen, wie man alle außerordentlichen Menschen, die etwas Großes, etwas Unmöglichscheinendes wirkten, von jeher für Trunkene und Wahnsinnige ausschreien mußte.

Aber auch im gemeinen Leben ists unerträglich, fast einem jeden bei halbweg einer freien, edlen, unerwarteten Tat nachrufen zu hören: der Mensch ist trunken, der ist närrisch! Schämt euch, ihr Nüchternen! Schämt euch, ihr Weisen!

Das sind nun wieder von deinen Grillen, sagte Albert, du überspannst alles und hast wenigstens hier gewiß unrecht, daß du den Selbstmord, wovon jetzt die Rede ist, mit großen Handlungen vergleichst: da man es doch für nichts anders als eine Schwäche halten kann. Denn freilich ist es leichter zu sterben, als ein qualvolles Leben standhaft zu ertragen.

Ich war im Begriff abzubrechen; denn kein Argument bringt mich so aus der Fassung, als wenn einer mit einem unbedeutenden Gemeinspruche angezogen kommt, wenn ich aus ganzem Herzen rede. Doch faßte ich mich, weil ichs schon oft gehört und mich öfter darüber geärgert hatte, und versetzte ihm mit einiger Lebhaftigkeit: Du nennst das Schwäche? Ich bitte dich, laß dich vom Anscheine nicht verführen. Ein Volk, das unter dem unerträglichen Joch eines Tyrannen seufzt, darfst du das schwach heißen, wenn es endlich aufgärt und seine Ketten zerreißt? Ein Mensch, der über dem Schrecken, daß Feuer sein Haus ergriffen hat, alle Kräfte gespannt fühlt und mit Leichtigkeit Lasten wegträgt, die er bei ruhigem Sinne kaum bewegen kann; einer, der in der Wut der Beleidigung es mit sechsen aufnimmt und sie überwältigt, sind die schwach zu nennen? Und, mein Guter, wenn Anstrengung Stärke ist, warum soll die Überspannung das Gegenteil sein? – Albert sah mich an und sagte: Nimm mirs nicht übel, die Beispiele, die du da gibst, scheinen hieher gar nicht zu gehören. – Es mag sein, sagte ich, man hat mir schon öfters vorgeworfen, daß meine Kombinationsart manchmal an

"That's something quite different," Albert retorted, "because
a person who's swept away by his passions loses all of his judgment and is looked upon as being intoxicated or insane."
"Oh, you rational people!" I exclaimed with a smile. "Passion!
Intoxication! Insanity! You stand there so calmly, so devoid of empathy, you moral people! You berate the drunkard, you loathe the
madman, you walk past like the priest, and like the Pharisee you
thank God that he didn't make you like one of those. I've been
drunk more than once, my passions have always been close to
madness, and I'm not repentant on either count: because, in my
measure, I have learned to understand why people have always
needed to decry as drunkards and madmen every extraordinary
person who accomplished anything great or seemingly impossible.

"But even in everyday life it's intolerable to see almost everyone who performs a halfway free, noble, or unexpected deed
pursued with the outcry: that fellow is drunk, that one's a fool!
Shame on you, you sober folk! Shame on you, you sages!"

"Those are just more of your lunacies," Albert said, "you ex-
aggerate everything, and in this case, at least, you're certainly
wrong in comparing suicide, which is the topic, with noble actions, whereas it can only be considered as a token of weakness.
Because it's surely easier to die than to bear up manfully under
a painful existence."

I was about to break off, because no line of reasoning makes
me lose my calm more than when someone flings a meaningless
cliché at me while I've been speaking out of the fullness of my
heart. But I controlled myself because I had heard that so often
before and had frequently been irritated by it; and I retorted
rather vigorously: "You call that weakness? Please don't be mis-
led by appearances. When a nation is groaning beneath the unbearable yoke of a tyrant, can you call it weak when it finally
rises up and breaks its chains? When a man, in his alarm because
his house has caught on fire, feels an onrush of strength and easily carries away loads that he could barely move if he were re-
laxed; when a man enraged by an affront faces six adversaries
and subdues them: are they to be called weak? And, my good
man, if exertion is strength, why should exaggerated action be
the opposite?" Albert looked at me and said: "Don't hold this
against me, but the examples you've just given seem to be out of
place here." "That may be," I said, "I've often been reproached
by people who said my method of associating ideas sometimes

Radotage grenze. Laßt uns denn sehen, ob wir uns auf eine andere
Weise vorstellen können, wie dem Menschen zumute sein mag, der
sich entschließt, die sonst angenehme Bürde des Lebens abzuwerfen.
Denn nur insofern wir mitempfinden, haben wir Ehre, von einer
Sache zu reden.

Die menschliche Natur, fuhr ich fort, hat ihre Grenzen: sie kann
Freude, Leid, Schmerzen bis auf einen gewissen Grad ertragen und
geht zugrunde, sobald *der* überstiegen ist. Hier ist also nicht die
Frage, ob einer schwach oder stark ist, sondern ob er das Maß seines
Leidens ausdauern kann – es mag nun moralisch oder körperlich sein;
und ich finde es ebenso wunderbar zu sagen: der Mensch ist feige,
der sich das Leben nimmt, als es ungehörig wäre, den einen Feigen
zu nennen, der an einem bösartigen Fieber stirbt.

Paradox! sehr paradox! rief Albert aus. – Nicht so sehr als du
denkst, versetzte ich. Du gibst mir zu: wir nennen das eine Krankheit
zum Tode, wodurch die Natur so angegriffen wird, daß teils ihre
Kräfte verzehrt, teils so außer Wirkung gesetzt werden, daß sie sich
nicht wieder aufzuhelfen, durch keine glückliche Revolution den
gewöhnlichen Umlauf des Lebens wiederherzustellen fähig ist.

Nun, mein Lieber, laß uns das auf den Geist anwenden. Sieh den
Menschen an in seiner Eingeschränktheit, wie Eindrücke auf ihn
wirken, Ideen sich bei ihm festsetzen, bis endlich eine wachsende
Leidenschaft ihn aller ruhigen Sinneskraft beraubt und ihn zugrunde
richtet.

Vergebens, daß der gelassene, vernünftige Mensch den Zustand
des Unglücklichen übersieht, vergebens, daß er ihm zuredet! Ebenso
wie ein Gesunder, der am Bette des Kranken steht, ihm von seinen
Kräften nicht das geringste einflößen kann.

Alberten war das zu allgemein gesprochen. Ich erinnerte ihn an ein
Mädchen, das man vor weniger Zeit im Wasser tot gefunden, und
wiederholte ihm ihre Geschichte. – Ein gutes junges Geschöpf, das in
dem engen Kreise häuslicher Beschäftigungen, wöchentlicher be-
stimmter Arbeit herangewachsen war, das weiter keine Aussicht von
Vergnügen kannte, als etwa Sonntags in einem nach und nach zusam-
mengeschafften Putz mit ihresgleichen um die Stadt spazierenzuge-
hen, vielleicht alle hohen Feste einmal zu tanzen, und übrigens mit
aller Lebhaftigkeit des herzlichsten Anteils manche Stunde über den
Anlaß eines Gezänkes, einer übeln Nachrede mit einer Nachbarin zu
verplaudern – deren feurige Natur fühlt nun endlich innigere
Bedürfnisse, die durch die Schmeicheleien der Männer vermehrt
werden; ihre vorigen Freuden werden ihr nach und nach unschmack-

came close to sheer babble. So, let's see whether we can picture to ourselves in a different way how a man must feel when he decides to cast off the burden of life, which is usually a pleasant one. Because only to the extent that we empathize can we discuss a matter without being presumptuous.

"The human constitution," I went on, "has its limits: it can bear joy, sorrow, and pain up to a certain degree, but it perishes once that degree is passed. Thus the question here is not whether a man is weak or strong, but whether he can endure the measure of his suffering, be it mental or physical; and I find it just as odd to say that a man who takes his life is a coward as it would be inappropriate to call someone a coward if he died from a malignant fever."

"Paradoxical! Most paradoxical!" Albert exclaimed. "Not as much as you think," I retorted. "You grant me this: we call it a mortal illness when a man's constitution is so strongly assailed that its strength is partly consumed and partly made so ineffectual that it's no longer capable of regaining its footing or restoring the normal course of life by means of any fortunate breakthrough.

"Now, my friend, let's apply that to the mind. Observe man in his limitations, see how impressions affect him, how ideas take root in him, until finally a growing passion robs him of all calm judgment and destroys him.

"It's of no use when a calm, rational person fully recognizes the poor man's condition; it's of no use when he gives him advice! Just as a healthy man at a sick man's bedside can't lend him the slightest amount of his own strength."

Albert found that too much of a generalization. I reminded him of a girl who was found drowned not long ago, and I repeated her history to him. "A good young person who had grown up in the narrow sphere of domestic occupations and a set amount of work every week, a girl who had no further prospects of amusement than, let's say, to stroll around town on Sunday with girls just like herself, wearing finery that she had accumulated little by little, maybe dancing on every big holiday, and otherwise chatting with a neighbor with all the vivacity of warm interest about some quarrel or some slander. Finally her fiery nature feels more intimate needs, which are heightened by the flattering words of men; her former friends become more and more distasteful to her until she finally meets a man to whom

haft, bis sie endlich einen Menschen antrifft, zu dem ein unbekanntes
Gefühl sie unwiderstehlich hinreißt, auf den sie nun alle ihre
Hoffnungen wirft, die Welt rings um sich vergißt, nichts hört, nichts
sieht, nichts fühlt als ihn, den Einzigen, sich nur sehnt nach ihm, dem
Einzigen. Durch die leeren Vergnügungen einer unbeständigen Eitelkeit nicht verdorben, zieht ihr Verlangen gerade nach dem Zweck, sie
will die Seinige werden, sie will in ewiger Verbindung all das Glück
antreffen, das ihr mangelt, die Vereinigung aller Freuden genießen,
nach denen sie sich sehnte. Wiederholtes Versprechen, das ihr die
Gewißheit aller Hoffnungen versiegelt, kühne Liebkosungen, die ihre
Begierden vermehren, umfangen ganz ihre Seele; sie schwebt in
einem dumpfen Bewußtsein, in einem Vorgefühl aller Freuden, sie ist
bis auf den höchsten Grad gespannt, sie streckt endlich ihre Arme
aus, all ihre Wünsche zu umfassen – und ihr Geliebter verläßt sie. –
Erstarrt, ohne Sinne, steht sie vor einem Abgrunde; alles ist Finsternis um sie her, keine Aussicht, kein Trost, keine Ahnung! denn *der*
hat sie verlassen, in dem sie allein ihr Dasein fühlte. Sie sieht nicht die
weite Welt, die vor ihr liegt, nicht die Vielen, die ihr den Verlust ersetzen könnten, sie fühlt sich allein, verlassen von aller Welt – und
blind, in die Enge gepreßt von der entsetzlichen Not ihres Herzens,
stürzt sie sich hinunter, um in einem rings umfangenden Tode alle
ihre Qualen zu ersticken. – Sieh, Albert; das ist die Geschichte so
manches Menschen! und sag, ist das nicht der Fall der Krankheit?
Die Natur findet keinen Ausweg aus dem Labyrinthe der verworre-
nen und widersprechenden Kräfte, und der Mensch muß sterben.

Wehe dem, der zusehen und sagen könnte: Die Törin! Hätte sie
gewartet, hätte sie die Zeit wirken lassen, die Verzweifelung würde
sich schon gelegt, es würde sich schon ein anderer sie zu trösten
vorgefunden haben. – Das ist eben, als wenn einer sagte: Der Tor,
stirbt am Fieber! Hätte er gewartet, bis seine Kräfte sich erholt, seine
Säfte sich verbessert, der Tumult seines Blutes sich gelegt hätten:
alles wäre gut gegangen, und er lebte bis auf den heutigen Tag!

Albert, dem die Vergleichung noch nicht anschaulich war, wandte
noch einiges ein, und unter andern: ich hätte nur von einem einfälti-
gen Mädchen gesprochen; wie aber ein Mensch von Verstande, der
nicht so eingeschränkt sei, der mehr Verhältnisse übersehe, zu
entschuldigen sein möchte, könne er nicht begreifen. – Mein
Freund, rief ich aus, der Mensch ist Mensch, und das bißchen
Verstand, das einer haben mag, kommt wenig oder nicht in Anschlag,
wenn Leidenschaft wütet und die Grenzen der Menschheit einen
drängen. Vielmehr – Ein andermal davon, sagte ich und griff nach

she's irresistibly attracted by some unknown feeling, a man on whom she now pins all her hopes, forgetting the world around her, hearing nothing, seeing nothing, feeling nothing but him and him alone, yearning for him and him alone. Unspoiled by the empty pleasures of inconstant vanity, her desire draws her right to the goal, she wants to become his, she wants to find in an eternal union all the happiness she has missed, to enjoy the combination of all the joys she has longed for. Repeated promises which seal the certainty of all her hopes, bold caresses which fuel her desires, occupy her entire soul; she floats in a vague awareness, a foretaste of every joy; she is in the highest degree of suspense; she finally holds out her arms to grasp all her wishes—and her lover deserts her.—Numb, her senses dulled, she is standing in front of a precipice; everything around her is darkness; there's no prospect, no consolation, no hope, because she has been deserted by the man on whom her whole life centered. She doesn't see the wide world that lies before her, or the many men who could make up her loss to her; she feels alone, abandoned by everyone—and blindly, pushed into a corner by the frightful distress in her heart, she plunges down, to stifle all her torments in a death that embraces her round about.—See, Albert, that's the history of so many people! Now tell me, isn't that the same case as the illness? Nature finds no way out of the labyrinth of tangled, contradictory forces, and the person must die.

"Woe to the man who could watch this and say: 'The fool! Had she only waited, had she let time do its work, her despair would have abated, another man would have showed up to comfort her.' That's just like saying: 'What a fool, to die of fever! Had he waited until his strength returned, his bodily fluids had cleared, the uproar in his blood had settled, everything would have been all right, and he'd still be alive today!'"

Albert, who still didn't see the analogy clearly, made a few more objections, including this: I had spoken merely about a simple girl; but he couldn't comprehend how an intelligent person who was not so circumscribed, who saw the larger connections of things, could be pardoned. "My friend," I exclaimed, "a person is a person, and the little bit of intelligence he may have is of little or no account when passion rages and the limits of humanity press in upon him. Rather— We'll talk about it some other time," I said, reaching for my hat. Oh, how

meinem Hute. O mir war das Herz so voll – Und wir gingen aus-
einander, ohne einander verstanden zu haben. Wie denn auf dieser
Welt keiner leicht den andern versteht.

Am 15. August.

Es ist doch gewiß, daß in der Welt den Menschen nichts notwendig
macht als die Liebe. Ich fühls an Lotten, daß sie mich ungerne ver-
löre, und die Kinder haben keinen andern Begriff, als daß ich immer
morgen wiederkommen würde. Heute war ich hinausgegangen,
Lottens Klavier zu stimmen, ich konnte aber nicht dazu kommen,
denn die Kleinen verfolgten mich um ein Märchen, und Lotte sagte
selbst, ich sollte ihnen den Willen tun. Ich schnitt ihnen das
Abendbrot, das sie nun fast so gern von mir als von Lotten annehmen,
und erzählte ihnen das Hauptstückchen von der Prinzessin, die von
Händen bedient wird. Ich lerne viel dabei, das versichre ich dich, und
ich bin erstaunt, was es auf sie für Eindrücke macht. Weil ich manchmal einen Inzidentpunkt erfinden muß, den ich beim zweiten Mal
vergesse, sagen sie gleich, das vorige Mal wär es anders gewesen, so
daß ich mich jetzt übe, sie unveränderlich in einem singenden
Silbenfall an einem Schnürchen weg zu rezitieren. Ich habe daraus
gelernt, wie ein Autor durch eine zweite veränderte Ausgabe seiner
Geschichte, und wenn sie poetisch noch so besser geworden wäre,
notwendig seinem Buche schaden muß. Der erste Eindruck findet
uns willig, und der Mensch ist gemacht, daß man ihn das
Abenteuerlichste überreden kann; das haftet aber auch gleich so fest,
und wehe dem, der es wieder auskratzen und austilgen will!

Am 18. August.

Mußte denn das so sein, daß das, was des Menschen Glückseligkeit
macht, wieder die Quelle seines Elendes würde?

Das volle, warme Gefühl meines Herzens an der lebendigen Natur,
das mich mit so vieler Wonne überströmte, das ringsumher die Welt
mir zu einem Paradiese schuf, wird mir jetzt zu einem unerträglichen
Peiniger, zu einem quälenden Geist, der mich auf allen Wegen verfolgt. Wenn ich sonst vom Felsen über den Fluß bis zu jenen Hügeln
das fruchtbare Tal überschaute und alles um mich her keimen und
quellen sah; wenn ich jene Berge, vom Fuße bis zum Gipfel, mit
hohen, dichten Bäumen bekleidet, jene Täler in ihren mannigfaltigen
Krümmungen von den lieblichsten Wäldern beschattet sah, und der
sanfte Fluß zwischen den lispelnden Rohren dahingleitete und die
lieben Wolken abspiegelte, die der sanfte Abendwind am Himmel

full my heart was!—And we separated without having understood each other. But who in this world can readily understand someone else?

It's a sure thing, after all, that nothing in the world makes a person as necessary as love does. I can tell from Lotte that she'd hate to lose me, and the children couldn't imagine me not returning day after day. Today I had gone out there to tune Lotte's clavier, but I couldn't get to it because the little ones begged me for a fairy tale, and Lotte herself said I should comply with their wishes. I sliced their bread for supper (now they take it from me almost as gladly as from Lotte), and I told them their favorite story about the princess who is waited on by disembodied hands. I learn a lot when I tell stories, I assure you, and I'm amazed at the impression it makes on them. Because I occasionally have to invent a secondary plot element, which I forget the second time I tell the story, they immediately say it was different the last time; so that I now practice reeling off the stories without change in a singsong tone. This has taught me that an author must of necessity harm his book by bringing out a second, revised edition, even if it's been greatly improved poetically. The first impression finds us receptive, and man is so constituted that he can be convinced of even the most outlandish things; but they become deeply rooted at once, and woe to the man who wants to scrape them away or erase them!

Was it necessarily so, that the source of man's bliss should become the source of his misery?

The full, warm joy my heart felt in the living nature which deluged me with so much rapture, which made the world around me a paradise, is now becoming an intolerable torturer to me, a tormenting spirit that pursues me on every path. Formerly, when I looked down from the cliff at the fertile valley, across the river all the way to the hills beyond, and saw everything around me burgeon and bubble up; when I saw those mountains clad with tall, dense trees from their foot to their summit, those valleys in their varied windings shaded by the loveliest woods; when the quiet river glided past the whispering reeds, reflecting the charming clouds which the soft evening breeze gently propelled through the

herüberwiegte; wenn ich dann die Vögel um mich den Wald beleben
hörte, und die Millionen Mückenschwärme im letzten roten Strahle
der Sonne mutig tanzten und ihr letzter zuckender Blick den sum-
menden Käfer aus seinem Grase befreite und das Schwirren und
Weben um mich her mich auf den Boden aufmerksam machte und
das Moos, das meinem harten Felsen seine Nahrung abzwingt, und
das Geniste, das den dürren Sandhügel hinunterwächst, mir das innere glühende, heilige Leben der Natur eröffnete: wie faßte ich das
alles in mein warmes Herz, fühlte mich in der überfließenden Fülle
wie vergöttert, und die herrlichen Gestalten der unendlichen Welt
bewegten sich allbelebend in meiner Seele. Ungeheure Berge um-
gaben mich, Abgründe lagen vor mir, und Wetterbäche stürzten
herunter, die Flüsse strömten unter mir, und Wald und Gebirg er-
klang; und ich sah sie wirken und schaffen ineinander in den Tiefen
der Erde, alle die unergründlichen Kräfte; und nun über der Erde
und unter dem Himmel wimmeln die Geschlechter der mannigfaltigen Geschöpfe. Alles, alles bevölkert mit tausendfachen Gestalten;
und die Menschen dann sich in Häuslein zusammen sichern und sich
annisten und herrschen in ihrem Sinne über die weite Welt! Armer
Tor! der du alles so gering achtest, weil du so klein bist. – Vom unzu-
gänglichen Gebirge über die Einöde, die kein Fuß betrat, bis ans
Ende des unbekannten Ozeans weht der Geist des Ewigschaffenden
und freut sich jedes Staubes, der ihn vernimmt und lebt. – Ach
damals, wie oft habe ich mich mit Fittichen eines Kranichs, der über
mich hinflog, zu dem Ufer des ungemessenen Meeres gesehnt, aus
dem schäumenden Becher des Unendlichen jene schwellende
Lebenswonne zu trinken und nur einen Augenblick, in der
eingeschränkten Kraft meines Busens, einen Tropfen der Seligkeit
des Wesens zu fühlen, das alles in sich und durch sich hervorbringt.

Bruder, nur die Erinnerung jener Stunden macht mir wohl. Selbst
diese Anstrengung, jene unsäglichen Gefühle zurückzurufen, wieder
auszusprechen, hebt meine Seele über sich selbst und läßt mich dann
das Bange des Zustandes doppelt empfinden, der mich jetzt umgibt.

Es hat sich vor meiner Seele wie ein Vorhang weggezogen, und der
Schauplatz des unendlichen Lebens verwandelt sich vor mir in den
Abgrund des ewig offenen Grabes. Kannst du sagen: *Das ist!* da alles
vorübergeht? da alles mit der Wetterschnelle vorüberrollt, so selten
die ganze Kraft seines Daseins ausdauert, ach! in den Strom fort-
gerissen, untergetaucht und an Felsen zerschmettert wird? Da ist
kein Augenblick, der nicht dich verzehrte und die Deinigen um dich
her, kein Augenblick, da du nicht ein Zerstörer bist, sein mußt; der

sky; when I then heard the songbirds enlivening the woods around me, and the millions of swarms of gnats danced cheerfully in the last red ray of sunshine, and the sun's last flashing glance freed the humming beetle from its grass, and the rustling and activity around me drew my attention to the ground; and the moss that with difficulty derives its nourishment from my rugged crag, and the brush that grows all the way down the barren sandy hill, exposed the glowing, sacred inner life of nature to me—how I clutched it all to my tender heart, feeling like a god amid that overflowing abundance, while the splendid forms of the infinite world stirred in my soul with universal vigor! Huge mountains surrounded me, abysses opened before me, and torrents plunged down; rivers flowed below me, and forest and hill resounded; and I saw them operate creatively on one another in the depths of the earth, all those unfathomable forces; and now on the earth's surface and beneath the sky, the races of the various creatures swarm. Everything, everything is populated by thousands of forms; and then people shelter together in little houses, settle in, and imagine that they rule the whole world! Poor fool, you look down at everything because you're so small.—From the inaccessible mountains, across the wilderness untouched by any foot, to the furthest limits of the unknown ocean, the spirit of the eternally creating One wafts and takes pleasure in every grain of dust that perceives him and lives.—Ah, in those days, how often I yearned for the wings of the crane that flew by over my head, so I could reach the shore of the unmeasured sea, to drink that swelling rapture of life from the foaming goblet of infinity, and just for a moment to feel in the limited strength of my breast one drop of the bliss of that Being who produces all this in himself and through himself.

My brother, only the recollection of those hours makes me feel good. Even this exertion to recall those ineffable emotions and express them again lifts my soul above itself, and then makes me feel doubly the terror of the situation I now find myself in.

It's as if a curtain had been drawn away before my soul, and the scene of infinite life is being transformed before my eyes into the abyss of the eternally open grave. Can you say "This is" when everything is transitory, when everything rolls by with the speed of a storm, and the full strength of its existence so seldom endures? Alas, it's swept away by the current, submerged, and shattered against the rocks! There's no instant which doesn't consume you and your loved ones around you, no instant when you yourself

harmloseste Spaziergang kostet tausend armen Würmchen das
Leben, es zerrüttet Ein Fußtritt die mühseligen Gebäude der
Ameisen und stampft eine kleine Welt in ein schmähliches Grab. Ha!
nicht die große seltne Not der Welt, diese Fluten, die eure Dörfer
wegspülen, diese Erdbeben, die eure Städte verschlingen, rühren
mich; mir untergräbt das Herz die verzehrende Kraft, die in dem All
der Natur verborgen liegt; die nichts gebildet hat, das nicht seinen
Nachbar, nicht sich selbst zerstörte. Und so taumle ich beängstigt!
Himmel und Erde und ihre webenden Kräfte um mich her: Ich sehe
nichts, als ein ewig verschlingendes, ewig wiederkäuendes
Ungeheuer.

Am 21. August.

Umsonst strecke ich meine Arme nach ihr aus, morgens, wenn ich von
schweren Träumen aufdämmre, vergebens suche ich sie nachts in
meinem Bette, wenn mich ein glücklicher unschuldiger Traum
getäuscht hat, als säß ich neben ihr auf der Wiese und hielte ihre
Hand und deckte sie mit tausend Küssen. Ach wenn ich dann noch
halb im Taumel des Schlafes nach ihr tappe und drüber mich ermuntere – ein Strom von Tränen bricht aus meinem gepreßten
Herzen, und ich weine trostlos einer finstern Zukunft entgegen.

Am 22. August.

Es ist ein Unglück, Wilhelm, meine tätigen Kräfte sind zu einer unruhigen Lässigkeit verstimmt, ich kann nicht müßig sein und kann
doch auch nichts tun. Ich habe keine Vorstellungskraft, kein Gefühl an
der Natur, und die Bücher ekeln mich an. Wenn wir uns selbst fehlen,
fehlt uns doch alles. Ich schwöre dir, manchmal wünschte ich ein
Tagelöhner zu sein, um nur des Morgens beim Erwachen eine
Aussicht auf den künftigen Tag, einen Drang, eine Hoffnung zu haben.
Oft beneide ich Alberten, den ich über die Ohren in Akten begraben
sehe, und bilde mir ein, mir wäre wohl, wenn ich an seiner Stelle wäre!
Schon etlichemal ist mirs so aufgefahren, ich wollte dir schreiben und
dem Minister, um die Stelle bei der Gesandtschaft anzuhalten, die, wie
du versicherst, mir nicht versagt werden würde. Ich glaube es selbst.
Der Minister liebt mich seit langer Zeit, hatte lange mir angelegen, ich
sollte mich irgendeinem Geschäfte widmen; und eine Stunde ist mirs
auch wohl drum zu tun. Hernach, wenn ich wieder dran denke und
mir die Fabel vom Pferde einfällt, das, seiner Freiheit ungeduldig, sich
Sattel und Zeug auflegen läßt und zuschanden geritten wird, – ich weiß
nicht, was ich soll – Und mein Lieber! ist nicht vielleicht das Sehnen

aren't, can help being, a destroyer; the most innocent stroll costs the lives of a thousand poor worms, one footstep demolishes the painstaking constructions of an anthill, treading that microcosm into a wretched grave. Ha! It's not the large-scale, rarely occurring disasters in the world, those floods which wash away your villages, those earthquakes which swallow up your cities, that affect me; my heart is undermined by the consuming force concealed in all of nature, which has created nothing that doesn't destroy its neighbor and itself. And so I reel about in anxiety! Heaven and earth and their creative forces all around me, and I see nothing but a monster eternally swallowing, eternally chewing its cud.

August 21

It's in vain that I hold my arms out to her in the morning when I hazily awaken from heavy dreams, in vain that I seek her at night in my bed when a happy, blameless dream has deceived me, as if I were sitting next to her in the meadow, holding her hand and covering it with a thousand kisses. Ah, when I then, still half-dazed by sleep, grope for her and then become wide awake—a torrent of tears wells up from my anguished heart, and I weep inconsolably as I face a gloomy future.

August 22

It's a terrible thing, Wilhelm, my active forces have been untuned into a restless indolence; I can't remain idle and yet I can't do a thing. I have no power to depict things, no feeling for nature, and books disgust me. When we lack ourselves, we lack everything. I swear to you, sometimes I wish I were a day laborer, just so I could wake up in the morning with the expectation of the day to come, with some drive or hope. Often I envy Albert, whom I see up to his ears in official documents; and I imagine I'd feel good if I were in his place! A few times now I've had a sudden urge to write to you and the minister to apply for the position in the embassy, which you assure me wouldn't be refused me. I think so too. The minister has been fond of me for some time, and had long been entreating me to dedicate myself to some occupation; and at times I'm even eager to do so. Later on, when I think it over and I remember the fable about the horse who was fed up with being free, allowed a saddle and harness to be placed on him, and was ridden till he was lame, I no longer know what I should do.—And, dear friend, isn't my long-

in mir nach Veränderung des Zustandes eine innere unbehagliche
Ungeduld, die mich überallhin verfolgen wird?

Am 28. August.

Es ist wahr, wenn meine Krankheit zu heilen wäre, so würden diese
Menschen es tun. Heute ist mein Geburtstag, und in aller Frühe empfange ich ein Päckchen von Alberten. Mir fällt beim Eröffnen sogleich
eine der blaßroten Schleifen in die Augen, die Lotte vorhatte, als ich
sie kennen lernte, und um die ich seither etlichemal gebeten hatte. Es
waren zwei Büchelchen in Duodez dabei, der kleine Wetsteinische
Homer, eine Ausgabe, nach der ich so oft verlangt, um mich auf dem
Spaziergange mit dem Ernestischen nicht zu schleppen. Sieh! so kommen sie meinen Wünschen zuvor, so suchen sie alle die kleinen
Gefälligkeiten der Freundschaft auf, die tausendmal werter sind als
jene blendenden Geschenke, wodurch uns die Eitelkeit des Gebers
erniedrigt. Ich küsse diese Schleife tausendmal, und mit jedem
Atemzuge schlürfe ich die Erinnerung jener Seligkeiten ein, mit
denen mich jene wenigen, glücklichen, unwiederbringlichen Tage
überfüllten. Wilhelm, es ist so, und ich murre nicht, die Blüten des
Lebens sind nur Erscheinungen! Wie viele gehn vorüber, ohne eine
Spur hinter sich zu lassen, wie wenige setzen Frucht an, und wie
wenige dieser Früchte werden reif! Und doch sind deren noch genug
da; und doch – O mein Bruder! – können wir gereifte Früchte ver-
nachlässigen, verachten, ungenossen verfaulen lassen?

Lebe wohl! Es ist ein herrlicher Sommer; ich sitze oft auf den
Obstbäumen in Lottens Baumstück mit dem Obstbrecher, der langen
Stange, und hole die Birnen aus dem Gipfel. Sie steht unten und
nimmt sie ab, wenn ich sie ihr herunterlasse.

Am 30. August.

Unglücklicher! Bist du nicht ein Tor? betrügst du dich nicht selbst? Was
soll diese tobende endlose Leidenschaft? Ich habe kein Gebet mehr als
an sie; meiner Einbildungskraft erscheint keine andere Gestalt als die
ihrige, und alles in der Welt um mich her sehe ich nur im Verhältnisse
mit ihr. Und das macht mir denn so manche glückliche Stunde – bis ich
mich wieder von ihr losreißen muß! Ach Wilhelm! wozu mich mein
Herz oft drängt! – Wenn ich bei ihr gesessen bin, zwei, drei Stunden,
und mich an ihrer Gestalt, an ihrem Betragen, an dem himmlischen

ing for a change of status perhaps an inner, uncomfortable impatience that will pursue me wherever I go?

August 28

It's true, if my illness were curable, these people would cure it. Today is my birthday,[13] and early in the morning I received a little parcel from Albert. As soon as I opened it I caught sight of one of the pink bows Lotte was wearing when I met her, and for which I had asked her a few times since then. There were also two little volumes in duodecimo, the little Wetstein Homer, an edition I had wanted so often, so I wouldn't have to drag along the Ernesti edition on my outings.[14] You see! That's how they make my wishes come true, that's how they perform all the little kindnesses that friends do, which are a thousand times more valuable than those eye-catching gifts with which the donor's vanity overwhelms us. I kiss that bow a thousand times, and with every breath I inhale the recollection of those blisses which those few happy, irretrievable days heaped upon me. Wilhelm, that's the way it is, and I'm not grumbling: the blossoms of life are merely apparitions! How many pass by without leaving a trace behind; how few of them form fruit, and how few of those fruits ripen! And yet there's still enough such fruit; and yet, my brother, can we neglect ripe fruit, despise it, and let it rot untasted?

Farewell! It's a splendid summer; I frequently sit up in the fruit trees in Lotte's orchard with the fruit picker, that long pole, fetching pears from the treetops. She stands below and receives them when I lower them to her.

August 30

Unhappy man! Aren't you a fool? Aren't you deceiving yourself? What does this unending, furious passion mean? My only prayers now are to her; no other form appears in my imagination but hers, and I see everything in the world around me only as it relates to her. And then that creates so many happy hours for me—until I have to tear myself away from her again! Ah, Wilhelm, what my heart often urges me to do!—When I've sat with her for two or three hours, enjoying her figure, her de-

13. August 28 was Goethe's birthday.   14. Wetstein was the printer/publisher of the 1707 Amsterdam edition; Ernesti was the editor of the five-volume quarto Leipzig edition, 1759–1764.

Ausdruck ihrer Worte geweidet habe und nun nach und nach alle
meine Sinnen aufgespannt werden, mir es düster vor den Augen wird,
ich kaum noch höre und es mich an die Gurgel faßt wie ein
Meuchelmörder, dann mein Herz in wilden Schlägen den bedrängten
Sinnen Luft zu machen sucht und ihre Verwirrung nur vermehrt –
Wilhelm, ich weiß oft nicht, ob ich auf der Welt bin! Und – wenn nicht
manchmal die Wehmut das Übergewicht nimmt und Lotte mir den
elenden Trost erlaubt, auf ihrer Hand meine Beklemmung
auszuweinen, – so muß ich fort, muß hinaus! und schweife dann weit im
Felde umher; einen jähen Berg zu klettern, ist dann meine Freude,
durch einen unwegsamen Wald einen Pfad durchzuarbeiten, durch die
Hecken, die mich verletzen, durch die Dornen, die mich zerreißen! Da
wird mirs etwas besser! Etwas! Und wenn ich vor Müdigkeit und Durst
manchmal unterwegs liegen bleibe, manchmal in der tiefen Nacht,
wenn der hohe Vollmond über mir steht, im einsamen Walde auf einen
krummgewachsenen Baum mich setze, um meinen verwundeten
Sohlen nur einige Linderung zu verschaffen, und dann in einer ermat-
tenden Ruhe in dem Dämmerschein hinschlummre! O Wilhelm! die
einsame Wohnung einer Zelle, das härene Gewand und der
Stachelgürtel wären Labsale, nach denen meine Seele schmachtet.
Adieu! Ich sehe dieses Elendes kein Ende als das Grab.

Am 3. September.

Ich muß fort! Ich danke dir, Wilhelm, daß du meinen wankenden
Entschluß bestimmt hast. Schon vierzehn Tage gehe ich mit dem
Gedanken um, sie zu verlassen. Ich muß fort. Sie ist wieder in der
Stadt bei einer Freundin. Und Albert – und – ich muß fort!

Am 10. September.

Das war eine Nacht! Wilhelm! nun überstehe ich alles. Ich werde sie
nicht wiedersehn! O daß ich nicht an deinen Hals fliegen, dir mit
tausend Tränen und Entzückungen ausdrücken kann, mein Bester,
die Empfindungen, die mein Herz bestürmen. Hier sitze ich und
schnappe nach Luft, suche mich zu beruhigen, erwarte den Morgen,
und mit Sonnenaufgang sind die Pferde bestellt.
    Ach, sie schläft ruhig und denkt nicht, daß sie mich nie wieder-
sehen wird. Ich habe mich losgerissen, bin stark genug gewesen, in
einem Gespräch von zwei Stunden mein Vorhaben nicht zu verraten.
Und Gott, welch ein Gespräch!
    Albert hatte mir versprochen, gleich nach dem Nachtessen mit
Lotten im Garten zu sein. Ich stand auf der Terrasse unter den hohen

meanor, the heavenly expression in her words, and all my senses
then gradually become tense and there's darkness in front of my
eyes, I can hardly hear any more, and I'm seized at the throat as
if by a strangler, when my heart then tries in its wild beating to
give vent to my oppressed senses but only increases their confusion— Wilhelm, I often don't know whether I'm still in the
world! And—unless at times melancholy gets the upper hand
and Lotte permits me the paltry comfort of pouring out my anguish in tears on her hand, I must take leave, I must get away!
Then I roam far and wide outdoors; then I take pleasure in
climbing a steep mountain, cutting a path through an impassable
forest, through the hedges that wound me, through the thorns
that lacerate me! Then I feel a little better! A little! And when at
times I lie down on the way from weariness and thirst, and when
sometimes late at night, with the full moon hanging high above
me, I sit down on a crooked tree in the solitary woods to give my
sore feet some relief, and then doze off in the half-light in an ex-
hausting repose! Oh, Wilhelm! A lonely residence in a hermit's
cell, a hair shirt and a girdle of thorns would be comforts for
which my soul languishes. Adieu! I see no end to this misery except the grave.

September 3

I must get away! I thank you, Wilhelm, for having strengthened
my faltering resolve. For two weeks now I've been thinking constantly about leaving her. I must get away. Once again she's in
town at a girl friend's house. And Albert—and—I must get away!

September 10

What a night this was! Wilhelm! After this I can get through anything. I won't see her again! Too bad I can't hug you, dear friend,
and let you know with a thousand tears and raptures the feelings
that are besieging my heart. I sit here gasping for air, I'm trying
to calm down, I'm waiting till morning comes, and I've ordered
horses for sunrise.

Ah, she's sleeping peacefully, not knowing she'll never see me
again. I've torn myself away, I've been strong enough to avoid
disclosing my intentions at any time during a two-hour conversation. And, God, what a conversation!

Albert had promised me to be in the garden with Lotte right
after supper. I stood on the terrace under the tall chestnut trees

Kastanienbäumen und sah der Sonne nach, die mir nun zum letzten Male über dem lieblichen Tale, über dem sanften Fluß unterging. So oft hatte ich hier gestanden mit ihr und ebendem herrlichen Schauspiele zugesehen, und nun – Ich ging in der Allee auf und ab, die mir so lieb war; ein geheimer sympathetischer Zug hatte mich hier so oft gehalten, ehe ich noch Lotten kannte, und wie freuten wir uns, als wir im Anfang unserer Bekanntschaft die wechselseitige Neigung zu diesem Plätzchen entdeckten, das wahrhaftig eins von den romantischsten ist, die ich von der Kunst hervorgebracht gesehen habe.

Erst hast du zwischen Kastanienbäumen die weite Aussicht – Ach, ich erinnere mich, ich habe dir, denk ich, schon viel davon geschrieben, wie hohe Buchenwände einen endlich einschließen und durch ein daran stoßendes Boskett die Allee immer düsterer wird, bis zuletzt alles sich in ein geschlossenes Plätzchen endigt, das alle Schauer der Einsamkeit umschweben. Ich fühle es noch, wie heimlich mirs ward, als ich zum ersten Male an einem hohen Mittage hineintrat; ich ahnete ganz leise, was für ein Schauplatz das noch werden sollte von Seligkeit und Schmerz.

Ich hatte mich etwa eine halbe Stunde in den schmachtend süßen Gedanken des Abscheidens, des Wiedersehens geweidet, als ich sie die Terrasse heraufsteigen hörte. Ich lief ihnen entgegen, mit einem Schauer faßte ich ihre Hand und küßte sie. Wir waren eben heraufgetreten, als der Mond hinter dem buschigen Hügel aufging; wir redeten mancherlei und kamen unvermerkt dem düstern Kabinette näher. Lotte trat hinein und setzte sich, Albert neben sie, ich auch; doch meine Unruhe ließ mich nicht lange sitzen; ich stand auf, trat vor sie, ging auf und ab, setzte mich wieder: es war ein ängstlicher Zustand. Sie machte uns aufmerksam auf die schöne Wirkung des Mondenlichtes, das am Ende der Buchenwände die ganze Terrasse vor uns erleuchtete: ein herrlicher Anblick, der um so viel frappanter war, weil uns rings eine tiefe Dämmerung einschloß. Wir waren still, und sie fing nach einer Weile an: Niemals gehe ich im Mondenlichte spazieren, niemals, daß mir nicht der Gedanke an meine Verstorbenen begegnete, daß nicht das Gefühl von Tod, von Zukunft über mich käme. Wir werden sein! fuhr sie mit der Stimme des herrlichsten Gefühls fort; aber, Werther, sollen wir uns wiederfinden? wiedererkennen? was ahnen Sie? was sagen Sie?

Lotte, sagte ich, indem ich ihr die Hand reichte und mir die Augen voll Tränen wurden, wir werden uns wiedersehen! hier und dort wiedersehen! – Ich konnte nicht weiterreden – Wilhelm, mußte sie mich das fragen, da ich diesen ängstlichen Abschied im Herzen hatte!

and watched the sun now setting for the last time for me over the lovely valley, over the gentle river. I had so often stood here with her watching the same splendid scene, and now— I walked up and down the avenue of trees I loved so much; a mysterious sympathetic inclination had held me fast here so often, even before I knew Lotte, and we used to be happy when, at the outset of our acquaintance, we discovered our mutual liking for this spot, which is truly one of the most romantic I've seen produced by art.

First you have the distant view between the chestnut trees.— Ah, I remember, I think I've already written you frequently how tall walls of beeches finally shut you in and the avenue is gradually darkened by an adjacent grove, until at last it ends in an enclosed spot surrounded by all the thrills of solitude. I still feel how uncanny it felt when I first entered that enclosure one day at high noon; I had the very quiet premonition of what a setting it would prove to be for bliss and grief.

I had enjoyed the yearningly sweet thoughts of leavetaking and reunion for about half an hour when I heard them ascending to the terrace. I ran to meet them, with a thrill of pleasure I grasped her hand and kissed it. We had just ascended when the moon rose behind the leafy hill; we spoke of all sorts of things and imperceptibly drew nearer to the dark pavilion. Lotte went in and sat down, Albert sat next to her, then I did the same; but my nerves didn't let me sit there long; I stood up, walked in front of her, paced to and fro, and sat back down: I was in a fearful state. She called our attention to the beautiful effect of the moonlight, which was illuminating the whole terrace before us at the end of the beechen walls: a splendid view, which was all the more striking because we were surrounded by deep dusk. We were silent, and after a while she began: "I never go walking in the moonlight, never, without thinking of my deceased dear ones, without the feeling of death and futurity coming over me. We shall still exist!" she continued with splendid emotion in her voice; "but, Werther, will we find one another again? Recognize one another? What do *you* think? What do *you* say?"

"Lotte," I said, holding out my hand to her as my eyes filled with tears, "we *will* meet again! Meet again in this world and the next!" I couldn't go on.—Wilhelm, did she have to ask me that while I had this fearful departure in my heart? "And do the dear

Und ob die lieben Abgeschiednen von uns wissen, fuhr sie fort, ob sie fühlen, wenns uns wohl geht, daß wir mit warmer Liebe uns ihrer erinnern? O! die Gestalt meiner Mutter schwebt immer um mich, wenn ich am stillen Abend unter ihren Kindern, unter meinen Kindern sitze und sie um mich versammelt sind, wie sie um sie versammelt waren. Wenn ich dann mit einer sehnenden Träne gen Himmel sehe und wünsche, daß sie hereinschauen könnte einen Augenblick, wie ich mein Wort halte, das ich ihr in der Stunde des Todes gab: die Mutter ihrer Kinder zu sein. Mit welcher Empfindung rufe ich aus: Verzeihe mirs, Teuerste, wenn ich ihnen nicht bin, was du ihnen warst. Ach! tue ich doch alles, was ich kann; sind sie doch gekleidet, genährt, ach, und was mehr ist als das alles, gepflegt und geliebt. Könntest du unsere Eintracht sehen, liebe Heilige! du würdest mit dem heißesten Danke den Gott verherrlichen, den du mit den letzten, bittersten Tränen un die Wohlfahrt deiner Kinder batest.
Sie sagte das! o Wilhelm, wer kann wiederholen, was sie sagte! Wie kann der kalte, tote Buchstabe diese himmlische Blüte des Geistes darstellen! Albert fiel ihr sanft in die Rede: Es greift Sie zu stark an, liebe Lotte! ich weiß, Ihre Seele hängt sehr nach diesen Ideen, aber ich bitte Sie – O Albert, sagte sie, ich weiß, du vergissest nicht die Abende, da wir zusammensaßen an dem kleinen runden Tischchen, wenn der Papa verreist war und wir die Kleinen schlafen geschickt hatten. Du hattest oft ein gutes Buch und kamst so selten dazu, etwas zu lesen – War der Umgang dieser herrlichen Seele nicht mehr als alles? die schöne, sanfte, muntere und immer tätige Frau! Gott kennt meine Tränen, mit denen ich mich oft in meinem Bette vor ihn hinwarf: er möchte mich ihr gleichmachen.
Lotte! rief ich aus, indem ich mich vor sie hinwarf, ihre Hand nahm und mit tausend Tränen netzte, Lotte! der Segen Gottes ruht über dir und der Geist deiner Mutter! – Wenn Sie sie gekannt hätten, sagte sie, indem sie mir die Hand drückte, – sie war wert, von Ihnen gekannt zu sein! – Ich glaubte zu vergehen. Nie war ein größeres, stolzeres Wort über mich ausgesprochen worden, – und sie fuhr fort: Und diese Frau mußte in der Blüte ihrer Jahre dahin, da ihr jüngster Sohn nicht sechs Monate alt war! Ihre Krankheit dauerte nicht lange; sie war ruhig, hingegeben, nur ihre Kinder taten ihr weh, besonders das kleine. Wie es gegen das Ende ging und sie zu mir sagte: Bringe mir sie herauf, und wie ich sie hereinführte, die kleinen, die nicht wußten, und die ältesten, die ohne Sinne waren, wie sie ums Bette standen, und wie sie die Hände aufhob und über

departed know about us?" she continued. "Are they aware when
things go well for us, that we remember them with tender love?
Oh! The image of my mother is always around me, when in the
quiet of the evening I sit among her children, my children, and
they're gathered around me as they were gathered around her.
When, at such moments, I look up to heaven with a tear of longing and wish that she could look in on us for a moment to see
how I'm keeping the promise I made her at the hour of her
death: to be a mother to her children. With what emotion I ex-
claim: 'Forgive me, dearest, if I'm not all to them that you were.
Ah, I *am* doing all I can; they *are* dressed, fed, ah, and what
counts more than all that, they're taken care of and loved. If you
could only see how well we get along, dear saint! You would
magnify God in deepest gratitude, God, to whom you prayed
with your last bitter tears for the welfare of your children.'"
    That's what she said! Oh, Wilhelm, who can repeat her words?
How can the cold, dead letter depict that heavenly blossom of
the spirit? Albert interrupted her quietly: "It's affecting you too
strongly, Lotte dear! I know your soul is greatly attached to those
ideas, but I beg of you—" "Oh, Albert," she said, "I know you
haven't forgotten those evenings when we sat together by the little round table, when Father was away on a trip and we had sent
the little ones off to bed. You often had a good book, but so
rarely got to to read anything.—Wasn't the company of that
splendid soul more than anything else? That beautiful, gentle,
lively, and always active woman! God knows with how many
tears I often prostrated myself before him in my bed, so that he
would make me resemble her!"
    "Lotte!" I exclaimed, casting myself down in front of her, seiz-
ing her hand, and moistening it with a thousand tears; "Lotte!
God's blessing rests on you, and so does your mother's spirit!" "If
you had only known her," she said, pressing my hand; "she was
worthy of your acquaintance!" I thought I'd perish. Never had a
finer, more flattering thing been said about me. She went on:
"And a woman like that had to die in the prime of life, when her
youngest son wasn't even six months old! Her illness didn't last
long; she was calm and resigned; she only felt bad for her children's sake, especially the infant. When it got near the end and
she said to me 'Bring them upstairs to me,' and I led them in, the
little ones, who couldn't understand, and the older ones, who
were in a daze; when they were standing around her bed, how

sie betete und sie küßte nacheinander und sie wegschickte und zu
mir sagte: Sei ihre Mutter! – Ich gab ihr die Hand drauf! – Du ver-
sprichst viel, meine Tochter, sagte sie, das Herz einer Mutter und das
Aug einer Mutter. Ich habe oft an deinen dankbaren Tränen gesehen, daß du fühlst, was das sei. Habe es für deine Geschwister, und
für deinen Vater die Treue und den Gehorsam einer Frau. Du wirst
ihn trösten. – Sie fragte nach ihm, er war ausgegangen, um uns den
unerträglichen Kummer zu verbergen, den er fühlte, der Mann war
ganz zerrissen.

Albert, du warst im Zimmer. Sie hörte jemand gehn und fragte und
forderte dich zu sich, und wie sie dich ansah und mich, mit dem
getrösteten, ruhigen Blicke, daß wir glücklich sein, zusammen glücklich sein würden – Albert fiel ihr um den Hals und küßte sie und rief:
Wir sind es! wir werden es sein! – Der ruhige Albert war ganz aus
seiner Fassung, und ich wußte nichts von mir selber.

Werther, fing sie an, und diese Frau sollte dahin sein! Gott, wenn
ich manchmal denke, wie man das Liebste seines Lebens wegtragen
läßt, und niemand als die Kinder das so scharf fühlt, die sich noch
lange beklagten, die schwarzen Männer hätten die Mama weggetra-
gen.

Sie stand auf, und ich ward erweckt und erschüttert, blieb sitzen
und hielt ihre Hand. – Wir wollen fort, sagte sie, es wird Zeit. – Sie
wollte ihre Hand zurückziehen, und ich hielt sie fester. – Wir werden
uns wiedersehen, rief ich, wir werden uns finden, unter allen
Gestalten werden wir uns erkennen. Ich gehe, fuhr ich fort, ich gehe
willig, und doch, wenn ich sagen sollte auf ewig, ich würde es nicht
aushalten. Leb wohl, Lotte! Leb wohl, Albert! Wir sehn uns wieder. –
Morgen, denke ich, versetzte sie scherzend. – Ich fühlte das Morgen!
Ach sie wußte nicht, als sie ihre Hand aus der meinen zog – Sie gingen die Allee hinaus, ich stand, sah ihnen nach im Mondscheine und
warf mich an die Erde und weinte mich aus und sprang auf und lief
auf die Terrasse hervor und sah noch dort unten im Schatten der
hohen Lindenbäume ihr weißes Kleid nach der Gartentür schim-
mern, ich streckte meine Arme aus, und es verschwand.

she lifted her hands and prayed over them and kissed each one in turn and sent them away and said to me: 'Be a mother to them!' I promised her I would. 'You're making an important promise, daughter,' she said, 'a mother's heart and a mother's watchful eye. I've often seen from your tears of gratitude that you feel what those things mean. Have them for your brothers and sisters, and for your father have a wife's fidelity and obedience. You'll console him.' She asked for him; he had gone out to hide from us the unbearable grief he felt; the man was all torn up.

"Albert, you were in the room. She heard someone's step and asked and called you over, and when she looked at you and at me, with a comforted, peaceful glance, seeing that we would be happy, happy together—" Albert hugged her, kissed her, and cried: "We are! We will be!" The usually calm Albert was quite beside himself, and, as for me, I was dead to the world.

"Werther," she began, "that such a woman should be gone! God, when I think sometimes how people let the dearest thing in their lives be carried away! And no one feels it as keenly as children do; for a long time they lamented that the men in black had carried away their mother."

She stood up; I came to my senses; deeply moved, I sat there holding her hand. "We must go," she said, "it's time." She tried to withdraw her hand, but I held it more tightly. "We *will* meet again," I cried, "we *will* find one another, we *will* recognize one another in any guise. I'm going," I continued, "I'm going willingly, and yet, if I were to say 'forever,' I couldn't bear it. Farewell, Lotte! Farewell, Albert! We'll meet again." "Tomorrow, I think," she replied jokingly. That "tomorrow" affected me! Ah, she was unaware, when she released her hand from mine— They left by way of the avenue; I stood there, watching them depart in the moonlight; then I threw myself to the ground and wept my fill, then leaped up and ran to the front of the terrace; down there, in the shadow of the tall lime trees, I still saw her white dress glimmering on the way to the garden door. I stretched out my arms, and it vanished.

Zweites Buch

Am 20. October 1771.

Gestern sind wir hier angelangt. Der Gesandte ist unpaß und wird sich also einige Tage einhalten. Wenn er nur nicht so unhold wäre, wär alles gut. Ich merke, ich merke, das Schicksal hat mir harte Prüfungen zugedacht. Doch gutes Muts! Ein leichter Sinn trägt alles! Ein leichter Sinn? das macht mich zu lachen, wie das Wort in meine Feder kommt. O ein bißchen leichteres Blut würde mich zum Glücklichsten unter der Sonne machen. Was! da, wo andere mit ihrem bißchen Kraft und Talent vor mir in behaglicher Selbstgefälligkeit herumschwadronieren, verzweifle ich an meiner Kraft, an meinen Gaben? Guter Gott, der du mir das alles schenktest, warum hieltest du nicht die Hälfte zurück und gabst mir Selbstvertrauen und Genügsamkeit!

Geduld! Geduld! es wird besser werden. Denn ich sage dir, Lieber, du hast recht. Seit ich unter dem Volke alle Tage herumgetrieben werde und sehe, was sie tun und wie sie's treiben, stehe ich viel besser mit mir selbst. Gewiß, weil wir doch einmal so gemacht sind, daß wir alles mit uns und uns mit allem vergleichen, so liegt Glück oder Elend in den Gegenständen, womit wir uns zusammenhalten, und da ist nichts gefährlicher als die Einsamkeit. Unsere Einbildungskraft, durch ihre Natur gedrungen, sich zu erheben, durch die phantastischen Bilder der Dichtkunst genährt, bildet sich eine Reihe Wesen hinauf, wo wir das unterste sind und alles außer uns herrlicher erscheint, jeder andere vollkommner ist. Und das geht ganz natürlich zu. Wir fühlen so oft, daß uns manches mangelt, und eben was uns fehlt, scheint uns oft ein anderer zu besitzen, dem wir denn auch alles dazugeben, was *wir* haben, und noch eine gewisse idealische Behaglichkeit dazu. Und so ist der Glückliche vollkommen fertig, das Geschöpf unserer selbst.

Dagegen wenn wir mit all unserer Schwachheit und Mühseligkeit nur gerade fortarbeiten, so finden wir gar oft, daß wir mit unserm

Book Two

October 20, 1771

We arrived here yesterday. The ambassador is unwell, and so
will remain at home for a few days. If he weren't so unfriendly,
everything would be all right. I can tell, I can tell, fate has severe
tribulations in store for me. But, be of good cheer! Cheerfulness
gets you through everything! Cheerfulness? It makes me laugh,
how the word flows from my pen. Oh, a little more easygoing-
ness would make me the happiest man under the sun. What!
While others parade their bit of strength and talent in front of
me with smug self-satisfaction, am I to despair of my strength
and endowments? Merciful God, you that gave me all this, why
didn't you retain half of it and give me self-confidence and contentment?

Patience! Patience! Things will get better. For I tell you, dear
friend, you're right. Ever since I've been rubbing elbows with the
populace daily, observing their doings and their habits, I appreciate
myself much more. Naturally, because we happen to be so constituted that we compare everything else to ourselves and ourselves to
everything else, happiness or misery lie in the objects we associate
with, and so nothing is more dangerous than solitude. Our imagination, compelled by its nature to seek higher spheres, nurtured by
the fantasy images of poetry, constructs an ascending order of beings in which we are the lowest and everything outside us seems
more splendid, everyone else more perfect. And that's the natural
process. We feel so often that we are lacking in many qualities, and
precisely what we lack someone else appears to possess; then we
also ascribe to that person everything that *we* possess, in addition to
a certain ideal feeling of comfort. Thus that lucky person becomes
perfect and complete, a person we ourselves have created.

On the other hand, if we merely push ahead despite all our weakness and our need to exert great efforts, we quite often find that our

Schlendern und Lavieren es weiter bringen als andere mit ihrem
Segeln und Rudern – und – das ist doch ein wahres Gefühl seiner
selbst, wenn man andern gleich- oder gar vorläuft.

Am 26. November.

Ich fange an, mich insofern ganz leidlich hier zu befinden. Das beste
ist, daß es zu tun genug gibt; und dann die vielerlei Menschen, die
allerlei neuen Gestalten machen mir ein buntes Schauspiel vor
meiner Seele. Ich habe den Grafen C . . . kennen lernen, einen Mann,
den ich jeden Tag mehr verehren muß, einen weiten, großen Kopf,
und der deswegen nicht kalt ist, weil er viel übersieht; aus dessen
Umgange so viel Empfindung für Freundschaft und Liebe hervor-
leuchtet. Er nahm teil an mir, als ich einen Geschäftsauftrag an ihn
ausrichtete und er bei den ersten Worten merkte, daß wir uns verstanden, daß er mit mir reden konnte wie nicht mit jedem. Auch kann
ich sein offenes Betragen gegen mich nicht genug rühmen. So eine
wahre warme Freude ist nicht in der Welt, als eine große Seele zu
sehen, die sich gegen einen öffnet.

Am 24. Dezember.

Der Gesandte macht mir viel Verdruß, ich habe es vorausgesehen. Er
ist der pünktlichste Narr, den es nur geben kann; Schritt vor Schritt
und umständlich wie eine Base; ein Mensch, der nie mit sich selbst
zufrieden ist, und dem es daher niemand zu Danke machen kann. Ich
arbeite gern leicht weg, und wie es steht, so steht es: da ist er imstande, mir einen Aufsatz zurückzugeben und zu sagen: Er ist gut,
aber sehen Sie ihn durch, man findet immer ein besseres Wort, eine
reinere Partikel. – Da möchte ich des Teufels werden. Kein Und,
kein Bindewörtchen darf außenbleiben, und von allen Inversionen,
die mir manchmal entfahren, ist er ein Todfeind; wenn man seinen
Perioden nicht nach der hergebrachten Melodie heraborgelt, so versteht er gar nichts drin. Das ist ein Leiden, mit so einem Menschen
zu tun zu haben.

Das Vetrauen des Grafen von C . . . ist noch das einzige, was mich
schadlos hält. Er sagte mir letzthin ganz aufrichtig, wie unzufrieden er
mit der Langsamkeit und Bedenklichkeit meines Gesandten sei. Die
Leute erschweren es sich und andern; doch, sagte er, man muß sich
darein resignieren, wie ein Reisender, der über einen Berg muß;
freilich, wäre der Berg nicht da, so wäre der Weg viel bequemer und
kürzer; er ist nun aber da, und man soll hinüber! –

Mein Alter spürt auch wohl den Vorzug, den mir der Graf vor ihm

sauntering and zigzagging produce greater results than the steady
sailing and rowing of others—and—after all, one truly esteems oneself when one keeps pace with others or even outraces them.

November 26
I'm beginning to feel tolerably at ease here to that extent. The
best thing is that there's plenty to do; besides that, the variety of
people, all sorts of new personalities, create a motley scene for
my mind. I've met Count C——, a man I must esteem more
daily, a man of extensive and serious intelligence, but who is nevertheless not distant just because he has so much responsibility;
his capacity for friendship and love is evident in my dealings
with him. He took notice of me when I delivered a professional
message to him and he realized at my first words that our minds
were akin, that he could speak with me as with few other people. Besides, I can't sufficiently praise his open demeanor with
me. There is no joy in the world so true and heartwarming as to
encounter a great soul that opens up to you.

December 24
The ambassador vexes me grievously; I foresaw it. He's the most
foolish stickler possible; he moves step by step, and he's as fussy
as an old lady; a man who's never satisfied with himself, and thus
never contented with anyone else. I like to work briskly, not worrying over tiny details; so he's liable to hand back a report to me
saying: "It's good, but look through it again; it's always possible
to find a better word, a more literate particle." At such times I
want to go crazy. No "and," no conjunction may be omitted, and
he's a mortal enemy of the free word placement I sometimes let
slip past me; if you don't rattle off his artificial sentences to the
traditional tune, he can't make them out at all. It's painful to
have to deal with such a person.

The confidence that Count von C—— places in me is still the
only thing that compensates me for it. Lately he told me straight
out how dissatisfied he is with my ambassador's slowness and
love of raising objections. People like that make things difficult
for themselves and for others; and yet, he said, one must resign
oneself to it, just like a traveler who has to cross a mountain;
naturally, if the mountain weren't there, the way would be much
easier and shorter; but it *is* there, and you've got to cross!—

My superior probably also detects the preference that the

gibt, und das ärgert ihn, und er ergreift jede Gelegenheit, Übels gegen mich vom Grafen zu reden: ich halte, wie natürlich, Widerpart, und dadurch wird die Sache nur schlimmer. Gestern gar brachte er mich auf, denn ich war mitgemeint: zu so Weltgeschäften sei der Graf ganz gut, er habe viele Leichtigkeit zu arbeiten und führe eine gute Feder, doch an gründlicher Gelehrsamkeit mangle es ihm wie allen Belletristen. Dazu machte er eine Miene, als ob er sagen wollte: Fühlst du den Stich? Aber es tat bei mir nicht die Wirkung; ich verachtete den Menschen, der so denken und sich so betragen konnte. Ich hielt ihm stand und focht mit ziemlicher Heftigkeit. Ich sagte, der Graf sei ein Mann, vor dem man Achtung haben müsse, wegen seines Charakters sowohl als wegen seiner Kenntnisse. Ich habe, sagt ich, niemand gekannt, dem es so geglückt wäre, seinen Geist zu erweitern, ihn über unzählige Gegenstände zu verbreiten und doch diese Tätigkeit fürs gemeine Leben zu behalten. – Das waren dem Gehirne spanische Dörfer, und ich empfahl mich, um nicht über ein weiteres Deraisonnement noch mehr Galle zu schlucken.

Und daran seid ihr alle schuld, die ihr mich in das Joch geschwatzt und mir so viel von Aktivität vorgesungen habt. Aktivität! Wenn nicht der mehr tut, der Kartoffeln legt und in die Stadt reitet, sein Korn zu verkaufen, als ich, so will ich zehn Jahre noch mich auf der Galeere abarbeiten, auf der ich nun angeschmiedet bin.

Und das glänzende Elend, die Langeweile unter dem garstigen Volke, das sich hier nebeneinander sieht! die Rangsucht unter ihnen, wie sie nur wachen und aufpassen, einander ein Schrittchen abzugewinnen; die elendesten, erbärmlichsten Leidenschaften, ganz ohne Röckchen. Da ist ein Weib, zum Exempel, die jedermann von ihrem Adel und ihrem Lande unterhält, so daß jeder Fremde denken muß: das ist eine Närrin, die sich auf das bißchen Adel und auf den Ruf ihres Landes Wunderstreiche einbildet. – Aber es ist noch viel ärger: eben das Weib ist hier aus der Nachbarschaft eine Amtschreiberstochter. – Sieh, ich kann das Menschengeschlecht nicht begreifen, das so wenig Sinn hat, um sich so platt zu prostituieren.

Zwar ich merke täglich mehr, mein Lieber, wie töricht man ist, andere nach sich zu berechnen. Und weil ich so viel mit mir selbst zu tun habe und dieses Herz so stürmisch ist – ach, ich lasse gern die andern ihres Pfades gehen, wenn sie mich nur auch könnten gehen lassen.

count gives me over him, and it irritates him, so he seizes every opportunity to malign the count to me; as is only natural, I take the opposing view, and that only makes the situation worse. Yesterday he really provoked me because he had me in mind, as well: the count was quite good in worldly matters, he said, he found work easy and wrote well, but, like all men of belles lettres, he was lacking in thorough scholarship. And he put on an expression which connoted: "Do you feel the sting?" But it didn't have the wanted effect on me; I despise a person who can think and act that way. I held my ground and disputed the matter rather hotly. I said that the count was a man who had to be esteemed for his character as well as his knowledge. I said that I had never met a man who had managed so successfully to broaden his mind, to extend it in countless directions, and yet to retain his effectiveness in everyday life.—That was Greek[15] to that mighty brain, and I took my leave, to avoid swallowing even more gall over additional senselessness.

And you and your crowd are to blame for this; you talked me into bearing this yoke by continually preaching "activity" to me. Activity! If more than this isn't accomplished by a man who plants potatoes and rides his horse into town to sell his grain, then I'll slave ten more years on the galley to which I'm now shackled!

And the magnificent poverty, the boredom amid the nasty people who consort together here! Their longing for higher rank, the way they lie in wait, on the watch, to steal a march on one another; the most wretched, pathetic passions, completely unconcealed. For example, there's a woman who speaks to everyone about her noble blood and her native country, so that any stranger must think: "She's a fool to be so amazingly conceited about her touch of nobility and her country's reputation." But things are even worse: this woman is a clerk's daughter from this very vicinity!—You see, I can't comprehend the human race, which is so mindless as to make such a sheer fool of itself.

To be sure, I notice more and more every day, dear friend, how silly it is to judge others by one's self. And because I commune so much with myself, and my heart is so impetuous—ah, I'd gladly let the others go their own way if they would only let me go mine.

15. Literally: "Spanish villages," i.e. names impossible to remember because they're so foreign; in more current German, the expression is *böhmische Dörfer* (Bohemian villages).

Was mich am meisten neckt, sind die fatalen bürgerlichen
Verhältnisse. Zwar weiß ich so gut als einer, wie nötig der Unterschied
der Stände ist, wie viel Vorteile er mir selbst verschafft: nur soll er mir
nicht eben gerade im Wege stehen, wo ich noch ein wenig Freude,
einen Schimmer von Glück auf dieser Erde genießen könnte. Ich
lernte neulich auf dem Spaziergange ein Fräulein von B . . . kennen,
ein liebenswürdiges Geschöpf, das sehr viel Natur mitten in dem
steifen Leben erhalten hat. Wir gefielen uns in unserem Gespräche,
und da wir schieden, bat ich sie um Erlaubnis, sie bei sich sehen zu
dürfen. Sie gestattete mir das mit so vieler Freimütigkeit, daß ich den
schicklichen Augenblick kaum erwarten konnte, zu ihr zu gehen. Sie
ist nicht von hier und wohnt bei einer Tante im Hause. Die Physiognomie der Alten gefiel mir nicht. Ich bezeigte ihr viel Aufmerksamkeit, mein Gespräch war meist an sie gewandt, und in minder als
einer halben Stunde hatte ich so ziemlich weg, was mir das Fräulein
nachher selbst gestand: daß die liebe Tante in ihrem Alter Mangel an
allem, kein anständiges Vermögen, keinen Geist und keine Stütze hat
als die Reihe ihrer Vorfahren, keinen Schirm als den Stand, in den sie
sich verpalisadiert, und kein Ergetzen, als von ihrem Stockwerk herab
über die bürgerlichen Häupter wegzusehen. In ihrer Jugend soll sie
schön gewesen sein und ihr Leben weggegaukelt, erst mit ihrem
Eigensinne manchen armen Jungen gequält und in den reiferen
Jahren sich unter den Gehorsam eines alten Offiziers geduckt haben,
der gegen diesen Preis und einen leidlichen Unterhalt das eherne
Jahrhundert mit ihr zubrachte und starb. Nun sieht sie im eisernen
sich allein und würde nicht angesehn, wär ihre Nichte nicht so
liebenswürdig.

Den 8. Januar 1772.

Was das für Menschen sind, deren ganze Seele auf dem Zeremoniell
ruht, deren Dichten und Trachten jahrelang dahin geht, wie sie um
einen Stuhl weiter hinauf bei Tische sich einschieben wollen! Und
nicht, daß sie sonst keine Angelegenheit hätten: nein, vielmehr
häufen sich die Arbeiten, eben weil man über den kleinen
Verdrießlichkeiten von Beförderung der wichtigen Sachen abgehalten
wird. Vorige Woche gab es bei der Schlittenfahrt Händel, und der
ganze Spaß wurde verdorben.

Die Toren, die nicht sehen, daß es eigentlich auf den Platz gar nicht
ankommt, und daß der, der den ersten hat, so selten die erste Rolle
spielt! Wie mancher König wird durch seinen Minister, wie mancher
Minister durch seinen Sekretär regiert! Und wer ist denn der Erste?

What bothers me most is the awful ways of the citizenry. Naturally, I know as well as anyone else how necessary the separation of social ranks is, and how many advantages accrue to *me* from it; but it shouldn't stand in my way when I might still taste a little joy, a gleam of happiness, in this world. Recently while strolling I met a Miss von B——, a charming creature, who has retained a great deal of naturalness amid this ceremonious life. We enjoyed our conversation and, on parting, I asked her permission to call on her. She consented with such openness that I was hardly able to wait for a suitable time to visit her. She's not a local, and she lives in the home of an aunt. I didn't like the old lady's face. I was very attentive to her, and my remarks were chiefly addressed to her, and in less than a half hour I had pretty much discovered what the young lady herself later confessed to me: that, in her old age, her dear aunt lacks everything; she has no decent fortune, no intelligence, and no other support than her ancestral lineage, no other protection than the social rank in which she has entrenched herself, no other pleasure than to look down from her upper story over and past the heads of the bourgeoisie. She is said to have been good-looking when young, and to have wasted her life, first by tormenting many unhappy young men with her obstinacy, and later, when more mature, by cringing under the thumb of an aged officer who, at that price and for being supported in passable comfort, spent the "bronze age" with her before he died. Now, in her "iron age," she finds herself alone, and no one would look at her if her niece weren't so charming.

January 8, 1772

What people these are! Their entire soul is attached to ceremonial, for years on end all their thoughts are only of how they can move up by one seat at the banquet table! And it's not that they have no other business to attend to: no, on the contrary, their work piles up for the very reason that their little vexations over advancement keep them from handling the important matters. Last week there was an argument during the sleigh ride and all the fun was spoiled.

What fools not to see that one's position is not what really matters, and that the man with the highest position so seldom plays the principal role! How many kings are ruled by their minister, how many ministers are ruled by their secretary! And then, who's

der, dünkt mich, der die anderen übersieht und so viel Gewalt oder
List hat, ihre Kräfte und Leidenschaften zu Ausführung seiner Plane
anzuspannen.

Am 20. Januar.

Ich muß Ihnen schreiben, liebe Lotte, hier in der Stube einer geringen Bauernherberge, in die ich mich vor einem schweren Wetter
geflüchtet habe. Solange ich in dem traurigen Neste D . . . , unter
dem fremden, meinem Herzen ganz fremden Volke herumziehe,
habe ich keinen Augenblick gehabt, keinen, an dem mein Herz mich
geheißen hätte, Ihnen zu schreiben; und jetzt in dieser Hütte, in
dieser Einsamkeit, in dieser Einschränkung, da Schnee und Schloßen
wider mein Fensterchen wüten, hier waren Sie mein erster Gedanke.
Wie ich hereintrat, überfiel mich Ihre Gestalt, Ihr Andenken, o Lotte!
so heilig, so warm! Guter Gott! der erste glückliche Augenblick
wieder.

Wenn Sie mich sähen, meine Beste, in dem Schwall von Zerstreu-
ung! wie ausgetrocknet meine Sinnen werden; nicht Einen
Augenblick der Fülle des Herzens, nicht Eine selige Stunde! nichts!
nichts! Ich stehe wie vor einem Raritätenkasten und sehe die
Männchen und Gäulchen vor mir herumrücken und frage mich oft,
ob es nicht optischer Betrug ist. Ich spiele mit, vielmehr ich werde
gespielt wie eine Marionette und fasse manchmal meinen Nachbar an
der hölzernen Hand und schaudere zurück. Des Abends nehme ich
mir vor, den Sonnenaufgang zu genießen, und komme nicht aus dem
Bette; am Tage hoffe ich, mich des Mondscheins zu erfreuen, und
bleibe in meiner Stube. Ich weiß nicht recht, warum ich aufstehe,
warum ich schlafen gehe.

Der Sauerteig, der mein Leben in Bewegung setzte, fehlt; der Reiz,
der mich in tiefen Nächten munter erhielt, ist hin, der mich des
Morgens aus dem Schlafe weckte, ist weg.

Ein einzig weibliches Geschöpf habe ich hier gefunden, eine
Fräulein von B . . . , sie gleicht Ihnen, liebe Lotte, wenn man Ihnen
gleichen kann. Ei! werden Sie sagen, der Mensch legt sich auf
niedliche Komplimente! Ganz unwahr ist es nicht. Seit einiger Zeit
bin ich sehr artig, weil ich doch nicht anders sein kann, habe viel Witz,
und die Frauenzimmer sagen: es wüßte niemand so fein zu loben als
ich (und zu lügen, setzen Sie hinzu, denn ohne das geht es nicht ab,

the "first"?—in my opinion, the man whose view encompasses all
the rest, and who has enough power or cunning to harness their
strength and passions to the execution of his own plans.

January 20
Dear Lotte, I must write to you here in the parlor of a petty rustic inn, where I have taken refuge from a heavy downpour. All the
while I've been roaming around in this pathetic dump, D——,
among people who are strangers, total strangers to my heart, I
haven't had a moment, not one, in which my heart bade me write
to you; and now in this hovel, in this solitude, in this confinement,
with snow and big hailstones assaulting my little window, here
you were my first thought. As I walked in, I was overcome with
your figure, with the memory of you, Lotte, so sacred, so warm!
Merciful God, my first happy moment in so long.

If you could see me, my good friend, in this surge of distrac-
tions! How arid my senses are becoming; not a moment of fullness of the heart, not one blissful hour! Nothing! Nothing! I
seem to be standing in front of a peepshow watching the tiny
people and horses jerking to and fro in front of me, and often
wondering whether it isn't an optical illusion. I play along—
rather, I'm played *with* like a marionette; and sometimes I take
hold of my neighbor's wooden hand and I recoil with a shudder.[16] In the evening I resolve to enjoy the sunrise, but I don't
get out of bed; during the day I look forward to take pleasure in
the moonlight, but I remain in my room. I don't rightly know
why I get up, why I go to bed.

The ferment that used to set my life in motion is missing; the
attraction that used to keep me awake late at night is gone, the
attraction that awoke me from sleep in the morning has
vanished.

I have found only one feminine being here, a Miss von B——;
she's like you, Lotte dear, if anyone can be. "Oh, my!" I can hear
you say; "the fellow now relies on pretty compliments!" It's not
completely untrue. For some time I've been very attentive to the
ladies, which I can't help being, and I have a ready tongue, so that
women say no one beats me at subtle praise (and at telling lies,
you add, because the one doesn't go without the other, does it?).

---

16. The remainder of this paragraph and all of the next one were newly added
to the 1787 edition.

verstehen Sie?). Ich wollte von Fräulein B . . . reden. Sie hat viel Seele, die voll aus ihren blauen Augen hervorblickt. Ihr Stand ist ihr zur Last, der keinen der Wünsche ihres Herzens befriedigt. Sie sehnt sich aus dem Getümmel, und wir verphantasieren manche Stunde in ländlichen Szenen von ungemischter Glückseligkeit; ach! und von Ihnen! Wie oft muß sie Ihnen huldigen; muß nicht, tut es freiwillig, hört so gern von Ihnen, liebt Sie. –

O säß ich zu Ihren Füßen in dem lieben vertraulichen Zimmerchen, und unsere kleinen Lieben wälzten sich miteinander um mich herum, und wenn sie Ihnen zu laut würden, wollte ich sie mit einem schauerlichen Märchen um mich zur Ruhe versammeln.

Die Sonne geht herrlich unter über der schneeglänzenden Gegend, der Sturm ist hinübergezogen, und ich – muß mich wieder in meinen Käfig sperren – Adieu! Ist Albert bei Ihnen? Und wie – ? Gott verzeihe mir diese Frage!

Den 8. Februar.

Wir haben seit acht Tagen das abscheulichste Wetter, und mir ist es wohltätig. Denn solang ich hier bin, ist mir noch kein schöner Tag am Himmel erschienen, den mir nicht jemand verdorben oder verleidet hätte. Wenns nun recht regnet und stöbert und fröstelt und taut – ha! denk ich, kanns doch zu Hause nicht schlimmer werden, als es draußen ist, oder umgekehrt, und so ists gut. Geht die Sonne des Morgens auf und verspricht einen feinen Tag, erwehr ich mir niemals auszurufen: da haben sie doch wieder ein himmlisches Gut, worum sie einander bringen können. Es ist nichts, worum sie einander nicht bringen. Gesundheit, guter Name, Freudigkeit, Erholung! Und meist aus Albernheit, Unbegriff und Enge, und, wenn man sie anhört, mit der besten Meinung. Manchmal möcht ich sie auf den Knien bitten, nicht so rasend in ihre eigenen Eingeweide zu wüten.

Am 17. Februar.

Ich fürchte, mein Gesandter und ich halten es zusammen nicht lange mehr aus. Der Mann ist ganz und gar unerträglich. Seine Art, zu arbeiten und Geschäfte zu treiben, ist so lächerlich, daß ich mich nicht enthalten kann, ihm zu widersprechen und oft eine Sache nach meinem Kopf und meiner Art zu machen, das ihm denn, wie natürlich, niemals recht ist. Darüber hat er mich neulich bei Hofe verklagt, und der Minister gab mir einen zwar sanften Verweis, aber es war

I wanted to discuss Miss B———. She's very soulful; her soul shines forth strongly from her blue eyes. Her social rank is a burden to her, not satisfying any wish of her heart. She longs to be free of the hubbub, and we dream away many an hour in rural scenery discussing unmitigated bliss—and discussing you! How often she has to pay homage to you; no, she isn't compelled to, she does it voluntarily; she likes to hear about you, she loves you.—

Oh, if I could only be sitting at your feet in that dear, cozy little room, with our dear little ones gamboling together around me! If they got too noisy for you, I'd gather them around me peacefully with a scary story.

The sun is setting in splendor over the scene outdoors, which is sparkling with snow; the storm has blown over, and I—must shut myself up in my cage again—. Adieu! Is Albert with you? And how—? May God forgive me for that question!

February 8[17]
For a week now we've had the most ghastly weather, but it's done me good. Because all the while I've been here, not one fine day has appeared in the sky that someone hasn't spoiled or embittered for me. Now that it's really raining, flurrying, freezing over, and thawing, I think: "Ha! After all, it can't be worse in the house than it is outside, or vice versa," and all is well. If the sun rises in the morning promising a fair day, I can never help exclaiming: "Now they have another heavenly blessing they can do each other out of!" There's nothing they don't do each other out of. Health, reputation, joy, relaxation! And mostly through stupidity, inability to understand, and narrowmindedness; and, to hear them tell it, always with the best intentions. At times I'd like to beg them on bended knee not to burrow in their own vitals with such savagery.

February 17
I'm afraid my ambassador and I won't be able to abide each other's company much longer. The man is absolutely unbearable. His way of working and doing business is so ludicrous that I can't help contradicting him and frequently doing a job as I see it, after my own fashion; of course, it never suits him when I do. Recently he complained about me at court, and the minister gave me a rebuke that was very gentle, to be sure, but still a re-

---

17. Entire letter new in the 1787 edition.

doch ein Verweis, und ich stand im Begriffe, meinen Abschied zu
begehren, als ich einen Privatbrief* von ihm erhielt, einen Brief, vor
dem ich niedergekniet und den hohen, edlen, weisen Sinn angebetet
habe. Wie er meine allzugroße Empfindlichkeit zurechtweiset, wie er
meine überspannten Ideen von Wirksamkeit, von Einfluß auf andere,
von Durchdringen in Geschäften als jugendlichen guten Mut zwar
ehrt, sie nicht auszurotten, nur zu mildern und dahin zu leiten sucht,
wo sie ihr wahres Spiel haben, ihre kräftige Wirkung tun können.
Auch bin ich auf acht Tage gestärkt und in mir selbst einig geworden.
Die Ruhe der Seele ist ein herrliches Ding und die Freude an sich
selbst. Lieber Freund, wenn nur das Kleinod nicht ebenso zerbrech-
lich wäre, als es schön und kostbar ist.

Am 20. Februar.

Gott segne euch, meine Lieben, gebe euch alle die guten Tage, die er
mir abzieht!

Ich danke dir, Albert, daß du mich betrogen hast: ich wartete auf
Nachricht, wann euer Hochzeittag sein würde, und hatte mir vorgenommen, feierlichst an demselben Lottens Schattenriß von der Wand
zu nehmen und ihn unter andere Papiere zu begraben. Nun seid ihr
ein Paar, und ihr Bild ist noch hier! Nun so soll es bleiben! Und
warum nicht? Ich weiß, ich bin ja auch bei euch, bin dir unbeschadet
in Lottens Herzen, habe, ja ich habe den zweiten Platz darin und will
und muß ihn behalten. O, ich würde rasend werden, wenn sie
vergessen könnte – Albert, in dem Gedanken liegt eine Hölle. Albert,
leb wohl! Leb wohl, Engel des Himmels! Leb wohl, Lotte!

Den 15. März.

Ich habe einen Verdruß gehabt, der mich von hier wegtreiben wird.
Ich knirsche mit den Zähnen! Teufel! er ist nicht zu ersetzen, und ihr
seid doch allein schuld daran, die ihr mich sporntet und triebt und
quältet, mich in einen Posten zu begeben, der nicht nach meinem
Sinne war. Nun habe ichs! nun habt ihrs! Und daß du nicht wieder
sagst, meine überspannten Ideen verdürben alles, so hast du hier,
lieber Herr, eine Erzählung, plan und nett, wie ein Chroniken-
schreiber das aufzeichnen würde.

Der Graf von C . . . liebt mich, distinguiert mich, das ist bekannt,

---

*Man hat aus Ehrfurcht für diesen trefflichen Herrn gedachten Brief und einen an-
dern, dessen weiter hinten erwähnt wird, dieser Sammlung entzogen, weil man nicht
glaubte, eine solche Kühnheit durch den wärmsten Dank des Publikums entschuldigen zu können.

buke; I was on the point of resigning when I received a private
letter° from him, a letter I knelt down to, worshipping its lofty,
noble, wise intelligence. In it he admonishes me for my exces-
sive sensitivity; he respects my exaggerated ideas of effectiveness, influence over others, and speedier accomplishment of
tasks as showing youthful high spirits; he seeks not to root them
out, merely to moderate them and guide them in a direction
where they can come into proper play and have their full effect.
Now I have been fortified for a week, and I have become one
with myself. Mental calm is a wonderful thing, as is joy in oneself. Dear friend, if only the jewel weren't just as fragile as it is
beautiful and precious.

February 20

God bless you, my dear ones, and give all of you the good days
he is taking away from me!

I thank you, Albert, for hoodwinking me: I was awaiting news
about the date of your wedding, and I had resolved to remove
the silhouette of Lotte from the wall on that day with great
solemnity and bury it among other papers. Now you're a married
couple, and her picture is still here! Now it will remain here!
Why not? I know that I'm with you, too, that I'm in Lotte's heart
without any detriment to you; yes, I'm in second place there,
and I will and must retain that place. Oh, I'd go raving mad if
she could forget— Albert, there's an inferno in that thought.
Albert, farewell! Farewell, heavenly angel! Farewell, Lotte!

March 15

I've had a vexation that will drive me away from here. I'm gnashing my teeth! Damn! There's no making it good, and the lot of
you are the only ones to blame, for having urged me and pushed
me and plagued me to accept a position that was uncongenial to
me. Now I've got mine! Now you've got yours! And so you don't
say again that my exaggerated ideas spoil everything, my fine
gentleman, here you have a crystal-clear recounting of the incident, just as a chronicler would register it.

The Count of C—— likes me and singles me out, that's well

°Out of respect for this excellent gentleman, the above-mentioned letter, and
another one, which is referred to later on, have been withdrawn from this collection, because the editor didn't believe that even the deepest gratitude of the
public warranted such an act of boldness. [Footnote in the original.]

das habe ich dir schon hundertmal gesagt. Nun war ich gestern bei
ihm zu Tafel, eben an dem Tage, da abends die noble Gesellschaft
von Herrn und Frauen bei ihm zusammenkommt, an die ich nie
gedacht habe, auch mir nie aufgefallen ist, daß wir Subalternen nicht
hineingehören. Gut. Ich speise bei dem Grafen, und nach Tische
gehn wir in dem großen Saal auf und ab, ich rede mit ihm, mit dem
Obristen B . . ., der dazukommt, und so rückt die Stunde der
Gesellschaft heran. Ich denke, Gott weiß, an nichts. Da tritt herein
die übergnädige Dame von S . . . mit Ihrem Herrn Gemahle und
wohlausgebrüteten Gänslein Tochter, mit der flachen Brust und
niedlichem Schnürleibe, machen en passant ihre hergebrachten
hochadeligen Augen und Naslöcher, und wie mir die Nation von
Herzen zuwider ist, wollte ich mich eben empfehlen und wartete
nur, bis der Graf vom garstigen Gewäsche frei wäre, als meine
Fräulein B . . . hereintrat. Da mir das Herz immer ein bißchen
aufgeht, wenn ich sie sehe, blieb ich eben, stellte mich hinter ihren
Stuhl und bemerkte erst nach einiger Zeit, daß sie mit weniger
Offenheit als sonst, mit einiger Verlegenheit mit mir redete. Das fiel
mir auf. Ist sie auch wie alle das Volk, dachte ich, und war
angestochen und wollte gehen, und doch blieb ich, weil ich sie gerne
entschuldigt hätte und es nicht glaubte und noch ein gut Wort von
ihr hoffte und – was du willst. Unterdessen füllt sich die Gesellschaft.
Der Baron F . . . mit der ganzen Garderobe von den Krönungszeiten
Franz des Ersten her, der Hofrat R . . ., hier aber in qualitate Herr
von R . . . genannt, mit seiner tauben Frau etc., den übelfournierten
J . . . nicht zu vergessen, der die Lücken seiner altfränkischen
Garderobe mit neumodischen Lappen ausflickt, das kommt zuhauf,
und ich rede mit einigen meiner Bekanntschaft, die alle sehr
lakonisch sind. Ich dachte – und gab nur auf meine B . . . acht. Ich
merkte nicht, daß die Weiber am Ende des Saales sich in die Ohren
flüsterten, daß es auf die Männer zirkulierte, daß Frau von S . . . mit
dem Grafen redete (das alles hat mir Fräulein B . . . nachher erzählt),
bis endlich der Graf auf mich losging und mich in ein Fenster nahm.
– Sie wissen, sagte er, unsere wunderbaren Verhältnisse; die
Gesellschaft ist unzufrieden, merke ich, Sie hier zu sehen; ich wollte
nicht um alles – Ihro Exzellenz, fiel ich ein, ich bitte tausendmal um
Verzeihung; ich hätte eher dran denken sollen, und ich weiß, Sie
vergeben mir diese Inkonsequenz; ich wollte schon vorhin mich
empfehlen, ein böser Genius hat mich zurückgehalten, setzte ich

known, I've already told you so a hundred times. Now, yesterday I
was his guest at lunch, on the very day when the noble company of
gentlemen and ladies assembles at his home in the afternoon. I
had never thought about them, and it had never occurred to me
that we lower clerks don't belong there. Fine! I ate with the count,
and after lunch we were walking to and fro in the big assembly
room; I was talking with him and with Colonel B——, who joined
us. Meanwhile the time for the assembly arrived. God knows, I
didn't have anything of the sort in mind. In came the over-gracious
Lady von S—— with her spouse and her well-hatched goose of a
daughter, with her flat chest and pretty laced bodice; while passing
by, their most noble and traditional eyes and nostrils glared and
flared, and since that class is deeply repugnant to me, I was just
about to take my leave, and was only waiting for the count to be
free of their disgusting babble, when Miss B—— came in. Since
my heart always leaps up a little whenever I see her, I lingered,
took my stand behind her chair, and only some time later noticed
that she was addressing me less openly than usual, and with some
embarrassment. That attracted my attention. "Is she like all the
rest?" I thought; I was peeved and wanted to go, but I stayed because I would have liked to find an excuse for her; in my disbelief
I still hoped for a kind word from her and—call it what you like. In
the meantime the assembly was filling up. Baron F——, with his
entire wardrobe dating from the coronation of Francis I;[18] Court
Councilor R——, called here by nature of his office Lord von R——,
with his deaf wife, and others; not forgetting the badly dressed
J——, who mends the holes in his outmoded clothing with newfangled patches—they all arrived together, and I spoke with some
of my acquaintances, who were not very talkative, any of them. I
thought my thoughts, and paid attention only to my B——. I failed
to notice that the women at the far end of the room were whispering into one another's ear, that the contagion spread to the men,
that Lady von S—— was speaking to the count (Miss B—— told me
all this later on), until the count finally headed in my direction and
drew me into a window embrasure. "You know," he said, "how peculiar our ways are; I can tell that my guests are unhappy to find
you here; I wouldn't for anything in the world—" "Your Excellence," I interrupted, "I ask pardon a thousand times over; I should
have thought about it earlier, and I know you'll forgive me for this

18. Holy Roman Emperor, crowned in 1745.

lächelnd hinzu, indem ich mich neigte. – Der Graf drückte meine
Hände mit einer Empfindung, die alles sagte. Ich strich mich sacht
aus der vornehmen Gesellschaft, ging, setzte mich in ein Kabriolett
und fuhr nach M . . ., dort vom Hügel die Sonne untergehen zu
sehen und dabei in meinem Homer den herrlichen Gesang zu lesen,
wie Ulyß von dem trefflichen Schweinhirten bewirtet wird. Das war
alles gut.

Des Abends komme ich zurück zu Tische, es waren noch wenige in
der Gaststube; die würfelten auf einer Ecke, hatten das Tischtuch
zurückgeschlagen. Da kommt der ehrliche A . . . hinein, legt seinen
Hut nieder, indem er mich ansieht, tritt zu mir und sagt leise: Du hast
Verdruß gehabt? – Ich? sagte ich. – Der Graf hat dich aus der
Gesellschaft gewiesen. – Hole sie der Teufel! sagt ich, mir wars lieb,
daß ich in die freie Luft kam. – Gut, sagte er, daß du es auf die leichte
Achsel nimmst. Nur verdrießt michs, es ist schon überall herum. –
Da fing mich das Ding erst an zu wurmen. Alle, die zu Tische kamen
und mich ansahen, dachte ich, die sehen dich darum an! Das gab
böses Blut.

Und da man nun heute gar, wo ich hintrete, mich bedauert, da ich
höre, daß meine Neider nun triumphieren und sagen: da sähe mans,
wo es mit den Übermütigen hinausginge, die sich ihres bißchen Kopfs
überhöben und glaubten, sich darum über alle Verhältnisse hinaus-
setzen zu dürfen, und was des Hundegeschwätzes mehr ist – da
möchte man sich ein Messer ins Herz bohren; denn man rede von
Selbständigkeit, was man will, den will ich sehen, der dulden kann,
daß Schurken über ihn reden, wenn sie einen Vorteil über ihn haben;
wenn ihr Geschwätze leer ist, ach, da kann man sie leicht lassen.

Am 16. März.

Es hetzt mich alles. Heute treffe ich die Fräulein B . . . in der Allee,
ich konnte mich nicht enthalten, sie anzureden und ihr, sobald wir
etwas entfernt von der Gesellschaft waren, meine Empfindlichkeit
über ihr neuliches Betragen zu zeigen. – O Werther, sagte sie mit
einem innigen Tone, konnten Sie meine Verwirrung so auslegen, da
Sie mein Herz kennen? Was ich gelitten habe um Ihrentwillen, von
dem Augenblicke an, da ich in den Saal trat! Ich sah alles voraus, hundertmal saß mirs auf der Zunge, es Ihnen zu sagen. Ich wußte, daß die
von S . . . und T . . . mit ihren Männern eher aufbrechen würden, als
in Ihrer Gesellschaft zu bleiben; ich wußte, daß der Graf es mit ihnen
nicht verderben darf – und jetzo der Lärm! – Wie, Fräulein? sagte ich
und verbarg meinen Schrecken; denn alles, was Adelin mir

tactlessness. I was about to take my leave sooner, but an evil genie held me back," I added with a smile, while bowing. The count squeezed my hands with an emotion that spoke worlds. I softly stole out of the aristocratic crowd, went out, hailed a cabriolet, and drove to M—— to see the sun set from the hill there while reading in my Homer the marvelous passage in which the excellent swineherd gives Ulysses hospitality. All of that was fine.

In the evening I came back to dine; only a few people were still in the dining room. They were playing dice on a corner of the table, they had pulled back the tablecloth. Then honest A—— came in, set down his hat, caught sight of me, walked over to me, and said quietly: "You've had some vexation?" "I?" I said. "The count asked you to leave the assembly." "The Devil take it!" I said; "I felt like getting some fresh air." "It's good," he said, "that you're taking it lightly. The only thing that bothers me is that the story has already spread everywhere." That's when the whole business really started to get to me. Everyone who came to the table and looked at me was looking at me for that reason, or so I imagined! That made me angry.

And since today, as well, people pity me wherever I go, and I hear that those who envy me are now triumphing and saying: "Now see what happens to arrogant folk who boast about their mite of intelligence and think they can disregard all propriety for that reason," and the rest of that drivel—then I'd like to jab a knife into my heart; because, say what you like about self-sufficiency, I want to see the man who can tolerate having scoundrels belittle him when they have some real advantage over him; when their babble is empty, yes, then you can readily let them have their say.

March 16

Everything is provoking me. Today I met Miss B—— in the avenue of trees; I couldn't refrain from addressing her and, once we were at some distance from her companions, telling her how hurt I was by her recent behavior. "Oh, Werther," she said in heartfelt tones, "could you interpret my embarrassment in that way, you who know my heart? What I suffered on your account from the moment I stepped into that room! I foresaw the whole thing, a hundred times I was on the point of telling you. I knew that Lady von S—— and Lady von T—— and their husbands would sooner leave than remain there in your company; I knew that the count can't afford to fall out with them—and now this hubbub!" "How is that, miss?" I said, concealing my alarm; be-

ehegestern gesagt hatte, lief mir wie siedend Wasser durch die Adern in diesem Augenblicke. – Was hat mich es schon gekostet! sagte das süße Geschöpf, indem ihr die Tränen in den Augen standen. – Ich war nicht Herr mehr von mir selbst, war im Begriffe, mich ihr zu Füßen zu werfen. – Erklären Sie sich, rief ich. – Die Tränen liefen ihr die Wangen herunter. Ich war außer mir. Sie trocknete sie ab, ohne sie verbergen zu wollen. – Meine Tante kennen Sie, fing sie an; sie war gegenwärtig und hat, o, mit was für Augen hat sie das angesehen! Werther, ich habe gestern nacht ausgestanden, und heute früh eine Predigt über meinen Umgang mit Ihnen, und ich habe müssen zuhören Sie herabsetzen, erniedrigen, und konnte und durfte Sie nur halb verteidigen.

Jedes Wort, das sie sprach, ging mir wie ein Schwert durchs Herz. Sie fühlte nicht, welche Barmherzigkeit es gewesen wäre, mir das alles zu verschweigen, und nun fügte sie noch dazu, was weiter würde geträtscht werden, was eine Art Menschen darüber triumphieren würde. Wie man sich nunmehr über die Strafe meines Übermuts und meiner Geringschätzung anderer, die sie mir schon lange vorwerfen, kitzeln und freuen würde. Das alles, Wilhelm, von ihr zu hören, mit der Stimme der wahresten Teilnehmung – Ich war zerstört und bin noch wütend in mir. Ich wollte, daß sich einer unterstünde, mir es vorzuwerfen, daß ich ihm den Degen durch den Leib stoßen könnte; wenn ich Blut sähe, würde mir es besser werden. Ach, ich habe hundertmal ein Messer ergriffen, um diesem gedrängten Herzen Luft zu machen. Man erzählt von einer edlen Art Pferde, die, wenn sie schrecklich erhitzt und aufgejagt sind, sich selbst aus Instinkt eine Ader aufbeißen, um sich zum Atem zu helfen. So ist mirs oft, ich möchte mir eine Ader öffnen, die mir die ewige Freiheit schaffte.

Am 24. März.

Ich habe meine Entlassung vom Hofe verlangt und werde sie, hoffe ich, erhalten, und ihr werdet mir verzeihen, daß ich nicht erst Erlaubnis dazu bei euch geholt habe. Ich mußte nun einmal fort, und was ihr zu sagen hattet, um mir das Bleiben einzureden, weiß ich alles, und also – Bringe das meiner Mutter in einem Säftchen bei, ich kann mir selbst nicht helfen, und sie mag sich gefallen lassen, wenn ich ihr auch nicht helfen kann. Freilich muß es ihr wehe tun. Den schönen Lauf, den ihr Sohn gerade zum Geheimenrat und Gesandten ansetzte, so auf einmal Halte zu sehen, und rückwärts mit dem Tierchen in den Stall! Macht nun daraus, was ihr wollt, und kombiniert die möglichen Fälle, unter denen ich hätte bleiben können

cause all that Adelin had told me the day before was coursing
through my veins like boiling water at that moment. "What it's
already cost me!" said the sweet woman, with tears welling up in
her eyes.—I was no longer in control of myself, I was about to
throw myself at her feet. "Explain yourself!" I cried. Tears ran
down her cheeks. I was beside myself. She dried them without
attempting to conceal them. "You know my aunt," she began;
"she was there and, oh, what eyes she made when she saw what
was going on! Werther, what I went through last night, and what
a sermon I received this morning about associating with you! I
was forced to hear you being degraded and belittled, and I was
only able, only permitted, to defend you halfway."

Every word she spoke pierced my heart like a sword. She
didn't feel how merciful it would have been to keep all that
from me; and then she even added all the other gossip about
me, and how a certain type of people would gloat over it all;
how they would now be tickled pink and happy over the punishment of my arrogance and my scorn of others, which they
have long reproached me with. Wilhelm, to hear all that from
her, in the tones of deepest sympathy—! I was crushed, and I'm
still furious. I'd like someone to dare reproach me with it, so I
could run my sword through his body; if I saw blood, I'd feel
better. Oh, a hundred times I've seized a knife, to give vent to
my suffocating heart. People tell of a noble breed of horses
which, when terribly heated and exhausted, instinctively bite
open a vein in order to recover their breath. That's how I frequently feel: I'd like to open a vein that would secure eternal
freedom for me.

March 24

I've asked the court to dismiss me, and I hope my request will
be granted; you and your friends will forgive me for not asking your permission first. I just had to get away, and I know all
your arguments to persuade me to stay; and so— Inform my
mother of this as diplomatically as you can; I can't help myself,
and she mustn't mind too much if I can't help her, either. Of
course it must grieve her. To see the lovely career her son was
beginning, which would lead him to a privy councilorship and
an embassy, called to a halt all at once, and the horse driven
back into its stable! Make whatever you will of it, and mull
over all the possible cases in which I could or should stay

und sollen; genug, ich gehe; und damit ihr wißt, wo ich hinkomme, so
ist hier der Fürst °°, der vielen Geschmack an meiner Gesellschaft
findet; der hat mich gebeten, da er von meiner Absicht hörte, mit ihm
auf seine Güter zu gehen und den schönen Frühling da zuzubringen.
Ich soll ganz mir selbst gelassen sein, hat er mir versprochen, und da
wir uns zusammen bis auf einen gewissen Punkt verstehn, so will ich
es denn auf gut Glück wagen und mit ihm gehen.

Am 19. April.
                        Zur Nachricht.
Danke für deine beiden Briefe. Ich antwortete nicht, weil ich dieses
Blatt liegen ließ, bis mein Abschied vom Hofe da wäre; ich fürchtete,
meine Mutter möchte sich an den Minister wenden und mir mein
Vorhaben erschweren. Nun aber ist es geschehen, mein Abschied ist
da. Ich mag euch nicht sagen, wie ungern man mir ihn gegeben hat,
und was mir der Minister schreibt – ihr würdet in neue Lamenta-
tionen ausbrechen. Der Erbprinz hat mir zum Abschiede fünfund-
zwanzig Dukaten geschickt, mit einem Worte, das mich bis zu Tränen
gerührt hat; also brauche ich von der Mutter das Geld nicht, um das
ich neulich schrieb.

Am 5. Mai.
Morgen gehe ich von hier ab, und weil mein Geburtsort nur sechs
Meilen vom Wege liegt, so will ich den auch wiedersehen, will mich
der alten, glücklich verträumten Tage erinnern. Zu eben dem Tore
will ich hineingehn, aus dem meine Mutter mit mir herausfuhr, als sie
nach dem Tode meines Vaters den lieben, vertraulichen Ort verließ,
um sich in ihre unerträgliche Stadt einzusperren. Adieu, Wilhelm, du
sollst von meinem Zuge hören.

Am 9. Mai.
Ich habe die Wallfahrt nach meiner Heimat mit aller Andacht eines
Pilgrims vollendet, und manche unerwarteten Gefühle haben mich
ergriffen. An der großen Linde, die eine Viertelstunde vor der Stadt
nach S . . . zu steht, ließ ich halten, stieg aus und hieß den Postillion
fortfahren, um zu Fuße jede Erinnerung ganz neu, lebhaft, nach
meinem Herzen zu kosten. Da stand ich nun unter der Linde, die
ehedem, als Knabe, das Ziel und die Grenze meiner Spaziergänge
gewesen. Wie anders! Damals sehnte ich mich in glücklicher Un-
wissenheit hinaus in die unbekannte Welt, wo ich für mein Herz so
viele Nahrung, so vielen Genuß hoffte, meinen strebenden, sehnen-

here—in a word, I'm leaving; and to let you know where I'm
going: Prince —— is here; he enjoys my company a great deal,
and, when he heard of my intentions, he invited me to accompany him to his estate and spend the lovely spring there.
I'll be left undisturbed, he promised me, and since we understand each other to a certain degree, I'll take my chances on it
and go with him.

April 19
For your information.
Thanks for your two letters. I didn't answer because I left this
sheet waiting until my discharge from the court had come
through; I was afraid my mother might apply to the minister and
make my decision hard to execute. But now it has happened, my
discharge is here. I don't feel like telling you how unwillingly
they gave it to me, and what the minister wrote to me—you'd
break out into new lamentations. The crown prince sent me
twenty-five ducats as a going-away present, along with a note
that moved me to tears; thus, my mother doesn't need to send
me the money I recently asked for.

May 5
I'm leaving tomorrow, and since the place where I was born is
only six miles off my path, I shall revisit it and recall the old days
that I dreamed away there happily. I'll enter by the same gate
through which my mother drove out with me when, after my father's death, she left that dear, homelike spot to shut herself up
in her own unbearable city. Adieu, Wilhelm, you'll hear about
my pilgrimage.

May 9
I have performed the pilgrimage to my birthplace with all of a pilgrim's piety, and many unexpected feelings came over me. I had
the coach stop by the old lime tree that stands at a quarter-hour's
distance from the city in the direction of S——, I got out, and I
bade the postillion drive on, so that, on foot, I could enjoy every
memory freshly, vividly, as my heart wished. There I stood beneath
the lime tree which, when I was a boy, was the goal and the limit
of my strolls. How different it was! Then, in my blissful ignorance,
I longed to go out into the unknown world, where I hoped for so
much nutriment, so much enjoyment for my heart, to fill and sat-

den Busen auszufüllen und zu befriedigen. Jetzt komme ich zurück aus der weiten Welt – o, mein Freund, mit wie viel fehlgeschlagenen Hoffnungen, mit wie viel zerstörten Planen! – Ich sah das Gebirge vor mir liegen, das so tausendmal der Gegenstand meiner Wünsche gewesen war. Stundenlang konnt ich hier sitzen und mich hinübersehnen, mit inniger Seele mich in den Wäldern, den Tälern verlieren, die sich meinen Augen so freundlich-dämmernd darstellten; und wenn ich dann um die bestimmte Zeit wieder zurückmußte, mit welchem Widerwillen verließ ich nicht den lieben Platz! – Ich kam der Stadt näher, alle die alten bekannten Gartenhäuschen wurden von mir gegrüßt, die neuen waren mir zuwider, so auch alle Veränderungen, die man sonst vorgenommen hatte. Ich trat zum Tor hinein und fand mich doch gleich und ganz wieder. Lieber, ich mag nicht ins Detail gehn; so reizend, als es mir war, so einförmig würde es in der Erzählung werden. Ich hatte beschlossen, auf dem Markte zu wohnen, gleich neben unserem alten Hause. Im Hingehen bemerkte ich, daß die Schulstube, wo ein ehrliches altes Weib unsere Kindheit zusammengepfercht hatte, in einen Kramladen verwandelt war. Ich erinnerte mich der Unruhe, der Tränen, der Dumpfheit des Sinnes, der Herzensangst, die ich in dem Loche ausgestanden hatte. – Ich tat keinen Schritt, der nicht merkwürdig war. Ein Pilger im heiligen Lande trifft nicht so viele Stätten religiöser Erinnerungen an, und seine Seele ist schwerlich so voll heiliger Bewegung. – Noch eins für tausend. Ich ging den Fluß hinab, bis an einen gewissen Hof; das war sonst auch mein Weg, und die Plätzchen, wo wir Knaben uns übten, die meisten Sprünge der flachen Steine im Wasser hervorzubringen. Ich erinnerte mich so lebhaft, wenn ich manchmal stand und dem Wasser nachsah, mit wie wunderbaren Ahnungen ich es verfolgte, wie abenteuerlich ich mir die Gegenden vorstellte, wo es nun hinflösse, und wie ich da so bald Grenzen meiner Vorstellungskraft fand; und doch mußte das weitergehen, immer weiter, bis ich mich ganz in dem Anchauen einer unsichtbaren Ferne verlor. – Sieh, mein Lieber, so beschränkt und so glücklich waren die herrlichen Altväter! so kindlich ihr Gefühl, ihre Dichtung! Wenn Ulyß von dem ungemeßnen Meer und von der unendlichen Erde spricht, das ist so wahr, menschlich, innig, eng und geheimnisvoll. Was hilft michs, daß ich jetzt mit jedem Schulknaben nachsagen kann, daß sie rund sei? Der Mensch braucht nur wenige Erdschollen, um drauf zu genießen, weniger, um drunter zu ruhen.

isfy my striving, yearning bosom. Now I was returning from the wide world—oh, my friend, with how many frustrated hopes, with how many ruined plans!—I saw before me the mountain range which had been the object of my wishes a thousand times over. I used to be able to sit here for hours on end, longing to be across that range, losing myself ardently in the forests and valleys that offered themselves to my gaze in such friendly dusk; and when I had to go back home at the promised time, how reluctantly I would leave the dear spot!—I approached the city; all the old, familiar summerhouses were greeted by me, I found the new ones repellent, as I found all the other innovations that had been undertaken. I walked through the city gate and, all the same, I immediately found myself right at home. Dear friend, I don't want to go into details; as charming as it was to me, that's how monotonous it would become if I narrated it. I had determined to live on the market square right next to our old house. On the way there I noticed that the schoolhouse, into which a respectable old lady had crammed us children together, had been transformed into a grocery. I remembered the restlessness, the tears, the emptyheadedness, and the anguish I had suffered in that hole.—I didn't take a step that wasn't noteworthy. A pilgrim in the Holy Land doesn't come across as many sites that evoke religious memories, and his soul is hardly so full of sacred agitation.—To give one more example out of a thousand: I walked downstream beside the river up to a certain farmyard; that was another customary stroll of mine, and the places where we boys vied to see who could make a flat stone thrown into the water skip the most times. I recalled so vividly how I often stood and watched the river, with what strange premonitions I pursued its course, how exciting I imagined those regions to be which it would reach as it kept flowing, and how soon I found limits set to my conceptions; and yet I had to continue, further and further, until I became completely lost in the contemplation of an invisible distance.—You see, dear friend, just so limited and so happy were the marvelous patriarchs! Their emotions, their poetry were just that childlike! When Ulysses speaks of the boundless sea and the infinite earth, it's so true, human, heartfelt, confined, and mysterious. What good does it do me to be able to repeat now, like any schoolboy, that the earth is round?[19] Man needs only a few clods of earth on which to enjoy himself, even less to rest under.

---

19. The following sentence is new in the 1787 edition.

Nun bin ich hier auf dem fürstlichen Jagdschloß. Es läßt sich noch ganz wohl mit dem Herrn leben, er ist wahr und einfach. Wunderliche Menschen sind um ihn herum, die ich gar nicht begreife. Sie scheinen keine Schelmen und haben doch auch nicht das Ansehen von ehrlichen Leuten. Manchmal kommen sie mir ehrlich vor, und ich kann ihnen doch nicht trauen. Was mir noch leid tut, ist, daß er oft von Sachen redet, die er nur gehört und gelesen hat, und zwar aus eben dem Gesichtspunkte, wie sie ihm der andere vorstellen mochte.

Auch schätzt er meinen Verstand und meine Talente mehr als dies Herz, das doch mein einziger Stolz ist, das ganz allein die Quelle von allem ist, aller Kraft, aller Seligkeit und alles Elendes. Ach, was ich weiß, kann jeder wissen – mein Herz habe ich allein.

Am 25. Mai.

Ich hatte etwas im Kopfe, davon ich euch nichts sagen wollte, bis es ausgeführt wäre: jetzt, da nichts draus wird, ist es ebenso gut. Ich wollte in den Krieg; das hat mir lange am Herzen gelegen. Vornehmlich darum bin ich dem Fürsten hierher gefolgt, der General in °°°schen Diensten ist. Auf einem Spaziergang entdeckte ich ihm mein Vorhaben; er widerriet mir es, und es müßte bei mir mehr Leidenschaft als Grille gewesen sein, wenn ich seinen Gründen nicht hätte Gehör geben wollen.

Am 11. Junius.

Sage, was du willst, ich kann nicht länger bleiben. Was soll ich hier? die Zeit wird mir lang. Der Fürst hält mich, so gut man nur kann, und doch bin ich nicht in meiner Lage. Wir haben im Grunde nichts gemein mit einander. Er ist ein Mann von Verstande, aber von ganz gemeinem Verstande; sein Umgang unterhält mich nicht mehr, als wenn ich ein wohlgeschriebenes Buch lese. Noch acht Tage bleibe ich, und dann ziehe ich wieder in der Irre herum. Das beste, was ich hier getan habe, ist mein Zeichnen. Der Fürst fühlt in der Kunst und würde noch stärker fühlen, wenn er nicht durch das garstige wissenschaftliche Wesen und durch die gewöhnliche Terminologie eingeschränkt wäre. Manchmal knirsche ich mit den Zähnen, wenn ich ihn mit warmer Imagination an Natur und Kunst herumführe und er es auf einmal recht gut zu machen denkt, wenn er mit einem gestempelten Kunstworte dreinstolpert.

Now I'm here in the prince's palatial hunting lodge. Life with this lord is still quite easy, he's sincere and natural.[20] There are peculiar people around him whom I totally fail to understand. They don't seem to be scoundrels, and yet they don't have the appearance of honest people. Sometimes they come across as being honest, but I can't trust them. What still grieves me is that he often speaks about things he has merely heard or read, and always from the viewpoint of the person who imparted them to him.

Besides, he values my intelligence and talents more than he does my heart, which after all is my only pride; it alone is the source of everything, all my strength, all my bliss, and all my misery. Ah, anyone can have the same knowledge that I have—I alone possess my heart.

May 25

I had something in mind that I didn't want to tell you about until I had actually done it; now that it has come to nought, it's just as well. I wanted to serve in the war; my heart was set on it for some time. It was principally for that reason that I followed the prince here, since he's a general in the service of ——. During an outing I disclosed my determination to him; he advised me against it, and it would have had to be more of a passion than a caprice of mine if I had refused to listen to his reasoning.

June 11

Say what you will, I can't stay here any longer. What is there for me here? I'm getting bored. The prince treats me as well as anybody can, and yet I'm out of place. Fundamentally we have nothing in common. He's a man of understanding, but of quite average understanding; his company doesn't entertain me more than reading a well-written book. I'll stay another week, then I'll start roaming around aimlessly again. The best thing I've done here is my drawing. The prince has a feeling for art, and his feeling would be deeper if he weren't limited by that repulsive scientific approach and the usual jargon. Sometimes I gnash my teeth when I expound nature and art to him with a fervent imagination and he suddenly thinks he's done something remarkable by stumbling into the discourse with a clichéd art term.

---

20. The following three sentences are new in the 1787 edition.

Am 16. Junius.

Ja wohl bin ich nur ein Wandrer, ein Waller auf der Erde! Seid ihr denn mehr?

Am 18. Junius.

Wo ich hin will? das laß dir im Vertrauen eröffnen. Vierzehn Tage muß ich doch noch hier bleiben, und dann habe ich mir weisgemacht, daß ich die Bergwerke im **schen besuchen wollte; ist aber im Grunde nichts dran, ich will nur Lotten wieder näher, das ist alles. Und ich lache über mein eignes Herz – und tu ihm seinen Willen.

Am 29. Junius.

Nein, es ist gut! es ist alles gut! – Ich – ihr Mann! O Gott, der du mich machtest, wenn du mir diese Seligkeit bereitet hättest, mein ganzes Leben sollte ein anhaltendes Gebet sein. Ich will nicht rechten, und verzeihe mir diese Tränen, verzeihe mir meine vergeblichen Wünsche! – Sie meine Frau! Wenn ich das liebste Geschöpf unter der Sonne in meine Arme geschlossen hätte – Es geht mir ein Schauder durch den ganzen Körper, Wilhelm, wenn Albert sie um den schlanken Leib faßt.

Und, darf ich es sagen? Warum nicht, Wilhelm? Sie wäre mit mir glücklicher geworden als mit ihm! O, er ist nicht der Mensch, die Wünsche dieses Herzens alle zu füllen. Ein gewisser Mangel an Fühlbarkeit, ein Mangel – nimm es, wie du willst; daß sein Herz nicht sympathetisch schlägt bei – oh! – bei der Stelle eines lieben Buches, wo mein Herz und Lottens in Einem zusammentreffen; in hundert andern Vorfällen, wenn es kommt, daß unsere Empfindungen über eine Handlung eines Dritten laut werden. Lieber Wilhelm! – Zwar er liebt sie von ganzer Seele, und so eine Liebe, was verdient die nicht! –

Ein unerträglicher Mensch hat mich unterbrochen. Meine Tränen sind getrocknet. Ich bin zerstreut. Adieu, Lieber.

Am 4. August.

Es geht mir nicht allein so. Alle Menschen werden in ihren Hoffnungen getäuscht, in ihren Erwartungen betrogen. Ich besuchte mein gutes Weib unter der Linde. Der älteste Junge lief mir entgegen, sein Freudengeschrei führte die Mutter herbei, die sehr niedergeschlagen aussah. Ihr erstes Wort war: Guter Herr, ach mein Hans ist mir gestorben! – Es war der jüngste ihrer Knaben. Ich war stille. – Und

June 16[21]

Yes, I'm merely a wanderer, a pilgrim on the earth! But are you and your friends anything more?

June 18

Where I intend to go? Let me reveal that to you in confidence. I must stay here another two weeks after all; then I've hoodwinked myself into believing that I want to visit the mines in —— territory; but basically it's nothing of the sort: I merely want to be closer to Lotte, that's all. And I laugh at my own heart—and I do its bidding.

July 29

No, it's all right! Everything is all right! I—her husband! O God, who created me, if you had ordained that bliss for me, my entire life would be one perpetual prayer. I don't want to dispute the matter; forgive me these tears, forgive me my fruitless wishes!— She my wife! If I had clasped in my arms the dearest being under the sun— A shudder runs all through me, Wilhelm, whenever Albert takes her around her slender waist.

And, may I say it? Why not, Wilhelm? She would have been happier with me than with him! Oh, he isn't man enough to fulfill all the wishes of that heart. A certain lack of the power to feel things, a lack—take it however you like; it's that his heart doesn't beat in sympathy at—oh!—at the passage in a beloved book, at which Lotte's heart and mine come together in a single point; in a hundred other instances when our feelings about a third party's actions happen to be expressed aloud. Dear Wilhelm!—Yes, he loves her with his whole soul, and what doesn't a love like that merit!—

An unbearable person interrupted me. My tears are dry. I'm distracted. Adieu, good friend.

August 4

Such things don't happen only to me. Everyone's hopes are disappointed, their expectations cheated. I visited that good woman under the lime tree. Her eldest boy ran to greet me; his cry of joy brought over his mother, who looked extremely depressed. Her first words were: "Kind gentleman, oh, my Hans has died!" He was the youngest of her boys. I was silent. "And

---

21. This entire letter is new in the 1787 edition.

mein Mann, sagte sie, ist aus der Schweiz zurück und hat nichts mit-
gebracht, und ohne gute Leute hätte er sich herausbetteln müssen, er
hatte das Fieber unterwegs gekriegt. – Ich konnte ihr nichts sagen
und schenkte dem Kleinen was, sie bat mich, einige Äpfel
anzunehmen, das ich tat, und den Ort des traurigen Andenkens verließ.

Am 21. August.

Wie man eine Hand umwendet, ist es anders mit mir. Manchmal will
wohl ein freudiger Blick des Lebens wieder aufdämmern, ach! nur für
einen Augenblick! – Wenn ich mich so in Träumen verliere, kann ich
mich des Gedankens nicht erwehren: wie, wenn Albert stürbe? Du
würdest! ja, sie würde – und dann laufe ich dem Hirngespinste nach,
bis es mich an Abgründe führet, vor denen ich zurückbebe.

Wenn ich zum Tor hinausgehe, den Weg, den ich zum ersten Mal
fuhr, Lotten zum Tanze zu holen, wie war das so ganz anders! Alles,
alles ist vorübergegangen! Kein Wink der vorigen Welt, kein
Pulsschlag meines damaligen Gefühles. Mir ist es, wie es einem
Geiste sein müßte, der in das ausgebrannte, zerstörte Schloß zurück-
kehrte, das er als blühender Fürst einst gebaut und, mit allen Gaben
der Herrlichkeit ausgestattet, sterbend seinem geliebten Sohne hoffnungsvoll hinterlassen hätte.

Am 3. September.

Ich begreife manchmal nicht, wie sie ein anderer lieb haben *kann*,
lieb haben *darf*, da ich sie so ganz allein, so innig, so voll liebe, nichts
anders kenne, noch weiß, noch habe als sie!

Am 4. September.

Ja, es ist so. Wie die Natur sich zum Herbste neigt, wird es Herbst in
mir und um mich her. Meine Blätter werden gelb, und schon sind die
Blätter der benachbarten Bäume abgefallen. Hab ich dir nicht einmal
von einem Bauerburschen geschrieben, gleich da ich herkam? Jetzt
erkundigte ich mich wieder nach ihm in Wahlheim; es hieß, er sei aus
dem Dienste gejagt worden, und niemand wollte was weiter von ihm
wissen. Gestern traf ich ihn von ungefähr auf dem Wege nach einem
andern Dorfe, ich redete ihn an, und er erzählte mir seine
Geschichte, die mich doppelt und dreifach gerührt hat, wie du leicht
begreifen wirst, wenn ich dir sie wiedererzähle. Doch wozu das alles,

my husband," she said, "is back from Switzerland and hasn't brought anything with him; if it weren't for some kind people, he would have had to beg his way out; he had caught a fever on the way." I couldn't say a thing to her; I gave the little one something; she asked me to accept a few apples, which I did; then I left that place of sad memories.

August 21

Things change for me as swiftly as turning over one's hand. Sometimes a joyous glimpse of life tries to dawn again—alas, only for a moment!—When I lose myself in dreams that way, I can't help thinking: what if Albert were to die? "You would . . . , yes, she would! . . ." And then I pursue that imaginary idea until it leads me to the edge of the abyss, from which I recoil trembling.

When I go out the town gate along the route I first drove over to pick up Lotte and take her to the ball, how totally different things were! Everything, everything has gone by! No hint of the previous world, no pulse beat of my emotion at that time. I feel how a man's ghost must feel on returning to his burnt-out, ruined castle, which he once built while a flourishing ruler, and which, when dying, he hopefully bequeathed to his beloved son equipped with every majestic furnishing.

September 3

Sometimes I can't understand how another man *can* love her, has the *right* to love her, when I love her so exclusively, so ardently, so completely, when I know, am aware of, and possess nothing but her!

September 4[22]

Yes, it's true. As nature is declining into autumn, it's becoming autumn in and around me. My leaves are turning yellow, and the leaves of the neighboring trees have already fallen. Didn't I once write you about a farmhand, right after my first arrival here? Now I inquired about him again in Wahlheim; I was told he had been dismissed from his job, and no one cared to say anything else about him. Yesterday I met him accidentally on the way to another village; I addressed him, and he told me his story, which moved me doubly and triply, as you'll readily understand when I repeat it to you. But what good is all this? Why don't I keep to

---

22. This entire long letter is new in the 1787 edition.

warum behalt ich nicht für mich, was mich ängstigt und kränkt? warum betrüb ich noch dich? warum geb ich dir immer Gelegenheit, mich zu bedauern und mich zu schelten? Sei's denn, auch das mag zu meinem Schicksal gehören!

Mit einer stillen Traurigkeit, in der ich ein wenig scheues Wesen zu bemerken schien, antwortete der Mensch mir erst auf meine Fragen; aber gar bald offner, als wenn er sich und mich auf einmal wieder erkennte, gestand er mir seine Fehler, klagte er mir sein Unglück. Könnt ich dir, mein Freund, jedes seiner Worte vor Gericht stellen! Er bekannte, ja er erzählte mit einer Art von Genuß und Glück der Wiedererinnerung, daß die Leidenschaft zu seiner Hausfrau sich in ihm tagtäglich vermehrt, daß er zuletzt nicht gewußt habe, was er tue, nicht, wie er sich ausdrückte, wo er mit dem Kopfe hin gesollt. Er habe weder essen noch trinken noch schlafen können, es habe ihm an der Kehle gestockt, er habe getan, was er nicht tun sollen, was ihm aufgetragen worden, hab er vergessen, er sei als wie von einem bösen Geist verfolgt gewesen, bis er eines Tags, als er sie in einer obern Kammer gewußt, ihr nachgegangen, ja vielmehr ihr nachgezogen worden sei; da sie seinen Bitten kein Gehör gegeben, hab er sich ihrer mit Gewalt bemächtigen wollen; er wisse nicht, wie ihm geschehen sei, und nehme Gott zum Zeugen, daß seine Absichten gegen sie immer redlich gewesen, und daß er nichts sehnlicher gewünscht, als daß sie ihn heiraten, daß sie mit ihm ihr Leben zubringen möchte. Da er eine Zeitlang geredet hatte, fing er an zu stocken, wie einer, der noch etwas zu sagen hat und sich es nicht herauszusagen getraut; endlich gestand er mir auch mit Schüchternheit, was sie ihm für kleine Vertraulichkeiten erlaubt, und welche Nähe sie ihm vergönnet. Er brach zwei-, dreimal ab und wiederholte die lebhaftesten Protestationen, daß er das nicht sage, um sie schlecht zu machen, wie er sich ausdrückte, daß er sie liebe und schätze wie vorher, daß so etwas nicht über seinen Mund gekommen sei und daß er es mir nur sage, um mich zu überzeugen, daß er kein ganz verkehrter und unsinniger Mensch sei. – Und hier, mein Bester, fang ich mein altes Lied wieder an, das ich ewig anstimmen werde: könnt ich dir den Menschen vorstellen, wie er vor mir stand, wie er noch vor mir steht! Könnt ich dir alles recht sagen, damit du fühltest, wie ich an seinem Schicksale teilnehme, teilnehmen muß! Doch genug, da du auch mein Schicksal kennst, auch mich kennst, so weißt du nur zu wohl, was mich zu allen Unglücklichen, was mich besonders zu diesem Unglücklichen hinzieht.

Da ich das Blatt wieder durchlese, seh ich, daß ich das Ende der

myself a thing that grieves and hurts me? Why should I make
you unhappy, too? Why do I always give you occasions to pity me
and scold me? Let it be! That, too, is probably part of my destiny!

With a quiet sadness in which I thought I detected some
timidity, the fellow first answered my questions; but very soon
more candidly, as if he suddenly recognized me and himself, he
confessed his faults and lamented his misfortune to me. My
friend, if I could only report each of his words to you accurately!
He confessed, yes, he told with a sort of enjoyment and happiness in the recollection, that his passion for his employer had increased within him daily, that finally he didn't know what he was
doing, or, as he expressed it, which way to turn. He was unable
to eat, drink, or sleep, his throat was constricted, he did things
he wasn't supposed to, he forgot the orders he had been given,
he seemed to be persecuted by an evil spirit, until one day, when
he knew she was in an upstairs room, he went up there after
her—or rather, was literally drawn to her; when she refused his
requests, he tried to subdue her by force. He told me that he
didn't know what had happened to him, and he called upon God
as his witness that his intentions with regard to her had always
been honorable, and that he had wished for nothing more ardently than for her to marry him and spend her life with him.
After he had spoken for a while, he began to falter, like a man
who still has something to say but can't trust himself to utter it;
finally he also confessed to me bashfully that she had allowed
him little intimacies, and had let him become quite familiar with
her. Two or three times he broke off, repeating the liveliest
protestations that he wasn't saying this to make her out a bad
woman, as he expressed it; he loved and esteemed her as much
as ever; he had never revealed those secrets to anyone and was
only telling them to me to convince me that he wasn't totally
perverted and mindless.—And here, dear friend, I once again
strike up my old song, which I shall always repeat: if I could only
depict the fellow for you as he stood in front of me, as he still
stands in front of me! If I could only tell you everything properly, so you could feel how I sympathize, how I must sympathize
with his fate! But enough! Since you know my fate also, me also,
you know all too well the attraction I feel for all unfortunate people, and for this unfortunate man in particular.

As I now reread this sheet, I see that I've forgotten to tell the

Geschichte zu erzählen vergessen habe, das sich aber leicht hinzu-
denken läßt. Sie erwehrte sich sein; ihr Bruder kam dazu, der ihn
schon lange gehaßt, der ihn schon lange aus dem Hause gewünscht
hatte, weil er fürchtet, durch eine neue Heirat der Schwester werde
seinen Kindern die Erbschaft entgehn, die ihnen jetzt, da sie kinder-
los ist, schöne Hoffnungen gibt; dieser habe ihn gleich zum Hause
hinausgestoßen und einen solchen Lärm von der Sache gemacht, daß
die Frau, auch selbst wenn sie gewollt, ihn nicht wieder hätte
aufnehmen können. Jetzo habe sie wieder einen andern Knecht
genommen, auch über den, sage man, sei sie mit dem Bruder zer-
fallen, und man behaupte für gewiß, sie werde ihn heiraten, aber er
sei fest entschlossen, das nicht zu erleben.

Was ich dir erzähle, ist nicht übertrieben, nichts verzärtelt, ja ich
darf wohl sagen: schwach, schwach hab ichs erzählt, und vergröbert
hab ichs, indem ichs mit unsern hergebrachten sittlichen Worten vor-
getragen habe.

Diese Liebe, diese Treue, diese Leidenschaft ist also keine dichte-
rische Erfindung. Sie lebt, sie ist in ihrer größten Reinheit unter der
Klasse von Menschen, die wir ungebildet, die wir roh nennen. Wir
Gebildeten – zu Nichts Verbildeten! Lies die Geschichte mit Andacht,
ich bitte dich. Ich bin heute still, indem ich das hinschreibe; du siehst
an meiner Hand, daß ich nicht so strudele und sudele wie sonst. Lies,
mein Geliebter, und denke dabei, daß es auch die Geschichte deines
Freundes ist. Ja, so ist mirs gegangen, so wird mirs gehn, und ich bin
nicht halb so brav, nicht halb so entschlossen als der arme Unglückliche,
mit dem ich mich zu vergleichen mich fast nicht getraue.

Am 5. September.

Sie hatte ein Zettelchen an ihren Mann aufs Land geschrieben, wo er
sich Geschäfte wegen aufhielt. Es fing an: Bester, Liebster, komme,
sobald du kannst, ich erwarte dich mit tausend Freuden. – Ein
Freund, der hereinkam, brachte Nachricht, daß er wegen gewisser
Umstände so bald noch nicht zurückkehren würde. Das Billett blieb
liegen und fiel mir abends in die Hände. Ich las es und lächelte; sie
fragte worüber? – Was die Einbildungskraft für ein göttliches
Geschenk ist, rief ich aus, ich konnte mir einen Augenblick vor-
spiegeln, als wäre es an mich geschrieben. – Sie brach ab, es schien
ihr zu mißfallen, und ich schwieg.

end of the story, though you can easily imagine it. She resisted his violence; her brother came in. He had long hated the farmhand and had long wished him out of the household out of fear that his sister's remarriage would deprive his children of her inheritance, of which they now have great expectations since she's childless. Her brother immediately threw him out of the house and raised such a hue and cry over the matter that the woman couldn't have taken him back even if she had wanted to. Now she has hired another hand, and people say that she has quarreled with her brother over *him*, too; people declare it's a sure thing she'll marry him, but my interlocutor says he's firmly resolved not to live to see that happen.

What I am telling you is in no way exaggerated or prettied up; in fact I may very well say it's weak; I have told it feebly and I have coarsened it by narrating it in terms of our traditional morality.

This love, this fidelity, this passion is thus no poetic invention. It lives, it exists in its purest form among the class of people we call uneducated, we call raw. We educated people—miseducated into nothingness! Read this story with piety, I beg of you. Today I am calm as I write it down; you can tell from my handwriting that I'm not writing so wildly and smearily as I usually do. Read it, dear friend, and, as you do, think that it's your friend's story, too. Yes, that's how it was with me, how it will be with me, and I'm not half so fine, not half so determined as that poor wretch whom I almost don't dare compare myself to.

September 5[23]

She had written a note to her husband in the country, where business affairs kept him. It began: "Best of men, dearest, come as soon as you can, I look forward to your return with a thousand pleasures." A friend who stopped by brought the news that, because of certain circumstances, he wouldn't be home so soon. The note was left around, and came into my hands that evening. I read it and smiled; she asked me why. "What a divine gift imagination is!" I exclaimed; "for a moment I was able to convince myself that it was addressed to me." She broke off, my words seemed to displease her, and I fell silent.

23. Entire letter new in 1787 edition.

Am 6. September.

Es hat schwer gehalten, bis ich mich entschloß, meinen blauen einfachen Frack, in dem ich mit Lotten zum ersten Male tanzte, abzulegen, er ward aber zuletzt gar unscheinbar. Auch habe ich mir einen machen lassen ganz wie den vorigen, Kragen und Aufschlag, und auch wieder so gelbe Weste und Beinkleider dazu.

Ganz will es doch die Wirkung nicht tun. Ich weiß nicht – Ich denke, mit der Zeit soll mir der auch lieber werden.

Am 12. September.

Sie war einige Tage verreist, Alberten abzuholen. Heute trat ich in ihre Stube, sie kam mir entgegen, und ich küßte ihre Hand mit tausend Freuden.

Ein Kanarienvogel flog von dem Spiegel ihr auf die Schulter. – Einen neuen Freund, sagte sie und lockte ihn auf ihre Hand, er ist meinen Kleinen zugedacht. Er tut gar zu lieb! Sehen Sie ihn! Wenn ich ihm Brot gebe, flattert er mit den Flügeln und pickt so artig. Er küßt mich auch, sehen Sie!

Als sie dem Tierchen den Mund hinhielt, drückte es sich so lieblich in die süßen Lippen, als wenn es die Seligkeit hätte fühlen können, die es genoß.

Er soll Sie auch küssen, sagte sie und reichte den Vogel herüber. – Das Schnäbelchen machte den Weg von ihrem Munde zu dem meinigen, und die pickende Berührung war wie ein Hauch, eine Ahnung liebevollen Genusses.

Sein Kuß, sagte ich, ist nicht ganz ohne Begierde, er sucht Nahrung und kehrt unbefriedigt von der leeren Liebkosung zurück.

Er ißt mir auch aus dem Munde, sagte sie. – Sie reichte ihm einige Brosamen mit ihren Lippen, aus denen die Freuden unschuldig teilnehmender Liebe in aller Wonne lächelten.

Ich kehrte das Gesicht weg. Sie sollte es nicht tun! sollte nicht meine Einbildungskraft mit diesen Bildern himmlischer Unschuld und Seligkeit reizen und mein Herz aus dem Schlafe, in den es manchmal die Gleichgültigkeit des Lebens wiegt, nicht wecken! – Und warum nicht? – Sie traut mir so! sie weiß, wie ich sie liebe!

September 6

It cost me a great effort until I decided to stop wearing that simple blue dress coat in which I danced with Lotte for the first time, yet it was recently becoming really unsightly. But I've had one made just like the old one, with collar and lapels, and, once again, a yellow waistcoat and breeches to go with it.[24]

But it doesn't have quite the same effect. I don't know . . . I think that in time I'll get to like the new one better, too.

September 12[25]

She had been away for a few days to go and pick up Albert. Today I walked into her parlor, she came to greet me, and I kissed her hand with a thousand joys.

A canary flew from the mirror onto her shoulder. "A new friend," she said, and called it onto her hand; "I intend him for my little ones. How sweet he is! Look at him! When I give him bread, he flaps his wings and pecks at it so darlingly. He kisses me, too, look!"

When she held out her lips to the little creature, it pressed those sweet lips as cunningly as if it could have felt the bliss it was enjoying.

"He must kiss you, too," she said, holding out the bird to me. Its little beak traveled from her lips to mine, and the pecking contact was like a breath, a foretaste of amorous pleasure.

"His kiss," I said, "isn't completely devoid of greed; he was looking for food, and he has come away unsatisfied by the empty caress."

"He eats from my mouth, too," she said. She offered it a few crumbs on her lips, from which the joys of innocently sympathetic love were smiling in full rapture.

I turned my face away. She shouldn't do that! She shouldn't provoke my imagination with those images of heavenly innocence and bliss, and awaken my heart from the slumber into which the even flow of life sometimes rocks it!—And why not?—She trusts me so! She knows how much I love her!

---

24. When the novel became wildly popular, many fashionable men adopted the outfit described here, and Goethe himself wore it at a fancy-dress ball years later.   25. The entire letter is new in the 1787 edition.

Am 15. September.

Man möchte rasend werden, Wilhelm, daß es Menschen geben soll
ohne Sinn und Gefühl an dem Wenigen, was auf Erden noch einen
Wert hat. Du kennst die Nußbäume, unter denen ich bei dem
ehrlichen Pfarrer zu St . . . mit Lotten gesessen, die herrlichen
Nußbäume! die mich, Gott weiß, immer mit dem größten Seelenver-
gnügen füllten! Wie vertraulich sie den Pfarrhof machten, wie kühl!
und wie herrlich die Äste waren! und die Erinnerung bis zu den
ehrlichen Geistlichen, die sie vor so vielen Jahren pflanzten. Der
Schulmeister hat uns den einen Namen oft genannt, den er von
seinem Großvater gehört hatte; und so ein braver Mann soll er gewesen sein, und sein Andenken war mir immer heilig unter den
Bäumen. Ich sage dir, dem Schulmeister standen die Tränen in den
Augen, da wir gestern davon redeten, daß sie abgehauen worden –
Abgehauen! Ich möchte toll werden, ich könnte den Hund ermorden,
der den ersten Hieb dran tat. Ich, der ich mich vertrauern könnte,
wenn so ein paar Bäume in meinem Hofe stünden und einer davon
stürbe vor Alter ab, ich muß zusehen. Lieber Schatz, eins ist doch
dabei! Was Menschengefühl ist! Das ganze Dorf murrt, und ich hoffe,
die Frau Pfarrerin soll es an Butter und Eiern und übrigem Zutrauen
spüren, was für eine Wunde sie ihrem Orte gegeben hat. Denn *sie* ist
es, die Frau des neuen Pfarrers (unser alter ist auch gestorben), ein
hageres, kränkliches Geschöpf, das sehr Ursache hat, an der Welt
keinen Anteil zu nehmen, denn niemand nimmt Anteil an ihr. Eine
Närrin, die sich abgibt, gelehrt zu sein, sich in die Untersuchung des
Kanons meliert, gar viel an der neumodischen moralisch-kritischen
Reformation des Christentumes arbeitet und über Lavaters
Schwärmereien die Achseln zuckt, eine ganz zerrüttete Gesundheit
hat und deswegen auf Gottes Erdboden keine Freude. So einer
Kreatur war es auch allein möglich, meine Nußbäume abzuhauen.
Siehst du, ich komme nicht zu mir! Stelle dir vor, die abfallenden
Blätter machen ihr den Hof unrein und dumpfig, die Bäume nehmen
ihr das Tageslicht, und wenn die Nüsse reif sind, so werfen die
Knaben mit Steinen darnach, und das fällt ihr auf die Nerven, das
stört sie in ihren tiefen Überlegungen, wenn sie Kennikot, Semler
und Michaelis gegen einander abwiegt. Da ich die Leute im Dorfe,

September 15

I could go crazy, Wilhelm, because there are people with no sense of, or feeling for, the few things on earth that still have some value. You remember the walnut trees I sat under with Lotte at the honest parson's place in St——, those magnificent walnut trees, which, God knows, always filled my soul with the greatest pleasure! How home-like they made the parsonage yard, how cool! And how splendid their boughs were! Not to mention the way they recalled the honest clergymen who planted them so many years ago. The schoolmaster often told us one of their names, which he had heard from his grand-father; he is said to have been such a fine man, and his memory was always sacred to me under those trees. I tell you, there were tears in the schoolmaster's eyes when he told me yesterday they had been cut down.—Cut down! I could go mad, I could kill the dog who struck the first blow at them. I, who could go into mourning if a pair of trees like that stood in my yard and one of them decayed from old age—I must stand by and watch. Beloved friend, there's still one good thing! Thank goodness for human warmth! The whole village is grumbling, and I hope the parson's wife will be able to tell from the amount of butter, eggs, and other contributions[26] she receives what a great wound she has inflicted on her locality. Because it was she, the wife of the new parson (our former one has died, too), a skinny, sickly creature who has great reason to remain aloof from the world because nobody cares about *her*. She's a fool who pretends to be learned, meddles with research on the canon of the Bible,[27] works hard for the newfangled moral and critical reformation of Christianity, and shrugs her shoulders at Lavater's extravagant theo-ries; her health is severely shaken, so she has no joy on God's earth. Only such a creature was capable of cutting down my walnut trees. You see, I can't get over it! Imagine: the falling leaves made her yard dirty and stuffy; the trees took away her sunlight; and when the nuts were ripe, boys would throw stones at them; all that got on her nerves, it disturbed her profound meditations when she was com-paring the relative merits of Kennicot, Semler, and Michaelis.[28] When I saw how discontented the villagers were, especially the el-derly ones, I said: "Why did you allow it?" They said: "In these parts,

---

26. Some editors believe the German word should be *Zutragen* instead of *Zutrauen*.   27. At this time Goethe had little use for the new Bible criticism, which he had become acquainted with in Leipzig.   28. Three theologians and Bible scholars: Benjamin Kennicot (1718–1783), Johann Salomo Semler (1725–1791), and Johann David Michaelis (1717–1791).

besonders die alten, so unzufrieden sah, sagte ich: Warum habt ihr es gelitten? – Wenn der Schulze will, hierzulande, sagten sie, was kann man machen? – Aber eins ist recht geschehen. Der Schulze und der Pfarrer, der doch auch von seiner Frauen Grillen, die ihm ohnedies die Suppen nicht fett machen, was haben wollte, dachten es mit einander zu teilen; da erfuhr es die Kammer und sagte: hier herein! denn sie hatte noch alte Prätensionen an den Teil des Pfarrhofes, wo die Bäume standen, und verkaufte sie an den Meistbietenden. Sie liegen! O wenn ich Fürst wäre! ich wollte die Pfarrerin, den Schulzen und die Kammer – Fürst! – Ja, wenn ich Fürst wäre, was kümmerten mich die Bäume in meinem Lande!

Am 10. October.

Wenn ich nur ihre schwarzen Augen sehe, ist mir es schon wohl! Sieh, und was mich verdrießt, ist daß Albert nicht so beglückt zu sein scheinet, als er – hoffte – als ich – zu sein glaubte – wenn – Ich mache nicht gern Gedankenstriche, aber hier kann ich mich nicht anders ausdrücken – und mich dünkt, deutlich genug.

Am 12. October.

Ossian hat in meinem Herzen den Homer verdrängt. Welch eine Welt, in die der Herrliche mich führt! Zu wandern über die Heide, umsaust vom Sturmwinde, der in dampfenden Nebeln die Geister der Väter im dämmernden Lichte des Mondes hinführt. Zu hören vom Gebirge her, im Gebrülle des Waldstroms, halb verwehtes Ächzen der Geister aus ihren Höhlen und die Wehklagen des zu Tode sich jammernden Mädchens um die vier moosbedeckten, grasbewachsenen Steine des Edelgefallnen, ihres Geliebten. Wenn ich ihn dann finde, den wandelnden grauen Barden, der auf der weiten Heide die Fußstapfen seiner Väter sucht und ach! ihre Grabsteine findet, und dann jammernd nach dem lieben Sterne des Abends hinblickt, der sich ins rollende Meer verbirgt, und die Zeiten der Vergangenheit in des Helden Seele lebendig werden, da noch der freundliche Strahl den Gefahren der Tapferen leuchtete und der Mond ihr bekränztes siegrückkehrendes Schiff beschien; wenn ich den tiefen Kummer auf seiner Stirn lese, den letzten verlaßnen Herrlichen in aller Ermattung dem Grabe zuwanken sehe, wie er immer neue, schmerzlich glühende Freuden in der kraftlosen Gegenwart der Schatten seiner Abgeschiedenen einsaugt und nach der kalten Erde, dem hohen, we-

when the mayor is in favor of something, what can be done?" But one thing turned out justly. The mayor and the parson, who after all wanted some profit out of his wife's caprices, which normally don't put bread on his table, intended to share the proceeds; then the treasury department heard about it and said: "This way with the cash!"[29] Because they already had longstanding claims to the portion of the parsonage grounds on which the trees stood, and they sold them to the highest bidder. The trees are on the ground! Oh, if I were the prince! I would take the parson's wife, the mayor, and the treasury and— Prince!—Yes, if I were the prince, what would I care about the trees in my country?

October 10

Whenever I catch sight of her dark eyes, I immediately feel good! You see? And what vexes me is that Albert doesn't seem to be as happy as he—hoped—as I—think I'd be—if— I don't like to draw dashes instead of spelling out my thoughts, but in this case it's the only way I can express what I'm feeling—and distinctly enough, it seems to me.

October 12

Ossian has supplanted Homer in my heart. What a world that wonderful poet leads me into! To wander over the heath, the storm wind raging about me and conveying the spirits of the ancestors in vaporous mists in the faint light of the moon. To hear coming from the mountains, in the roar of the forest stream, the half-trailed-away moaning of the spirits from their caves and the laments of the girl grieving herself to death over the four moss-covered, grass-overgrown stones where the noble fallen warrior, her beloved, is buried. When I then find him, the wandering gray bard, seeking the footprints of his fathers on the broad heath and, alas, finding their tombstones, and then gazing up in sorrow at the lovely evening star which hides itself in the rolling sea; when past eras live again in the hero's soul, eras when that friendly beam still pointed out brave men's dangers to them and the moon illuminated their bewreathed ship as it sailed home victorious; when I read the deep grief on his brow, and see the last great man, abandoned, tottering to his grave in complete exhaustion, imbibing ever-new, painfully fervent joys in the

---

29. The following sentence is new in the 1787 edition.

henden Grase niedersieht und ausruft: Der Wanderer wird kommen,
kommen, der mich kannte in meiner Schönheit, und fragen: Wo ist
der Sänger, Fingals trefflicher Sohn? Sein Fußtritt geht über mein
Grab hin, und er fragt vergebens nach mir auf der Erde. – O Freund!
ich möchte gleich einem edlen Waffenträger das Schwert ziehen,
meinen Fürsten von der zückenden Qual des langsam absterbenden
Lebens auf einmal befreien und dem befreiten Halbgott meine Seele
nachsenden.

Am 19. October.

Ach, diese Lücke! diese entsetzliche Lücke, die ich hier in meinem
Busen fühle! – Ich denke oft: wenn du sie nur einmal, nur einmal an
dieses Herz drücken könntest, diese ganze Lücke würde ausgefüllt
sein.

Am 26. October.

Ja, es wird mir gewiß, Lieber! gewiß und immer gewisser, daß an dem
Dasein eines Geschöpfes wenig gelegen ist, ganz wenig. Es kam eine
Freundin zu Lotten, und ich ging herein ins Nebenzimmer, ein Buch
zu nehmen, und konnte nicht lesen, und dann nahm ich eine Feder,
zu schreiben. Ich hörte sie leise reden; sie erzählten einander unbe-
deutende Sachen, Stadtneuigkeiten: wie diese heiratet, wie jene
krank, sehr krank ist. – Sie hat einen trocknen Husten, die Knochen
stehn ihr zum Gesichte heraus, und kriegt Ohnmachten; ich gebe
keinen Kreuzer für ihr Leben, sagte die eine. Der N. N. ist auch so
übel dran, sagte Lotte. Er ist schon geschwollen, sagte die andere. –
Und meine lebhafte Einbildungskraft versetzte mich ans Bett dieser
Armen; ich sah sie, mit welchem Widerwillen sie dem Leben den
Rücken wandten, wie sie – Wilhelm! und meine Weibchen redeten
davon, wie man eben davon redet – daß ein Fremder stirbt. – Und
wenn ich mich umsehe und sehe das Zimmer an und rings um mich
Lottens Kleider und Alberts Skripturen und diese Möbeln, denen ich
nun so befreundet bin, sogar diesem Tintenfasse, und denke: Siehe,
was du nun diesem Hause bist! Alles in allem. Deine Freunde ehren
dich! du machst oft ihre Freude, und deinem Herzen scheint es, als
wenn es ohne sie nicht sein könnte, und doch – wenn du nun gingst,
wenn du aus diesem Kreise schiedest? würden sie, wie lange würden
sie die Lücke fühlen, die dein Verlust in ihr Schicksal reißt? wie
lange? – O, so vergänglich ist der Mensch, daß er auch da, wo er
seines Daseins eigentliche Gewißheit hat, da, wo er den einzigen
wahren Eindruck seiner Gegenwart macht, in dem Andenken, in der

strengthless presence of the shades of his departed ones, looking down at the cold earth, at the tall, waving grass, and exclaiming: "The wanderer will come, come, he who knew me in
my beauty, and he will ask: 'Where is the bard, Fingal's excellent
son?' His steps walk over my grave, and he inquires after me on
the earth in vain." Oh, my friend, like a noble arms-bearer, I'd
like to draw my sword, liberate my prince at once from the
twitching torment of slowly ebbing life, and send my own soul
after the liberated demigod!

October 19

Oh, this void! This horrible void I feel here in my bosom!—I
often think: "If you could press her to your heart just once, just
once, that whole void would be filled."

October 26

Yes, I'm becoming certain, dear friend, ever more certain that
any one being's existence is of little account, very little. A lady
friend of Lotte's visited her, and I went into the adjacent room
to get a book, but I couldn't read; then I picked up a pen to
write. I heard them talking softly; they were telling each other
insignificant things, town news: that one woman was getting
married, that another was ill, very ill. "She has a dry cough, her
bones are standing out in her face, and she has fainting fits; I
wouldn't give a nickel for her life," the visitor said. "So-and-so is
also in bad shape," Lotte said. "He's already all bloated," her
friend said. And my vivid imagination carried me to the bedside
of those unfortunates; I saw how reluctantly they were turning
their back on life, how they— Wilhelm! And my little females
were talking about it just the way people generally do: a stranger
is dying. When I look around and study the room, with Lotte's
clothes and Albert's paperwork all around me, and that furniture
I'm now so fond of, even this inkwell, and when I think: "See
what you now mean to this household! You're everything to
them. Your friends respect you! You often give them happiness,
and your heart believes that it couldn't exist without them, and
yet—if you were to go now, if you were to leave this circle, would
they feel—how long would they feel—the gap which the loss of
you would create in their destiny? How long?" Oh, man is so
transitory that even where he is most fully certain of his existence, where his presence makes its only real impression, in the

Seele seiner Lieben, daß er auch da verlöschen, verschwinden muß, und das so bald!

Am 27. October.

Ich möchte mir oft die Brust zerreißen und das Gehirn einstoßen, daß man einander so wenig sein kann. Ach, die Liebe, Freude, Wärme und Wonne, die ich nicht hinzubringe, wird mir der andere nicht geben, und mit einem ganzen Herzen voll Seligkeit werde ich den andern nicht beglücken, der kalt und kraftlos vor mir steht.

Abends.

Ich habe so viel, und die Empfindung an ihr verschlingt alles; ich habe so viel, und ohne sie wird mir alles zu nichts.

Am 30. October.

Wenn ich nicht schon hundertmal auf dem Punkte gestanden bin, ihr um den Hals zu fallen! Weiß der große Gott, wie einem das tut, so viele Liebenswürdigkeit vor einem herumkreuzen zu sehen und nicht zugreifen zu dürfen; und das Zugreifen ist doch der natürlichste Trieb der Menschheit. Greifen die Kinder nicht nach allem, was ihnen in den Sinn fällt? – Und ich?

Am 3. November.

Weiß Gott! ich lege mich so oft zu Bette mit dem Wunsche, ja manchmal mit der Hoffnung, nicht wieder zu erwachen: und morgens schlage ich die Augen auf, sehe die Sonne wieder und bin elend. O daß ich launisch sein könnte, könnte die Schuld aufs Wetter, auf einen Dritten, auf eine fehlgeschlagene Unternehmung schieben, so würde die unerträgliche Last des Unwillens doch nur halb auf mir ruhen. Wehe mir! ich fühle zu wahr, daß an mir allein alle Schuld liegt, – nicht Schuld! Genug, daß in mir die Quelle alles Elendes verborgen ist, wie ehemals die Quelle aller Seligkeiten. Bin ich nicht noch eben derselbe, der ehemals in aller Fülle der Empfindung herumschwebte, dem auf jedem Tritte ein Paradies folgte, der ein Herz hatte, eine ganze Welt liebevoll zu umfassen? Und dies Herz ist jetzt tot, aus ihm fließen keine Entzückungen mehr, meine Augen sind trocken, und meine Sinnen, die nicht mehr von erquickenden Tränen gelabt werden, ziehen ängstlich meine Stirn zusammen. Ich leide viel, denn ich habe verloren, was meines Lebens einzige Wonne war, die heilige

memory, in the soul of those dear to him, even there he must be extinguished, must disappear, and so quickly!

October 27
Often I'd like to tear my chest open and knock my brains out, when I consider how little people can mean to one another. Ah, the love, joy, warmth, and bliss that I don't contribute myself won't be given to me by anyone else; and with a heart full of rapture I won't make anyone else happy when they stand before me cold and powerless.

In the evening[30]
I have so much, and my feelings for her engulf it all; I have so much, and without her it all becomes nothing to me.

October 30
If I haven't been, a hundred times already, on the point of throwing my arms around her shoulders! God above knows how a man feels when he sees so much sweetness milling around in front of him, and mustn't reach out and grab it; and yet to seize something is the most natural human urge. Don't children reach for anything that comes into their head?—What about me?

November 3
God knows! I go to bed so often wishing—yes, sometimes expecting—I'll never wake up again; and in the morning I open my eyes, I see the sun again, and I'm miserable. Oh, if I could only be capricious, and blame it on the weather, on some third party, on the failure of some enterprise, the unbearable burden of my indignation would only weigh on me half as much. Woe is me! I feel too clearly that I alone bear all the blame—no, not blame! Suffice it to say that the source of all this misery is hidden within me, just as the source of all bliss used to be. Am I not still the same man who once hovered about in an abundance of feelings, a paradise following my every step? The same man whose heart was capable of encompassing an entire world lovingly? And that heart is now dead, no more raptures flow from it; my eyes are dry, and my senses, no longer refreshed by stimulating tears, compress my brow in anguish. I suffer much, for I have lost that which was my life's sole bliss, the sacred energizing

---

30. This postscript to the letter of October 27 is new in the 1787 edition.

belebende Kraft, mit der ich Welten um mich schuf; sie ist dahin! – Wenn ich zu meinem Fenster hinaus an den fernen Hügel sehe, wie die Morgensonne über ihn her den Nebel durchbricht und den stillen Wiesengrund bescheint und der sanfte Fluß zwischen seinen entblätterten Weiden zu mir herschlängelt, – o! wenn da diese herrliche Natur so starr vor mir steht wie ein lackiertes Bildchen und alle die Wonne keinen Tropfen Seligkeit aus meinem Herzen herauf in das Gehirn pumpen kann und der ganze Kerl vor Gottes Angesicht steht wie ein versiegter Brunn, wie ein verlechter Eimer. Ich habe mich oft auf den Boden geworfen und Gott um Tränen gebeten, wie ein Ackersmann um Regen, wenn der Himmel ehern über ihm ist und um ihn die Erde verdürstet.

Aber ach! ich fühle es, Gott gibt Regen und Sonnenschein nicht unserm ungestümen Bitten, und jene Zeiten, deren Andenken mich quält, warum waren sie so selig? als weil ich mit Geduld seinen Geist erwartete und die Wonne, die er über mich ausgoß, mit ganzem, innig dankbarem Herzen aufnahm.

Am 8. November.

Sie hat mir meine Exzesse vorgeworfen! ach, mit so viel Liebenswürdigkeit! Meine Exzesse, daß ich mich manchmal von einem Glase Wein verleiten lasse, eine Bouteille zu trinken. – Tun Sie es nicht! sagte sie, denken Sie an Lotten! – Denken! sagte ich, brauchen Sie mir das zu heißen? Ich denke! – ich denke nicht! Sie sind immer vor meiner Seele. Heute saß ich an dem Flecke, wo Sie neulich aus der Kutsche stiegen – Sie redete was anders, um mich nicht tiefer in den Text kommen zu lassen. Bester, ich bin dahin! sie kann mit mir machen, was sie will.

Am 15. November.

Ich danke dir, Wilhelm, für deinen herzlichen Anteil, für deinen wohlmeinenden Rat, und bitte dich, ruhig zu sein. Laß mich ausdulden, ich habe bei aller meiner Müdseligkeit noch Kraft genug durchzusetzen. Ich ehre die Religion, das weißt du, ich fühle, daß sie manchem Ermatteten Stab, manchem Verschmachtenden Erquickung ist. Nur – kann sie denn, muß sie denn das einem jeden sein? Wenn du die große Welt ansiehst, so siehst du Tausende, denen sie es nicht war, Tausende, denen sie es nicht sein wird, gepredigt oder ungepredigt, und muß sie mir es denn sein? Sagt nicht selbst der Sohn Gottes, daß die um ihn sein würden, die ihm der Vater gegeben hat? Wenn ich ihm nun nicht gegeben bin? wenn mich nun der Vater

power with which I created worlds around me; it's gone!—
When I look out my window at the distant hill and see how the
morning sun breaks through the mist across it, shining on the
quiet meadow, and how the gentle river winds its way to me between its leafless willows—oh, when this magnificent nature
lies before me as rigid as a little lacquered picture, and all that
bliss can't pump one drop of happiness from my heart up into
my brain, and I stand before God's countenance altogether like
a dried-up well, like a leaky bucket! I have often thrown myself
onto the floor and begged God for tears, as a farmer prays for
rain when the sky above him is brazen and the earth around
him parched.

But, alas, I feel it, God doesn't apportion rain and sunshine to
our reckless prayers; and why were those times, the memory of
which tortures me, so blissful, if not because I was patiently
awaiting his spirit, and because I received the rapture he poured
down on me with a whole, inwardly thankful heart?

November 8

She has upbraided me for my excesses! Ah, with so much deli-
cate charm! My excesses: that I sometimes am led astray by a
glass of wine to drink a whole bottle. "Don't do it," she said,
"think of Lotte!" "Think!" I said; "do you need to tell me that?
Whether I think, or don't think, you are constantly on my mind.
Today I sat down on the spot where you recently got out of the
coach." She changed the subject so that I wouldn't elaborate on
what I had started to say. My dear friend, I'm lost! She can do
whatever she wants with me.

November 15

I thank you, Wilhelm, for your sincere sympathy, for your well-
intentioned advice, and I urge you to be calm. Let me ride this out;
despite all my weariness I still have strength enough to get through
it. I revere religion, as you know; I feel that it is a staff for many an
exhausted man, refreshment for many a one who languishes. Only—
can it, must it for that reason be that for everyone? When you observe the wide world, you see thousands for whom religion was nothing of the sort, thousands for whom it won't be, whether or not they
hear its preachings, so must it be a staff and refreshment for me?
Doesn't the Son of God himself say that those will be about him
whom his Father has given him? What if I haven't been given to

für sich behalten will, wie mir mein Herz sagt? – Ich bitte dich, lege
das nicht falsch aus; sieh nicht etwa Spott in diesen unschuldigen
Worten; es ist meine ganze Seele, die ich dir vorlege; sonst wollte ich
lieber, ich hätte geschwiegen: wie ich denn über alles das, wovon jedermann so wenig weiß als ich, nicht gern ein Wort verliere. Was ist
es anders als Menschenschicksal, sein Maß auszuleiden, seinen
Becher auszutrinken? – Und ward der Kelch dem Gott vom Himmel
auf seiner Menschenlippe zu bitter, warum soll ich großtun und mich
stellen, als schmeckte er mir süß? Und warum sollte ich mich schämen, in dem schrecklichen Augenblick, da mein ganzes Wesen zwischen Sein und Nichtsein zittert, da die Vergangenheit wie ein Blitz
über dem finstern Abgrunde der Zukunft leuchtet und alles um mich
her versinkt und mit mir die Welt untergeht – Ist es da nicht die
Stimme der ganz in sich gedrängten, sich selbst ermangelnden und
unaufhaltsam hinabstürzenden Kreatur, in den innern Tiefen ihrer
vergebens aufarbeitenden Kräfte zu knirschen: Mein Gott! mein
Gott! warum hast du mich verlassen? Und sollt' ich mich des Aus-
druckes schämen, sollte mir es vor dem Augenblicke bange sein, da
ihm der nicht entging, der die Himmel zusammenrollt wie ein Tuch?

Am 21. November.

Sie sieht nicht, sie fühlt nicht, daß sie ein Gift bereitet, das mich und
sie zugrunde richten wird; und ich mit voller Wollust schlürfe den
Becher aus, den sie mir zu meinem Verderben reicht. Was soll der
gütige Blick, mit dem sie mich oft – oft? – nein, nicht oft, aber doch
manchmal ansieht, die Gefälligkeit, womit sie einen unwillkürlichen
Ausdruck meines Gefühles aufnimmt, das Mitleiden mit meiner
Duldung, das sich auf ihrer Stirne zeichnet?

Gestern, als ich wegging, reichte sie mir die Hand und sagte:
Adieu, lieber Werther! – Lieber Werther! Es war das erste Mal, daß
sie mich Lieber hieß, und es ging mir durch Mark und Bein. Ich habe
es mir hundertmal wiederholt, und gestern Nacht, da ich zu Bette
gehen wollte und mit mir selbst allerlei schwatzte, sagte ich so auf einmal: Gute Nacht, lieber Werther! und mußte hernach selbst über
mich lachen.

Am 22. November.

Ich kann nicht beten: Laß mir sie! und doch kommt sie mir oft als die
Meine vor. Ich kann nicht beten: Gib mir sie! denn sie ist eines an-

him? What if the Father wants to keep me for himself, as my heart tells me?—I beg of you, don't misconstrue this; don't see mockery in these innocent words; it's my whole soul I'm laying bare before you; otherwise I would prefer to have remained silent: just as I dislike wasting words over all these matters that everyone is as ignorant of as I am. What else is it but man's fate to endure his measure of suffering, to drain his goblet?—And if God from heaven found the chalice too bitter for his human lips, why should I boast and pretend it tastes sweet to me? And why should I be ashamed, at that awful moment when my entire being trembles between existence and nonexistence, when the past flashes like lightning over the dark abyss of the future, and everything around me subsides and the world perishes along with me— Isn't it the true voice of the creature totally driven inside itself, lacking its own resources, and inexorably plunging downward, when in the innermost depths of its fruitlessly upward-striving strength it gnashes its teeth and cries: "My God! My God! Why have you forsaken me?" And should I be ashamed of that expression, should I hang back at that moment, when even he was forced to utter it who can roll the heavens up like a cloth?

November 21
She doesn't see, she doesn't feel that she's mixing a poison that will destroy her and me both; and with the deepest pleasure I drain the goblet she hands me for my undoing. Why that friendly glance she often gives me? Often? No, not often, but sometimes. Why that obligingness with which she accepts an involuntary expression of my emotions, that sympathy with my long-suffering which can be read on her brow?

Yesterday when I left she gave me her hand and said: "Adieu, dear Werther!" Dear Werther! It was the first time she called me "dear," and it went right to the heart of me. I repeated it to myself a hundred times, and last night when I wanted to go to bed and was prattling to myself about all sorts of things, I suddenly said: "Good night, dear Werther!" and later I had to laugh at myself.

November 22[31]
I can't pray: "Relinquish her to me!" and yet I often think of her as being mine. I can't pray: "Give her to me!" because she be-

---

31. Entire letter new in 1787 edition.

dern. Ich witzle mich mit meinen Schmerzen herum; wenn ich mirs nachließe, es gäbe eine ganze Litanei von Antithesen.

Am 24. November.

Sie fühlt, was ich dulde. Heute ist mir ihr Blick tief durchs Herz gedrungen. Ich fand sie allein; ich sagte nichts, und sie sah mich an. Und ich sah nicht mehr in ihr die liebliche Schönheit, nicht mehr das Leuchten des trefflichen Geistes; das war alles vor meinen Augen verschwunden. Ein weit herrlicherer Blick wirkte auf mich, voll Ausdruck des innigsten Anteils, des süßesten Mitleidens. Warum durfte ich mich nicht ihr zu Füßen werfen? warum durfte ich nicht an ihrem Halse mit tausend Küssen antworten? Sie nahm ihre Zuflucht zum Klavier und hauchte mit süßer, leiser Stimme harmonische Laute zu ihrem Spiele. Nie habe ich ihre Lippen so reizend gesehen; es war, als wenn sie sich lechzend öffneten, jene süßen Töne in sich zu schlürfen, die aus dem Instrument hervorquollen, und nur der heimliche Widerschall aus dem reinen Munde zurückklänge – Ja wenn ich dir das so sagen könnte! – Ich widerstand nicht länger, neigte mich und schwur: nie will ich es wagen, einen Kuß euch aufzudrücken, Lippen! auf denen die Geister des Himmels schweben – Und doch – ich will – Ha! siehst du, das steht wie eine Scheidewand vor meiner Seele – diese Seligkeit – und dann untergegangen, diese Sünde abzubüßen – Sünde?

Am 26. November.

Manchmal sag ich mir: Dein Schicksal ist einzig; preise die übrigen glücklich – so ist noch keiner gequält worden. Dann lese ich einen Dichter der Vorzeit, und es ist mir, als säh ich in mein eignes Herz. Ich habe so viel auszustehen! Ach, sind denn Menschen vor mir schon so elend gewesen?

Am 30. November.

Ich soll, ich soll nicht zu mir selbst kommen! wo ich hintrete, begegnet mir eine Erscheinung, die mich aus aller Fassung bringt. Heute! o Schicksal! o Menschheit!

Ich gehe an dem Wasser hin in der Mittagsstunde, ich hatte keine Lust zu essen. Alles war öde, ein naßkalter Abendwind blies vom Berge, und die grauen Regenwolken zogen das Tal hinein. Von fern sah ich einen Menschen in einem grünen schlechten Rocke, der zwi-

longs to another. I make jokes of my sorrows; if I allowed myself, there would be a whole litany of contradictions.

November 24

She feels what I'm going through. Today her gaze pierced deeply into my heart. I found her alone; I said nothing, and she looked at me. And I no longer saw in her the lovely beauty, no longer the glow of her excellent mind; all that had disappeared from my sight. A far more splendid view affected me, full of the expression of the most heartfelt sympathy, of the sweetest compassion. Why was I not allowed to fling myself at her feet? Why was I not allowed to respond by embracing her and giving her a thousand kisses? She took refuge in the clavier, her sweet, quiet voice breathing harmonious sounds as she played. I've never seen her lips so alluring; it was as if they opened longingly to imbibe those sweet tones which were pouring from the instrument and only the secret echo from her pure mouth were reverberating— Yes, if I could only describe it to you!—I couldn't resist any longer, I bent my head, and I swore: "Never will I dare to implant a kiss on those lips, above which the heavenly spirits hover!"—And yet—I want— Ha! You see, it's like a partition in front of my soul—that bliss—and then: perish, to atone for the sin!—sin?

November 26[32]

Sometimes I tell myself: "Your destiny is unique; count others fortunate—no one else has ever been tortured this way." Then I read an ancient author, and I feel as if I were looking into my own heart. I must endure so much! Ah, were people before me already so miserable?

November 30

It's not to be, I'll never get a grip on myself! Wherever I go, I see an apparition that totally deranges me. Today! O fate! O mankind!

At the noon hour I was walking by the water, I had no appetite. Everything was bleak, a cold, wet evening wind was blowing from the mountains, and gray rainclouds moved into the valley. From far off I saw a man in a shabby green jacket scrambling among

---

32. Letter new in 1787.

schen den Felsen herumkrabbelte und Kräuter zu suchen schien. Als ich näher zu ihm kam und er sich auf das Geräusch, das ich machte, herumdrehte, sah ich eine interessante Physiognomie, darin eine stille Trauer den Hauptzug machte, die aber sonst nichts als einen geraden guten Sinn ausdrückte; seine schwarzen Haare waren mit Nadeln in zwei Rollen gesteckt, und die übrigen in einen starken Zopf geflochten, der ihm den Rücken herunterhing. Da mir seine Kleidung einen Menschen von geringem Stande zu bezeichnen schien, glaubte ich, er würde es nicht übelnehmen, wenn ich auf seine Beschäftigung aufmerksam wäre, und daher fragte ich ihn, was er suchte? – Ich suche, antwortete er mit einem tiefen Seufzer, Blumen – und finde keine. – Das ist auch die Jahrszeit nicht, sagte ich lächelnd. – Es gibt so viele Blumen, sagte er, indem er zu mir herunterkam. In meinem Garten sind Rosen und Jelängerjelieber zweierlei Sorten, eine hat mir mein Vater gegeben, sie wachsen wie Unkraut; ich suche schon zwei Tage darnach und kann sie nicht finden. Da haußen sind auch immer Blumen, gelbe und blaue und rote, und das Tausendgüldenkraut hat ein schönes Blümchen. Keines kann ich finden. – Ich merkte was Unheimliches, und drum fragte ich durch einen Umweg: Was will Er denn mit den Blumen? – Ein wunderbares, zuckendes Lächeln verzog sein Gesicht. – Wenn Er mich nicht verraten will, sagte er, indem er den Finger auf den Mund drückte, ich habe meinem Schatz einen Strauß versprochen. – Das ist brav, sagte ich. – O, sagte er, sie hat viel andere Sachen, sie ist reich. – Und doch hat sie Seinen Strauß lieb, versetzte ich. – O! fuhr er fort, sie hat Juwelen und eine Krone. – Wie hießt sie denn? – Wenn mich die Generalstaaten bezahlen wollten, versetzte er, ich wär ein anderer Mensch! Ja, es war einmal eine Zeit, da mir es so wohl war! Jetzt ist es aus mit mir. Ich bin nun – Ein nasser Blick zum Himmel drückte alles aus. – Er war also glücklich? fragte ich. – Ach, ich wollte, ich wäre wieder so! sagte er. Da war mir es so wohl, so lustig, so leicht wie einem Fisch im Wasser! – Heinrich! rief eine alte Frau, die den Weg herkam, Heinrich, wo steckst du? wir haben dich überall gesucht, komm zum Essen! – Ist das Euer Sohn? fragt ich, zu ihr tretend. – Wohl, mein armer Sohn! versetzte sie. Gott hat mir ein schweres Kreuz aufgelegt. – Wie lange ist er so? fragte ich. – So stille, sagte sie, ist er nun ein halbes Jahr. Gott sei Dank, daß er nur so weit ist, vorher war er ein ganzes Jahr rasend, da hat er an Ketten im Tollhause gelegen. Jetzt tut er niemand nichts, nur hat er immer mit Königen und Kaisern zu schaffen. Es war ein so guter, stiller Mensch, der mich ernähren half, seine schöne Hand schrieb, und auf einmal wird er tiefsinnig, fällt in ein hitziges Fieber, daraus in

the boulders, apparently seeking herbs. When I got nearer to him and he turned around at the noise I made, I saw an interesting physiognomy in which a quiet sadness was the principal feature, but which otherwise merely expressed a good, honest mind; his black hair was parted in two at the sides with pins, in back it was twisted into a heavy braid which hung down over his shoulders. Since his attire seemed to indicate a person of a lower class, I thought he wouldn't take it badly if I paid attention to his occupation; so I asked him what he was looking for. He replied with a deep sigh: "I'm looking for flowers—and I can't find any." "It's the wrong season," I said with a smile. "There are so many flowers," he said, as he came down to join me; "in my garden there are roses and nasturtiums of two varieties; one, my father gave me, and they grow like weeds; it's two days now that I've been looking for them but can't find them. Out here there are always flowers, too, yellow and blue and red ones, and the centaury has a pretty little flower. I can't find any at all." I noticed something uncanny, so I asked in a roundabout way: "What do you want to do with the flowers?" A strange twitching smile distorted his face. "If you won't give me away," he said, pressing a finger to his lips, "I promised my sweetheart a bouquet." "That's gentlemanly," I said. "Oh," he replied, "she has many other things, she's rich." "And yet she's fond of a bouquet from you," was my response. "Oh," he continued, "she has jewels and a crown." "What's her name?" "If Holland would only pay me," he replied, "I'd be a different person! Yes, there once was a time when I was so prosperous! Now it's all over for me. Now I'm—" A tear-dimmed glance at the sky expressed it all. "So you were happy?" I asked. "Oh, I wish I were that way again!" he said; "I felt so good then, so merry, as brisk as a fish in the water!" "Heinrich!" called an old woman who was coming down the path; "Heinrich, where are you? We've been looking for you all over, come home for lunch!" "Is he your son?" I asked, walking over to her. "Yes, my poor son!" she replied. "God has laid a heavy cross on me." "How long has he been this way?" I asked. She said: "Quiet like this, for six months now. Thank God that he's come this far; previously he was raving mad for a whole year, then he was chained up in the madhouse. Now he does nobody any harm, but he's always dealing with kings and emperors. He was such a good, quiet boy; he helped support me, he wrote a good hand; then all at once he became melancholy, broke out into a burning fever, from that into

Raserei, und nun ist er, wie Sie ihn sehen. Wenn ich Ihm erzählen sollte, Herr – Ich unterbrach den Strom ihrer Worte mit der Frage: Was war denn das für eine Zeit, von der er rühmt, daß er so glücklich, so wohl darin gewesen sei? – Der törichte Mensch! rief sie mit mitleidigem Lächeln, da meint er die Zeit, da er von sich war, das rühmt er immer; das ist die Zeit, da er im Tollhause war, wo er nichts von sich wußte – Das fiel mir auf wie ein Donnerschlag, ich drückte ihr ein Stück Geld in die Hand und verließ sie eilend.

Da du glücklich warst! rief ich aus, schnell vor mich hin nach der Stadt zu gehend, da dir es wohl war wie einem Fisch im Wasser! – Gott im Himmel! hast du das zum Schicksale der Menschen gemacht, daß sie nicht glücklich sind, als ehe sie zu ihrem Verstande kommen und wenn sie ihn wieder verlieren! – Elender! und auch wie beneide ich deinen Trübsinn, die Verwirrung deiner Sinne, in der du verschmachtest! Du gehst hoffnungsvoll aus, deiner Königin Blumen zu pflücken – im Winter – und trauerst, da du keine findest, und begreifst nicht, warum du keine finden kannst. Und ich – und ich gehe ohne Hoffnung, ohne Zweck heraus und kehre wieder heim, wie ich gekommen bin. – Du wähnst, welcher Mensch du sein würdest, wenn die Generalstaaten dich bezahlten. Seliges Geschöpf! das den Mangel seiner Glückseligkeit einer irdischen Hindernis zuschreiben kann. Du fühlst nicht! du fühlst nicht, daß in deinem zerstörten Herzen, in deinem zerrütteten Gehirne dein Elend liegt, wovon alle Könige der Erde dir nicht helfen können.

Müsse der trostlos umkommen, der eines Kranken spottet, der nach der entferntesten Quelle reist, die seine Krankheit vermehren, sein Ausleben schmerzhafter machen wird! der sich über das bedrängte Herz erhebt, das, um seine Gewissensbisse loszuwerden und die Leiden seiner Seele abzutun, eine Pilgrimschaft nach dem heiligen Grabe tut. Jeder Fußtritt, der seine Sohlen auf ungebahntem Wege durchschneidet, ist ein Linderungstropfen der geängsteten Seele, und mit jeder ausgedauerten Tagereise legt sich das Herz um viele Bedrängnisse leichter nieder. – Und dürft ihr das Wahn nennen, ihr Wortkrämer auf euren Polstern? – Wahn! – O Gott! du siehst meine Tränen! Mußtest du, der du den Menschen arm genug erschufst, ihm auch Brüder zugeben, die ihm das bißchen Armut, das bißchen Vertrauen noch raubten, das er auf dich hat, auf dich, du Allliebender! Denn das Vertrauen zu einer heilenden Wurzel, zu den Tränen des Weinstockes, was ist es als Vertrauen zu dir, daß du in alles, was uns umgibt, Heil- und Linderungskraft gelegt hast, der wir so stündlich bedürfen? Vater! den ich nicht kenne! Vater! der sonst meine ganze Seele füllte und nun sein Angesicht von mir gewendet

raving madness, and now he's as you see him. If I were to tell you, sir—" I interrupted her flow of words with the question: "What sort of time was it in which he claims to have been so happy and contented?" "The fool!" she cried with a compassionate smile, "he means the time when he was out of his mind, he always praises that; it was the time when he was in the madhouse, when he knew nothing of himself." That dismayed me like a thunder-clap; I pressed a coin into her hand and left her hastily.

"When you were happy!" I exclaimed, swiftly proceeding straight ahead back to town; "when you were as contented as a fish in the water!—God in heaven! Have you made that people's destiny: that they aren't happy except before they have the use of their mind, and when they lose it again!—Poor wretch! And how I envy your muddled head, the confusion of your senses, in which you languish! You set out with high hopes of picking flow-ers for your queen—in winter—and you mourn when you can't find any, not understanding why you can't find any. And I—I go out with no hope, no purpose, and return home just as I left it.—You have delusions about what a fine man you'd be if Holland paid you. Fortunate creature, who can ascribe his lack of good fortune to a terrestrial obstacle! You don't sense, you don't sense that your misery lies in your shattered heart, in your addled brain, and that all the kings on earth can't help you out of it!"

May that man perish without consolation who mocks a sick per-son that travels to the remotest spa, which will only make his illness worse and his last days more painful! Curse him who looks down upon the oppressed heart which, to free itself of its pangs of con-science and slough off the suffering of its soul, makes a pilgrimage to the holy sepulcher! Every step that lacerates his feet on the trackless journey is a drop of balm to that anguished soul, and with every day's march that has been endured, that heart lies down un-burdened of many oppressions.—And are you to be allowed to call that a delusion, you wordmongers on your upholstered sofas?—A delusion!—O God, you see my tears! After creating man poor enough, did you also have to give him brothers who deprive him of that little which he possesses, of that bit of trust he has in you, in you, the All-Loving One? Because what is trust in a healing root, in the tears of the vine, if it isn't trust in you, the confidence that in all that surrounds us you have placed that power to heal and relieve which we need hourly? Father whom I know not! Father who once filled my whole soul and has now turned his face away from me!

hat! rufe mich zu dir! schweige nicht länger! dein Schweigen wird diese dürstende Seele nicht aufhalten – Und würde ein Mensch, ein Vater zürnen können, dem sein unvermutet rückkehrender Sohn um den Hals fiele und riefe: Ich bin wieder da, mein Vater! Zürne nicht, daß ich die Wanderschaft abbreche, die ich nach deinem Willen länger aushalten sollte. Die Welt ist überall einerlei, auf Mühe und Arbeit Lohn und Freude; aber was soll mir das? mir ist nur wohl, wo du bist, und vor deinem Angesichte will ich leiden und genießen. – Und du, lieber himmlischer Vater, solltest ihn von dir weisen?

Am 1. Dezember.

Wilhelm! der Mensch, von dem ich dir schrieb, der glückliche Unglückliche, war Schreiber bei Lottens Vater, und eine Leidenschaft zu ihr, die er nährte, verbarg, entdeckte und worüber er aus dem Dienst geschickt wurde, hat ihn rasend gemacht. Fühle, bei diesen trocknen Worten, mit welchem Unsinne mich die Geschichte ergriffen hat, da mir sie Albert ebenso gelassen erzählte, als du sie vielleicht liesest.

Am 4. Dezember.

Ich bitte dich – Siehst du, mit mir ists aus, ich trag es nicht länger! Heute saß ich bei ihr – saß, sie spielte auf ihrem Klavier, mannigfaltige Melodieen, und all den Ausdruck! all! – all! – Was willst du? – Ihr Schwesterchen putzte ihre Puppe auf meinem Knie. Mir kamen die Tränen in die Augen. Ich neigte mich, und ihr Trauring fiel mir ins Gesicht – meine Tränen flossen – Und auf einmal fiel sie in die alte himmelsüße Melodie ein, so auf einmal, und mir durch die Seele gehn ein Trostgefühl und eine Erinnerung des Vergangenen, der Zeiten, da ich das Lied gehört, der düstern Zwischenräume, des Verdrusses, der fehlgeschlagenen Hoffnungen, und dann – Ich ging in der Stube auf und nieder, mein Herz erstickte unter dem Zudringen. – Um Gottes willen, sagte ich, mit einem heftigen Ausbruch hin gegen sie fahrend, um Gottes willen hören Sie auf! – Sie hielt und sah mich starr an. – Werther, sagte sie, mit einem Lächeln, das mir durch die Seele ging – Werther, Sie sind sehr krank, Ihre Lieblingsgerichte widerstehen Ihnen. Gehen Sie! Ich bitte Sie, beruhigen Sie sich. – Ich riß mich von ihr weg, und – Gott! du siehst mein Elend und wirst es enden.

Am 6. Dezember.

Wie mich die Gestalt verfolgt! Wachend und träumend füllt sie meine

Summon me to you! Be silent no longer! Your silence won't restrain this thirsting soul— And could a man, a father, be angry if
his son came back home unexpectedly, threw his arms around his
shoulders, and called: "I'm home again, father! Don't be angry because I cut short the wandering which it was your will that I should
continue to endure! The world is the same everywhere, payment
and joy for effort and labor; but what is that to me? I'm only happy
where you are, and I want to suffer and rejoice in your sight." And
you, dear heavenly Father, will you turn him away?

December 1

Wilhelm! The man I wrote to you about, the happy unfortunate,
was a clerk working for Lotte's father, and it was a passion for her
which he nurtured, concealed, and disclosed, and for which he
was discharged from his position, that drove him mad. From
these dry words imagine how the story robbed me of my senses
when it was told to me by Albert just as calmly as you may be
reading it now.

December 4

I beg of you— You see, it's all over for me, I can't bear it any
longer! Today I was sitting with her—sitting while she played
the clavier, various melodies, with so much expressiveness! So
much! So much!—What do you want?—Her little sister was sitting on my knee, dressing her doll. Tears came to my eyes. I bent
over and caught sight of her wedding ring—my tears flowed—
And all at once she began to play that old, heavenly-sweet
melody, all at once, and a feeling of consolation shot through my
soul, and a recollection of the past, of the times when I had
heard that song, of the gloomy periods in between, of my vexation, of my frustrated hopes, and then— I paced to and fro in
the parlor, my heart suffocating under that crowd of images.
"For God's sake," I said, assailing her with a violent outburst,
"for God's sake, stop!" She stopped and stared at me. "Werther,"
she said with a smile that pierced my soul, "Werther, you're very
ill, your favorite dishes disagree with you. Go home! I implore
you, calm down!" I tore myself away from her, and— God, you
see my misery and you'll put an end to it!

December 6

How her image persecutes me! Waking and dreaming, it fills my

ganze Seele! Hier, wenn ich die Augen schließe, hier in meiner Stirne, wo die innere Sehkraft sich vereinigt, stehn ihre schwarzen Augen. Hier! ich kann dir es nicht ausdrücken. Mache ich meine Augen zu, so sind sie da; wie ein Meer, wie ein Abgrund ruhen sie vor mir, in mir, füllen die Sinne meiner Stirn.

Was ist der Mensch, der gepriesene Halbgott! Ermangeln ihm nicht eben da die Kräfte, wo er sie am nötigsten braucht? Und wenn er in Freude sich aufschwingt oder im Leiden versinkt, wird er nicht in beiden eben da aufgehalten, eben da zu dem stumpfen, kalten Bewußtsein wieder zurückgebracht, da er sich in der Fülle des Unendlichen zu verlieren sehnte?

Der Herausgeber an den Leser.

Wie sehr wünscht' ich, daß uns von den letzten merkwürdigen Tagen unseres Freundes so viel eigenhändige Zeugnisse übrig geblieben wären, daß ich nicht nötig hätte, die Folge seiner hinterlaßnen Briefe durch Erzählung zu unterbrechen.

Ich habe mir angelegen sein lassen, genaue Nachrichten aus dem Munde derer zu sammeln, die von seiner Geschichte wohl unterrichtet sein konnten; sie ist einfach, und es kommen alle Erzählungen davon bis auf wenige Kleinigkeiten miteinander überein; nur über die Sinnesarten der handelnden Personen sind die Meinungen verschieden und die Urteile geteilt.

Was bleibt uns übrig, als dasjenige, was wir mit wiederholter Mühe erfahren können, gewissenhaft zu erzählen, die von dem Abscheidenden hinterlaßnen Briefe einzuschalten und das kleinste aufgefundene Blättchen nicht geringzuachten; zumal da es so schwer ist, die eigensten, wahren Triebfedern auch nur einer einzelnen Handlung zu entdecken, wenn sie unter Menschen vorgeht, die nicht gemeiner Art sind.

Unmut und Unlust hatten in Werthers Seele immer tiefer Wurzel geschlagen, sich fester untereinander verschlungen und sein ganzes Wesen nach und nach eingenommen. Die Harmonie seines Geistes war völlig zerstört, eine innerliche Hitze und Heftigkeit, die alle Kräfte seiner Natur durcheinanderarbeitete, brachte die widrigsten Wirkungen hervor und ließ ihm zuletzt nur eine Ermattung übrig, aus der er noch ängstlicher emporstrebte, als er mit allen Übeln bisher gekämpft hatte. Die Beängstigung seines Herzens zehrte die übrigen

whole soul! Here, when I close my eyes, here in my forehead, where the powers of inward vision gather, I see her dark eyes. Here! I can't describe it to you. When I shut my eyes, they're there; like an ocean, like an abyss they lie before me, in me, filling the senses of my brow.

What is man, that highly praised demigod? Doesn't he lack strength precisely when he needs it most? And when he's exalted by joy or immersed in sorrow, isn't he in both cases arrested and dragged back to his dull, cold consciousness precisely when he was yearning to lose himself in the fullness of infinity?

The Editor to the Reader.[33]

How I wish that so many autograph testimonies had remained to us from the final remarkable days of our friend that I would not need to interrupt the sequence of the letters he has left us with narrative of my own!

I have felt it my duty to collect information from the lips of those who were in a position to know his story well; it is simple, and all the recountings of it agree with one another except for a few trifling details; only on the way of thinking of the various people involved do opinions diverge and are judgments divided.

What remains for us, except to narrate conscientiously whatever we were able to learn from repeated efforts, inserting the letters which the deceased has left us, without neglecting the slightest little note we have found? Especially since it is so difficult to discover the true, deep-seated motives of even a single action when it occurs among people who are not of a common stamp.

Indignation and aversion had taken ever deeper root in Werther's soul, combining more and more thoroughly and gradually taking over his entire being. The harmony of his mind was completely destroyed; an inner heat and violence, which jumbled all his natural powers, produced the most repellent effects, and finally left him with nothing but exhaustion, from which he strove to free himself with even greater anxiety than that with which he had previously fought against all his woes. The oppression of his

---

33. From here to the end of the novel, the 1787 version (printed here) is a major revision and expansion of the 1774 text; no details will be given.

Kräfte seines Geistes, seine Lebhaftigkeit, seinen Scharfsinn auf, er ward ein trauriger Gesellschafter, immer unglücklicher, und immer ungerechter, je unglücklicher er ward. Wenigstens sagen dies Alberts Freunde; sie behaupten, daß Werther einen reinen, ruhigen Mann, der nun eines lang gewünschten Glückes teilhaftig geworden, und sein Betragen, sich dieses Glück auch auf die Zukunft zu erhalten, nicht habe beurteilen können, er, der gleichsam mit jedem Tage sein ganzes Vermögen verzehrte, um an dem Abend zu leiden und zu darben. Albert, sagen sie, hatte sich in so kurzer Zeit nicht verändert, er war noch immer derselbige, den Werther so vom Anfang her kannte, so sehr schätzte und ehrte. Er liebte Lotten über alles, er war stolz auf sie und wünschte sie auch von jedermann als das herrlichste Geschöpf anerkannt zu wissen. War es ihm daher zu verdenken, wenn er auch jeden Schein des Verdachtes abzuwenden wünschte, wenn er in dem Augenblicke mit niemand diesen köstlichen Besitz auch auf die unschuldigste Weise zu teilen Lust hatte? Sie gestehen ein, daß Albert oft das Zimmer seiner Frau verlassen, wenn Werther bei ihr war, aber nicht aus Haß noch Abneigung gegen seinen Freund, sondern nur, weil er gefühlt habe, daß dieser von seiner Gegenwart gedrückt sei.

Lottens Vater war von einem Übel befallen worden, das ihn in der Stube hielt; er schickte ihr seinen Wagen, und sie fuhr hinaus. Es war ein schöner Wintertag, der erste Schnee war stark gefallen und deckte die ganze Gegend.

Werther ging ihr den andern Morgen nach, um, wenn Albert sie nicht abzuholen käme, sie hereinzubegleiten.

Das klare Wetter konnte wenig auf sein trübes Gemüt wirken, ein dumpfer Druck lag auf seiner Seele, die traurigen Bilder hatten sich bei ihm festgesetzt, und sein Gemüt kannte keine Bewegung als von einem schmerzlichen Gedanken zum andern.

Wie er mit sich in ewigem Unfrieden lebte, schien ihm auch der Zustand andrer nur bedenklicher und verworrener, er glaubte, das schöne Verhältnis zwischen Albert und seiner Gattin gestört zu haben, er machte sich Vorwürfe darüber, in die sich ein heimlicher Unwille gegen den Gatten mischte.

Seine Gedanken fielen auch unterwegs auf diesen Gegenstand. Ja, ja, sagte er zu sich selbst mit heimlichem Zähnknirschen: das ist der vertraute, freundliche, zärtliche, an allem teilnehmende Umgang, die ruhige, dauernde Treue! Sattigkeit ists und Gleichgültigkeit! Zieht ihn nicht jedes elende Geschäft mehr an als die teure, köstliche Frau? Weiß er sein Glück zu schätzen? Weiß er sie zu achten, wie sie es verdient? Er hat sie, nun gut, er hat sie – Ich weiß das, wie ich was an-

heart consumed the remaining strength of his mind, his vivacity, and his acumen; he became a sad companion, unhappier all the time, and more unjust as he became more unhappy. At least that is what Albert's friends say; they assert that Werther was unable to judge properly a pure, calm man, who had now won a long-sought happiness, and his efforts to hold onto that happiness in the future, because he himself seemed to be using up all that he possessed every day, only to suffer and feel want at night. Albert, they say, had not changed in such a short time, he was still the same man that Werther knew from the outset, the man he had esteemed and respected. He loved Lotte above all else, he was proud of her and wanted her to be acknowledged by everyone else as the most splendid of women. Therefore was it to be held against him if he wished to avert any shadow of suspicion, if at that moment he had no mind to share that priceless possession with anyone else, even in the most innocent way? They admit that Albert often left his wife's room when Werther was with her, but not out of hatred or dislike of his friend, merely because he felt that Werther was uncomfortable in his presence.

Lotte's father had fallen ill with an ailment that kept him indoors; he sent her his carriage, and she drove out to see him. It was a fine winter's day, the first snowfall had been heavy and the whole neighborhood was covered with snow.

Werther followed her there the next morning to accompany her home in case Albert didn't come to get her.

The clear weather had little power to affect his gloomy mood, a numb pressure lay on his soul, mournful images had become fixed in his mind, and his spirits knew no motion except from one painful thought to another.

Since he lived in perpetual war with himself, the condition of others seemed all the more dubious and confused to him; he believed he had disrupted the beautiful relationship between Albert and his wife; he reproached himself for it, but a secret indignation against the husband mingled with the reproaches.

On this journey, too, his thoughts turned to that subject. "Yes, yes," he said to himself, secretly gnashing his teeth, "that's a trusting, friendly, loving helpmate, always sympathetic! Calm and lasting fidelity! It's really satedness and indifference! Isn't he more attracted by every wretched piece of business than by his dear, precious wife? Can he appreciate his good luck? Can he esteem her as she deserves? He has her, well and good, he has

ders auch weiß, ich glaube an den Gedanken gewöhnt zu sein, er wird mich noch rasend machen, er wird mich noch umbringen – Und hat denn die Freundschaft zu mir Stich gehalten? Sieht er nicht in meiner Anhänglichkeit an Lotten schon einen Eingriff in seine Rechte, in meiner Aufmerksamkeit für sie einen stillen Vorwurf? Ich weiß es wohl, ich fühl es, er sieht mich ungern, er wünscht meine Entfernung, meine Gegenwart ist ihm beschwerlich.

Oft hielt er seinen raschen Schritt an, oft stand er stille und schien umkehren zu wollen; allein er richtete seinen Gang immer wieder vorwärts und war mit diesen Gedanken und Selbstgesprächen endlich gleichsam wider Willen bei dem Jagdhause angekommen.

Er trat in die Tür, fragte nach dem Alten und nach Lotten, er fand das Haus in einiger Bewegung. Der älteste Knabe sagte ihm, es sei drüben in Wahlheim ein Unglück geschehn, es sei ein Bauer erschlagen worden! – Es machte das weiter keinen Eindruck auf ihn. – Er trat in die Stube und fand Lotten beschäftigt, dem Alten zuzureden, der ungeachtet seiner Krankheit hinüber wollte, um an Ort und Stelle die Tat zu untersuchen. Der Täter war noch unbekannt, man hatte den Erschlagenen des Morgens vor der Haustür gefunden, man hatte Mutmaßungen: der Entleibte war Knecht einer Witwe, die vorher einen andern im Dienste gehabt, der mit Unfrieden aus dem Hause gekommen war.

Da Werther dieses hörte, fuhr er mit Heftigkeit auf. – Ists möglich! rief er aus, ich muß hinüber, ich kann nicht einen Augenblick ruhn. – Er eilte nach Wahlheim zu, jede Erinnerung ward ihm lebendig, und er zweifelte nicht einen Augenblick, daß jener Mensch die Tat begangen, den er so manchmal gesprochen, der ihm so wert geworden war.

Da er durch die Linden mußte, um nach der Schenke zu kommen, wo sie den Körper hingelegt hatten, entsetzt' er sich vor dem sonst so geliebten Platze. Jene Schwelle, worauf die Nachbarskinder so oft gespielt hatten, war mit Blut besudelt. Liebe und Treue, die schönsten menschlichen Empfindungen, hatten sich in Gewalt und Mord verwandelt. Die starken Bäume standen ohne Laub und bereift, die schönen Hecken, die sich über die niedrige Kirchhofmauer wölbten, waren entblättert, und die Grabsteine sahen mit Schnee bedeckt durch die Lücken hervor.

Als er sich der Schenke näherte, vor welcher das ganze Dorf versammelt war, entstand auf einmal ein Geschrei. Man erblickte von fern einen Trupp bewaffneter Männer, und ein jeder rief, daß man den Täter herbeiführe. Werther sah hin und blieb nicht lange zweifel-

her— I know that, just as I also know something else; I think I've grown used to the idea, but it will still drive me crazy, it will still be the death of me— And has his friendship for me kept up? Doesn't he see in my attachment to Lotte an invasion of his rights, doesn't he detect a silent reproach in my attentions to her? I know it, I feel it, he hates the sight of me, he'd like me to be far away, my presence is hard for him to take."

Often he slackened his rapid pace, often he halted and seemed to want to go back; but he proceeded forward each time and, despite those ideas and soliloquies, he finally arrived at the hunting lodge, as if against his will.

He went in, inquired after the old man and Lotte, and found the house in some agitation. The eldest boy told him that a disaster had occurred over in Wahlheim, a farmer had been killed! —That made no special impression on him.—He entered the parlor and found Lotte busy arguing with the old man, who despite his illness wanted to ride over and investigate the crime right on the spot. The perpetrator was still unknown, the murdered man had been found in front of his house door in the morning, and people had assumptions: the victim was the servant of a widow who had previously employed another man, one that had left the household under a cloud.

When Werther heard this, he reacted violently. "Is it possible?" he exclaimed; "I must go out there, I can't rest for a minute." He hurried over to Wahlheim; every memory came to him vividly, and he didn't doubt for a moment that the crime had been committed by that fellow he had spoken with so often and had become so fond of.

When he had to pass by the lime trees to reach the inn, where the body had been brought, he was horrified by that spot he formerly loved so well. That threshold on which the local children had played so often was sullied with blood. Love and fidelity, the most beautiful human emotions, had changed into violence and murder. The mighty trees stood there leafless, covered with hoarfrost; the lovely hedges which arched over the low wall of the churchyard had no foliage, and the tombstones, covered with snow, appeared through the gaps.

When he approached the inn, in front of which the entire village was assembled, an outcry suddenly arose. In the distance could be seen a troop of armed men, and everyone shouted that they were bringing back the criminal. Werther saw him and

haft. Ja! es war der Knecht, der jene Witwe so sehr liebte, den er vor einiger Zeit mit dem stillen Grimme, mit der heimlichen Verzweiflung umhergehend angetroffen hatte.

Was hast du begangen, Unglücklicher! rief Werther aus, indem er auf den Gefangnen losging. – Dieser sah ihn still an, schwieg und versetzte endlich ganz gelassen: Keiner wird sie haben, sie wird keinen haben. – Man brachte den Gefangnen in die Schenke, und Werther eilte fort.

Durch die entsetzliche, gewaltige Berührung war alles, was in seinem Wesen lag, durcheinandergeschüttelt worden. Aus seiner Trauer, seinem Mißmut, seiner gleichgültigen Hingegebenheit wurde er auf einen Augenblick herausgerissen; unüberwindlich bemächtigte sich die Teilnehmung seiner, und es ergriff ihn eine unsägliche Begierde, den Menschen zu retten. Er fühlte ihn so unglücklich, er fand ihn als Verbrecher selbst so schuldlos, er setzte sich so tief in seine Lage, daß er gewiß glaubte, auch andere davon zu überzeugen. Schon wünschte er für ihn sprechen zu können, schon drängte sich der lebhafteste Vortrag nach seinen Lippen, er eilte nach dem Jagdhause und konnte sich unterwegs nicht enthalten, alles das, was er dem Amtmann vorstellen wollte, schon halb laut auszusprechen.

Als er in die Stube trat, fand er Alberten gegenwärtig, dies verstimmte ihn einen Augenblick; doch faßte er sich bald wieder und trug dem Amtmanne feurig seine Gesinnungen vor. Dieser schüttelte einigemal den Kopf, und obgleich Werther mit der größten Lebhaftigkeit, Leidenschaft und Wahrheit alles vorbrachte, was ein Mensch zur Entschuldigung eines Menschen sagen kann, so war doch, wie sichs leicht denken läßt, der Amtmann dadurch nicht gerührt. Er ließ vielmehr unsern Freund nicht ausreden, widersprach ihm eifrig und tadelte ihn, daß er einen Meuchelmörder in Schutz nehme! er zeigte ihm, daß auf diese Weise jedes Gesetz aufgehoben, alle Sicherheit des Staats zugrund gerichtet werde, auch setzte er hinzu, daß er in einer solchen Sache nichts tun könne, ohne sich die größte Verantwortung aufzuladen, es müsse alles in der Ordnung, in dem vorgeschriebenen Gang gehen.

Werther ergab sich noch nicht, sondern bat nur, der Amtmann möchte durch die Finger sehn, wenn man dem Menschen zur Flucht behülflich wäre! Auch damit wies ihn der Amtmann ab. Albert, der sich endlich ins Gespräch mischte, trat auch auf des Alten Seite; Werther wurde überstimmt, und mit einem entsetzlichen Leiden machte er sich auf den Weg, nachdem ihm der Amtmann einigemal gesagt hatte: Nein, er ist nicht zu retten!

Wie sehr ihm diese Worte aufgefallen sein müssen, sehn wir aus

didn't have doubts for very long. Yes, it was the farmhand who loved that widow so much, the man he had met some time before going around with that silent fury and secret despair. "What have you done, unlucky man!" Werther exclaimed as he walked up to the prisoner. The fellow looked at him quietly, remained silent, and finally replied with total calm: "No one will have her, she won't have anybody." The prisoner was led into the inn, and Werther left hastily.

His entire being was shaken up by that terrible, violent contact. For a moment he was plucked out of his sadness, moroseness, and indifferent resignation; irresistibly sympathy overpowered him, and he was gripped by an inexpressible urge to rescue the fellow. He felt him to be so unhappy, he found him so innocent even as a criminal, he put himself in his place so completely, that he surely believed he could convince others as well. He was already wishing he could speak in his behalf, the liveliest speech was already rising to his lips; he hastened to the hunting lodge and, on the way, he couldn't help pronouncing softly every allegation he wanted to make to the bailiff.

When he entered the parlor, he found Albert there, which spoiled his mood for a moment; but he soon regained his self-control and expounded his principles to the bailiff fervently. The bailiff shook his head a few times, and though Werther uttered all that one man can say to excuse another, as vivaciously, passionately, and sincerely as possible, nevertheless, as may well be imagined, the bailiff was completely unmoved. On the contrary, he didn't let our friend finish speaking, he contradicted him enthusiastically, and censured him for protecting an assassin! He pointed out to him that, by such doings, every law is abrogated, the entire security of the state is destroyed; he added that in such a case he could do nothing without incurring the gravest blame; everything must take its course in the prescribed manner.

Werther still didn't give up, but asked only that the bailiff wink an eye if someone helped the fellow escape! This, too, the bailiff rejected. Albert, who finally joined the conversation, took the old man's part; Werther was outvoted, and in terrific sorrow he set out again, after the bailiff had told him a few times: "No, he can't be saved!"

How strong an impression those words must have made on

einem Zettelchen, das sich unter seinen Papieren fand, und das gewiß
an dem nämlichen Tage geschrieben worden:
    Du bist nicht zu retten, Unglücklicher! ich sehe wohl, daß wir nicht
zu retten sind.

    Was Albert zuletzt über die Sache des Gefangenen in Gegenwart
des Amtmanns gesprochen, war Werthern höchst zuwider gewesen:
er glaubte einige Empfindlichkeit gegen sich darin bemerkt zu haben,
und wenn gleich bei mehrerem Nachdenken seinem Scharfsinne
nicht entging, daß beide Männer recht haben möchten, so war es ihm
doch, als ob er seinem innersten Dasein entsagen müßte, wenn er es
gestehen, wenn er es zugeben sollte.
    Ein Blättchen, das sich darauf bezieht, das vielleicht sein ganzes
Verhältnis zu Albert ausdrückt, finden wir unter seinen Papieren:
    Was hilft es, daß ich mirs sage und wieder sage, er ist brav und gut, aber
es zerreißt mir mein inneres Eingeweide; ich kann nicht gerecht sein.

    Weil es ein gelinder Abend war und das Wetter anfing, sich zum
Tauen zu neigen, ging Lotte mit Alberten zu Fuße zurück. Unterwegs
sah sie sich hier und da um, eben als wenn sie Werthers Begleitung
vermißte. Albert fing von ihm an zu reden, er tadelte ihn, indem er
ihm Gerechtigkeit widerfahren ließ. Er berührte seine unglückliche
Leidenschaft und wünschte, daß es möglich sein möchte, ihn zu entfernen. – Ich wünsch es auch um unsertwillen, sagt' er, und ich bitte
dich, fuhr er fort, siehe zu, seinem Betragen gegen dich eine andere
Richtung zu geben, seine öftern Besuche zu vermindern. Die Leute
werden aufmerksam, und ich weiß, daß man hier und da drüber
gesprochen hat. – Lotte schwieg, und Albert schien ihr Schweigen
empfunden zu haben; wenigstens seit der Zeit erwähnte er Werthers
nicht mehr gegen sie, und wenn sie seiner erwähnte, ließ er das
Gespräch fallen oder lenkte es wo anders hin.
    Der vergebliche Versuch, den Werther zur Rettung des Unglück-
lichen gemacht hatte, war das letzte Auflodern der Flamme eines ver-
löschenden Lichtes; er versank nur desto tiefer in Schmerz und
Untätigkeit; besonders kam er fast außer sich, als er hörte, daß man
ihn vielleicht gar zum Zeugen gegen den Menschen, der sich nun aufs
Leugnen legte, auffordern könnte.
    Alles, was ihm Unangenehmes jemals in seinem wirksamen Leben
begegnet war, der Verdruß bei der Gesandtschaft, alles, was ihm sonst
mißlungen war, was ihn je gekränkt hatte, ging in seiner Seele auf und
nieder. Er fand sich durch alles dieses wie zur Untätigkeit berechtigt,

him we can gather from a note that was found among his papers, and which was surely written on the same day:

"You can't be saved, unlucky man! I see clearly that we can't be saved."

What Albert had finally said about the prisoner's case in the bailiff's presence had been extremely repugnant to Werther: he thought he could detect in it some resentment against himself, and even though, after some reflection, it couldn't escape his good sense that the two men might be right, nevertheless he felt as if he'd have to renounce his fundamental character if he admitted it and conceded their point.

A little note with regard to this, which perhaps expresses his entire relationship to Albert, was found among his papers:

"What good is it if I tell myself over and over again that he's steady and kind? It rips up my vitals, I can't be fair about it."

Because it was a mild evening and a thaw was setting in, Lotte walked back home with Albert. On the way she looked around here and there, just as if she missed Werther's company. Albert began talking about him, censuring him but also doing him justice. He mentioned his unfortunate passion and wished it were possible to be rid of him. "I also wish it for our own sake," he said, and he continued: "Please make an effort to give another direction to his behavior toward you and cut down on the number of his visits. People are starting to notice, and I know it's been discussed here and there." Lotte was silent, and Albert seemed to have taken her silence to heart; anyway, after that time, he no longer mentioned Werther to her, and if *she* mentioned him, he let the subject drop or changed it to something else.

The fruitless attempt Werther had made to save the unfortunate farmhand was the final flaring up of a light that was going out; he sank all the more deeply into sorrow and inactivity; in particular, he was nearly beside himself when he heard that he might even be summoned as a witness against the man, who was now denying his guilt.

Everything unpleasant that had ever happened to him in his active existence, his vexation at the embassy, everything else that had gone wrong for him, that had ever hurt him, was constantly on his mind. He found that all this justified his inactiv-

er fand sich abgeschnitten von aller Aussicht, unfähig, irgend eine
Handhabe zu ergreifen, mit denen man die Geschäfte des gemeinen
Lebens anfaßt, und so rückte er endlich, ganz seiner wunderbaren
Empfindung, Denkart und einer endlosen Leidenschaft hingegeben,
in dem ewigen Einerlei eines traurigen Umgangs mit dem liebens-
würdigen und geliebten Geschöpfe, dessen Ruhe er störte, in seine
Kräfte stürmend, sie ohne Zweck und Aussicht abarbeitend, immer
einem traurigen Ende näher.

Von seiner Verworrenheit, Leidenschaft, von seinem rastlosen
Treiben und Streben, von seiner Lebensmüde sind einige hinterlaßne
Briefe die stärksten Zeugnisse, die wir hier einrücken wollen:

Am 12. Dezember.

Lieber Wilhelm, ich bin in einem Zustande, in dem jene Unglücklichen gewesen sein müssen, von denen man glaubte, sie würden von
einem bösen Geiste umhergetrieben. Manchmal ergreift michs; es ist
nicht Angst, nicht Begier – es ist ein inneres unbekanntes Toben, das
meine Brust zu zerreißen droht, das mir die Gurgel zupreßt! Wehe!
wehe! und dann schweife ich umher in den furchtbaren nächtlichen
Szenen dieser menschenfeindlichen Jahrszeit.

Gestern abend mußte ich hinaus. Es war plötzlich Tauwetter einge-
fallen, ich hatte gehört, der Fluß sei übergetreten, alle Bäche
geschwollen und von Wahlheim herunter mein liebes Tal überschwemmt! Nachts nach eilfe rannte ich hinaus. Ein fürchterliches
Schauspiel, vom Fels herunter die wühlenden Fluten in dem
Mondlichte wirbeln zu sehen, über Äcker und Wiesen und Hecken
und alles, und das weite Tal hinauf und hinab Eine stürmende See im
Sausen des Windes! Und wenn dann der Mond wieder hervortrat und
über der schwarzen Wolke ruhte und vor mir hinaus die Flut in
fürchterlich herrlichem Widerschein rollte und klang: da überfiel
mich ein Schauer und wieder ein Sehnen! Ach, mit offenen Armen
stand ich gegen den Abgrund und atmete hinab! hinab! und verlor
mich in der Wonne, meine Qualen, mein Leiden da hinabzustürmen!
dahinzubrausen wie die Wellen! Oh! – und den Fuß vom Boden zu
heben vermochtest du nicht und alle Qualen zu enden! – Meine Uhr
ist noch nicht ausgelaufen, ich fühle es! O Wilhelm! Wie gern hätte
ich mein Menschsein drum gegeben, mit jenem Sturmwinde die
Wolken zu zerreißen, die Fluten zu fassen! Ha! und wird nicht vielleicht dem Eingekerkerten einmal diese Wonne zuteil? –

Und wie ich wehmütig hinabsah auf ein Plätzchen, wo ich mit
Lotten unter einer Weide geruht, auf einem heißen Spaziergange, –

ity, he found himself cut off from all prospects, unable to grasp any handle on the business of everyday life, and so finally, completely the prisoner of his odd emotions, way of thinking, and endless passion, in the eternal monotony of a dream intercourse with the lovable and beloved woman whose repose he was disturbing, raging against his powers and consuming them without a goal or prospects, he drew ever closer to a sad ending.

The most eloquent witnesses to his confusion and passion, his unceasing stirring and striving, and his weariness of life are some of the letters he left behind, which we insert in this place:

"December 12
"Dear Wilhelm, I'm in a state that those unfortunates must have been in who were thought to be possessed by an evil spirit. Sometimes it comes over me; it's not fear, it's not desire—it's an unknown inward raging that threatens to tear open my breast, that squeezes my gullet shut! Woe! Woe! And then I roam about in the fearful nocturnal scenes of this season so hostile to man.

"Last night I had to get out. A thaw had suddenly set in; I had heard the river had overflowed, all the brooks were swollen, and my lovely valley submerged below Wahlheim! After eleven at night I dashed out. A frightful scene, to see the churning waters eddying in the moonlight down from the crag, over cultivated fields, meadows, hedges, and all, and up and down the wide valley a single raging sea in the roaring of the wind! And when the moon came out again, resting above the dark clouds, and the waters rolled past in front of me with a terribly magnificent reflection and bellow: I was overcome by a shudder and again by a longing! Ah, I stood there with open eyes facing the abyss and breathed 'Down! Down!' and I was lost in the rapture of freeing myself from torment and sorrow by leaping down and flowing away with the noisy billows! Oh—and you were unable to lift a foot from the ground and end all your torture!—My time has not yet run out, I feel it! Oh, Wilhelm! How gladly I would have given up my human existence to be able to rip apart the clouds along with that storm wind, to embrace the waters! Ha! Won't that rapture ever fall to the lot of this prisoner?—

"And as I looked down in melancholy at a spot where I had rested with Lotte under a willow during one warm stroll—it,

das war auch überschwemmt, und kaum daß ich die Weide erkannte!
Wilhelm! Und ihre Wiesen, dachte ich, die Gegend um ihr Jagdhaus!
wie verstört jetzt vom reißenden Strome unsere Laube! dacht ich.
Und der Vergangenheit Sonnenstrahl blickte herein wie einem
Gefangenen ein Traum von Herden, Wiesen und Ehrenämtern! Ich
stand! – Ich schelte mich nicht, denn ich habe Mut zu sterben. – Ich
hätte – Nun sitze ich hier wie ein altes Weib, das ihr Holz von
Zäunen stoppelt und ihr Brot an den Türen, um ihr hinsterbendes
freudeloses Dasein noch einen Augenblick zu verlängern und zu
erleichtern.

Am 14. Dezember.

Was ist das, mein Lieber? Ich erschrecke vor mir selbst! Ist nicht
meine Liebe zu ihr die heiligste, reinste, brüderlichste Liebe? Habe
ich jemals einen strafbaren Wunsch in meiner Seele gefühlt? – Ich will
nicht beteuern – Und nun, Träume! O wie wahr fühlten die Menschen,
die so widersprechende Wirkungen fremden Mächten zuschrieben!
Diese Nacht! ich zittere, es zu sagen, hielt ich sie in meinen Armen,
fest an meinen Busen gedrückt, und deckte ihren liebelispelnden
Mund mit unendlichen Küssen; mein Auge schwamm in der
Trunkenheit des ihrigen! Gott! bin ich strafbar, daß ich auch jetzt noch
eine Seligkeit fühle, mir diese glühenden Freuden mit voller Innigkeit
zurückzurufen? Lotte! Lotte! – Und mit mir ist es aus! meine Sinnen
verwirren sich, schon acht Tage habe ich keine Besinnungskraft mehr,
meine Augen sind voll Tränen. Ich bin nirgend wohl und überall wohl.
Ich wünsche nichts, ich verlange nichts. Mir wäre besser, ich ginge.

Der Entschluß, die Welt zu verlassen, hatte in dieser Zeit, unter
solchen Umständen in Werthers Seele immer mehr Kraft gewonnen.
Seit der Rückkehr zu Lotten war es immer seine letzte Aussicht und
Hoffnung gewesen; doch hatte er sich gesagt, es solle keine übereilte,
keine rasche Tat sein, er wolle mit der besten Überzeugung, mit der
möglichst ruhigen Entschlossenheit diesen Schritt tun.
    Seine Zweifel, sein Streit mit sich selbst blicken aus einem Zettel-
chen hervor, das wahrscheinlich ein angefangener Brief an Wilhelm
ist und ohne Datum unter seinen Papieren gefunden worden:

Ihre Gegenwart, ihr Schicksal, ihre Teilnehmung an dem meinigen
preßt noch die letzten Tränen aus meinem versengten Gehirne.
    Den Vorhang aufzuheben und dahinterzutreten! Das ist alles! Und
warum das Zaudern und Zagen? Weil man nicht weiß, wie es dahin-

too, was submerged and I could hardly make out the willow! Wilhelm! 'And her meadows,' I thought 'the area around her hunting lodge! How wrecked our arbor must now be by the raging river!' I thought. And the sunbeam of the past shone on me, as a dream of flocks, meadows, and honorable positions shines on a prisoner! I stood there!—I don't upbraid myself, because I have the courage to die.—I could have— Now I'm sitting here like an old woman who gathers her firewood from fences and begs for bread at doorways in order to prolong her declining, joyless existence by another minute, and make it easier."

"December 14
"What's this, dear friend? I'm frightened at myself! Isn't my love for her the most sacred, pure, and brotherly love? Have I ever felt a blameworthy wish in my soul?—I won't asseverate— And now, dreams! Oh, how truly those people felt things who ascribed such contradictory effects to outside powers! Last night—I tremble to say it—I held her in my arms, pressed tightly to my breast, and I covered her lips, which whispered of love, with infinite kisses; my eyes were rolling in the intoxication of hers! God! Am I blameworthy if I still feel bliss in recalling those ardent joys with the deepest intimacy? Lotte! Lotte!—And it's all over for me! My senses are confused, for a week I haven't really been conscious, my eyes are filled with tears. I don't feel good anywhere I am, and I feel good everywhere. I wish for nothing, I ask for nothing. It would be better for me if I left."

In these circumstances the decision to leave the world had taken an increasingly firm hold of Werther's soul during those days. Ever since he had returned to Lotte, it had always been his final prospect and hope, but he had told himself that it mustn't be a hasty, swift action; he wanted to take that step with the fullest conviction and with the calmest determination possible.

His doubts, his fight with himself, can be seen in a note that was probably the beginning of a letter to Wilhelm; it was undated and found among his papers:

"Her presence, her destiny, her sympathy for mine, can still squeeze the last tears out of my scorched brain.

"To lift the curtain and step behind it! That's all! Why this timid shilly-shallying? Because no one knows what's behind it

ten aussieht? und man nicht wiederkehrt? Und daß das nun die
Eigenschaft unseres Geistes ist, da Verwirrung und Finsternis zu
ahnen, wovon wir nichts Bestimmtes wissen. –

Endlich ward er mit dem traurigen Gedanken immer mehr ver-
wandt und befreundet, und sein Vorsatz fest und unwiderruflich,
wovon folgender zweideutige Brief, den er an seinen Freund schrieb,
ein Zeugnis abgibt:

Am 20. Dezember.
Ich danke deiner Liebe, Wilhelm, daß du das Wort so aufgefangen
hast. Ja, du hast recht: mir wäre besser, ich ginge. Der Vorschlag, den
du zu einer Rückkehr zu euch tust, gefällt mir nicht ganz; wenigstens
möchte ich noch gern einen Umweg machen, besonders da wir an-
haltenden Frost und gute Wege zu hoffen haben. Auch ist mir es sehr
lieb, daß du kommen willst, mich abzuholen; verziehe nur noch
vierzehn Tage und erwarte noch einen Brief von mir mit dem
Weiteren. Es ist nötig, daß nichts gepflückt werde, ehe es reif ist. Und
vierzehn Tage auf oder ab tun viel. Meiner Mutter sollst du sagen: daß
sie für ihren Sohn beten soll und daß ich sie um Vergebung bitte
wegen alles Verdrusses, den ich ihr gemacht habe. Das war nun mein
Schicksal, die zu betrüben, denen ich Freude schuldig war. Leb wohl,
mein Teuerster! Allen Segen des Himmels über dich! Leb wohl!

Was in dieser Zeit in Lottens Seele vorging, wie ihre Gesinnungen
gegen ihren Mann, gegen ihren unglücklichen Freund gewesen, ge-
trauen wir uns kaum mit Worten auszudrücken, ob wir uns gleich
davon, nach der Kenntnis ihres Charakters, wohl einen stillen Begriff
machen können und eine schöne weibliche Seele sich in die ihrige
denken und mit ihr empfinden kann.

Soviel ist gewiß, sie war fest bei sich entschlossen, alles zu tun, um
Werthern zu entfernen, und wenn sie zauderte, so war es eine herz-
liche, freundschaftliche Schonung, weil sie wußte, wie viel es ihm
kosten, ja daß es ihm beinahe unmöglich sein würde. Doch ward sie
in dieser Zeit mehr gedrängt, Ernst zu machen; es schwieg ihr Mann
ganz über dies Verhältnis, wie sie auch immer darüber geschwiegen
hatte, und um so mehr war ihr angelegen, ihm durch die Tat zu be-
weisen, wie ihre Gesinnungen der seinigen wert seien.

An demselben Tage, als Werther den zuletzt eingeschalteten Brief
an seinen Freund geschrieben, es war der Sonntag vor Weihnachten,
kam er abends zu Lotten und fand sie allein. Sie beschäftigte sich,

and no one returns? And because our mind is so constituted that it has a foreboding of chaos and darkness when confronted by things of which we have no definite knowledge.—"

Finally he became more and more attuned and at home with that sad idea, and his resolve became firm and irrevocable, as shown by the following ambiguous letter he wrote to his friend:

"*December 20*

"I gratefully attribute it to your love for me, Wilhelm, that you understood my words in that sense. Yes, you're right: it would be better for me if I left. Your proposal that I rejoin you and your circle doesn't quite please me; at least, I'd still like to make a detour, especially since we have hopes of steady frost and good roads. It's also very gratifying to me that you're willing to come and pick me up; but wait another two weeks; I'll send you a letter with further details. It's important for nothing to be gathered before it's ripe. And two weeks one way or another make a big difference. Please tell my mother to pray for her son; say I ask her forgiveness for all the vexation I've caused her. It was simply my fate to sadden those to whom I owed joy. Farewell, dearest friend! All the blessings of heaven on you! Farewell!"

We scarcely dare to express in words what was going on in Lotte's soul during this time, what her attitude was toward her husband and her unhappy friend, although we can surely conceive of this tacitly from our knowledge of her character, and a beautiful feminine soul can both think and feel in sympathetic vibration with hers.

This much is certain: she was firmly resolved to do everything to keep Werther at a distance; if she hesitated, it was to spare him in a cordial, friendly way, because she knew how much it would cost him, she knew it would be nearly impossible for him. But during this time there was more pressure on her to take a serious step; her husband was totally silent about that relationship, just as she had always been, and this made her more concerned to prove to him by some actual deed that her principles were as noble as his.

On the very day that Werther wrote his friend the letter that has just been inserted—it was the Sunday before Christmas—he visited Lotte in the evening and found her alone. She was busy

einige Spielwerke in Ordnung zu bringen, die sie ihren kleinen Geschwistern zum Christgeschenke zurechtgemacht hatte. Er redete
von dem Vergnügen, das die Kleinen haben würden, und von den
Zeiten, da einen die unerwartete Öffnung der Tür und die
Erscheinung eines aufgeputzten Baumes mit Wachslichtern,
Zuckerwerk und Äpfeln in paradiesische Entzückung setzte. – Sie
sollen, sagte Lotte, indem sie ihre Verlegenheit unter ein liebes
Lächeln verbarg, Sie sollen auch beschert kriegen, wenn Sie recht
geschickt sind; ein Wachsstöckchen und noch was. – Und was heißen
Sie geschickt sein? rief er aus; wie soll ich sein? wie kann ich sein?
beste Lotte! – Donnerstag abend, sagte sie, ist Weihnachtsabend, da
kommen die Kinder, mein Vater auch, da kriegt jedes das seinige, da
kommen Sie auch – aber nicht eher. – Werther stutzte. – Ich bitte Sie,
fuhr sie fort, es ist nun einmal so, ich bitte Sie um meiner Ruhe
willen, es kann nicht, es kann nicht so bleiben. – Er wendete seine
Augen von ihr und ging in der Stube auf und ab und murmelte das:
‚Es kann nicht so bleiben!‘ zwischen den Zähnen. Lotte, die den
schrecklichen Zustand fühlte, worein ihn diese Worte versetzt hatten,
suchte durch allerlei Fragen seine Gedanken abzulenken, aber
vergebens. – Nein, Lotte, rief er aus, ich werde Sie nicht wiedersehen! – Warum das? versetzte sie, Werther, Sie können, Sie müssen
uns wiedersehen, nur mäßigen Sie sich. O, warum mußten Sie mit
dieser Heftigkeit, dieser unbezwinglich haftenden Leidenschaft für
alles, was Sie einmal anfassen, geboren werden! Ich bitte Sie, fuhr sie
fort, indem sie ihn bei der Hand nahm, mäßigen Sie sich! Ihr Geist,
Ihre Wissenschaften, Ihre Talente, was bieten die Ihnen für mannigfaltige Ergetzungen dar! Sein Sie ein Mann! Wenden Sie diese traurige Anhänglichkeit von einem Geschöpf, das nichts tun kann als Sie
bedauern. – Er knirrte mit den Zähnen und sah sie düster an. Sie
hielt seine Hand: Nur einen Augenblick ruhigen Sinn, Werther! sagte
sie. Fühlen Sie nicht, daß Sie sich betrügen, sich mit Willen zugrunde
richten! Warum denn mich, Werther? just mich, das Eigentum eines
andern? just das? Ich fürchte, ich fürchte, es ist nur die Unmöglich-
keit, mich zu besitzen, die Ihnen diesen Wunsch so reizend macht. –
Er zog seine Hand aus der ihrigen, indem er sie mit einem starren,
unwilligen Blick ansah. – Weise! rief er, sehr weise! hat vielleicht
Albert diese Anmerkung gemacht? Politisch! sehr politisch! – Es kann
sie jeder machen, versetzte sie drauf. Und sollte denn in der weiten
Welt kein Mädchen sein, das die Wünsche Ihres Herzens erfüllte?
Gewinnen Sie's über sich, suchen Sie darnach, und ich schwöre
Ihnen, Sie werden sie finden; denn schon lange ängstet mich, für Sie

arranging some toys which she had prepared as holiday gifts for her little brothers and sisters. He spoke about the pleasure they would give the children and about the days when the unexpected opening of the door and the revelation of an ornamented tree with wax candles, candy, and apples sent a child off into heavenly rapture. Lotte, concealing her embarrassment with a charming smile, said: "You'll get a present, too, if you behave properly: a wax light and more." "And what do you call behaving?" he exclaimed. "How should I be? How can I be? Dear Lotte!" She replied: "Thursday night is Christmas Eve; the children will come, and so will my father; then everyone will get his own present. You come, too—but not before then." Werther gave a start. "I implore you," she continued, "that's the way it must be, I implore you for my peace of mind, things just can't remain this way." He averted his eyes from her and paced up and down the parlor, muttering between his teeth: "Things can't remain this way!" Lotte, who sensed the dreadful state her words had put him in, tried to divert his thoughts with all sorts of questions, but in vain. "No, Lotte," he exclaimed, "I'll never see you again!" "Why?" she replied. "Werther, you can, you must see us again, only in moderation. Oh, why did you have to be born with such impetuousness, such uncontrollably clinging passion for everything you once touch! I implore you," she continued, taking him by the hand, "use moderation! Your mind, your knowledge, your talents offer you so many delights! Be a man! Get rid of this unhappy attachment for a person who can only pity you!" He gnashed his teeth and looked at her gloomily. She was holding his hand. "Just one moment of calm thinking, Werther!" she said. "Don't you sense that you're deceiving yourself, voluntarily destroying yourself? And why me, Werther? Why me, when I belong to another man? This, and nothing else? I fear, I fear that it's only the impossibility of possessing me which makes that desire so alluring to you." He drew his hand away from hers, staring at her with a rigid, indignant gaze. "Prudent!" he cried. "Very prudent! Did Albert make that remark, perhaps? Diplomatic! Very diplomatic!" "Anyone can make that observation," she retorted. "In the whole wide world can't there be some single girl who could make the wishes of your heart come true? Make up your mind to it, look for her, and I swear to you that you'll find her; because, for your sake and ours, I've long been worried about the seclusion in which you've

und uns, die Einschränkung, in die Sie sich diese Zeit her selbst
gebannt haben. Gewinnen Sie es über sich! eine Reise wird Sie, muß
Sie zerstreuen! Suchen Sie, finden Sie einen werten Gegenstand
Ihrer Liebe und kehren Sie zurück, und lassen Sie uns zusammen die
Seligkeit einer wahren Freundschaft genießen.

Das könnte man, sagte er mit einem kalten Lachen, drucken lassen
und allen Hofmeistern empfehlen. Liebe Lotte! lassen Sie mir noch
ein klein wenig Ruh, es wird alles werden! – Nur das, Werther, daß Sie
nicht eher kommen als Weihnachtsabend! – Er wollte antworten, und
Albert trat in die Stube. Man bot sich einen frostigen Guten Abend
und ging verlegen im Zimmer neben einander auf und nieder.
Werther fing einen unbedeutenden Diskurs an, der bald aus war,
Albert desgleichen, der sodann seine Frau nach gewissen Aufträgen
fragte und, als er hörte, sie seien noch nicht ausgerichtet, ihr einige
Worte sagte, die Werthern kalt, ja gar hart vorkamen. Er wollte gehen,
er konnte nicht und zauderte bis acht, da sich denn sein Unmut und
Unwillen immer vermehrte, bis der Tisch gedeckt wurde und er Hut
und Stock nahm. Albert lud ihn zu bleiben, er aber, der nur ein unbedeutendes Kompliment zu hören glaubte, dankte kalt dagegen und
ging weg.

Er kam nach Hause, nahm seinem Burschen, der ihm leuchten
wollte, das Licht aus der Hand und ging allein in sein Zimmer, weinte
laut, redete aufgebracht mit sich selbst, ging heftig die Stube auf und
ab und warf sich endlich in seinen Kleidern aufs Bette, wo ihn der
Bediente fand, der es gegen eilfe wagte hineinzugehen, um zu fragen,
ob er dem Herrn die Stiefeln ausziehen sollte? das er denn zuließ und
dem Bedienten verbot, den andern Morgen ins Zimmer zu kommen,
bis er ihm rufen würde.

Montags früh, den einundzwanzigsten Dezember, schrieb er folgenden Brief an Lotten, den man nach seinem Tode versiegelt auf
seinem Schreibtische gefunden und ihr überbracht hat und den ich
absatzweise hier einrücken will, so wie aus den Umständen erhellet,
daß er ihn geschrieben habe.

Es ist beschlossen, Lotte, ich will sterben, und das schreibe ich dir
ohne romantische Überspannung, gelassen, an dem Morgen des
Tages, an dem ich dich zum letzten Male sehen werde. Wenn du
dieses liesest, meine Beste, deckt schon das kühle Grab die erstarrten
Reste des Unruhigen, Unglücklichen, der für die letzten Augenblicke
seines Lebens keine größere Süßigkeit weiß, als sich mit dir zu un-

confined yourself for some time now. Make up your mind to it! A journey will distract you, it must! Seek and find a worthy object of your love and then come back so we can enjoy the bliss of a true friendship, all of us together."

With a cold laugh he said: "That's a fine text for a book, which could be recommended to every tutor. Lotte dear! Leave me just a little more time, and it will all come about!" "Just one thing, Werther: don't come here before Christmas Eve!" He wanted to reply when Albert entered the parlor. They said good evening frostily and, in embarrassment, paced up and down the room side by side. Werther began an insignificant conversation, which was soon over, and Albert did the same; then he asked his wife about certain chores and, hearing that they had not yet been done, he said a few words to her which struck Werther as being cold or even harsh. He wanted to leave, but couldn't, and lingered till eight; then his distress and indignation increased, until the table was set and he picked up his hat and stick. Albert invited him to stay, but he, thinking it was merely an insincere courtesy, declined coldly and left.

He came home, took the candle out of the hand of his young servant, who wanted to light his way, and went alone to his room, where he wept aloud, talked excitedly to himself, paced up and down the room impetuously, and finally flung himself onto his bed fully dressed. There he was found by his servant, who ventured to go in at about eleven to ask whether he should pull off his master's boots. Werther allowed him to do so, then he forbade the servant to enter his room the following morning until he was called.

Early Monday morning, December twenty-first, he wrote the following letter to Lotte, which after his death was found sealed on his desk and was delivered to her. I wish to insert this letter here in the separate sections in which he wrote it, as the circumstances make clear.

"I'm determined, Lotte, I want to die, and I'm writing to tell you this without any romantic exaggeration, calmly, on the morning of the day on which I shall see you for the last time. When you read this, dearest, the cold grave will already cover the stiff remains of the restless, unfortunate man who knows of no greater pleasure in the final moments of his life than to speak

terhalten. Ich habe eine schreckliche Nacht gehabt und ach! eine wohltätige Nacht. Sie ist es, die meinen Entschluß befestigt, bestimmt hat: ich will sterben! Wie ich mich gestern von dir riß, in der fürchterlichen Empörung meiner Sinnen, wie sich alles das nach meinem Herzen drängte und mein hoffnungsloses, freudeloses Dasein neben dir in gräßlicher Kälte mich anpackte – ich erreichte kaum mein Zimmer, ich warf mich außer mir auf meine Knie, und o Gott! du gewährtest mir das letzte Labsal der bittersten Tränen! Tausend Anschläge, tausend Aussichten wüteten durch meine Seele, und zuletzt stand er da, fest, ganz, der letzte, einzige Gedanke: ich will sterben! – Ich legte mich nieder, und morgens, in der Ruhe des Erwachens, steht er noch fest, noch ganz stark in meinem Herzen: ich will sterben! – Es ist nicht Verzweiflung, es ist Gewißheit, daß ich ausgetragen habe und daß ich mich opfere für dich. Ja, Lotte! warum sollte ich es verschweigen? Eins von uns dreien muß hinweg, und das will ich sein! O meine Beste! in diesem zerrissenen Herzen ist es wütend herumgeschlichen, oft – deinen Mann zu ermorden! – dich! mich! – So sei es! – Wenn du hinaufsteigst auf den Berg, an einem schönen Sommerabende, dann erinnere dich meiner, wie ich so oft das Tal heraufkam, und dann blicke nach dem Kirchhofe hinüber nach meinem Grabe, wie der Wind das hohe Gras im Scheine der sinkenden Sonne hin- und herwiegt – Ich war ruhig, da ich anfing; nun, nun weine ich wie ein Kind, da alles das so lebhaft um mich wird. –

Gegen zehn Uhr rief Werther seinem Bedienten, und unter dem Anziehen sagte er ihm: wie er in einigen Tagen verreisen würde, er solle daher die Kleider auskehren und alles zum Einpacken zurechtmachen; auch gab er ihm Befehl, überall Kontos zu fordern, einige ausgeliehene Bücher abzuholen und einigen Armen, denen er wöchentlich etwas zu geben gewohnt war, ihr Zugeteiltes auf zwei Monate voraus zu bezahlen.

Er ließ sich das Essen auf die Stube bringen, und nach Tische ritt er hinaus zum Amtmanne, den er nicht zu Hause antraf. Er ging tiefsinnig im Garten auf und ab und schien noch zuletzt alle Schwermut der Erinnerung auf sich häufen zu wollen.

Die Kleinen ließen ihn nicht lange in Ruhe, sie verfolgten ihn, sprangen an ihm hinauf, erzählten ihm: daß, wenn morgen, und wieder morgen, und noch ein Tag wäre, sie die Christgeschenke bei Lotten holten, und erzählten ihm Wunder, die sich ihre kleine Einbildungskraft versprach. – Morgen! rief er aus, und wieder morgen! und noch ein Tag! – und küßte sie alle herzlich und wollte sie ver-

with you. I had a terrible night, but also a beneficial night. It is
this night which has fortified my resolve and made it firm: I want
to die! When I tore myself away from you yesterday, all my
senses in a fearful frenzy, when everything you said crowded in
on my heart and I was gripped by a gruesome chill at the real-
ization that my existence alongside you was hopeless and joyless—as soon as I reached my room, I fell on my knees, beside
myself, and, O God, you granted me that final consolation: the
bitterest tears! A thousand plans, a thousand prospects were raging in my soul, and finally there it was, firm, entire, the last, the
sole thought: I want to die!—I lay down and now, in the morning, in the calm of awakening, it's still firm and very strong in my
heart: I want to die!—It's not despair, it's the certainty that my
suffering is over and that I'm sacrificing myself for you. Yes,
Lotte! Why should I conceal it? One of us three must disappear,
and I want it to be me! Oh, my dearest! In my confused heart
the furious idea has often lurked—to kill your husband!—or
you!—or myself!—So be it!—When you climb the mountain
some fine summer afternoon, remember me, how often I came
up the valley, and then look across to the churchyard at my
grave, where the wind is blowing the tall grass back and forth in
the glow of the setting sun.—I was calm when I began this; now,
now I'm weeping like a child, with all this coming to my mind so
vividly."

About ten, Werther summoned his valet and, while dressing,
he told him he'd make a trip in a few days, so he should brush
his clothes and prepare everything for packing; he also ordered
him to ask for all his bills, to retrieve some books he had lent
people, and to make a two-months' advance payment to some
paupers whom he customarily gave something weekly.

He had his breakfast brought to the parlor and, after eating,
he rode out to visit the bailiff, who wasn't home. He walked up
and down the garden pensively, seemingly wishing to heap all
the melancholy of recollection onto himself at the last.

The children didn't give him peace for very long; they dogged his
steps, they jumped onto him, and they told him: after tomorrow,
and another tomorrow, and one more day, they'd get their
Christmas gifts at Lotte's house; they told him of the marvels their
young imagination led them to expect. "Tomorrow!" he exclaimed.
"And another tomorrow! And one more day!" And he kissed them

lassen, als ihm der Kleine noch etwas in das Ohr sagen wollte. Der verriet ihm, die großen Brüder hätten schöne Neujahrswünsche geschrieben, *so* groß! und einen für den Papa, für Albert und Lotte einen und auch einen für Herrn Werther; die wollten sie am Neujahrstage früh überreichen. Das übermannte ihn, er schenkte jedem etwas, setzte sich zu Pferde, ließ den Alten grüßen und ritt mit Tränen in den Augen davon.

Gegen fünf kam er nach Hause, befahl der Magd, nach dem Feuer zu sehen und es bis in die Nacht zu unterhalten. Den Bedienten hieß er Bücher und Wäsche unten in den Koffer packen und die Kleider einnähen. Darauf schrieb er wahrscheinlich folgenden Absatz seines letzten Briefes an Lotten:

Du erwartest mich nicht! du glaubst, ich würde gehorchen und erst Weihnachtsabend dich wiedersehn. O, Lotte! heut oder nie mehr. Weihnachtsabend hältst du dieses Papier in deiner Hand, zitterst und benetzest es mit deinen lieben Tränen. Ich will, ich muß! O, wie wohl ist es mir, daß ich entschlossen bin. –

Lotte war indes in einen sonderbaren Zustand geraten. Nach der letzten Unterredung mit Werthern hatte sie empfunden, wie schwer es ihr fallen werde, sich von ihm zu trennen, was er leiden würde, wenn er sich von ihr entfernen sollte.

Es war wie im Vorübergehn in Alberts Gegenwart gesagt worden, daß Werther vor Weihnachtsabend nicht wiederkommen werde, und Albert war zu einem Beamten in der Nachbarschaft geritten, mit dem er Geschäfte abzutun hatte und wo er über Nacht ausbleiben mußte.

Sie saß nun allein, keins von ihren Geschwistern war um sie, sie überließ sich ihren Gedanken, die stille über ihren Verhältnissen herumschweiften. Sie sah sich nun mit dem Mann auf ewig verbunden, dessen Liebe und Treue sie kannte, dem sie von Herzen zugetan war, dessen Ruhe, dessen Zuverlässigkeit recht vom Himmel dazu bestimmt zu sein schien, daß eine wackere Frau das Glück ihres Lebens darauf gründen sollte; sie fühlte, was er ihr und ihren Kindern auf immer sein würde. Auf der andern Seite war ihr Werther so teuer geworden, gleich von dem ersten Augenblick ihrer Bekanntschaft an hatte sich die Übereinstimmung ihrer Gemüter so schön gezeigt, der lange dauernde Umgang mit ihm, so manche durchlebten Situationen hatten einen unauslöschlichen Eindruck auf ihr Herz gemacht. Alles, was sie Interessantes fühlte und dachte, war sie gewohnt mit ihm zu teilen, und seine Entfernung drohete in ihr ganzes Wesen eine Lücke

all warmly, and was about to leave them when one boy still wanted to whisper something in his ear. He revealed that his older brothers had written beautiful New Year's greetings, as big as *that!* One for Father, one for Albert and Lotte, and also one for Mr. Werther; they intended to deliver them early on New Year's Day. That news was too much for him; he gave each of them a gift, mounted his horse, left his regards for the old man, and rode away with tears in his eyes.

About five he returned home and ordered the maid to see to the fire and keep it going until nighttime. He told his valet to pack his books and linens at the bottom of the trunk, and to sew up his clothes in a cloth. It was probably then that he wrote the following paragraph of his last letter to Lotte:

"You're not expecting me! You thought I'd obey you and not see you again until Christmas Eve. Oh, Lotte, today or never again! On Christmas Eve you'll be holding this paper in your hands, you'll be trembling and moistening it with your dear tears. I want to, I must! Oh, how good I feel now that I'm resolved.—"

Meanwhile, Lotte had gotten into a peculiar state. After her last conversation with Werther she had sensed how hard it would be for her to be separated from him, and how he'd suffer if he had to keep away from her.

It had been mentioned, as if casually, in Albert's presence that Werther wouldn't return until Christmas Eve, and Albert had ridden over to the home of an official in the neighborhood with whom he had business to conduct; he'd have to be away from home overnight.

Now she was sitting alone; none of her siblings was with her; she abandoned herself to her thoughts, which quietly circled around her circumstances. She now saw herself eternally linked with her husband, whose love and fidelity she recognized, for whom she had a sincere affection, whose calm and reliability seemed truly ordained by heaven to be the basis of an honest woman's lifetime happiness; she sensed what he would always mean to her and her little ones. On the other hand, Werther had become so precious to her; from the very first moment of their acquaintance the harmony of their minds had been so evident; her long-lasting relations to him, and so many events they had experienced, had made an indelible impression on her heart. Every intriguing feeling and thought that she had, she was accustomed to share with him, and his absence

zu reißen, die nicht wieder ausgefüllt werden konnte. O, hätte sie ihn in dem Augenblick zum Bruder unwandeln können! wie glücklich wäre sie gewesen! – hätte sie ihn einer ihrer Freundinnen verheiraten dürfen, hätte sie hoffen können, auch sein Verhältnis gegen Albert ganz wieder herzustellen!

Sie hatte ihre Freundinnen der Reihe nach durchgedacht und fand bei einer jeglichen etwas auszusetzen, fand keine, der sie ihn gegönnt hätte.

Über allen diesen Betrachtungen fühlte sie erst tief, ohne sich es deutlich zu machen, daß ihr herzliches heimliches Verlangen sei, ihn für sich zu behalten, und sagte sich daneben, daß sie ihn nicht behalten könne, behalten dürfe; ihr reines, schönes, sonst so leichtes und leicht sich helfendes Gemüt empfand den Druck einer Schwermut, dem die Aussicht zum Glück verschlossen ist. Ihr Herz war gepreßt, und eine trübe Wolke lag über ihrem Auge.

So war es halb sieben geworden, als sie Werthern die Treppe heraufkommen hörte und seinen Tritt, seine Stimme, die nach ihr fragte, bald erkannte. Wie schlug ihr Herz, und wir dürfen fast sagen zum ersten Mal, bei seiner Ankunft. Sie hätte sich gern vor ihm verleugnen lassen, und als er hereintrat, rief sie ihm mit einer Art von leidenschaftlicher Verwirrung entgegen: Sie haben nicht Wort gehalten. – Ich habe nichts versprochen, war seine Antwort. – So hätten Sie wenigstens meiner Bitte stattgeben sollen, versetzte sie, ich bat Sie um unser beider Ruhe.

Sie wußte nicht recht, was sie sagte, ebensowenig was sie tat, als sie nach einigen Freundinnen schickte, um nicht mit Werthern allein zu sein. Er legte einige Bücher hin, die er gebracht hatte, fragte nach andern, und sie wünschte, bald daß ihre Freundinnen kommen, bald daß sie wegbleiben möchten. Das Mädchen kam zurück und brachte die Nachricht, daß sich beide entschuldigen ließen.

Sie wollte das Mädchen mit ihrer Arbeit in das Nebenzimmer sitzen lassen; dann besann sie sich wieder anders. Werther ging in der Stube auf und ab, sie trat ans Klavier und fing eine Menuett an, sie wollte nicht fließen. Sie nahm sich zusammen und setzte sich gelassen zu Werthern, der seinen gewöhnlichen Platz auf dem Kanapee eingenommen hatte.

Haben Sie nichts zu lesen? sagte sie. – Er hatte nichts. – Da drin in meiner Schublade, fing sie an, liegt Ihre Übersetzung einiger Gesänge Ossians; ich habe sie noch nicht gelesen, denn ich hoffte immer, sie von Ihnen zu hören; aber zeither hat sichs nicht finden, nicht machen wollen. – Er lächelte, holte die Lieder, ein Schauer

threatened to create a void in her whole being which couldn't be refilled. Oh, if she could only have transformed him into a brother at that moment, how happy she would have been!—If she had been allowed to marry him off to one of her friends; if she could have hoped to reestablish completely his good footing with Albert!

She had thought about each of her women friends one by one, but found some objection in each case; there wasn't one of them she'd have gladly given him to.

Amid all these contemplations she began to sense profoundly, without making it clear in her mind, that her sincere, secret desire was to keep him for herself; at the same time she told herself that she couldn't and shouldn't keep him; her pure, lovely mind, usually so cheerful and self-sufficient, felt the pressure of a melancholy that has no prospect of happiness. Her heart was oppressed, and a gloomy cloud shadowed her eyes.

In that way, six-thirty had arrived when she heard Werther coming up the stairs and soon recognized his footsteps and his voice, as he inquired after her. How her heart beat at his arrival—for the first time, we may almost say! She would gladly have had him told she was out, and when he walked in, she called to him in a sort of passionate confusion: "You didn't keep your word!" "I made no promises," he replied. "Then at least you should have complied with my request," she retorted; "I implored you for the sake of your peace of mind and mine."

She wasn't fully aware of what she was saying, or of what she was doing, for that matter, when she sent for a few women friends to avoid being alone with Werther. He set down a few books that he had brought and asked about others, and at some moments she wished her friends would come; at others, that they'd stay away. Her maid returned with the news that both of them had begged off.

She wanted to have the maid sit in the adjacent room with her needlework, then she changed her mind again. Werther paced up and down the room, she stepped to the clavier and began a minuet, but it had no flow to it. She pulled herself together and sat down calmly beside Werther, who had occupied his customary place on the sofa.

"You have nothing to read to me?" she asked. He had nothing. "In my drawer over there," she began, "you'll find your translation of some of the songs of Ossian; I haven't read it yet, because I kept hoping to hear *you* read it; but since then there just hasn't been an opportunity." He smiled and went to get the songs; a thrill of emo-

überfiel ihn, als er sie in die Hände nahm, und die Augen standen ihm
voll Tränen, als er hineinsah. Er setzte sich nieder und las:

Stern der dämmernden Nacht, schön funkelst du in Westen, hebst
dein strahlend Haupt aus deiner Wolke, wandelst stattlich deinen
Hügel hin. Wornach blickst du auf die Heide? Die stürmenden
Winde haben sich gelegt; von ferne kommt des Gießbachs Murmeln;
rauschende Wellen spielen am Felsen ferne; das Gesumme der
Abendfliegen schwärmt übers Feld. Wornach siehst du, schönes
Licht? Aber du lächelst und gehst, freudig umgeben dich die Wellen
und baden dein liebliches Haar. Lebe wohl, ruhiger Strahl. Erscheine,
du herrliches Licht von Ossians Seele!
    Und es erscheint in seiner Kraft. Ich sehe meine geschiedenen
Freunde, sie sammeln sich auf Lora, wie in den Tagen, die vorüber
sind. – Fingal kommt wie eine feuchte Nebelsäule; um ihn sind seine
Helden, und, siehe! die Barden des Gesanges: Grauer Ullin! statt-
licher Ryno! Alpin, lieblicher Sänger! und du, sanft klagende Minona!
– Wie verändert seid ihr, meine Freunde, seit den festlichen Tagen
auf Selma, da wir buhlten um die Ehre des Gesanges, wie Frühlings-
lüfte den Hügel hin wechselnd beugen das schwach lispelnde Gras.
    Da trat Minona hervor in ihrer Schönheit, mit niedergeschlagenem
Blick und tränenvollem Auge, schwer floß ihr Haar im unsteten
Winde, der von dem Hügel herstieß. – Düster wards in der Seele der
Helden, als sie die liebliche Stimme erhob; denn oft hatten sie das
Grab Salgars gesehen, oft die finstere Wohnung der weißen Colma.
Colma, verlassen auf dem Hügel, mit der harmonischen Stimme;
Salgar versprach zu kommen; aber ringsum zog sich die Nacht. Höret
Colmas Stimme, da sie auf dem Hügel allein saß.

COLMA:

Es ist Nacht! – ich bin allein, verloren auf dem stürmischen Hügel.
Der Wind saust im Gebirge. Der Strom heult den Felsen hinab.
Keine Hütte schützt mich vor dem Regen, mich Verlaßne auf dem
stürmischen Hügel.
    Tritt, o Mond, aus deinen Wolken! erscheinet, Sterne der Nacht!
Leite mich irgendein Strahl zu dem Orte, wo meine Liebe ruht von
den Beschwerden der Jagd, sein Bogen neben ihm abgespannt, seine

tion came over him when he picked them up, and his eyes were
filled with tears when he looked into them. He sat down and read:[34]

"Star of the darkening night, already you sparkle in the west,
raising your radiant head from your cloud, and proceeding in
stately fashion up your hill. What do you seek as you look down
at the heath? The stormy winds have abated; from afar comes
the murmur of the torrent; lapping waves play in the distance by
the crag; the buzzing of the evening flies swarms over the field.
What are you looking for, lovely light? But you smile and depart;
joyfully the waves surround you, washing your charming hair.
Farewell, calm ray! Appear, splendid light of Ossian's soul!

"And it appears in its might. I see my departed friends, they
gather on Lora as in the days that are gone.—Fingal comes like
a moist pillar of mist; around him are his heroes, and behold, the
bards of song: gray Ullin! Handsome Ryno! Alpin, charming
singer! And you, gently lamenting Minona!—How changed you
are, my friends, since those festive days on Selma when we vied
for the honor of the song, while spring breezes in alternation
bowed down the feebly whispering grass all along the hillside.

"Then Minona stepped forward in her beauty, with downcast
glance and tear-filled eyes; heavily waved her hair in the inconstant wind that blew from the hill.—Gloom overcame the soul of
the heroes when she raised her lovely voice; for often had they
seen the grave of Salgar, often the dark residence of white
Colma. Colma, forsaken on the hill, with the harmonious voice;
Salgar promised to come; but night closed in round about. Hear
Colma's voice as she sat alone on the hill.

"COLMA:
"'It is night!—I am alone, lost on the stormy hill. The wind is
roaring in the mountains. The river howls down the crags. No
cabin protects me from the rain, the deserted one on the stormy
hill.

"'Moon, emerge from your clouds! Appear, stars of the night!
Let some ray guide me to the place where my love reposes from
the exertions of the hunt, his bow unstrung beside him, his

---

34. For reasons that will be evident, considering the nature of this edition,
Goethe's very free rendering of Ossian will be translated literally on the English
pages that face the German text. The original English wording of the corre-
sponding passages will be found in Appendix Two at the end of this volume.

Hunde schnobend um ihn! Aber hier muß ich sitzen allein auf dem Felsen des verwachsenen Stroms. Der Strom und der Sturm saust, ich höre nicht die Stimme meines Geliebten.

Warum zaudert mein Salgar? Hat er sein Wort vergessen? – Da ist der Fels und der Baum und hier der rauschende Strom! Mit einbrechender Nacht versprachst du hier zu sein; ach! wohin hat sich mein Salgar verirrt? Mit dir wollt ich fliehen, verlassen Vater und Bruder! die Stolzen! Lange sind unsere Geschlechter Feinde, aber wir sind keine Feinde, o Salgar!

Schweig eine Weile, o Wind! still eine kleine Weile, o Strom! daß meine Stimme klinge durchs Tal, daß mein Wanderer mich höre. Salgar! ich bins, die ruft! Hier ist der Baum und der Fels! Salgar! mein Lieber! hier bin ich; warum zauderst du zu kommen?

Sieh, der Mond erscheint, die Flut glänzt im Tale, die Felsen stehen grau den Hügel hinauf; aber ich seh ihn nicht auf der Höhe, seine Hunde vor ihm her verkündigen nicht seine Ankunft. Hier muß ich sitzen allein.

Aber wer sind, die dort unten liegen auf der Heide? – Mein Geliebter? Mein Bruder? – Redet, o meine Freunde! Sie antworten nicht. Wie geängstet ist meine Seele! – Ach sie sind tot! Ihre Schwerter rot vom Gefechte! O mein Bruder, mein Bruder! warum hast du meinen Salgar erschlagen? O mein Salgar! warum hast meinen Bruder erschlagen? Ihr wart mir beide so lieb! O du warst schön an dem Hügel unter Tausenden! Er war schrecklich in der Schlacht. Antwortet mir! hört meine Stimme, meine Geliebten! Aber ach! sie sind stumm! stumm auf ewig! kalt, wie die Erde, ist ihr Busen!

O, von dem Felsen des Hügels, von dem Gipfel des stürmenden Berges, redet, Geister der Toten! redet! mir soll es nicht grausen! – Wohin seid ihr zur Ruhe gegangen? in welcher Gruft des Gebirges soll ich euch finden! – Keine schwache Stimme vernehme ich im Winde, keine wehende Antwort im Sturme des Hügels.

Ich sitze in meinem Jammer, ich harre auf den Morgen in meinen Tränen. Wühlet das Grab, ihr Freunde der Toten, aber schließt es nicht, bis ich komme. Mein Leben schwindet wie ein Traum, wie sollt' ich zurückbleiben. Hier will ich wohnen mit meinen Freunden an dem Strome des klingenden Felsens – Wenns Nacht wird auf dem Hügel und Wind kommt über die Heide, soll mein Geist im Winde stehn und trauern den Tod meiner Freunde. Der Jäger hört mich aus seiner Laube, fürchtet meine Stimme und liebt sie; denn süß soll meine Stimme sein um meine Freunde, sie waren mir beide so lieb!

hounds panting around him! But here I must sit alone on the crag by the swollen river. The river and the storm roar; I hear not the voice of my beloved.

"'Why does my Salgar delay? Has he forgotten his word?— There stand the crag and the tree, and here the noisy river! You promised to be here at nightfall; ah, where has my Salgar strayed to? I wanted to run away with you, to abandon my father and brother, those proud men! Long have our families been enemies, but you and I are not enemies, O Salgar!

"'Be silent a while, wind! Tranquil a brief while, river, so my voice can resound through the valley and my wandering one can hear me! Salgar, it's I calling! Here are the tree and the crag! Salgar, my dear one! I am here; why do you delay in coming?

"'See, the moon appears, the waters shine in the valley, the crags stand gray up along the hillside; but I see him not on the heights, his hounds do not precede him announcing his arrival. I must sit here alone.

"'But who are they that lie upon the heath there below?—My beloved? My brother?—Speak, my friends! They do not answer. How anguished my soul is!—Ah, they are dead! Their swords red from their combat! O my brother, my brother, why did you slay my Salgar? O my Salgar, why did you slay my brother? You were both so dear to me! You, Salgar, were the handsomest on the hill among thousands! *He* was fearsome in battle. Answer me! Hear my voice, my loved ones! But alas, they are mute, eternally mute! Cold as the earth is their bosom!

"'Oh, from the crag of the hill, from the peak of the stormy mountain, speak, spirits of the dead! Speak! I shall not be horror-stricken!—Where have you gone to rest? In what mountain tomb will I find you?—I perceive no weak voice in the wind, no blowing reply in the storm on the hill.

"'I sit in my grief, I await the morning in my tears. Dig the grave, friends of the dead, but do not close it until I arrive. My life is fading like a dream, how can I remain behind? Here I shall dwell with my friends by the river of the resounding crag— When night falls on the hill and wind comes over the heath, my spirit shall hover in the wind and mourn the death of my friends. The hunter will hear me from his arbor; he will fear my voice and love it, for my voice will be sweet as it laments my friends, both of whom I loved so much!'

Das war dein Gesang, o Minona, Tormans sanft errötende Tochter. Unsere Tränen flossen um Colma, und unsere Seele ward düster. Ullin trat auf mit der Harfe und gab uns Alpins Gesang – Alpins Stimme war freundlich, Rynos Seele ein Feuerstrahl. Aber schon ruhten sie im engen Hause, und ihre Stimme war verhallet in Selma. Einst kehrte Ullin zurück von der Jagd, ehe die Helden noch fielen. Er hörte ihren Wettegesang auf dem Hügel. Ihr Lied war sanft, aber traurig. Sie klagten Morars Fall, des ersten der Helden. Seine Seele war wie Fingals Seele, sein Schwert wie das Schwert Oskars – Aber er fiel, und sein Vater jammerte, und seiner Schwester Augen waren voll Tränen, Minonas Augen waren voll Tränen, der Schwester des herrlichen Morars. Sie trat zurück vor Ullins Gesang, wie der Mond in Westen, der den Sturmregen voraussieht und sein schönes Haupt in eine Wolke verbirgt. – Ich schlug die Harfe mit Ullin zum Gesange des Jammers.

RYNO:

Vorbei sind Wind und Regen, der Mittag ist so heiter, die Wolken teilen sich. Fliehend bescheint den Hügel die unbeständige Sonne. Rötlich fließt der Strom des Berges im Tale hin. Süß ist dein Murmeln, Strom; doch süßer die Stimme, die ich höre. Es ist Alpins Stimme, er bejammert den Toten. Sein Haupt ist vor Alter gebeugt, und rot sein tränendes Auge. Alpin! trefflicher Sänger! warum allein auf dem schweigenden Hügel? warum jammerst du wie ein Windstoß im Walde, wie eine Welle am fernen Gestade?

ALPIN:

Meine Tränen, Ryno, sind für den Toten, meine Stimme für die Bewohner des Grabs. Schlank bist du auf dem Hügel, schön unter den Söhnen der Heide. Aber du wirst fallen wie Morar, und auf deinem Grabe der Trauernde sitzen. Die Hügel werden dich vergessen, dein Bogen in der Halle liegen ungespannt.

Du warst schnell, o Morar, wie ein Reh auf dem Hügel, schrecklich wie die Nachtfeuer am Himmel. Dein Grimm war ein Sturm, dein Schwert in der Schlacht wie Wetterleuchten über der Heide. Deine Stimme glich dem Waldstrome nach dem Regen, dem Donner auf fernen Hügeln. Manche fielen vor deinem Arm, die Flamme deines Grimmes verzehrte sie. Aber wenn du wiederkehrtest vom Kriege, wie friedlich war deine Stirne! dein Angesicht war gleich der Sonne nach dem Gewitter, gleich dem Monde in der schweigenden Nacht, ruhig deine Brust wie der See, wenn sich des Windes Brausen gelegt hat.

"That was your song, Minona, Torman's gently blushing daughter. Our tears flowed for Colma's sake, and our soul became gloomy.

"Ullin stepped forward with his harp and gave us Alpin's song—Alpin's voice was friendly, Ryno's soul was a fiery ray. But by now they rested in their narrow house, and their voices had faded away in Selma. Once Ullin returned from the hunt, before those heroes fell. He heard their song competition on the hill. Their song was gentle, but sad. They were lamenting the death in battle of Morar, first of heroes. His soul was like Fingal's soul, his sword like Oscar's sword— But he fell, and his father grieved, and his sister's eyes were filled with tears, Minona's eyes were filled with tears; she was the sister of splendid Morar. She withdrew at Ullin's song, like the moon in the west which foresees the rainstorm and conceals its lovely head in a cloud.—I played the harp with Ullin to accompany the song of grief.

"RYNO:

"'Wind and rain have passed, the noon is so clear, the clouds are breaking up. As it flees by, the inconstant sun illuminates the hill. The mountain stream is reddish as it flows down the valley. Sweet is your murmur, stream; but sweeter the voice that I hear. It is the voice of Alpin bewailing the dead man. His head is bowed with age, and his weeping eyes are red. Alpin, excellent singer! Why alone on the silent hill? Why do you lament like a gust of wind in the forest, like a wave on the distant shore?'

"ALPIN:

"'My tears, Ryno, are for the dead man, my voice for the dwellers in the grave. Slender are you on the hill, handsome among the sons of the heath. But you will fall like Morar, and the mourner will sit on your grave. The hills will forget you, your bow will lie unstrung in the great hall.

"'You were swift, Morar, like a roebuck on the hill, fearsome as the night fires in the sky. Your ire was a storm, your sword in battle like lightning over the heath. Your voice resembled the forest stream after rain, or thunder on distant hills. Many fell before your arm, the flame of your ire consumed them. But when you returned from war, how peaceful was your brow! Your face was like sunshine after storm, like moonlight in the silent night; your bosom, like the lake after the roar of the wind has abated.

Eng ist nun deine Wohnung! finster deine Stätte! mit drei Schritten
meß ich dein Grab, o du! der du ehe so groß warst! vier Steine mit
moosigen Häuptern sind dein einziges Gedächtnis, ein entblätterter
Baum, langes Gras, das im Winde wispelt, deutet dem Auge des
Jägers das Grab des mächtigen Morars. Keine Mutter hast du, dich zu
beweinen, kein Mädchen mit Tränen der Liebe. Tot ist, die dich
gebar, gefallen die Tochter von Morglan.

Wer auf seinem Stabe ist das? Wer ist es, dessen Haupt weiß ist vor
Alter, dessen Augen rot sind von Tränen? es ist dein Vater, o Morar!
der Vater keines Sohnes außer dir. Er hörte von deinem Ruf in der
Schlacht, er hörte von zerstobenen Feinden; er hörte Morars Ruhm!
Ach! nichts von seiner Wunde? Weine, Vater Morars! weine! aber
dein Sohn hört dich nicht. Tief ist der Schlaf der Toten, niedrig ihr
Kissen von Staube. Nimmer achtet er auf die Stimme, nie erwacht er
auf deinen Ruf. O, wann wird es Morgen im Grabe, zu bieten dem
Schlummerer: Erwache!

Lebe wohl! edelster der Menschen, du Eroberer im Felde! Aber
nimmer wird dich das Feld sehen! Nimmer der düstere Wald
leuchten vom Glanze deines Stahls. Du hinterließest keinen Sohn,
aber der Gesang soll deinen Namen erhalten, künftige Zeiten sollen
von dir hören, hören von dem gefallenen Morar.

Laut war die Trauer der Helden, am lautesten Armins berstender
Seufzer. Ihn erinnerte es an den Tod seines Sohnes, er fiel in den
Tagen der Jugend. Carmor saß nah bei dem Helden, der Fürst des
hallenden Galmal. Warum schluchzet der Seufzer Armins? sprach er,
was ist hier zu weinen? Klingt nicht Lied und Gesang, die Seele zu
schmelzen und zu ergetzen? sie sind wie sanfter Nebel, der steigend
vom See aufs Tal sprüht, und die blühenden Blumen füllet das Naß;
aber die Sonne kommt wieder in ihrer Kraft, und der Nebel ist gegangen. Warum bist du so jammervoll, Armin, Herrscher des seeum-
flossenen Gorma?

Jammervoll! Wohl, das bin ich, und nicht gering die Ursache
meines Wehs. – Carmor, du verlorst keinen Sohn, verlorst keine
blühende Tochter; Colgar, der Tapfere, lebt, und Annira, die schönste
der Mädchen. Die Zweige deines Hauses blühen, o Carmor; aber
Armin ist der Letzte seines Stammes. Finster ist dein Bett, o Daura!
dumpf ist dein Schlaf im Grabe – Wann erwachst du mit deinen
Gesängen, mit deiner melodischen Stimme? Auf! ihr Winde des
Herbstes! auf! stürmt über die finstere Heide! Waldströme, braust!
heult, Stürme, im Gipfel der Eichen! Wandle durch gebrochene
Wolken, o Mond, zeige wechselnd dein bleiches Gesicht! Erinnre

"'Narrow is your dwelling now, dark your abode! With three paces I measure your grave, and you were once so great! Four stones with mossy heads are your only memorial, a leafless tree; tall grass whispering in the wind indicates mighty Morar's grave to the eyes of the hunter. You have no mother to weep over you, no girl with tears of love. Dead is she who bore you, fallen is the daughter of Morglan.

"'Who is this leaning on his staff? Who is this whose head is white with age, whose eyes are red with tears? It is your father, O Morar! The father of no other son besides you. He heard of your reputation in battle, he heard of the enemies you dispersed; he heard Morar's fame! Ah, but nothing about his wound? Weep, father of Morar, weep! But your son hears you not. Deep is the sleep of the dead, low their pillow of dust. Never will he heed your voice, never will he awaken to your call. Oh, when will it be morning in the grave, to cry to the slumberer: "Awaken!"?

"'Farewell, noblest of men, conqueror in the field! But never will the field see you! Never will the gloomy forest shine with the gleam of your steel. You left no son behind, but song will preserve your name, future eras will hear of you, hear of Morar the fallen.'

"Loud was the mourning of the heroes, loudest of all Armin's explosive sigh. He was reminded of the death of his own son, who fell in the days of his youth. Carmor sat near the hero, Carmor, prince of resounding Galmal. 'Why does Armin's sigh sob?' he asked. 'What calls for weeping here? Do not song and chant resound to melt the soul and delight it? They are like gentle mist that rises from the lake and besprinkles the valley, and the blossoming flowers feel the moisture; but the sun returns in its strength, and the mist is gone. Why are you so grief-stricken, Armin, ruler of sea-girt Gorma?'

"'Grief-stricken! Yea, that am I, and not trivial the cause of my woe.—Carmor, you never lost a son, never lost a blossoming daughter; Colgar the brave lives, as does Annira, fairest of maidens. The branches of your house are in bloom, Carmor, but Armin is the last of his line. Dark is your bed, O Daura! Dull is your sleep in the grave— When will you awaken with your songs, with your melodious voice? Arise, you winds of autumn! Arise! Rage across the dark heath! Forest streams, roar! Howl, storms, in the tops of the oaks! Move through broken clouds, moon, show and hide your pale face in alternation! Remind me

mich der schrecklichen Nacht, da meine Kinder umkamen, da Arindal, der Mächtige, fiel, Daura, die Liebe, verging. Daura, meine Tochter, du warst schön! schön wie der Mond auf den Hügeln von Fura, weiß wie der gefallene Schnee, süß wie die atmende Luft! Arindal, dein Bogen war stark, dein Speer schnell auf dem Felde, dein Blick wie Nebel auf der Welle, dein Schild eine Feuerwolke im Sturme!

Armar, berühmt im Kriege, kam und warb um Dauras Liebe; sie widerstand nicht lange. Schön waren die Hoffnungen ihrer Freunde. Erath, der Sohn Odgals, grollte, denn sein Bruder lag erschlagen von Armar. Er kam, in einen Schiffer verkleidet. Schön war sein Nachen auf der Welle, weiß seine Locken vor Alter, ruhig sein ernstes Gesicht. Schönste der Mädchen, sagte er, liebliche Tochter von Armin, dort am Felsen, nicht fern in der See, wo die rote Frucht vom Baume herblinkt, dort wartet Armar auf Daura; ich komme, seine Liebe zu führen über die rollende See.

Sie folgt' ihm und rief nach Armar; nichts antwortete als die Stimme des Felsens. Armar! mein Lieber! mein Lieber! warum ängstest du mich so? Höre, Sohn Arnaths! höre! Daura ists, die dich ruft!

Erath, der Verräter, floh lachend zum Lande. Sie erhob ihre Stimme, rief nach ihrem Vater und Bruder: Arindal! Armin! Ist keiner, seine Daura zu retten?

Ihre Stimme kam über die See. Arindal, mein Sohn, stieg vom Hügel herab, rauh in der Beute der Jagd, seine Pfeile rasselten an seiner Seite, seinen Bogen trug er in der Hand, fünf schwarzgraue Doggen waren um ihn. Er sah den kühnen Erath am Ufer, faßte und band ihn an die Eiche, fest umflocht er seine Hüften, der Gefesselte füllte mit Ächzen die Winde.

Arindal betritt die Wellen in seinem Boote, Daura herüberzubringen. Armar kam in seinem Grimme, drückt' ab den graubefiederten Pfeil, er klang, er sank in dein Herz, o Arindal, mein Sohn! Statt Erath, des Verräters, kamst du um, das Boot erreichte den Felsen, er sank dran nieder und starb. Zu deinen Füßen floß deines Bruders Blut, welch war dein Jammer, o Daura!

Die Wellen zerschmetterten das Boot. Armar stürzte sich in die See, seine Daura zu retten oder zu sterben. Schnell stürmte ein Stoß vom Hügel in die Wellen, er sank und hob sich nicht wieder.

Allein auf dem seebespülten Felsen hörte ich die Klagen meiner Tochter. Viel und laut war ihr Schreien, doch konnte sie ihr Vater nicht retten. Die ganze Nacht stand ich am Ufer, ich sah sie im

of the terrible night when my children perished, when Arindal the mighty fell and Daura the lovely passed away.

"'Daura, my daughter, you were beautiful! Beautiful as the moon on the hills of Fura, white as the fallen snow, sweet as the breathing air! Arindal, your bow was strong, your spear swift in the field, your gaze like mist on the waves, your shield a fiery cloud in the storm!

"'Armar, famed in war, came and sued for Daura's love; she did not long resist. Beautiful were the hopes of her friends.

"'Erath, son of Odgal, bore a grudge, for his brother had been slain by Armar. He came, disguised as a boatman. Lovely was his vessel on the waves, white with age his tresses, calm his grave countenance. "Fairest of maidens," he said, "lovely daughter of Armin: there by the crag, not far from here on the sea, where the red fruit shines on the tree, there Armar awaits Daura; I have come to guide his beloved over the rolling sea."

"'She followed him and called to Armar; there was no reply but the voice of the crag. "Armar, beloved, beloved, why are you frightening me so? Hear me, son of Arnath, hear me! It is Daura who calls you!"

"'Erath the betrayer fled to the land, laughing. She raised her voice, called to her father and brother: "Arindal! Armin! Is there no one to rescue Daura?"

"'Her voice came across the sea. Arindal, my son, descended from the hill, rough with the quarry from his hunt; his arrows rattled by his side, he carried his bow in his hand, five dark-gray mastiffs were around him. He saw bold Erath on the shore, seized him and tied him to the oak; tightly he wound the rope around his hips, the bound man filled the winds with groans.

"'Arindal entered the waters in his boat to bring Daura across. Armar came in his wrath, he let fly the gray-feathered arrow, which rang and sank into your heart, Arindal, my son! Instead of Erath the betrayer it was you that perished; the boat reached the crag, then he collapsed beside it and died. At your feet your brother's blood flowed; what was your grief, O Daura!

"'The waves shattered the boat. Armar plunged into the sea to save his Daura or die. Swiftly a gust raged from the hill into the waves; he sank and rose not again.

"'Alone on the sea-washed crag I heard the lamenting of my daughter. Much and loudly she cried, but her father could not save her. All night I stood on the shore, I saw her in the feeble

schwachen Strahle des Mondes, die ganze Nacht hörte ich ihr
Schreien, laut war der Wind, und der Regen schlug scharf nach der
Seite des Berges. Ihre Stimme ward schwach, ehe der Morgen er-
schien, sie starb weg wie die Abendluft zwischen dem Grase der
Felsen. Beladen mit Jammer starb sie und ließ Armin allein! Dahin ist
meine Stärke im Kriege, gefallen mein Stolz unter den Mädchen.
Wenn die Stürme des Berges kommen, wenn der Nord die Wellen
noch hebt, sitze ich am schallenden Ufer, schaue nach dem schreck-
lichen Felsen. Oft im sinkenden Monde sehe ich die Geister meiner
Kinder, halb dämmernd wandeln sie zusammen in trauriger
Eintracht. – –

Ein Strom von Tränen, der aus Lottens Augen brach und ihrem
gepreßten Herzen Luft machte, hemmte Werthers Gesang. Er warf
das Papier hin, faßte ihre Hand und weinte die bittersten Tränen.
Lotte ruhte auf der andern und verbarg ihre Augen ins Schnupftuch.
Die Bewegung beider war fürchterlich. Sie fühlten ihr eignes Elend
in dem Schicksale der Edlen, fühlten es zusammen, und ihre Tränen
vereinigten sie. Die Lippen und Augen Werthers glühten an Lottens
Arme; ein Schauer überfiel sie; sie wollte sich entfernen, und
Schmerz und Anteil lagen betäubend wie Blei auf ihr. Sie atmete, sich
zu erholen, und bat ihn schluchzend, fortzufahren, bat mit der ganzen
Stimme des Himmels! Werther zitterte, sein Herz wollte bersten, er
hob das Blatt auf und las halb gebrochen:

Warum weckst du mich, Frühlingsluft? Du buhlst und sprichst: Ich
betaue mit Tropfen des Himmels! Aber die Zeit meines Welkens ist
nahe, nahe der Sturm, der meine Blätter herabstört! Morgen wird der
Wanderer kommen, kommen der mich sah in meiner Schönheit,
ringsum wird sein Auge im Felde mich suchen und wird mich nicht
finden. –

Die ganze Gewalt dieser Worte fiel über den Unglücklichen. Er
warf sich vor Lotten nieder in der vollsten Verzweifelung, faßte ihre
Hände, drückte sie in seine Augen, wider seine Stirn, und ihr schien
eine Ahnung seines schrecklichen Vorhabens durch die Seele zu
fliegen. Ihre Sinnen verwirrten sich, sie drückte seine Hände, drückte
sie wider ihre Brust, neigte sich mit einer wehmütigen Bewegung zu
ihm, und ihre glühenden Wangen berührten sich. Die Welt verging
ihnen. Er schlang seine Arme um sie her, preßte sie an seine Brust
und deckte ihre zitternden, stammelnden Lippen mit wütenden

rays of the moon; all night I heard her cries; loud was the wind, and the rain gave sharp strokes at the side of the mountain. Her voice became weak; before morning appeared she died away like the evening breeze amid the grass on the crags. Laden with grief she died, leaving Armin alone! Gone is my strength in war, fallen my pride among maidens.

"'When the mountain storms come, when the north wind raises the waves high, I sit on the resounding shore and gaze at the fearsome crag. Often in the sinking moon I see the spirits of my children; in semidarkness they walk together in mournful harmony.——'"

A flood of tears bursting from Lotte's eyes, giving vent to her oppressed heart, interrupted Werther's chant. He flung down the paper, took her hand, and wept the bitterest tears. Lotte supported herself on her other arm, hiding her eyes in her handkerchief. The agitation they both felt was frightful. They sensed their own misery in the fate of those noble heroes, they sensed it together, and their tears united them. Werther's lips and eyes were burning on Lotte's arm; a thrill ran through her; she wanted to move away, and sorrow and sympathy lay numbingly on her like lead. She breathed heavily, to recover, and with sobs she asked him to continue, asked him with the very voice of heaven! Werther trembled, his heart was about to crack; he picked up the sheet and read in a broken voice:

"Why do you awaken me, spring breeze? You play wantonly and say: 'I bedew you with drops from heaven!' But the time of my withering is nigh, nigh is the storm that will tear off my leaves! Tomorrow the wanderer will come, he will come who saw me in my beauty; his eyes will seek me round about in the field and will not find me.——"

The full force of those words overcame the unfortunate man. He flung himself down in front of Lotte in the most total desperation; he seized her hands and pressed them to his eyes, against his forehead, and a foreboding of his terrible intentions seemed to shoot through her soul. Her senses became confused, she squeezed his hands, pressed them against her bosom, and stooped down to him with a melancholy motion; their burning cheeks touched. The world no longer existed for them. He threw his arms around her, clasped her to his breast, and covered her trembling, stammering

Küssen. – Werther! rief sie mit erstickter Stimme, sich abwendend,
Werther! – und drückte mit schwacher Hand seine Brust von der ihrigen; – Werther! rief sie mit dem gefaßten Tone des edelsten Gefühles.
– Er widerstand nicht, ließ sie aus seinen Armen und warf sich unsin-
nig vor sie hin. Sie riß such auf, und in ängstlicher Verwirrung,
bebend zwischen Liebe und Zorn, sagte sie: Das ist das letzte Mal!
Werther! Sie sehn mich nicht wieder. – Und mit dem vollsten Blick
der Liebe auf den Elenden eilte sie ins Nebenzimmer und schloß hinter sich zu. Werther streckte ihr die Arme nach, getraute sich nicht,
sie zu halten. Er lag an der Erde, den Kopf auf dem Kanapee, und in
dieser Stellung blieb er über eine halbe Stunde, bis ihn ein Geräusch
zu sich selbst rief. Es war das Mädchen, das den Tisch decken wollte.
Er ging im Zimmer auf und ab, und da er sich wieder allein sah, ging
er zur Türe des Kabinetts und rief mit leiser Stimme: Lotte! Lotte!
nur noch Ein Wort! ein Lebewohl! – Sie schwieg. Er harrte und bat
und harrte; dann riß er sich weg und rief: Lebe wohl, Lotte! auf ewig
lebe wohl!

Er kam ans Stadttor. Die Wächter, die ihn schon gewohnt waren,
ließen ihn stillschweigend hinaus. Es stiebte zwischen Regen und
Schnee, und erst gegen eilfe klopfte er wieder. Sein Diener bemerkte, als Werther nach Hause kam, daß seinem Herrn der Hut
fehlte. Er getraute sich nicht, etwas zu sagen, entkleidete ihn, alles
war naß. Man hat nachher den Hut auf einem Felsen, der an dem
Abhange des Hügels ins Tal sieht, gefunden, und es ist unbegreiflich,
wie er ihn in einer finstern, feuchten Nacht, ohne zu stürzen, er-
stiegen hat.

Er legte sich zu Bette und schlief lange. Der Bediente fand ihn
schreibend, als er ihm den andern Morgen auf sein Rufen den Kaffee
brachte. Er schrieb folgendes am Briefe an Lotten:

Zum letzten Male denn, zum letzten Male schlage ich diese Augen
auf. Sie sollen, ach, die Sonne nicht mehr sehen, ein trüber neblichter
Tag hält sie bedeckt. So traure denn, Natur! dein Sohn, dein Freund,
dein Geliebter naht sich seinem Ende. Lotte, das ist ein Gefühl ohne-
gleichen, und doch kommt es dem dämmernden Traum am nächsten,
zu sich zu sagen: das ist der letzte Morgen. Der letzte! Lotte, ich habe
keinen Sinn für das Wort: der letzte! Stehe ich nicht da in meiner
ganzen Kraft, und morgen liege ich ausgestreckt und schlaff am
Boden. Sterben! was heißt das? Siehe, wir träumen, wenn wir vom
Tode reden. Ich habe manchen sterben sehen; aber so eingeschränkt
ist die Menschheit, daß sie für ihres Daseins Anfang und Ende keinen

lips with furious kisses. "Werther!" she cried in a stifled voice, turning away. "Werther!" And with a weak hand she pushed his bosom
away from hers. "Werther!" she cried with the composed tone of the
noblest feelings. He didn't resist, he released her from his arms and
flung himself down before her madly. She leaped up and in fearful
confusion, wavering between love and anger, she said: "This is the
last time! Werther, you'll never see me again!" And with the most
heartfelt loving glance at the wretched man she dashed into the next
room and locked the door behind her. Werther held out his arms to
her, but didn't venture to hold her back. He lay on the floor, his head
on the sofa, and remained in that position for a half-hour, until a
sound recalled him to his senses. It was the maid, who wanted to set
the table. He paced up and down the room, and when he found
himself alone again, he went to the door of the little room and called
softly: "Lotte! Lotte! Just one more word! To say farewell!" She was
silent. He lingered and urged her and lingered; then he tore himself
away, crying: "Farewell, Lotte! Farewell forever!"

He arrived at the town gate. The guards, already used to him, let
him out in silence. There were flurries of snow mixed with rain, and
it was already about eleven when he knocked at his own door again.
His servant noticed that his master's hat was missing when he came
home. He didn't dare remark on it; he undressed him; everything
was wet. Later the hat was found on a crag on the slope of the hill
with a view of the valley; it is incomprehensible how he could have
climbed it on a dark, damp night without falling to his death.

He went to bed and slept a long time. His valet found him
writing when he answered his call on the following morning and
brought him his coffee. He was writing the next portion of his
letter to Lotte:

"For the last time, then, for the last time I have opened these
eyes. Alas, they will never see the sun again, they're covered by
a gloomy, foggy day. Mourn then, nature! Your son, your friend,
your beloved is nearing his end. Lotte, this is a feeling like no
other, and yet to say 'This is my last morning' comes closest to a
twilight dream. My last! Lotte, I can't understand the word 'last'!
Am I not here in my full vigor? And tomorrow I'll be stretched
out, limp, on the floor. To die! What does that mean? You see,
we dream when we speak of death. I've seen many people die;
but mankind is so circumscribed that it has no understanding of
the beginning or end of its existence. I still belong to myself, and

Sinn hat. Jetzt noch mein, dein! dein, o Geliebte! Und einen Augenblick – getrennt, geschieden – vielleicht auf ewig? – Nein, Lotte, nein – Wie kann ich vergehen? wie kannst du vergehen? Wir *sind* ja! – Vergehen! – Was heißt das? Das ist wieder ein Wort! ein leerer Schall! ohne Gefühl für mein Herz. – – Tot, Lotte! eingescharrt der kalten Erde, so eng! so finster! – Ich hatte eine Freundin, die mein Alles war meiner hülflosen Jugend; sie starb, und ich folgte ihrer Leiche und stand an dem Grabe, wie sie den Sarg hinunterließen und die Seile schnurrend unter ihm weg- und wieder heraufschnellten, dann die erste Schaufel hinunterschollerte und die ängstliche Lade einen dumpfen Ton wiedergab, und dumpfer und immer dumpfer, und endlich bedeckt war! – Ich stürzte neben das Grab hin – ergriffen, erschüttert, geängstet, zerrissen mein Innerstes, aber ich wußte nicht, wie mir geschah – wie mir geschehen wird – Sterben! Grab! ich verstehe die Worte nicht!

O vergib mir! vergib mir! Gestern! Es hätte der letzte Augenblick meines Lebens sein sollen. O du Engel! zum ersten Male, zum ersten Male ganz ohne Zweifel durch mein innig Innerstes durchglühte mich das Wonnegefühl: Sie liebt mich! sie liebt mich! Es brennt noch auf meinen Lippen das heilige Feuer, das von den deinigen strömte; neue warme Wonne ist in meinem Herzen. Vergib mir! vergib mir!

Ach ich wußte, daß du mich liebtest, wußte es an den ersten seelenvollen Blicken, an dem ersten Händedruck, und doch, wenn ich wieder weg war, wenn ich Alberten an deiner Seite sah, verzagte ich wieder in fieberhaften Zweifeln.

Erinnerst du dich der Blumen, die du mir schicktest, als du in jener fatalen Gesellschaft mir kein Wort sagen, keine Hand reichen konntest? o ich habe die halbe Nacht davor gekniet, und sie versiegelten mir deine Liebe. Aber ach! diese Eindrücke gingen vorüber, wie das Gefühl der Gnade seines Gottes allmählich wieder aus der Seele des Gläubigen weicht, die ihm mit ganzer Himmelsfülle in heiligen sichtbaren Zeichen gereicht ward.

Alles das ist vergänglich, aber keine Ewigkeit soll das glühende Leben auslöschen, das ich gestern auf deinen Lippen genoß, das ich in mir fühle! Sie liebt mich! Dieser Arm hat sie umfaßt, diese Lippen haben auf ihren Lippen gezittert, dieser Mund hat an dem ihrigen gestammelt. Sie ist mein! du bist mein! ja, Lotte, auf ewig.

Und was ist das, daß Albert dein Mann ist? Mann! Das wäre denn für diese Welt – und für diese Welt Sünde, daß ich dich liebe, daß ich dich aus seinen Armen in die meinigen reißen möchte? Sünde? Gut, und ich strafe mich dafür; ich habe sie in ihrer ganzen Himmels-

to you, to you, my beloved! Another moment—parted, separated—perhaps forever?—No, Lotte, no—How can I perish?
How can you perish? We *exist!*—Perish!—What does that
mean? That's just another word! An empty sound! It arouses no
feeling in my heart.——Dead, Lotte! Shoveled into the cold
ground, so narrow, so dark!—I had a lady friend, who was everything to me in my helpless youth; she died, and I walked behind
her body and stood at the grave as they lowered the coffin and
the ropes under it sprung away and upward again with a hum; as
the first shovelful rumbled down and that dreadful box emitted
a muffled sound, which became ever more muffled until it was
finally covered!—I fell down next to the grave—moved, shaken,
anguished, my whole being torn apart, but I didn't know what
was happening to me—what *will* happen to me— To die! The
grave! I don't understand those words!

"Oh, forgive me! Forgive me! Yesterday! It should have been
the last moment of my life. You angel! For the first time, for the
first time without any doubts, the depths of my soul were
warmed by the rapturous feeling: 'She loves me! She loves me!'
The sacred fire that emanated from your lips still burns on mine;
a new, warm rapture is in my heart. Forgive me! Forgive me!

"Ah, I knew you loved me, I could tell from those first soulful
glances, from the first time you pressed my hand, and yet, when
I was away again, when I saw Albert by your side, I grew timid
again in feverish doubting.

"Do you remember the flowers you sent me when at that terrible party you were unable to say a word to me or give me your
hand? Oh, I knelt in front of them half the night, and they assured me of your love. But, alas, those impressions passed by,
just as the feeling of God's mercy gradually fades again from the
believer's soul, that mercy which is offered to him in heavenly
abundance by visible holy signs.

"All of that is perishable, but no eternity will extinguish the
glowing life which I tasted on your lips yesterday, which I feel
within me! She loves me! This arm has embraced her, these lips
have trembled on her lips, this mouth has stammered next to
hers. She is mine! You are mine! Yes, Lotte, forever.

"And what does it mean if Albert is your husband? Husband!
That would count for this world—and would it be a sin for this
world that I love you, that I want to tear you out of his arms and
clasp you in mine? A sin? Very well, and I'm punishing myself

wonne geschmeckt, diese Sünde, habe Lebensbalsam und Kraft in
mein Herz gesaugt. Du bist von diesem Augenblicke mein! mein, o
Lotte! Ich gehe voran! gehe zu meinem Vater, zu deinem Vater. Dem
will ichs klagen, und er wird mich trösten, bis du kommst, und ich
fliege dir entgegen und fasse dich und bleibe bei dir vor dem
Angesichte des Unendlichen in ewigen Umarmungen.
Ich träume nicht, ich wähne nicht! nahe am Grabe wird mir es
heller. Wir werden sein! wir werden uns wiedersehen! Deine Mutter
sehen! ich werde sie sehen, werde sie finden, ach und vor ihr mein
ganzes Herz ausschütten! Deine Mutter, dein Ebenbild. –

Gegen eilfe fragte Werther seinen Bedienten, ob wohl Albert zu-
rückgekommen sei? Der Bediente sagte: ja, er habe dessen Pferd
dahinführen sehen. Drauf gibt ihm der Herr ein offenes Zettelchen
des Inhalts:

Wollten Sie mir wohl zu einer vorhabenden Reise Ihre Pistolen lei-
hen? Leben Sie recht wohl!

Die liebe Frau hatte die letzte Nacht wenig geschlafen; was sie
gefürchtet hatte, war entschieden, auf eine Weise entschieden, die sie
weder ahnen noch fürchten konnte. Ihr sonst so rein und leicht
fließendes Blut war in einer fieberhaften Empörung, tausenderlei
Empfindungen zerrütteten das schöne Herz. War es das Feuer von
Werthers Umarmungen, das sie in ihrem Busen fühlte? war es
Unwille über seine Verwegenheit? war es eine unmutige Vergleichung ihres gegenwärtigen Zustandes mit jenen Tagen ganz unbefan-
gener freier Unschuld und sorglosen Zutrauens an sich selbst? Wie
sollte sie ihrem Manne entgegengehen? wie ihm eine Szene bekennen, die sie so gut gestehen durfte und die sie sich doch zu gestehen
nicht getraute? Sie hatten so lange gegen einander geschwiegen, und
sollte sie die erste sein, die das Stillschweigen bräche und eben zur
unrechten Zeit ihrem Gatten eine so unerwartete Entdeckung
machte? Schon fürchtete sie, die bloße Nachricht von Werthers
Besuch werde ihm einen unangenehmen Eindruck machen, und nun
gar diese unerwartete Katastrophe! Konnte sie wohl hoffen, daß ihr
Mann sie ganz im rechten Lichte sehen, ganz ohne Vorurteil
aufnehmen würde? und konnte sie wünschen, daß er in ihrer Seele

for it; I've tasted it in all its heavenly bliss, that sin, I've drawn the balm of life, and strength, into my heart. From this moment on, you are mine! Mine, Lotte! I'm leading the way, going to my Father, to your Father. I shall make my complaint to him, and he will comfort me until you come and I fly to meet you, and I take hold of you, and I remain with you before the face of the Eternal One in everlasting embraces.

"I'm not dreaming, I'm not having delusions! Close to the grave, I see things more clearly. We shall exist! We shall meet again! We shall see your mother! I'll see her, find her, ah, and pour out my whole heart to her! Your mother, the image of you.—"

About eleven Werther asked his valet whether Albert had returned. His valet said yes, he had seen his horse being led away. Thereupon his master handed him an open note, which read:

"Would you lend me your pistols for a trip I intend to make? Farewell and be happy!"[35]

The dear woman had slept very little the previous night; what she had feared had come to pass, come to pass in a way that she had been unable to foresee or guard against. Her blood, which normally flowed so purely and lightly, was in feverish turmoil, emotions of a thousand kinds were upsetting her lovely heart. Was it the fire of Werther's embraces that she felt in her bosom? Was it indignation at his boldness? Was it a vexatious comparison between her present state and those days of totally carefree candid innocence and untroubled self-confidence? How should she greet her husband? How should she disclose to him a scene which she could confess to him so safely, but which she didn't dare to confess? They had kept silent on that subject for so long, and was she to be the first one to break that silence and make so unexpected a revelation to her husband at a very inopportune time? She was already afraid that the mere report of Werther's visit would make an unpleasant impression on him, and now this unexpected catastrophe to boot! Could she really expect her husband to see her in exactly the right light and accept her without prejudice? And could she wish he would want to delve into

35. The exact wording of Jerusalem's real note to Kestner! The formal *Sie* for "you" is in contradiction to the *du*-basis between Werther and Albert in the novel.

lesen möchte? Und doch wieder, konnte sie sich verstellen gegen den Mann, vor dem sie immer wie ein kristallhelles Glas offen und frei gestanden war und dem sie keine ihrer Empfindungen jemals verheimlicht noch verheimlichen können? Eins und das andre machte ihr Sorgen und setzte sie in Verlegenheit; und immer kehrten ihre Gedanken wieder zu Werthern, der für sie verloren war, den sie nicht lassen konnte, den sie leider! sich selbst überlassen mußte und dem, wenn er sie verloren hatte, nichts mehr übrig blieb.

Wie schwer lag jetzt, was sie sich in dem Augenblick nicht deutlich machen konnte, die Stockung auf ihr, die sich unter ihnen festgesetzt hatte! So verständige, so gute Menschen fingen wegen gewisser heimlicher Verschiedenheiten unter einander zu schweigen an, jedes dachte seinem Recht und dem Unrechte des andern nach, und die Verhältnisse verwickelten und verhetzten sich dergestalt, daß es unmöglich ward, den Knoten eben in dem kritischen Momente, von dem alles abhing, zu lösen. Hätte eine glückliche Vertraulichkeit sie früher wieder einander näher gebracht, wäre Liebe und Nachsicht wechselsweise unter ihnen lebendig worden und hätte ihre Herzen aufgeschlossen, vielleicht wäre unser Freund noch zu retten gewesen.

Noch ein sonderbarer Umstand kam dazu. Werther hatte, wie wir aus seinen Briefen wissen, nie ein Geheimnis daraus gemacht, daß er sich, diese Welt zu verlassen, sehnte. Albert hatte ihn oft bestritten, auch war zwischen Lotten und ihrem Mann manchmal die Rede davon gewesen. Dieser, wie er einen entschiedenen Widerwillen gegen die Tat empfand, hatte auch gar oft mit einer Art von Empfindlichkeit, die sonst ganz außer seinem Charakter lag, zu erkennen gegeben, daß er an dem Ernst eines solchen Vorsatzes sehr zu zweifeln Ursach finde, er hatte sich sogar darüber einigen Scherz erlaubt und seinen Unglauben Lotten mitgeteilt. Dies beruhigte sie zwar von einer Seite, wenn ihre Gedanken ihr das traurige Bild vorführten, von der andern aber fühlte sie sich auch dadurch gehindert, ihrem Manne die Besorgnisse mitzuteilen, die sie in dem Augenblicke quälten.

Albert kam zurück, und Lotte ging ihm mit einer verlegnen Hastigkeit entgegen, er war nicht heiter, sein Geschäft war nicht vollbracht, er hatte an dem benachbarten Amtmanne einen unbiegsamen, kleinsinnigen Menschen gefunden. Der üble Weg auch hatte ihn verdrießlich gemacht.

Er fragte, ob nichts vorgefallen sei, und sie antwortete mit Übereilung: Werther sei gestern abends dagewesen. Er fragte, ob Briefe gekommen, und er erhielt zur Antwort, daß ein Brief und Pakete auf seiner Stube lägen. Er ging hinüber, und Lotte blieb

her soul? Then again, could she put on a pretense to the man before whom she had always stood as open and candid as a crystalline glass, from whom she had never concealed any of her feelings, or had been able to? Both one and the other worried and embarrassed her; and her thoughts constantly returned to Werther, who was lost to her, whom she couldn't do without, whom she, alas, had to abandon to himself, and who had nothing else left once he had lost her.

Though she couldn't make it clear to herself at that moment, how grievously she now felt the deadlock that had established itself between her and her husband! Because of certain secret differences, such intelligent and kind people began to keep things from each other; each one brooded on his own rightness and the other's wrongness, and the circumstances became so tangled and harried that it was impossible to undo the knot at the critical moment on which everything depended. Had a fortunate trustfulness brought them closer together again sooner, had love and consideration revived mutually between them, opening their hearts, perhaps our friend could still have been saved.

There was one other peculiar circumstance. As we know from Werther's letters, he had never made a secret of his longing to leave this world. Albert had often argued with him about it, and Lotte and her husband had discussed it at times. Albert, who felt decided repugnance to suicide, had even frequently, with a sort of resentment quite out of character, made it known that he had reason to have strong doubts about the seriousness of such intentions; he had even allowed himself a few jokes on the subject and had communicated his disbelief to Lotte. This, to be sure, calmed her down on the one hand, when her thoughts depicted that mournful image to her, but on the other hand she felt herself thereby prevented from sharing with her husband the worries tormenting her at such times.

Albert returned, and Lotte met him with embarrassed haste; he wasn't in a good mood; his business hadn't been settled; he had found the neighboring bailiff to be an inflexible, narrow-minded person. The badness of the roads had made him peevish, as well.

He asked whether anything had occurred, and she answered, too hastily, that Werther had come the evening before. He asked whether letters had arrived, and received the reply that a letter and some parcels were in his room. He went there, and Lotte re-

allein. Die Gegenwart des Mannes, den sie liebte und ehrte, hatte
einen neuen Eindruck in ihr Herz gemacht. Das Andenken seines
Edelmuts, seiner Liebe und Güte hatte ihr Gemüt mehr beruhigt,
sie fühlte einen heimlichen Zug, ihm zu folgen, sie nahm ihre
Arbeit und ging auf sein Zimmer, wie sie mehr zu tun pflegte. Sie
fand ihn beschäftigt, die Pakete zu erbrechen und zu lesen. Einige
schienen nicht das Angenehmste zu enthalten. Sie tat einige
Fragen an ihn, die er kurz beantwortete, und sich an den Pult
stellte, zu schreiben.

Sie waren auf diese Weise eine Stunde nebeneinander gewesen,
und es ward immer dunkler in Lottens Gemüt. Sie fühlte, wie schwer
es ihr werden würde, ihrem Mann, auch wenn er bei dem besten
Humor wäre, das zu entdecken, was ihr auf dem Herzen lag: sie verfiel in eine Wehmut, die ihr um desto ängstlicher ward, als sie solche
zu verbergen und ihre Tränen zu verschlucken suchte.

Die Erscheinung von Werthers Knaben setzte sie in die größte
Verlegenheit; er überreichte Alberten das Zettelchen, der sich
gelassen nach seiner Frau wendete und sagte: Gib ihm die Pistolen. –
Ich lasse ihm glückliche Reise wünschen, sagte er zum Jungen. – Das
fiel auf sie wie ein Donnerschlag, sie schwankte aufzustehen, sie
wußte nicht, wie ihr geschah. Langsam ging sie nach der Wand, zit-
ternd nahm sie das Gewehr herunter, putzte den Staub ab und zauderte und hätte noch lange gezögert, wenn nicht Albert durch einen
fragenden Blick sie gedrängt hätte. Sie gab das unglückliche Werkzeug dem Knaben, ohne ein Wort vorbringen zu können, und als der
zum Hause hinaus war, machte sie ihre Arbeit zusammen, ging in ihr
Zimmer, in dem Zustande der unaussprechlichsten Ungewißheit. Ihr
Herz weissagte ihr alle Schrecknisse. Bald war sie im Begriffe, sich zu
den Füßen ihres Mannes zu werfen, ihm alles zu entdecken, die
Geschichte des gestrigen Abends, ihre Schuld und ihre Ahnungen.
Dann sah sie wieder keinen Ausgang des Unternehmens, am wenigsten konnte sie hoffen, ihren Mann zu einem Gange nach Werthern
zu bereden. Der Tisch ward gedeckt, und eine gute Freundin, die nur
etwas zu fragen kam, gleich gehen wollte – und blieb, machte die
Unterhaltung bei Tische erträglich; man zwang sich, man redete, man
erzählte, man vergaß sich.

Der Knabe kam mit den Pistolen zu Werthern, der sie ihm mit
Entzücken abnahm, als er hörte, Lotte habe sie ihm gegeben. Er ließ
sich Brot und Wein bringen, hieß den Knaben zu Tische gehen und
setzte sich nieder, zu schreiben:

mained alone. The presence of the man she loved and honored
had made a new impression on her heart. The recollection of his
nobility of character, his love, and his kindness had further
calmed her mind; she felt a secret urge to go after him; she took
her needlework and went to his room, as she was accustomed to
do frequently. She found him busy opening the parcels and
reading the messages. Some of them apparently didn't contain
the most pleasant of news. She asked him a few questions, which
he answered briefly, and he sat down at his desk to write.

They had been together that way for an hour, and Lotte's spirits were getting gloomier all the time. She felt how difficult it
would be for her, even if her husband were in the best humor,
to reveal to him what was oppressing her heart; she lapsed into
a melancholy which became all the more of an anguish to her
when she attempted to conceal it and blink back her tears.

The arrival of Werther's young valet gave her the greatest embarrassment; he handed Albert the note; Albert turned calmly to
his wife, saying: "Give him the pistols." "I wish him a good journey," he said to the boy. That affected her like a thunderclap; she
stood up shakily, not knowing what had come over her. Slowly
she went to the wall, tremblingly she took down the weapons;
she dusted them off, hesitated, and would have tarried longer
had Albert not hurried her with an inquisitive glance. She gave
the unlucky things to the boy without being able to utter a word;
when he had left the house, she gathered together her needlework and went to her room in a state of the most indescribable
uncertainty. Her heart predicted every horror to her. At one
point she was about to fling herself at her husband's feet, to reveal everything to him, the story of the previous evening, her
guilt, and her forebodings. Then, she no longer foresaw any result even if she tried; the last thing she could hope for was to talk
her husband into going to Werther's place. The table was set,
and a good woman friend arrived; she had merely come to ask
some question and intended to leave at once—but she stayed,
and that made the mealtime conversation bearable; they forced
themselves, they told stories, they forgot their worries.

The boy brought the pistols to Werther, who took them from
him with delight when he heard that Lotte had handed them to
him. He called for bread and wine, ordered the boy to have a
meal, and sat down to write:

Sie sind durch deine Hände gegangen, du hast den Staub davon
geputzt, ich küsse sie tausendmal, du hast sie berührt: und du, Geist
des Himmels, begünstigst meinen Entschluß! und du, Lotte, reichst
mir das Werkzeug, du, von deren Händen ich den Tod zu empfangen
wünschte und ach! nun empfange. O ich habe meinen Jungen ausge-
fragt. Du zittertest, als du sie ihm reichtest, du sagtest kein Lebewohl!
– Wehe! wehe! kein Lebewohl! – Solltest du dein Herz für mich verschlossen haben, um des Augenblicks willen, der mich ewig an dich
befestigte? Lotte, kein Jahrtausend vermag den Eindruck auszulöschen! und ich fühle es, du kannst den nicht hassen, der so für dich
glüht.

Nach Tische hieß er den Knaben alles vollends einpacken, zerriß
viele Papiere, ging aus und brachte noch kleine Schulden in Ordnung.
Er kam wieder nach Hause, ging wieder aus, vors Tor, ungeachtet des
Regens, in den gräflichen Garten, schweifte weiter in der Gegend
umher und kam mit anbrechender Nacht zurück und schrieb:

Wilhelm, ich habe zum letzten Male Feld und Wald und den
Himmel gesehen. Lebe wohl auch du! Liebe Mutter, verzeiht mir!
Tröste sie, Wilhelm! Gott segne euch! Meine Sachen sind alle in
Ordnung. Lebt wohl! wir sehen uns wieder und freudiger.

Ich habe dir übel gelohnt, Albert, und du vergibst mir. Ich habe
den Frieden deines Hauses gestört, ich habe Mißtrauen zwischen
euch gebracht. Lebe wohl! ich will es enden. O daß ihr glücklich
wäret durch meinen Tod! Albert! Albert! mache den Engel glücklich!
Und so wohne Gottes Segen über dir! –

Er kramte den Abend noch viel in seinen Papieren, zerriß vieles
und warf es in den Ofen, versiegelte einige Päcke mit den Adressen
an Wilhelm. Sie enthielten kleine Aufsätze, abgerissene Gedanken,
deren ich verschiedene gesehen habe; und nachdem er um zehn Uhr
Feuer hatte nachlegen und sich eine Flasche Wein geben lassen,
schickte er den Bedienten, dessen Kammer wie auch die Schlaf-
zimmer der Hausleute weit hinten hinaus waren, zu Bette, der sich
dann in seinen Kleidern niederlegte, um frühe bei der Hand zu sein;
denn sein Herr hatte gesagt, die Postpferde würden vor sechse vors
Haus kommen.

"They passed through your hands, you cleaned the dust off them; I kiss them a thousand times: you touched them. And you, heavenly spirit, you favor my decision! And you, Lotte, you hand me the implements, you from whose hands I wished to receive death, and, alas, I now do receive it! Oh, I questioned my boy thoroughly. You were trembling when you handed them to him, you didn't say farewell.—Woe! Woe! No farewell!—Can you have closed your heart to me because of the moment that united you to me eternally? Lotte, not even a thousand years can wipe out that impression! And I feel it, you can't hate the man who is on fire for you like this."

After eating, he ordered the boy to pack up everything; he tore up many papers, went out, and settled a few more small debts. He returned home and went out again, out the town gate, despite the rain, to the count's gardens; he roamed around the vicinity some more, returning home at nightfall, when he wrote the following two notes:

"Wilhelm, I've seen the fields and the woods and the sky for the last time. Farewell to you, too! Mother dear, forgive me! Console her, Wilhelm! God bless you all! My affairs are all in order. Farewell! We'll meet again, when we'll be happier."

"Albert, I've paid you back badly, but you'll forgive me. I disturbed the peace of your household, and I've brought distrust between you and your wife. Farewell! I'm putting an end to it. I hope my death can make you both happy! Albert! Albert! Make that angel happy! And so, may God's blessing repose on you!—"

That evening he still spent a lot of time rummaging in his papers; he tore up many things and threw them in the stove; he sealed a few parcels and addressed them to Wilhelm. They contained short essays and disconnected thoughts, several of which I have seen. Around ten, after he had had the fire replenished and a bottle of wine brought, he sent his valet, whose room, like the other tenants' bedrooms, was far in the back, to bed. The boy lay down fully dressed so he could be available at once in the morning, because his master had said that the post horses would arrive at the house before six.

Nach Eilfe.

Alles ist so still um mich her, und so ruhig meine Seele. Ich danke dir,
Gott, der du diesen letzten Augenblicken diese Wärme, diese Kraft
schenkest.

Ich trete an das Fenster, meine Beste! und sehe, und sehe noch
durch die stürmenden, vorüberfliehenden Wolken einzelne Sterne
des ewigen Himmels! Nein, ihr werdet nicht fallen! der Ewige trägt
euch an seinem Herzen, und mich. Ich sehe die Deichselsterne des
Wagens, des liebsten unter allen Gestirnen. Wenn ich nachts von dir
ging, wie ich aus deinem Tore trat, stand er gegen mir über. Mit
welcher Trunkenheit habe ich ihn oft angesehen! oft mit aufgehobe-
nen Händen ihn zum Zeichen, zum heiligen Merksteine meiner
gegenwärtigen Seligkeit gemacht! und noch – O Lotte, was erinnert
mich nicht an dich! umgibst du mich nicht! und habe ich nicht, gleich
einem Kinde, ungenügsam allerlei Kleinigkeiten zu mir gerissen, die
du Heilige berührt hattest!

Liebes Schattenbild! Ich vermache dir es zurück, Lotte, und bitte
dich, es zu ehren. Tausend, tausend Küsse habe ich drauf gedrückt,
tausend Grüße ihm zugewinkt, wenn ich ausging oder nach Hause
kam.

Ich habe deinen Vater in einem Zettelchen gebeten, meine Leiche
zu schützen. Auf dem Kirchhofe sind zwei Lindenbäume, hinten in
der Ecke nach dem Felde zu; dort wünsche ich zu ruhen. Er kann, er
wird das für seinen Freund tun. Bitte ihn auch. Ich will frommen
Christen nicht zumuten, ihren Körper neben einen armen Unglücklichen zu legen. Ach ich wollte, ihr begrübt mich am Wege, oder im
einsamen Tale, daß Priester und Levit vor dem bezeichneten Steine
sich segnend vorübergingen und der Samariter eine Träne weinte.

Hier, Lotte! Ich schaudere nicht, den kalten, schrecklichen Kelch
zu fassen, aus dem ich den Taumel des Todes trinken soll! Du reichtest mir ihn, und ich zage nicht. All! all! So sind alle die Wünsche und
Hoffnungen meines Lebens erfüllt! So kalt, so starr an der ehernen
Pforte des Todes anzuklopfen.

Daß ich des Glückes hätte teilhaftig werden können, für *dich* zu
sterben! Lotte, für *dich* mich hinzugeben! Ich wollte mutig, ich
wollte freudig sterben, wenn ich dir die Ruhe, die Wonne deines
Lebens wieder schaffen könnte. Aber ach! das ward nur wenigen

"After eleven
"Everything around me is so quiet, and my soul is so calm. I thank you, God, for granting these last moments this warmth, this strength.

"I step to the window, dearest woman, and I see, I still see a few stars of eternal heaven through the stormy clouds scudding by! No, you stars won't fall! The Eternal One carries you, and me, next to his heart. I see the handle of the Big Dipper,[36] that loveliest of constellations. When I used to leave your house at night, when I stepped out of your garden gate, it used to be facing me. With what enthusiasm I often beheld it! Often with uplifted hands I made it the symbol, the sacred sign of the bliss I was feeling! And still— Oh, Lotte, what doesn't remind me of you? Don't you encompass me? And haven't I, like a child, greedily snatched every trifling thing that was touched by your holy hands?

"Dear silhouette! I bequeath it to you, Lotte, and I implore you to revere it. I've given it a thousand, thousand kisses, waved a thousand greetings to it, whenever I went out or came home.

"In a note I've asked your father to protect my body. In the churchyard there are two lime trees, in the back, in the corner near the field; there I wish to rest. He can, he will do that for his friend. You ask him, too! I don't want to give pious Christians the unpleasantness of laying their bodies down next to an unfortunate wretch. Ah, I'd like you to bury me by the wayside, or in the lonely valley, so that the priest and the Levite might bless themselves as they pass the marked stone, and the Samaritan might shed a tear.[37]

"Here, Lotte! I don't shudder to grasp the cold, terrible chalice from which I shall drink the dizziness of death! You are handing it to me, and I am unafraid. Over! Over! Thus all the wishes and hopes of my life have come true! To knock at the bronze portal of death, so cold, so rigid.

"To think I've been able to taste the happiness of dying for *you!* To sacrifice myself for *you,* Lotte! I wanted to die courageously, joyfully, if I could restore to you the repose and bliss of your life. But, alas, it is given to only a very few noble souls to

---

36. Literally: "the stars that form the shaft of the Chariot" (the German equivalent of the Dipper).   37. A reference to the parable of the Good Samaritan (Luke 10:31–33).

Edeln gegeben, ihr Blut für die Ihrigen zu vergießen und durch ihren
Tod ein neues hundertfältiges Leben ihren Freunden anzufachen.

In diesen Kleidern, Lotte, will ich begraben sein, du hast sie berührt, geheiligt; ich habe auch deinen Vater *da*rum gebeten. Meine
Seele schwebt über dem Sarge. Man soll meine Taschen nicht aus-
suchen. Diese blaßrote Schleife, die du am Busen hattest, als ich dich
zum ersten Male unter deinen Kindern fand – O küsse sie tausendmal
und erzähle ihnen das Schicksal ihres unglücklichen Freundes. Die
Lieben! sie wimmeln um mich. Ach wie ich mich an dich schloß! seit
dem ersten Augenblicke dich nicht lassen konnte! – Diese Schleife
soll mit mir begraben werden. An meinem Geburtstage schenktest du
mir sie! Wie ich das alles verschlang! – Ach ich dachte nicht, daß mich
der Weg hierher führen sollte! – – Sei ruhig! ich bitte dich, sei ruhig! –
Sie sind geladen – Es schlägt zwölfe! So sei es denn! – Lotte! Lotte,
lebe wohl! lebe wohl! –

Ein Nachbar sah den Blick vom Pulver und hörte den Schuß fallen;
da aber alles stille blieb, achtete er nicht weiter drauf.

Morgens um sechse tritt der Bediente herein mit dem Lichte. Er
findet seinen Herrn an der Erde, die Pistole und Blut. Er ruft, er faßt
ihn an; keine Antwort, er röchelte nur noch. Er läuft nach den Ärzten,
nach Alberten. Lotte hört die Schelle ziehen, ein Zittern ergreift alle
ihre Glieder. Sie weckt ihren Mann, sie stehen auf, der Bediente
bringt heulend und stotternd die Nachricht, Lotte sinkt ohnmächtig
vor Alberten nieder.

Als der Medikus zu dem Unglücklichen kam, fand er ihn an der
Erde ohne Rettung, der Puls schlug, die Glieder waren alle gelähmt.
Über dem rechten Auge hatte er sich durch den Kopf geschossen, das
Gehirn war herausgetrieben. Man ließ ihm zum Überfluß eine Ader
am Arme, das Blut lief, er holte noch immer Atem.

Aus dem Blut auf der Lehne des Sessels konnte man schließen, er
habe sitzend vor dem Schreibtische die Tat vollbracht, dann ist er
heruntergesunken, hat sich konvulsivisch um den Stuhl herum-
gewälzt. Er lag gegen das Fenster entkräftet auf dem Rücken, war in
völliger Kleidung, gestiefelt, im blauen Frack mit gelber Weste.

Das Haus, die Nachbarschaft, die Stadt kam in Aufruhr. Albert trat
herein. Werthern hatte man auf das Bette gelegt, die Stirn verbunden,
sein Gesicht schon wie eines Toten, er rührte kein Glied. Die Lunge
röchelte noch fürchterlich, bald schwach, bald stärker; man erwartete
sein Ende.

shed their blood for their loved ones and incite by their death a new hundredfold life for their friends.

"Lotte, I wish to be buried in these clothes; you touched them and consecrated them; I've asked your father for that favor, as well. My soul is hovering over the coffin. I don't want my pockets searched. This pink bow which you wore on your bosom when I first found you in the midst of your children—oh, kiss it a thousand times and tell them the fate of their unlucky friend. The dear ones! They're swarming around me. Oh, how I tied myself to you, unable to leave you from the first moment on!—This bow is to be buried with me. You gave it to me on my birthday! How greedily I gulped everything down!—Ah, I never thought the way would lead me here!——Be calm, I implore you, be calm!—

"They're loaded— It's striking twelve! So be it, then!—Lotte! Lotte, farewell, farewell!—"

A neighbor saw the powder flash and heard the shot; but when everything was quiet after that, he paid no further attention to it.

In the morning about six the servant came in with the candle. He found his master on the floor, he saw the pistol and blood. He cried out, he took hold of him; no answer, just a continuing death rattle. He ran for the doctors, for Albert. Lotte heard the doorbell being pulled, and began to tremble all over. She woke up her husband, they got out of bed, and the valet, howling and stuttering, told the news. Lotte swooned away in front of Albert.

When the physician came to the unhappy man, he found him on the floor, past hope; his pulse was beating, but all his limbs were paralyzed. He had shot himself in the head over the right eye; his brain had been dashed out. Needlessly they bled him on the arm, the blood flowed, he was still breathing.

From the blood on the back of the chair it could be deduced that he had done the deed sitting at his desk; then he had fallen and rolled around the chair in convulsions. He was lying against the window on his back, he was fully dressed in boots, his blue dress coat, and his yellow waistcoat.

The house, the neighborhood, the town were thrown into an uproar. Albert came in. Werther had been placed on his bed; his forehead bandaged, his face was already like a dead man's; he didn't move a muscle. His lungs were still rattling horribly, now feebly, now more strongly. His death was expected.

Von dem Weine hatte er nur ein Glas getrunken. Emilia Galotti lag auf dem Pulte aufgeschlagen.

Von Alberts Bestürzung, von Lottens Jammer laßt mich nichts sagen.

Der alte Amtmann kam auf die Nachricht hereingesprengt, er küßte den Sterbenden unter den heißesten Tränen. Seine ältesten Söhne kamen bald nach ihm zu Fuße, sie fielen neben dem Bette nieder im Ausdrucke des unbändigsten Schmerzens, küßten ihm die Hände und den Mund, und der ältste, den er immer am meisten geliebt, hing an seinen Lippen, bis er verschieden war und man den Knaben mit Gewalt wegriß. Um zwölfe mittags starb er. Die Gegenwart des Amtmannes und seine Anstalten tuschten einen Auflauf. Nachts gegen eilfe ließ er ihn an die Stätte begraben, die er sich erwählt hatte. Der Alte folgte der Leiche und die Söhne, Albert vermochts nicht. Man fürchtete für Lottens Leben. Handwerker trugen ihn. Kein Geistlicher hat ihn begleitet.

He had drunk only one glass of the wine. *Emilia Galotti*[38] lay open on his desk.

Allow me to say nothing about Albert's dismay and Lotte's grief.

On hearing the news, the old bailiff came hurrying over; with hot tears he kissed the dying man. His eldest sons arrived on foot soon after he did; they sank down beside the bed, displaying the most uncontrollable sorrow; they kissed Werther's hands and lips, and the oldest one, whom Werther had always loved most, hung on his lips until he died and the boy was pulled away forcibly. He died at twelve noon. The presence of the bailiff, and the measures he took, prevented a crowd from assembling. About eleven at night he had him buried in the place he had chosen for himself. The old man accompanied the body, as did his sons; Albert couldn't. There was fear for Lotte's life.[39] Laborers carried the bier. No clergyman attended.

---

38. A play by Gotthold Ephraim Lessing (1729–1781) which was new in 1772, the year in which the latter part of the novel takes place. Lessing was a patron of the real-life Jerusalem; he *had* been reading the play, which concerns a girl who kills herself rather than be dishonored.   39. The original 1774 edition made it clear that Lotte's life wasn't in danger, and that she survived.

APPENDIX ONE

Poem Written by Goethe for a 1775 Printing[40]

(The first quatrain preceded Book One; the second, Book Two.)

Jeder Jüngling sehnt sich, so zu lieben,
Jedes Mädchen, so geliebt zu sein;
Ach, der heiligste von unsern Trieben,
Warum quillt aus ihm die grimme Pein?

Du beweinst, du liebst ihn, liebe Seele,
Rettest sein Gedächtnis von der Schmach;
Sieh, dir winkt sein Geist aus seiner Höhle:
Sei ein Mann, und folge mir nicht nach.

(Every young man yearns to love in that way; every girl yearns to be loved in that way; ah, that most sacred of our urges: why does fierce sorrow stem from it? / You mourn him, you love him, dear soul, you rescue his memory from disgrace; behold, his spirit beckons to you from his grave: "Be a man, and do not follow me!")

APPENDIX TWO

Original English Text of the Principal Ossian Passage[41]

Star of descending night! fair is thy light in the west! thou liftest thy unshorn head from thy cloud: thy steps are stately on thy hill. What dost thou behold in the plain? The stormy winds are laid. The murmur of the torrent comes from afar. Roaring waves climb the distant rock. The flies of evening are on their feeble wings; the hum of their course is on the field. What dost thou behold, fair light? But thou dost smile and depart. The waves come with joy around thee: they bathe

---

40. See Introduction, page vii.   41. See footnote 34, page 175.

thy lovely hair. Farewell, thou silent beam! Let the light of Ossian's soul arise!

And it does arise in its strength! I behold my departed friends. Their gathering is on Lora, as in the days of other years. Fingal comes like a watery column of mist; his heroes are around. And see the bards of song, grey-haired Ullin! stately Ryno! Alpin, with the tuneful voice! the soft complaint of Minona! How are ye changed, my friends, since the days of Selma's feast? when we contended, like gales of spring, as they fly along the hill, and bend by turns the feebly-whistling grass.

Minona came forth in her beauty; with down-cast look and tearful eye. Her hair flew slowly on the blast, that rushed unfrequent from the hill. The souls of the heroes were sad when she raised the tuneful voice. Often had they seen the grave of Salgar, the dark dwelling of white-bosomed Colma. Colma left alone on the hill, with all her voice of song! Salgar promised to come: but the night descended around. Hear the voice of Colma, when she sat alone on the hill!

COLMA.
It is night; I am alone, forlorn on the hill of storms. The wind is heard in the mountain. The torrent pours down the rock. No hut receives me from the rain, forlorn on the hill of winds.

Rise, moon! from behind thy clouds. Stars of the night, arise! Lead me, some light, to the place where my love rests from the chase alone! his bow near him, unstrung: his dogs panting around him. But here I must sit alone, by the rock of the mossy stream. The stream and the wind roar aloud. I hear not the voice of my love! Why delays my Salgar, why the chief of the hill, his promise? Here is the rock, and here the tree! here is the roaring stream! Thou didst promise with night to be here. Ah! whither is my Salgar gone? With thee I would fly, from my father; with thee, from my brother of pride. Our race have long been foes; we are not foes, O Salgar!

Cease a little while, O wind! stream, be thou silent a while! let my voice be heard around. Let my wanderer hear me! Salgar! it is Colma who calls. Here is the tree, and the rock. Salgar, my love! I am here. Why delayest thou thy coming? Lo! the calm moon comes forth. The flood is bright in the vale. The rocks are grey on the steep. I see him not on the brow. His dogs come not before him, with tidings of his near approach. Here I must sit alone!

Who lie on the heath beside me? Are they my love and my brother? Speak to me, O my friends! To Colma they give no reply. Speak to me: I am alone! My soul is tormented with fears! Ah! they are dead! Their

swords are red from the fight. O my brother! my brother! why hast
thou slain my Salgar? why, O Salgar! hast thou slain my brother? Dear
were ye both to me! what shall I say in your praise? Thou wert fair on
the hill among thousands! he was terrible in fight. Speak to me; hear
my voice; hear me, sons of my love! They are silent; silent for ever!
Cold, cold are their breasts of clay! Oh! from the rock on the hill; from
the top of the windy steep, speak, ye ghosts of the dead! speak, I will
not be afraid! Whither are ye gone to rest? In what cave of the hill
shall I find the departed? No feeble voice is on the gale; no answer
half-drowned in the storm!

I sit in my grief! I wait for morning in my tears! Rear the tomb, ye
friends of the dead. Close it not till Colma come. My life flies away
like a dream! why should I stay behind? Here shall I rest with my
friends, by the stream of the sounding rock. When night comes on the
hill; when the loud winds arise; my ghost shall stand in the blast, and
mourn the death of my friends. The hunter shall hear from his booth.
He shall fear, but love my voice! For sweet shall my voice be for my
friends: pleasant were her friends to Colma!

Such was thy song, Minona, softly-blushing daughter of Torman.
Our tears descended from Colma, and our souls were sad! Ullin came
with his harp; he gave the song of Alpin. The voice of Alpin was pleasant; the soul of Ryno was a beam of fire! But they had rested in the narrow house: their voice had ceased in Selma. Ullin had returned, one
day, from the chase, before the heroes fell. He heard their strife on the
hill; their song was soft but sad. They mourned the fall of Morar, first
of mortal men! His soul was like the soul of Fingal; his sword like the
sword of Oscar. But he fell, and his father mourned: his sister's eyes
were full of tears. Minona's eyes were full of tears, the sister of car-
borne Morar. She retired from the song of Ullin, like the moon in the
west, when she foresees the shower, and hides her fair head in a cloud.
I touched the harp, with Ullin; the song of mourning rose!

RYNO.   .

The wind and the rain are past: calm is the noon of day. The clouds
are divided in heaven. Over the green hills flies the inconstant sun.
Red through the stony vale comes down the stream of the hill. Sweet
are thy murmurs, O stream! but more sweet is the voice I hear. It is
the voice of Alpin, the son of song, mourning for the dead! Bent is his
head of age; red his tearful eye. Alpin, thou son of song, why alone on
the silent hill? why complainest thou, as a blast in the wood; as a wave
on the lonely shore?

ALPIN.

My tears, O Ryno! are for the dead; my voice for those that have passed away. Tall thou art on the hill; fair among the sons of the vale. But thou shalt fall like Morar; the mourner shall sit on thy tomb. The hills shall know thee no more; thy bow shall lie in thy hall unstrung!

Thou wert swift, O Morar! as a roe on the desert; terrible as a meteor of fire. Thy wrath was as the storm. Thy sword in battle, as lightning in the field. Thy voice was a stream after rain; like thunder on distant hills. Many fell by thy arm; they were consumed in the flames of thy wrath. But when thou didst return from war, how peaceful was thy brow! Thy face was like the sun after rain; like the moon in the silence of night; calm as the breast of the lake when the loud wind is laid.

Narrow is thy dwelling now! dark the place of thine abode! With three steps I compass thy grave, O thou who wast so great before! Four stones, with their heads of moss, are the only memorial of thee. A tree with scarce a leaf, long grass which whistles in the wind, mark to the hunter's eye the grave of the mighty Morar. Morar! thou art low indeed. Thou hast no mother to mourn thee; no maid with her tears of love. Dead is she that brought thee forth. Fallen is the daughter of Morglan.

Who on his staff is this? who is this, whose head is white with age? whose eyes are red with tears? who quakes at every step? It is thy father, O Morar! the father of no son but thee. He heard of thy fame in war; he heard of foes dispersed. He heard of Morar's renown; why did he not hear of his wound? Weep, thou father of Morar! weep; but thy son heareth thee not. Deep is the sleep of the dead; low their pillow of dust. No more shall he hear thy voice; no more awake at thy call. When shall it be morn in the grave, to bid the slumberer awake? Farewell, thou bravest of men! thou conqueror in the field! but the field shall see thee no more; nor the dark wood be lightened with the splendour of thy steel. Thou has left no son. The song shall preserve thy name. Future times shall hear of thee; they shall hear of the fallen Morar!

The grief of all arose, but most the bursting sigh of Armin. He remembers the death of his son, who fell in the days of his youth. Carmor was near the hero, the chief of the echoing Galmal. Why bursts the sigh of Armin? he said. Is there a cause to mourn? The song comes, with its music, to melt and please the soul. It is like soft mist, that, rising from a lake, pours on the silent vale; the green flowers are filled with dew, but the sun returns in his strength, and the mist is gone. Why art thou sad, O Armin! chief of sea-surrounded Gorma?

Sad I am! nor small is my cause of woe! Carmor, thou hast lost no son; thou hast lost no daughter of beauty. Colgar the valiant lives; and Annira, fairest maid. The boughs of thy house ascend, O Carmor! but Armin is the last of his race. Dark is thy bed, O Daura! deep thy sleep in the tomb! When shalt thou awake with thy songs? with all thy voice of music?

Arise, winds of autumn, arise; blow along the heath! streams of the mountains roar! roar, tempests, in the groves of my oaks! walk through broken clouds, O moon! show thy pale face, at intervals! bring to my mind the night, when all my children fell; when Arindal the mighty fell; when Daura the lovely failed! Daura, my daughter! thou wert fair; fair as the moon on Fura; white as the driven snow; sweet as the breathing gale. Arindal, thy bow was strong. Thy spear was swift in the field. Thy look was like mist on the wave; thy shield, a red cloud in a storm. Armar, renowned in war, came, and sought Daura's love. He was not long refused: fair was the hope of their friends!

Erath, son of Odgal, repined: his brother had been slain by Armar. He came disguised like a son of the sea: fair was his skiff on the wave; white his locks of age; calm his serious brow. Fairest of women, he said, lovely daughter of Armin! a rock not distant in the sea bears a tree on its side; red shines the fruit afar. There Armar waits for Daura. I come to carry his love! She went; she called on Armar. Nought answered, but the son of the rock, Armar, my love! my love! why tormentest thou me with fear? hear, son of Arnart, hear: it is Daura who calleth thee! Erath the traitor fled laughing to the land. She lifted up her voice; she called for her brother and her father. Arindal! Armin! none to relieve your Daura!

Her voice came over the sea. Arindal my son descended from the hill; rough in the spoils of the chase. His arrows rattled by his side; his bow was in his hand: five dark grey dogs attend his steps. He saw fierce Erath on the shore: he seized and bound him to an oak. Thick wind the thongs of the hide around his limbs; he loads the wind with his groans. Arindal ascends the deep in his boat, to bring Daura to land. Armar came in his wrath, and let fly the grey-feathered shaft. It sung; it sunk in thy heart, O Arindal, my son! for Erath the traitor thou diedst. The oar is stopped at once; he panted on the rock and expired. What is thy grief, O Daura, when round thy feet is poured thy brother's blood! The boat is broken in twain. Armar plunges into the sea, to rescue his Daura, or die. Sudden a blast from the hill came over the waves. He sank, and he rose no more.

Alone, on the sea-beat rock, my daughter was heard to complain.

Frequent and loud were her cries. What could her father do? All night I stood on the shore. I saw her by the faint beam of the moon. All night I heard her cries. Loud was the wind; the rain beat hard on the hill. Before morning appeared her voice was weak. It died away, like the evening-breeze among the grass of the rocks. Spent with grief she expired; and left thee, Armin, alone. Gone is my strength in war! fallen my pride among women! When the storms aloft arise; when the north lifts the wave on high; I sit by the sounding shore, and look on the fatal rock. Often by the setting moon, I see the ghosts of my children. Half viewless, they walk in mournful conference together.

A CATALOG OF SELECTED

DOVER BOOKS

IN ALL FIELDS OF INTEREST

A CATALOG OF SELECTED DOVER BOOKS IN ALL FIELDS OF INTEREST

100 BEST-LOVED POEMS, Edited by Philip Smith. "The Passionate Shepherd to His Love," "Shall I compare thee to a summer's day?" "Death, be not proud," "The Raven," "The Road Not Taken," plus works by Blake, Wordsworth, Byron, Shelley, Keats, many others. 96pp. 5$\frac{3}{16}$ x 8¼. 0-486-28553-7

100 SMALL HOUSES OF THE THIRTIES, Brown-Blodgett Company. Exterior photographs and floor plans for 100 charming structures. Illustrations of models accompanied by descriptions of interiors, color schemes, closet space, and other amenities. 200 illustrations. 112pp. 8⅜ x 11. 0-486-44131-8

1000 TURN-OF-THE-CENTURY HOUSES: With Illustrations and Floor Plans, Herbert C. Chivers. Reproduced from a rare edition, this showcase of homes ranges from cottages and bungalows to sprawling mansions. Each house is meticulously illustrated and accompanied by complete floor plans. 256pp. 9⅜ x 12¼. 0-486-45596-3

101 GREAT AMERICAN POEMS, Edited by The American Poetry & Literacy Project. Rich treasury of verse from the 19th and 20th centuries includes works by Edgar Allan Poe, Robert Frost, Walt Whitman, Langston Hughes, Emily Dickinson, T. S. Eliot, other notables. 96pp. 5$\frac{3}{16}$ x 8¼. 0-486-40158-8

101 GREAT SAMURAI PRINTS, Utagawa Kuniyoshi. Kuniyoshi was a master of the warrior woodblock print — and these 18th-century illustrations represent the pinnacle of his craft. Full-color portraits of renowned Japanese samurais pulse with movement, passion, and remarkably fine detail. 112pp. 8⅜ x 11. 0-486-46523-3

ABC OF BALLET, Janet Grosser. Clearly worded, abundantly illustrated little guide defines basic ballet-related terms: arabesque, battement, pas de chat, relevé, sissonne, many others. Pronunciation guide included. Excellent primer. 48pp. 4$\frac{5}{16}$ x 5¾. 0-486-40871-X

ACCESSORIES OF DRESS: An Illustrated Encyclopedia, Katherine Lester and Bess Viola Oerke. Illustrations of hats, veils, wigs, cravats, shawls, shoes, gloves, and other accessories enhance an engaging commentary that reveals the humor and charm of the many-sided story of accessorized apparel. 644 figures and 59 plates. 608pp. 6 ⅛ x 9¼. 0-486-43378-1

ADVENTURES OF HUCKLEBERRY FINN, Mark Twain. Join Huck and Jim as their boyhood adventures along the Mississippi River lead them into a world of excitement, danger, and self-discovery. Humorous narrative, lyrical descriptions of the Mississippi valley, and memorable characters. 224pp. 5$\frac{3}{16}$ x 8¼. 0-486-28061-6

ALICE STARMORE'S BOOK OF FAIR ISLE KNITTING, Alice Starmore. A noted designer from the region of Scotland's Fair Isle explores the history and techniques of this distinctive, stranded-color knitting style and provides copious illustrated instructions for 14 original knitwear designs. 208pp. 8⅜ x 10⅞. 0-486-47218-3

Browse over 9,000 books at www.doverpublications.com

CATALOG OF DOVER BOOKS

ALICE'S ADVENTURES IN WONDERLAND, Lewis Carroll. Beloved classic about a little girl lost in a topsy-turvy land and her encounters with the White Rabbit, March Hare, Mad Hatter, Cheshire Cat, and other delightfully improbable characters. 42 illustrations by Sir John Tenniel. 96pp. 5³⁄₁₆ x 8¼. 0-486-27543-4

AMERICA'S LIGHTHOUSES: An Illustrated History, Francis Ross Holland. Profusely illustrated fact-filled survey of American lighthouses since 1716. Over 200 stations — East, Gulf, and West coasts, Great Lakes, Hawaii, Alaska, Puerto Rico, the Virgin Islands, and the Mississippi and St. Lawrence Rivers. 240pp. 8 x 10¾. 0-486-25576-X

AN ENCYCLOPEDIA OF THE VIOLIN, Alberto Bachmann. Translated by Frederick H. Martens. Introduction by Eugene Ysaye. First published in 1925, this renowned reference remains unsurpassed as a source of essential information, from construction and evolution to repertoire and technique. Includes a glossary and 73 illustrations. 496pp. 6½ x 9¼. 0-486-46618-3

ANIMALS: 1,419 Copyright-Free Illustrations of Mammals, Birds, Fish, Insects, etc., Selected by Jim Harter. Selected for its visual impact and ease of use, this outstanding collection of wood engravings presents over 1,000 species of animals in extremely lifelike poses. Includes mammals, birds, reptiles, amphibians, fish, insects, and other invertebrates. 284pp. 9 x 12. 0-486-23766-4

THE ANNALS, Tacitus. Translated by Alfred John Church and William Jackson Brodribb. This vital chronicle of Imperial Rome, written by the era's great historian, spans A.D. 14-68 and paints incisive psychological portraits of major figures, from Tiberius to Nero. 416pp. 5³⁄₁₆ x 8¼. 0-486-45236-0

ANTIGONE, Sophocles. Filled with passionate speeches and sensitive probing of moral and philosophical issues, this powerful and often-performed Greek drama reveals the grim fate that befalls the children of Oedipus. Footnotes. 64pp. 5³⁄₁₆ x 8 ¼. 0-486-27804-2

ART DECO DECORATIVE PATTERNS IN FULL COLOR, Christian Stoll. Reprinted from a rare 1910 portfolio, 160 sensuous and exotic images depict a breathtaking array of florals, geometrics, and abstracts — all elegant in their stark simplicity. 64pp. 8⅜ x 11. 0-486-44862-2

THE ARTHUR RACKHAM TREASURY: 86 Full-Color Illustrations, Arthur Rackham. Selected and Edited by Jeff A. Menges. A stunning treasury of 86 full-page plates span the famed English artist's career, from *Rip Van Winkle* (1905) to masterworks such as *Undine, A Midsummer Night's Dream,* and *Wind in the Willows* (1939). 96pp. 8⅜ x 11. 0-486-44685-9

THE AUTHENTIC GILBERT & SULLIVAN SONGBOOK, W. S. Gilbert and A. S. Sullivan. The most comprehensive collection available, this songbook includes selections from every one of Gilbert and Sullivan's light operas. Ninety-two numbers are presented uncut and unedited, and in their original keys. 410pp. 9 x 12. 0-486-23482-7

THE AWAKENING, Kate Chopin. First published in 1899, this controversial novel of a New Orleans wife's search for love outside a stifling marriage shocked readers. Today, it remains a first-rate narrative with superb characterization. New introductory Note. 128pp. 5³⁄₁₆ x 8¼. 0-486-27786-0

BASIC DRAWING, Louis Priscilla. Beginning with perspective, this commonsense manual progresses to the figure in movement, light and shade, anatomy, drapery, composition, trees and landscape, and outdoor sketching. Black-and-white illustrations throughout. 128pp. 8⅜ x 11. 0-486-45815-6

Browse over 9,000 books at www.doverpublications.com

THE BATTLES THAT CHANGED HISTORY, Fletcher Pratt. Historian profiles 16 crucial conflicts, ancient to modern, that changed the course of Western civilization. Gripping accounts of battles led by Alexander the Great, Joan of Arc, Ulysses S. Grant, other commanders. 27 maps. 352pp. 5⅜ x 8½. 0-486-41129-X

BEETHOVEN'S LETTERS, Ludwig van Beethoven. Edited by Dr. A. C. Kalischer. Features 457 letters to fellow musicians, friends, greats, patrons, and literary men. Reveals musical thoughts, quirks of personality, insights, and daily events. Includes 15 plates. 410pp. 5⅜ x 8½. 0-486-22769-3

BERNICE BOBS HER HAIR AND OTHER STORIES, F. Scott Fitzgerald. This brilliant anthology includes 6 of Fitzgerald's most popular stories: "The Diamond as Big as the Ritz," the title tale, "The Offshore Pirate," "The Ice Palace," "The Jelly Bean," and "May Day." 176pp. 5⅜ x 8½. 0-486-47049-0

BESLER'S BOOK OF FLOWERS AND PLANTS: 73 Full-Color Plates from Hortus Eystettensis, 1613, Basilius Besler. Here is a selection of magnificent plates from the *Hortus Eystettensis,* which vividly illustrated and identified the plants, flowers, and trees that thrived in the legendary German garden at Eichstätt. 80pp. 8⅜ x 11. 0-486-46005-3

THE BOOK OF KELLS, Edited by Blanche Cirker. Painstakingly reproduced from a rare facsimile edition, this volume contains full-page decorations, portraits, illustrations, plus a sampling of textual leaves with exquisite calligraphy and ornamentation. 32 full-color illustrations. 32pp. 9⅜ x 12¼. 0-486-24345-1

THE BOOK OF THE CROSSBOW: With an Additional Section on Catapults and Other Siege Engines, Ralph Payne-Gallwey. Fascinating study traces history and use of crossbow as military and sporting weapon, from Middle Ages to modern times. Also covers related weapons: balistas, catapults, Turkish bows, more. Over 240 illustrations. 400pp. 7¼ x 10⅛. 0-486-28720-3

THE BUNGALOW BOOK: Floor Plans and Photos of 112 Houses, 1910, Henry L. Wilson. Here are 112 of the most popular and economic blueprints of the early 20th century — plus an illustration or photograph of each completed house. A wonderful time capsule that still offers a wealth of valuable insights. 160pp. 8⅜ x 11. 0-486-45104-6

THE CALL OF THE WILD, Jack London. A classic novel of adventure, drawn from London's own experiences as a Klondike adventurer, relating the story of a heroic dog caught in the brutal life of the Alaska Gold Rush. Note. 64pp. 5³⁄₁₆ x 8¼. 0-486-26472-6

CANDIDE, Voltaire. Edited by Francois-Marie Arouet. One of the world's great satires since its first publication in 1759. Witty, caustic skewering of romance, science, philosophy, religion, government — nearly all human ideals and institutions. 112pp. 5³⁄₁₆ x 8¼. 0-486-26689-3

CELEBRATED IN THEIR TIME: Photographic Portraits from the George Grantham Bain Collection, Edited by Amy Pastan. With an Introduction by Michael Carlebach. Remarkable portrait gallery features 112 rare images of Albert Einstein, Charlie Chaplin, the Wright Brothers, Henry Ford, and other luminaries from the worlds of politics, art, entertainment, and industry. 128pp. 8⅜ x 11. 0-486-46754-6

CHARIOTS FOR APOLLO: The NASA History of Manned Lunar Spacecraft to 1969, Courtney G. Brooks, James M. Grimwood, and Loyd S. Swenson, Jr. This illustrated history by a trio of experts is the definitive reference on the Apollo spacecraft and lunar modules. It traces the vehicles' design, development, and operation in space. More than 100 photographs and illustrations. 576pp. 6¾ x 9¼. 0-486-46756-2

Browse over 9,000 books at www.doverpublications.com

A CHRISTMAS CAROL, Charles Dickens. This engrossing tale relates Ebenezer Scrooge's ghostly journeys through Christmases past, present, and future and his ultimate transformation from a harsh and grasping old miser to a charitable and compassionate human being. 80pp. 5⅜₆ x 8¼. 0-486-26865-9

COMMON SENSE, Thomas Paine. First published in January of 1776, this highly influential landmark document clearly and persuasively argued for American separation from Great Britain and paved the way for the Declaration of Independence. 64pp. 5⅜₆ x 8¼. 0-486-29602-4

THE COMPLETE SHORT STORIES OF OSCAR WILDE, Oscar Wilde. Complete texts of "The Happy Prince and Other Tales," "A House of Pomegranates," "Lord Arthur Savile's Crime and Other Stories," "Poems in Prose," and "The Portrait of Mr. W. H." 208pp. 5⅜₆ x 8¼. 0-486-45216-6

COMPLETE SONNETS, William Shakespeare. Over 150 exquisite poems deal with love, friendship, the tyranny of time, beauty's evanescence, death, and other themes in language of remarkable power, precision, and beauty. Glossary of archaic terms. 80pp. 5⅜₆ x 8¼. 0-486-26686-9

THE COUNT OF MONTE CRISTO: Abridged Edition, Alexandre Dumas. Falsely accused of treason, Edmond Dantès is imprisoned in the bleak Chateau d'If. After a hair-raising escape, he launches an elaborate plot to extract a bitter revenge against those who betrayed him. 448pp. 5⅜₆ x 8¼. 0-486-45643-9

CRAFTSMAN BUNGALOWS: Designs from the Pacific Northwest, Yoho & Merritt. This reprint of a rare catalog, showcasing the charming simplicity and cozy style of Craftsman bungalows, is filled with photos of completed homes, plus floor plans and estimated costs. An indispensable resource for architects, historians, and illustrators. 112pp. 10 x 7. 0-486-46875-5

CRAFTSMAN BUNGALOWS: 59 Homes from "The Craftsman," Edited by Gustav Stickley. Best and most attractive designs from Arts and Crafts Movement publication — 1903–1916 — includes sketches, photographs of homes, floor plans, descriptive text. 128pp. 8¼ x 11. 0-486-25829-7

CRIME AND PUNISHMENT, Fyodor Dostoyevsky. Translated by Constance Garnett. Supreme masterpiece tells the story of Raskolnikov, a student tormented by his own thoughts after he murders an old woman. Overwhelmed by guilt and terror, he confesses and goes to prison. 480pp. 5⅜₆ x 8¼. 0-486-41587-2

THE DECLARATION OF INDEPENDENCE AND OTHER GREAT DOCUMENTS OF AMERICAN HISTORY: 1775-1865, Edited by John Grafton. Thirteen compelling and influential documents: Henry's "Give Me Liberty or Give Me Death," Declaration of Independence, The Constitution, Washington's First Inaugural Address, The Monroe Doctrine, The Emancipation Proclamation, Gettysburg Address, more. 64pp. 5⅜₆ x 8¼. 0-486-41124-9

THE DESERT AND THE SOWN: Travels in Palestine and Syria, Gertrude Bell. "The female Lawrence of Arabia," Gertrude Bell wrote captivating, perceptive accounts of her travels in the Middle East. This intriguing narrative, accompanied by 160 photos, traces her 1905 sojourn in Lebanon, Syria, and Palestine. 368pp. 5⅜ x 8¼.
0-486-46876-3

A DOLL'S HOUSE, Henrik Ibsen. Ibsen's best-known play displays his genius for realistic prose drama. An expression of women's rights, the play climaxes when the central character, Nora, rejects a smothering marriage and life in "a doll's house." 80pp. 5⅜₆ x 8¼. 0-486-27062-9

CATALOG OF DOVER BOOKS

DOOMED SHIPS: Great Ocean Liner Disasters, William H. Miller, Jr. Nearly 200 photographs, many from private collections, highlight tales of some of the vessels whose pleasure cruises ended in catastrophe: the *Morro Castle, Normandie, Andrea Doria, Europa,* and many others. 128pp. 8⅞ x 11¾. 0-486-45366-9

THE DORÉ BIBLE ILLUSTRATIONS, Gustave Doré. Detailed plates from the Bible: the Creation scenes, Adam and Eve, horrifying visions of the Flood, the battle sequences with their monumental crowds, depictions of the life of Jesus, 241 plates in all. 241pp. 9 x 12. 0-486-23004-X

DRAWING DRAPERY FROM HEAD TO TOE, Cliff Young. Expert guidance on how to draw shirts, pants, skirts, gloves, hats, and coats on the human figure, including folds in relation to the body, pull and crush, action folds, creases, more. Over 200 drawings. 48pp. 8¼ x 11. 0-486-45591-2

DUBLINERS, James Joyce. A fine and accessible introduction to the work of one of the 20th century's most influential writers, this collection features 15 tales, including a masterpiece of the short-story genre, "The Dead." 160pp. 5³⁄₁₆ x 8¼. 0-486-26870-5

EASY-TO-MAKE POP-UPS, Joan Irvine. Illustrated by Barbara Reid. Dozens of wonderful ideas for three-dimensional paper fun — from holiday greeting cards with moving parts to a pop-up menagerie. Easy-to-follow, illustrated instructions for more than 30 projects. 299 black-and-white illustrations. 96pp. 8⅜ x 11. 0-486-44622-0

EASY-TO-MAKE STORYBOOK DOLLS: A "Novel" Approach to Cloth Dollmaking, Sherralyn St. Clair. Favorite fictional characters come alive in this unique beginner's dollmaking guide. Includes patterns for Pollyanna, Dorothy from *The Wonderful Wizard of Oz,* Mary of *The Secret Garden,* plus easy-to-follow instructions, 263 black-and-white illustrations, and an 8-page color insert. 112pp. 8¼ x 11. 0-486-47360-0

EINSTEIN'S ESSAYS IN SCIENCE, Albert Einstein. Speeches and essays in accessible, everyday language profile influential physicists such as Niels Bohr and Isaac Newton. They also explore areas of physics to which the author made major contributions. 128pp. 5 x 8. 0-486-47011-3

EL DORADO: Further Adventures of the Scarlet Pimpernel, Baroness Orczy. A popular sequel to *The Scarlet Pimpernel,* this suspenseful story recounts the Pimpernel's attempts to rescue the Dauphin from imprisonment during the French Revolution. An irresistible blend of intrigue, period detail, and vibrant characterizations. 352pp. 5³⁄₁₆ x 8¼. 0-486-44026-5

ELEGANT SMALL HOMES OF THE TWENTIES: 99 Designs from a Competition, Chicago Tribune. Nearly 100 designs for five- and six-room houses feature New England and Southern colonials, Normandy cottages, stately Italianate dwellings, and other fascinating snapshots of American domestic architecture of the 1920s. 112pp. 9 x 12. 0-486-46910-7

THE ELEMENTS OF STYLE: The Original Edition, William Strunk, Jr. This is the book that generations of writers have relied upon for timeless advice on grammar, diction, syntax, and other essentials. In concise terms, it identifies the principal requirements of proper style and common errors. 64pp. 5⅜ x 8½. 0-486-44798-7

THE ELUSIVE PIMPERNEL, Baroness Orczy. Robespierre's revolutionaries find their wicked schemes thwarted by the heroic Pimpernel — Sir Percival Blakeney. In this thrilling sequel, Chauvelin devises a plot to eliminate the Pimpernel and his wife. 272pp. 5³⁄₁₆ x 8¼. 0-486-45464-9

AN ENCYCLOPEDIA OF BATTLES: Accounts of Over 1,560 Battles from 1479 B.C. to the Present, David Eggenberger. Essential details of every major battle in recorded history from the first battle of Megiddo in 1479 B.C. to Grenada in 1984. List of battle maps. 99 illustrations. 544pp. 6½ x 9¼. 0-486-24913-1

ENCYCLOPEDIA OF EMBROIDERY STITCHES, INCLUDING CREWEL, Marion Nichols. Precise explanations and instructions, clearly illustrated, on how to work chain, back, cross, knotted, woven stitches, and many more — 178 in all, including Cable Outline, Whipped Satin, and Eyelet Buttonhole. Over 1400 illustrations. 219pp. 8⅜ x 11¼. 0-486-22929-7

ENTER JEEVES: 15 Early Stories, P. G. Wodehouse. Splendid collection contains first 8 stories featuring Bertie Wooster, the deliciously dim aristocrat and Jeeves, his brainy, imperturbable manservant. Also, the complete Reggie Pepper (Bertie's prototype) series. 288pp. 5⅜ x 8½. 0-486-29717-9

ERIC SLOANE'S AMERICA: Paintings in Oil, Michael Wigley. With a Foreword by Mimi Sloane. Eric Sloane's evocative oils of America's landscape and material culture shimmer with immense historical and nostalgic appeal. This original hardcover collection gathers nearly a hundred of his finest paintings, with subjects ranging from New England to the American Southwest. 128pp. 10⅝ x 9. 0-486-46525-X

ETHAN FROME, Edith Wharton. Classic story of wasted lives, set against a bleak New England background. Superbly delineated characters in a hauntingly grim tale of thwarted love. Considered by many to be Wharton's masterpiece. 96pp. 5³⁄₁₆ x 8 ¼. 0-486-26690-7

THE EVERLASTING MAN, G. K. Chesterton. Chesterton's view of Christianity — as a blend of philosophy and mythology, satisfying intellect and spirit — applies to his brilliant book, which appeals to readers' heads as well as their hearts. 288pp. 5⅜ x 8½. 0-486-46036-3

THE FIELD AND FOREST HANDY BOOK, Daniel Beard. Written by a co-founder of the Boy Scouts, this appealing guide offers illustrated instructions for building kites, birdhouses, boats, igloos, and other fun projects, plus numerous helpful tips for campers. 448pp. 5³⁄₁₆ x 8¼. 0-486-46191-2

FINDING YOUR WAY WITHOUT MAP OR COMPASS, Harold Gatty. Useful, instructive manual shows would-be explorers, hikers, bikers, scouts, sailors, and survivalists how to find their way outdoors by observing animals, weather patterns, shifting sands, and other elements of nature. 288pp. 5⅜ x 8½. 0-486-40613-X

FIRST FRENCH READER: A Beginner's Dual-Language Book, Edited and Translated by Stanley Appelbaum. This anthology introduces 50 legendary writers — Voltaire, Balzac, Baudelaire, Proust, more — through passages from *The Red and the Black, Les Misérables, Madame Bovary,* and other classics. Original French text plus English translation on facing pages. 240pp. 5⅜ x 8½. 0-486-46178-5

FIRST GERMAN READER: A Beginner's Dual-Language Book, Edited by Harry Steinhauer. Specially chosen for their power to evoke German life and culture, these short, simple readings include poems, stories, essays, and anecdotes by Goethe, Hesse, Heine, Schiller, and others. 224pp. 5⅜ x 8½. 0-486-46179-3

FIRST SPANISH READER: A Beginner's Dual-Language Book, Angel Flores. Delightful stories, other material based on works of Don Juan Manuel, Luis Taboada, Ricardo Palma, other noted writers. Complete faithful English translations on facing pages. Exercises. 176pp. 5⅜ x 8½. 0-486-25810-6

Browse over 9,000 books at www.doverpublications.com

CATALOG OF DOVER BOOKS

FIVE ACRES AND INDEPENDENCE, Maurice G. Kains. Great back-to-the-land classic explains basics of self-sufficient farming. The one book to get. 95 illustrations. 397pp. 5⅜ x 8½. 0-486-20974-1

FLAGG'S SMALL HOUSES: Their Economic Design and Construction, 1922, Ernest Flagg. Although most famous for his skyscrapers, Flagg was also a proponent of the well-designed single-family dwelling. His classic treatise features innovations that save space, materials, and cost. 526 illustrations. 160pp. 9⅜ x 12¼. 0-486-45197-6

FLATLAND: A Romance of Many Dimensions, Edwin A. Abbott. Classic of science (and mathematical) fiction — charmingly illustrated by the author — describes the adventures of A. Square, a resident of Flatland, in Spaceland (three dimensions), Lineland (one dimension), and Pointland (no dimensions). 96pp. 5³⁄₁₆ x 8¼. 0-486-27263-X

FRANKENSTEIN, Mary Shelley. The story of Victor Frankenstein's monstrous creation and the havoc it caused has enthralled generations of readers and inspired countless writers of horror and suspense. With the author's own 1831 introduction. 176pp. 5³⁄₁₆ x 8¼. 0-486-28211-2

THE GARGOYLE BOOK: 572 Examples from Gothic Architecture, Lester Burbank Bridaham. Dispelling the conventional wisdom that French Gothic architectural flourishes were born of despair or gloom, Bridaham reveals the whimsical nature of these creations and the ingenious artisans who made them. 572 illustrations. 224pp. 8⅜ x 11. 0-486-44754-5

THE GIFT OF THE MAGI AND OTHER SHORT STORIES, O. Henry. Sixteen captivating stories by one of America's most popular storytellers. Included are such classics as "The Gift of the Magi," "The Last Leaf," and "The Ransom of Red Chief." Publisher's Note. 96pp. 5³⁄₁₆ x 8¼. 0-486-27061-0

THE GOETHE TREASURY: Selected Prose and Poetry, Johann Wolfgang von Goethe. Edited, Selected, and with an Introduction by Thomas Mann. In addition to his lyric poetry, Goethe wrote travel sketches, autobiographical studies, essays, letters, and proverbs in rhyme and prose. This collection presents outstanding examples from each genre. 368pp. 5⅜ x 8½. 0-486-44780-4

GREAT EXPECTATIONS, Charles Dickens. Orphaned Pip is apprenticed to the dirty work of the forge but dreams of becoming a gentleman — and one day finds himself in possession of "great expectations." Dickens' finest novel. 400pp. 5³⁄₁₆ x 8¼. 0-486-41586-4

GREAT WRITERS ON THE ART OF FICTION: From Mark Twain to Joyce Carol Oates, Edited by James Daley. An indispensable source of advice and inspiration, this anthology features essays by Henry James, Kate Chopin, Willa Cather, Sinclair Lewis, Jack London, Raymond Chandler, Raymond Carver, Eudora Welty, and Kurt Vonnegut, Jr. 192pp. 5⅜ x 8½. 0-486-45128-3

HAMLET, William Shakespeare. The quintessential Shakespearean tragedy, whose highly charged confrontations and anguished soliloquies probe depths of human feeling rarely sounded in any art. Reprinted from an authoritative British edition complete with illuminating footnotes. 128pp. 5³⁄₁₆ x 8¼. 0-486-27278-8

THE HAUNTED HOUSE, Charles Dickens. A Yuletide gathering in an eerie country retreat provides the backdrop for Dickens and his friends — including Elizabeth Gaskell and Wilkie Collins — who take turns spinning supernatural yarns. 144pp. 5⅜ x 8½. 0-486-46309-5

CATALOG OF DOVER BOOKS

HEART OF DARKNESS, Joseph Conrad. Dark allegory of a journey up the Congo River and the narrator's encounter with the mysterious Mr. Kurtz. Masterly blend of adventure, character study, psychological penetration. For many, Conrad's finest, most enigmatic story. 80pp. 5³⁄₁₆ x 8¼. 0-486-26464-5

HENSON AT THE NORTH POLE, Matthew A. Henson. This thrilling memoir by the heroic African-American who was Peary's companion through two decades of Arctic exploration recounts a tale of danger, courage, and determination. "Fascinating and exciting." — *Commonweal.* 128pp. 5⅜ x 8½. 0-486-45472-X

HISTORIC COSTUMES AND HOW TO MAKE THEM, Mary Fernald and E. Shenton. Practical, informative guidebook shows how to create everything from short tunics worn by Saxon men in the fifth century to a lady's bustle dress of the late 1800s. 81 illustrations. 176pp. 5⅜ x 8½. 0-486-44906-8

THE HOUND OF THE BASKERVILLES, Arthur Conan Doyle. A deadly curse in the form of a legendary ferocious beast continues to claim its victims from the Baskerville family until Holmes and Watson intervene. Often called the best detective story ever written. 128pp. 5³⁄₁₆ x 8¼. 0-486-28214-7

THE HOUSE BEHIND THE CEDARS, Charles W. Chesnutt. Originally published in 1900, this groundbreaking novel by a distinguished African-American author recounts the drama of a brother and sister who "pass for white" during the dangerous days of Reconstruction. 208pp. 5⅜ x 8½. 0-486-46144-0

THE HUMAN FIGURE IN MOTION, Eadweard Muybridge. The 4,789 photographs in this definitive selection show the human figure — models almost all undraped — engaged in over 160 different types of action: running, climbing stairs, etc. 390pp. 7⅞ x 10⅝. 0-486-20204-6

THE IMPORTANCE OF BEING EARNEST, Oscar Wilde. Wilde's witty and buoyant comedy of manners, filled with some of literature's most famous epigrams, reprinted from an authoritative British edition. Considered Wilde's most perfect work. 64pp. 5³⁄₁₆ x 8¼. 0-486-26478-5

THE INFERNO, Dante Alighieri. Translated and with notes by Henry Wadsworth Longfellow. The first stop on Dante's famous journey from Hell to Purgatory to Paradise, this 14th-century allegorical poem blends vivid and shocking imagery with graceful lyricism. Translated by the beloved 19th-century poet, Henry Wadsworth Longfellow. 256pp. 5³⁄₁₆ x 8¼. 0-486-44288-8

JANE EYRE, Charlotte Brontë. Written in 1847, *Jane Eyre* tells the tale of an orphan girl's progress from the custody of cruel relatives to an oppressive boarding school and its culmination in a troubled career as a governess. 448pp. 5³⁄₁₆ x 8¼.
0-486-42449-9

JAPANESE WOODBLOCK FLOWER PRINTS, Tanigami Kônan. Extraordinary collection of Japanese woodblock prints by a well-known artist features 120 plates in brilliant color. Realistic images from a rare edition include daffodils, tulips, and other familiar and unusual flowers. 128pp. 11 x 8¼. 0-486-46442-3

JEWELRY MAKING AND DESIGN, Augustus F. Rose and Antonio Cirino. Professional secrets of jewelry making are revealed in a thorough, practical guide. Over 200 illustrations. 306pp. 5⅜ x 8½. 0-486-21750-7

JULIUS CAESAR, William Shakespeare. Great tragedy based on Plutarch's account of the lives of Brutus, Julius Caesar and Mark Antony. Evil plotting, ringing oratory, high tragedy with Shakespeare's incomparable insight, dramatic power. Explanatory footnotes. 96pp. 5³⁄₁₆ x 8¼. 0-486-26876-4

Browse over 9,000 books at www.doverpublications.com

CATALOG OF DOVER BOOKS

THE JUNGLE, Upton Sinclair. 1906 bestseller shockingly reveals intolerable labor practices and working conditions in the Chicago stockyards as it tells the grim story of a Slavic family that emigrates to America full of optimism but soon faces despair. 320pp. 5³⁄₁₆ x 8¼. 0-486-41923-1

THE KINGDOM OF GOD IS WITHIN YOU, Leo Tolstoy. The soul-searching book that inspired Gandhi to embrace the concept of passive resistance, Tolstoy's 1894 polemic clearly outlines a radical, well-reasoned revision of traditional Christian thinking. 352pp. 5³⁄₁₆ x 8¼. 0-486-45138-0

THE LADY OR THE TIGER?: and Other Logic Puzzles, Raymond M. Smullyan. Created by a renowned puzzle master, these whimsically themed challenges involve paradoxes about probability, time, and change; metapuzzles; and self-referentiality. Nineteen chapters advance in difficulty from relatively simple to highly complex. 1982 edition. 240pp. 5⅜ x 8½. 0-486-47027-X

LEAVES OF GRASS: The Original 1855 Edition, Walt Whitman. Whitman's immortal collection includes some of the greatest poems of modern times, including his masterpiece, "Song of Myself." Shattering standard conventions, it stands as an unabashed celebration of body and nature. 128pp. 5³⁄₁₆ x 8¼. 0-486-45676-5

LES MISÉRABLES, Victor Hugo. Translated by Charles E. Wilbour. Abridged by James K. Robinson. A convict's heroic struggle for justice and redemption plays out against a fiery backdrop of the Napoleonic wars. This edition features the excellent original translation and a sensitive abridgment. 304pp. 6⅛ x 9¼. 0-486-45789-3

LILITH: A Romance, George MacDonald. In this novel by the father of fantasy literature, a man travels through time to meet Adam and Eve and to explore humanity's fall from grace and ultimate redemption. 240pp. 5⅜ x 8½. 0-486-46818-6

THE LOST LANGUAGE OF SYMBOLISM, Harold Bayley. This remarkable book reveals the hidden meaning behind familiar images and words, from the origins of Santa Claus to the fleur-de-lys, drawing from mythology, folklore, religious texts, and fairy tales. 1,418 illustrations. 784pp. 5⅜ x 8½. 0-486-44787-1

MACBETH, William Shakespeare. A Scottish nobleman murders the king in order to succeed to the throne. Tortured by his conscience and fearful of discovery, he becomes tangled in a web of treachery and deceit that ultimately spells his doom. 96pp. 5³⁄₁₆ x 8¼. 0-486-27802-6

MAKING AUTHENTIC CRAFTSMAN FURNITURE: Instructions and Plans for 62 Projects, Gustav Stickley. Make authentic reproductions of handsome, functional, durable furniture: tables, chairs, wall cabinets, desks, a hall tree, and more. Construction plans with drawings, schematics, dimensions, and lumber specs reprinted from 1900s The Craftsman magazine. 128pp. 8⅛ x 11. 0-486-25000-8

MATHEMATICS FOR THE NONMATHEMATICIAN, Morris Kline. Erudite and entertaining overview follows development of mathematics from ancient Greeks to present. Topics include logic and mathematics, the fundamental concept, differential calculus, probability theory, much more. Exercises and problems. 641pp. 5⅜ x 8½. 0-486-24823-2

MEMOIRS OF AN ARABIAN PRINCESS FROM ZANZIBAR, Emily Ruete. This 19th-century autobiography offers a rare inside look at the society surrounding a sultan's palace. A real-life princess in exile recalls her vanished world of harems, slave trading, and court intrigues. 288pp. 5⅜ x 8½. 0-486-47121-7

Browse over 9,000 books at www.doverpublications.com

THE METAMORPHOSIS AND OTHER STORIES, Franz Kafka. Excellent new English translations of title story (considered by many critics Kafka's most perfect work), plus "The Judgment," "In the Penal Colony," "A Country Doctor," and "A Report to an Academy." Note. 96pp. 5³⁄₁₆ x 8¼. 0-486-29030-1

MICROSCOPIC ART FORMS FROM THE PLANT WORLD, R. Anheisser. From undulating curves to complex geometrics, a world of fascinating images abound in this classic, illustrated survey of microscopic plants. Features 400 detailed illustrations of nature's minute but magnificent handiwork. The accompanying CD-ROM includes all of the images in the book. 128pp. 9 x 9. 0-486-46013-4

A MIDSUMMER NIGHT'S DREAM, William Shakespeare. Among the most popular of Shakespeare's comedies, this enchanting play humorously celebrates the vagaries of love as it focuses upon the intertwined romances of several pairs of lovers. Explanatory footnotes. 80pp. 5³⁄₁₆ x 8¼. 0-486-27067-X

THE MONEY CHANGERS, Upton Sinclair. Originally published in 1908, this cautionary novel from the author of *The Jungle* explores corruption within the American system as a group of power brokers joins forces for personal gain, triggering a crash on Wall Street. 192pp. 5⅜ x 8½. 0-486-46917-4

THE MOST POPULAR HOMES OF THE TWENTIES, William A. Radford. With a New Introduction by Daniel D. Reiff. Based on a rare 1925 catalog, this architectural showcase features floor plans, construction details, and photos of 26 homes, plus articles on entrances, porches, garages, and more. 250 illustrations, 21 color plates. 176pp. 8⅜ x 11. 0-486-47028-8

MY 66 YEARS IN THE BIG LEAGUES, Connie Mack. With a New Introduction by Rich Westcott. A Founding Father of modern baseball, Mack holds the record for most wins — and losses — by a major league manager. Enhanced by 70 photographs, his warmhearted autobiography is populated by many legends of the game. 288pp. 5⅜ x 8½. 0-486-47184-5

NARRATIVE OF THE LIFE OF FREDERICK DOUGLASS, Frederick Douglass. Douglass's graphic depictions of slavery, harrowing escape to freedom, and life as a newspaper editor, eloquent orator, and impassioned abolitionist. 96pp. 5³⁄₁₆ x 8¼. 0-486-28499-9

THE NIGHTLESS CITY: Geisha and Courtesan Life in Old Tokyo, J. E. de Becker. This unsurpassed study from 100 years ago ventured into Tokyo's red-light district to survey geisha and courtesan life and offer meticulous descriptions of training, dress, social hierarchy, and erotic practices. 49 black-and-white illustrations; 2 maps. 496pp. 5⅜ x 8½. 0-486-45563-7

THE ODYSSEY, Homer. Excellent prose translation of ancient epic recounts adventures of the homeward-bound Odysseus. Fantastic cast of gods, giants, cannibals, sirens, other supernatural creatures — true classic of Western literature. 256pp. 5³⁄₁₆ x 8¼. 0-486-40654-7

OEDIPUS REX, Sophocles. Landmark of Western drama concerns the catastrophe that ensues when King Oedipus discovers he has inadvertently killed his father and married his mother. Masterly construction, dramatic irony. Explanatory footnotes. 64pp. 5³⁄₁₆ x 8¼. 0-486-26877-2

ONCE UPON A TIME: The Way America Was, Eric Sloane. Nostalgic text and drawings brim with gentle philosophies and descriptions of how we used to live — self-sufficiently — on the land, in homes, and among the things built by hand. 44 line illustrations. 64pp. 8⅜ x 11. 0-486-44411-2

Browse over 9,000 books at www.doverpublications.com

CATALOG OF DOVER BOOKS

ONE OF OURS, Willa Cather. The Pulitzer Prize–winning novel about a young Nebraskan looking for something to believe in. Alienated from his parents, rejected by his wife, he finds his destiny on the bloody battlefields of World War I. 352pp. 5³⁄₁₆ x 8¼. 0-486-45599-8

ORIGAMI YOU CAN USE: 27 Practical Projects, Rick Beech. Origami models can be more than decorative, and this unique volume shows how! The 27 practical projects include a CD case, frame, napkin ring, and dish. Easy instructions feature 400 two-color illustrations. 96pp. 8¼ x 11. 0-486-47057-1

OTHELLO, William Shakespeare. Towering tragedy tells the story of a Moorish general who earns the enmity of his ensign Iago when he passes him over for a promotion. Masterly portrait of an archvillain. Explanatory footnotes. 112pp. 5³⁄₁₆ x 8¼. 0-486-29097-2

PARADISE LOST, John Milton. Notes by John A. Himes. First published in 1667, *Paradise Lost* ranks among the greatest of English literature's epic poems. It's a sublime retelling of Adam and Eve's fall from grace and expulsion from Eden. Notes by John A. Himes. 480pp. 5³⁄₁₆ x 8¼. 0-486-44287-X

PASSING, Nella Larsen. Married to a successful physician and prominently ensconced in society, Irene Redfield leads a charmed existence — until a chance encounter with a childhood friend who has been "passing for white." 112pp. 5⅜ x 8½. 0-486-43713-2

PERSPECTIVE DRAWING FOR BEGINNERS, Len A. Doust. Doust carefully explains the roles of lines, boxes, and circles, and shows how visualizing shapes and forms can be used in accurate depictions of perspective. One of the most concise introductions available. 33 illustrations. 64pp. 5⅜ x 8½. 0-486-45149-6

PERSPECTIVE MADE EASY, Ernest R. Norling. Perspective is easy; yet, surprisingly few artists know the simple rules that make it so. Remedy that situation with this simple, step-by-step book, the first devoted entirely to the topic. 256 illustrations. 224pp. 5⅜ x 8½. 0-486-40473-0

THE PICTURE OF DORIAN GRAY, Oscar Wilde. Celebrated novel involves a handsome young Londoner who sinks into a life of depravity. His body retains perfect youth and vigor while his recent portrait reflects the ravages of his crime and sensuality. 176pp. 5³⁄₁₆ x 8¼. 0-486-27807-7

PRIDE AND PREJUDICE, Jane Austen. One of the most universally loved and admired English novels, an effervescent tale of rural romance transformed by Jane Austen's art into a witty, shrewdly observed satire of English country life. 272pp. 5³⁄₁₆ x 8¼. 0-486-28473-5

THE PRINCE, Niccolò Machiavelli. Classic, Renaissance-era guide to acquiring and maintaining political power. Today, nearly 500 years after it was written, this calculating prescription for autocratic rule continues to be much read and studied. 80pp. 5³⁄₁₆ x 8¼. 0-486-27274-5

QUICK SKETCHING, Carl Cheek. A perfect introduction to the technique of "quick sketching." Drawing upon an artist's immediate emotional responses, this is an extremely effective means of capturing the essential form and features of a subject. More than 100 black-and-white illustrations throughout. 48pp. 11 x 8¼. 0-486-46608-6

RANCH LIFE AND THE HUNTING TRAIL, Theodore Roosevelt. Illustrated by Frederic Remington. Beautifully illustrated by Remington, Roosevelt's celebration of the Old West recounts his adventures in the Dakota Badlands of the 1880s, from round-ups to Indian encounters to hunting bighorn sheep. 208pp. 6¼ x 9¼. 0-486-47340-6

CATALOG OF DOVER BOOKS

THE RED BADGE OF COURAGE, Stephen Crane. Amid the nightmarish chaos of a Civil War battle, a young soldier discovers courage, humility, and, perhaps, wisdom. Uncanny re-creation of actual combat. Enduring landmark of American fiction. 112pp. 5³⁄₁₆ x 8¼.   0-486-26465-3

RELATIVITY SIMPLY EXPLAINED, Martin Gardner. One of the subject's clearest, most entertaining introductions offers lucid explanations of special and general theories of relativity, gravity, and spacetime, models of the universe, and more. 100 illustrations. 224pp. 5⅜ x 8½.   0-486-29315-7

REMBRANDT DRAWINGS: 116 Masterpieces in Original Color, Rembrandt van Rijn. This deluxe hardcover edition features drawings from throughout the Dutch master's prolific career. Informative captions accompany these beautifully reproduced landscapes, biblical vignettes, figure studies, animal sketches, and portraits. 128pp. 8⅜ x 11.   0-486-46149-1

THE ROAD NOT TAKEN AND OTHER POEMS, Robert Frost. A treasury of Frost's most expressive verse. In addition to the title poem: "An Old Man's Winter Night," "In the Home Stretch," "Meeting and Passing," "Putting in the Seed," many more. All complete and unabridged. 64pp. 5³⁄₁₆ x 8¼.   0-486-27550-7

ROMEO AND JULIET, William Shakespeare. Tragic tale of star-crossed lovers, feuding families and timeless passion contains some of Shakespeare's most beautiful and lyrical love poetry. Complete, unabridged text with explanatory footnotes. 96pp. 5³⁄₁₆ x 8¼.   0-486-27557-4

SANDITON AND THE WATSONS: Austen's Unfinished Novels, Jane Austen. Two tantalizing incomplete stories revisit Austen's customary milieu of courtship and venture into new territory, amid guests at a seaside resort. Both are worth reading for pleasure and study. 112pp. 5⅜ x 8½.   0-486-45793-1

THE SCARLET LETTER, Nathaniel Hawthorne. With stark power and emotional depth, Hawthorne's masterpiece explores sin, guilt, and redemption in a story of adultery in the early days of the Massachusetts Colony. 192pp. 5³⁄₁₆ x 8¼.
                                                                            0-486-28048-9

THE SEASONS OF AMERICA PAST, Eric Sloane. Seventy-five illustrations depict cider mills and presses, sleds, pumps, stump-pulling equipment, plows, and other elements of America's rural heritage. A section of old recipes and household hints adds additional color. 160pp. 8⅜ x 11.   0-486-44220-9

SELECTED CANTERBURY TALES, Geoffrey Chaucer. Delightful collection includes the General Prologue plus three of the most popular tales: "The Knight's Tale," "The Miller's Prologue and Tale," and "The Wife of Bath's Prologue and Tale." In modern English. 144pp. 5³⁄₁₆ x 8¼.   0-486-28241-4

SELECTED POEMS, Emily Dickinson. Over 100 best-known, best-loved poems by one of America's foremost poets, reprinted from authoritative early editions. No comparable edition at this price. Index of first lines. 64pp. 5³⁄₁₆ x 8¼. 0-486-26466-1

SIDDHARTHA, Hermann Hesse. Classic novel that has inspired generations of seekers. Blending Eastern mysticism and psychoanalysis, Hesse presents a strikingly original view of man and culture and the arduous process of self-discovery, reconciliation, harmony, and peace. 112pp. 5³⁄₁₆ x 8¼.   0-486-40653-9

SKETCHING OUTDOORS, Leonard Richmond. This guide offers beginners step-by-step demonstrations of how to depict clouds, trees, buildings, and other outdoor sights. Explanations of a variety of techniques include shading and constructional drawing. 48pp. 11 x 8¼.   0-486-46922-0

Browse over 9,000 books at www.doverpublications.com

SMALL HOUSES OF THE FORTIES: With Illustrations and Floor Plans, Harold E. Group. 56 floor plans and elevations of houses that originally cost less than $15,000 to build. Recommended by financial institutions of the era, they range from Colonials to Cape Cods. 144pp. 8⅜ x 11. 0-486-45598-X

SOME CHINESE GHOSTS, Lafcadio Hearn. Rooted in ancient Chinese legends, these richly atmospheric supernatural tales are recounted by an expert in Oriental lore. Their originality, power, and literary charm will captivate readers of all ages. 96pp. 5⅜ x 8½. 0-486-46306-0

SONGS FOR THE OPEN ROAD: Poems of Travel and Adventure, Edited by The American Poetry & Literacy Project. More than 80 poems by 50 American and British masters celebrate real and metaphorical journeys. Poems by Whitman, Byron, Millay, Sandburg, Langston Hughes, Emily Dickinson, Robert Frost, Shelley, Tennyson, Yeats, many others. Note. 80pp. 5³⁄₁₆ x 8¼. 0-486-40646-6

SPOON RIVER ANTHOLOGY, Edgar Lee Masters. An American poetry classic, in which former citizens of a mythical midwestern town speak touchingly from the grave of the thwarted hopes and dreams of their lives. 144pp. 5³⁄₁₆ x 8¼. 0-486-27275-3

STAR LORE: Myths, Legends, and Facts, William Tyler Olcott. Captivating retellings of the origins and histories of ancient star groups include Pegasus, Ursa Major, Pleiades, signs of the zodiac, and other constellations. "Classic." — *Sky & Telescope.* 58 illustrations. 544pp. 5⅜ x 8½. 0-486-43581-4

THE STRANGE CASE OF DR. JEKYLL AND MR. HYDE, Robert Louis Stevenson. This intriguing novel, both fantasy thriller and moral allegory, depicts the struggle of two opposing personalities — one essentially good, the other evil — for the soul of one man. 64pp. 5³⁄₁₆ x 8¼. 0-486-26688-5

SURVIVAL HANDBOOK: The Official U.S. Army Guide, Department of the Army. This special edition of the Army field manual is geared toward civilians. An essential companion for campers and all lovers of the outdoors, it constitutes the most authoritative wilderness guide. 288pp. 5³⁄₁₆ x 8¼. 0-486-46184-X

A TALE OF TWO CITIES, Charles Dickens. Against the backdrop of the French Revolution, Dickens unfolds his masterpiece of drama, adventure, and romance about a man falsely accused of treason. Excitement and derring-do in the shadow of the guillotine. 304pp. 5³⁄₁₆ x 8¼. 0-486-40651-2

TEN PLAYS, Anton Chekhov. *The Sea Gull, Uncle Vanya, The Three Sisters, The Cherry Orchard,* and *Ivanov,* plus 5 one-act comedies: *The Anniversary, An Unwilling Martyr, The Wedding, The Bear,* and *The Proposal.* 336pp. 5³⁄₁₆ x 8¼. 0-486-46560-8

THE FLYING INN, G. K. Chesterton. Hilarious romp in which pub owner Humphrey Hump and friend take to the road in a donkey cart filled with rum and cheese, inveighing against Prohibition and other "oppressive forms of modernity." 320pp. 5⅜ x 8½. 0-486-41910-X

THIRTY YEARS THAT SHOOK PHYSICS: The Story of Quantum Theory, George Gamow. Lucid, accessible introduction to the influential theory of energy and matter features careful explanations of Dirac's anti-particles, Bohr's model of the atom, and much more. Numerous drawings. 1966 edition. 240pp. 5⅜ x 8½. 0-486-24895-X

TREASURE ISLAND, Robert Louis Stevenson. Classic adventure story of a perilous sea journey, a mutiny led by the infamous Long John Silver, and a lethal scramble for buried treasure — seen through the eyes of cabin boy Jim Hawkins. 160pp. 5³⁄₁₆ x 8¼. 0-486-27559-0

THE TRIAL, Franz Kafka. Translated by David Wyllie. From its gripping first sentence onward, this novel exemplifies the term "Kafkaesque." Its darkly humorous narrative recounts a bank clerk's entrapment in a bureaucratic maze, based on an undisclosed charge. 176pp. 5³⁄₁₆ x 8¼. 0-486-47061-X

THE TURN OF THE SCREW, Henry James. Gripping ghost story by great novelist depicts the sinister transformation of 2 innocent children into flagrant liars and hypocrites. An elegantly told tale of unspoken horror and psychological terror. 96pp. 5³⁄₁₆ x 8¼. 0-486-26684-2

UP FROM SLAVERY, Booker T. Washington. Washington (1856-1915) rose to become the most influential spokesman for African-Americans of his day. In this eloquently written book, he describes events in a remarkable life that began in bondage and culminated in worldwide recognition. 160pp. 5³⁄₁₆ x 8¼. 0-486-28738-6

VICTORIAN HOUSE DESIGNS IN AUTHENTIC FULL COLOR: 75 Plates from the "Scientific American – Architects and Builders Edition," 1885-1894, Edited by Blanche Cirker. Exquisitely detailed, exceptionally handsome designs for an enormous variety of attractive city dwellings, spacious suburban and country homes, charming "cottages" and other structures — all accompanied by perspective views and floor plans. 80pp. 9¼ x 12¼. 0-486-29438-2

VILLETTE, Charlotte Brontë. Acclaimed by Virginia Woolf as "Brontë's finest novel," this moving psychological study features a remarkably modern heroine who abandons her native England for a new life as a schoolteacher in Belgium. 480pp. 5³⁄₁₆ x 8¼. 0-486-45557-2

THE VOYAGE OUT, Virginia Woolf. A moving depiction of the thrills and confusion of youth, Woolf's acclaimed first novel traces a shipboard journey to South America for a captivating exploration of a woman's growing self-awareness. 288pp. 5³⁄₁₆ x 8¼. 0-486-45005-8

WALDEN; OR, LIFE IN THE WOODS, Henry David Thoreau. Accounts of Thoreau's daily life on the shores of Walden Pond outside Concord, Massachusetts, are interwoven with musings on the virtues of self-reliance and individual freedom, on society, government, and other topics. 224pp. 5³⁄₁₆ x 8¼. 0-486-28495-6

WILD PILGRIMAGE: A Novel in Woodcuts, Lynd Ward. Through startling engravings shaded in black and red, Ward wordlessly tells the story of a man trapped in an industrial world, struggling between the grim reality around him and the fantasies his imagination creates. 112pp. 6⅛ x 9¼. 0-486-46583-7

WILLY POGÁNY REDISCOVERED, Willy Pogány. Selected and Edited by Jeff A. Menges. More than 100 color and black-and-white Art Nouveau–style illustrations from fairy tales and adventure stories include scenes from Wagner's "Ring" cycle, *The Rime of the Ancient Mariner, Gulliver's Travels,* and *Faust.* 144pp. 8⅜ x 11. 0-486-47046-6

WOOLLY THOUGHTS: Unlock Your Creative Genius with Modular Knitting, Pat Ashforth and Steve Plummer. Here's the revolutionary way to knit — easy, fun, and foolproof! Beginners and experienced knitters need only master a single stitch to create their own designs with patchwork squares. More than 100 illustrations. 128pp. 6½ x 9¼. 0-486-46084-3

WUTHERING HEIGHTS, Emily Brontë. Somber tale of consuming passions and vengeance — played out amid the lonely English moors — recounts the turbulent and tempestuous love story of Cathy and Heathcliff. Poignant and compelling. 256pp. 5³⁄₁₆ x 8¼. 0-486-29256-8

Browse over 9,000 books at www.doverpublications.com